KT-398-697

GOOD TIME GIRL

Kate O'Mara has been a well known theatrical actress for many years, acclaimed for such roles as Cleopatra, Kate in *The Taming of the Shrew*, and her recent success in Melvyn Bragg's *King Lear in New York*. She founded the British Actors Theatre company in 1987, and has starred on television in *The Brothers* and *Howards' Way*. She shot to international stardom at the age of 46, playing the role of Caress in *Dynasty*.

By the same author

WHEN SHE WAS BAD

GAME PLAN - A MODERN WOMAN'S SURVIVAL KIT

KATE O'MARA

Good Time Girl

This edition published 1995 for
Parrallel Books
Units 13–17 Avonbridge Industrial Estate
Atlantic Road
Avonmouth, Bristol BS11 9QD
by Diamond Books
77–85 Fulham Palace Road
Hammersmith, London W6 8JB

First published 1993

Copyright © Kate O'Mara 1993
The Author asserts the moral right
to be identified as the author of this work

ISBN 0 261 66697 5

Set in Baskerville by Avocet Typesetters, Bicester, Oxon
Printed in Great Britain

All rights reserved. No part of this publication may be
reproduced, stored in a retrieval system, or transmitted,
in any form, or by any means, electronic, mechanical,
photocopying, recording or otherwise, without the prior
permission of the publishers.

CONDITIONS OF SALE
This book is sold subject to the condition that it shall not,
by way of trade or otherwise, be lent, re-sold, hired out or
otherwise circulated without the publisher's prior consent
in any form of binding or cover other than that in which it
is published and without a similar condition including this
condition being imposed on the subsequent purchaser.

To Ted Rhodes, in happy memory

1

The studio was dark, silent and tense. The crew, technicians and production team were shrouded in shadow. Only the actors in their little world of a make-believe art gallery were illuminated in a bright pool of light. They stood poised ready to spring into life at a given cue – a flamboyant wave of a white handkerchief from Larry Matthews, the highly eccentric, camp floor manager/PA/script editor/general right-hand man to Hugh Travis, the producer. Larry always used this rather overt method of cueing, claiming that the actors could see it easily in their peripheral line of vision. He was right, of course; the slightest movement from anyone on the studio floor could be misinterpreted as a cue by an actor already fraught with nerves. Larry was usually right about most things. He ran the studio, and indeed the series, like a tight ship, loved and feared by actors and technicians alike. Now he stood, his head encased by 'cans', keeping an ever-vigilant eye on the monitor that was suspended above his head. The cameramen adjusted focus. The boom operators pushed the microphones in and out of the set, paying them out and winding them in again like trout flies, checking and rechecking for shadows. It was the soundmen's difficult task to position the booms so as to be able to pick up every nuance from the actors. They had to achieve this without getting into shot, yet be near enough to hear even the most inaudible player. There was no difficulty with the experienced performers but the newcomers and those who had not had theatrical experience always posed problems.

Larry, ever watchful, glanced briefly around the studio, then up again at the monitor. Where –

> A tall fine figure of a man, with a remarkably even golden tan and deep-set vivid blue eyes was threading his way through the hustle and bustle of Mayfair. His silver hair was a touch too long for a banker or a barrister, and proclaimed him at once a man connected with the arts. Women's heads turned as he strode confidently along, his gaze firmly fixed ahead, a slightly worried look on his handsome chiselled features.

Back on the studio floor, Larry suddenly yelled, 'Coming out of telecine in two minutes,' thereby quelling even the faintest murmur of chatter and quiver of movement. The brightly lit actors braced themselves for the fray. The trick was to look and act perfectly naturally in a completely unnatural situation, the actor having to start exactly on Larry's cue. In this instance, the responsibility lay with Geoffrey Armitage, an old hand at the game, who played Paul McMaster in the series, and Amy Brindle, a relative newcomer, who played Sophie, his receptionist, and who was learning fast.

> Paul arrived at his destination and glanced up briefly with an air of ill-concealed pride at the name displayed above the premises. 'McMasters' it announced in discreet gold roman lettering on a very dark green ground. He paused for a moment to glance at the superb seventeenth-century Flemish painting that was the sole exhibit in the window,

8

then pressed the intercom. A distorted voice responded immediately.

'Good morning, sir.' A buzzing sound indicated that he was given admittance.

'Stand by, studio. Coming out of telecine in one minute!' Larry's voice was now lower both in volume and pitch, and had the effect of concentrating everyone wonderfully. His eyes were staring at the monitor.

'Morning, Sophie.'

'Paul, thank goodness you're here. Helen has been on the phone. There's been some sort of mix-up over the German consignment.'

Paul McMaster put a weary hand to his brow. 'Oh God, can't she handle it? I've got a meeting this morning.'

'There's a fax from Mr Van Geldes from Amsterdam, about the exhibition at the Rijksmuseum.'

'Yes, good. I was expecting that, anything else?'

'Yes,' said Sophie, looking embarrassed, 'your brother . . .'

'What's he done now?'

'I'm afraid he may be responsible for the confusion over the Hamburg shipment,' she replied, becoming more flustered by the minute.

Paul sighed heavily. 'All right, I'll deal with it,' he said resignedly, and crossed to the back of the shop. Sophie watched him go, then turned back to her desk with a troubled expression on her face.

There was a door leading to an outer office and a further door to an outhouse where restoration work and packing was carried out.

9

'Coming out of telecine in ten seconds, nine, eight, seven, six, five . . .' Five to zero were mimed by Larry using the fingers of one hand followed by the famous flourish of the white handkerchief descending in the manner of one starting a race and Geoffrey Armitage slipped smoothly and expertly through the studio office door, which exactly corresponded with the one in the telecine, and so achieved the transition from film to live studio. He spoke his lines on cue easily and effortlessly, with just the right amount of energy and charm to make him immensely watchable and adored by several thousand female admirers.

'Who said you could use my office?' snapped Paul McMaster.

An extremely good-looking man in his middle thirties was lounging nonchalantly in the leather captain's chair with his feet up on the desk in front of him.

Paul's errant younger brother, Tom, was played by Simon Lavell, a dark and rather arrogant young man who seemed to find difficulty in separating his screen persona from that of his own. Used to acting opposite each other, Simon and Geoff played to the end of the scene expertly.

'And we have a recording break there. Reposition cameras three and four in the McMaster apartment – as quickly as you can and no talking, PLEASE.' Larry's stentorian tones produced an immediate effect and there was absolute silence. He was tall, blond, good-looking, in his early forties, an ex-actor who possessed those magical qualities so necessary in the aspiring thespian, confidence, authority and charisma. The whole studio, actors and crew alike, recognized it and respected it. The change-over to the McMaster flat was effected very quickly and quietly. Helen McMaster, Paul's

10

estranged wife, played by Bella Shand, an extremely glamorous brunette in her middle forties, was reclining on a chaise longue, sumptuously clad in coral-pink chiffon and feathers. *The McMasters* was originally created for her by Hugh seven years ago and she revelled in her position as star of the show.

'Ready treasure?' asked Larry affectionately. Bella was an old trouper and they enjoyed a mutual respect.

Bella, who was entangled in a telephone flex, whilst attempting to look sultry and poised, said, 'I look and feel extremely awkward and uncomfortable, but apart from that, I'm raring to go.'

'You don't actually, darling. You look lovely as always,' replied Larry soothingly. 'Ready everyone?' He did not wait for a reply. 'And standby in the office set, we're coming straight over to you after this – no pause take your cue from Terri,' Larry had raised his voice so as to be heard by the actors on the nearby set, where the cameras were all ready for the opening shot. 'You look gorgeous, darling,' repeated Larry, as he observed Bella still wriggling surreptitiously.

'I look like a fucking flamingo, and you know it,' she muttered under her breath.

'Agreed, but a very lovely one.'

Larry's hand swept dramatically down. Bella glided effortlessly into the telephone conversation, any problem with the offending wire completely forgotten.

'Paul?' Her voice was a deep rich contralto, the voice of a woman who was either a chain smoker or imbibed heavily in gin, vodka or possibly both. 'Paul? Thank God – no listen. Trouble . . .Yes. Big trouble . . .Yes, yes . . .' She sighed dramatically. 'Of course, what else? Just keep quiet

11

and listen. De La Tour . . . Yes, the one that went
to Hamburg. Yes. Are you sitting down? Well,
you'd better. It's a fake.'

As Bella finished the sentence, Terri, the assistant floor
manager on the adjoining set, cued Geoff, who, as Paul
McMaster, had been perched on the edge of the desk and now
rose like a pheasant rocketing from a hedgerow.

'What!'
   Tom, who was wandering aimlessly around the
office with his hands in his pockets, stopped in his
tracks at his brother's outburst. At this moment, the
outer office door opened and a petite blonde entered.
She was gorgeously pretty, like a Barbie doll. Paul
cupped his hand over the phone.
   'Yes, Gemma. What is it?'
   'Sorry to interrupt you s-sir,' lisped Gemma
breathlessly, 'but there's been an accident in the
workroom. Young Billy's cut his hand on the gilly
   – guillotine.'

Patsy Hall, playing Gemma, was regarded by the rest of the
cast as a nonactress. She had been cast by Hugh in a weak
moment, having been totally bowled over by her undeniably
gorgeous looks and figure. He had felt, rightly, as it
transpired, that she would boost the series' ratings.
Unfortunately, she was virtually talentless. As soon as she
made her entrance it became apparent that she was ill at ease
– and she had fluffed her first line.
   Larry, watching like a hawk, but all the while listening
on his head-cans to the candid comments coming from the
gallery, waited to be told to suspend operations. The gallery
was the enclosed glass sanctum high above the studio floor

from which the production team directed the show. The director, in this instance, Scott Dudley, quite literally called the shots. Larry rolled his eyes with a 'Gawd help us' expression as Patsy then bumped into the filing cabinet, and the scene jerked awkwardly on, the other actors attempting to rescue it, but the rhythm and flow had been disturbed and much to everyone's relief the sound boom appeared in shot.

'Okay, hold it everyone,' intoned Larry, listening to the string of expletives from his earphones. 'Yes – yes – uh-huh . . . Yes, I couldn't have phrased it better myself . . . Patsy, dear,' said Larry loudly, turning his attention to the miscreant, 'the director says we're going again, and can you possibly manage even an approximation of the text – it's vital, dear, as we're using one of your lines to cut to another shot. Oh, never mind,' he amended as he saw Patsy's look of total bewilderment. 'Just remember the lines and don't bump into the furniture.'

This last was delivered in the clipped tones of Noël Coward. The whole studio chuckled quietly and there was a shout of raucous laughter from Bella, still on her chaise longue, waiting to do another very brief cutaway scene.

'Standby to go again, studio,' said Larry in a long-suffering voice. The boom operator shrugged his apologies to Larry. 'Don't mention it, dear,' was the swift reply. 'It was as welcome as the relief of Mafeking.'

The next time Patsy got it right, but her performance was dull and wooden. Up in the gallery, Scott Dudley was making his opinions known.

'She's appalling! She can't move, she can't speak, she can't act – what the fuck can she do?' he asked, clutching his forehead in disbelief. 'I mean apart from that,' he added, seeing the expressions of his colleagues. 'Look at her, it's

13

pathetic. Oh God, I can't bear it. Cut to camera one,' he said curtly to his assistant, Pam.

'It's not his shot yet,' replied Pam instantly.

'I can't help it. Punch up one,' he insisted.

The remainder of Patsy's speech was heard out of vision over a close-reaction shot on Tom.

Pam was Scott's girlfriend. He was heavily married with teenage children, but his affair with Pam had been progressing steadily now for three years. She was devoted to him and was also very good at her job.

'And cut to Paul,' barked Scott, switching to a reaction shot on Geoff earlier than was planned.

Geoff noted the red light on the camera that was trained on him come on and reacted accordingly. He was secretly pleased; he was having a very intermittent affair with Patsy, but knew she was totally untalented.

The scene finally finished.

'Thank you, studio, that's a clear!' Larry bellowed. Then: 'God, what a load of bullshit!' he muttered to himself as he removed the head-cans. 'I hope this looks better than it plays.'

2

'Yes, that's right, McMasters, Cork Street, as soon as you can.' A shot of an ambulance tearing across London from McMasters as the theme music surged accompanied the closing credit titles. Claire Jenner switched off the TV with the remote control unit and sank back against the pillows. *The McMasters* had deteriorated over the years, she thought. There was a time when she had wanted to be in it. It had been a terrific series when it had first started, full of drive, with punchy and original dialogue. Now the actors were still doing their best with the scripts they were given, but it was becoming decidedly cosy. It needed a kick up the arse, an injection of new life, a sparkling new character perhaps, or story line.

Claire gazed listlessly around the room. Why the hell was she worrying about a TV series? She was quite convinced she would never work again. Anyway, how could she? She was unattractive, undesirable – unnecessary. No one wanted her. Well, Roger didn't at any rate. The tears started to well up inside her. She heard the clatter of her friend Sal in the kitchen making soup. Dear Sal. Claire would never have come through this without her. The tears coursed unbidden down her cheeks at the thought of her friend's cheerfulness and kind understanding. The door of the bedroom burst open.

'Have I missed the end? Damn. What happened?' Sal

demanded, entering and plonking herself down on the end of the bed. 'Soup won't be a moment.'

'Nothing much,' replied Claire, trying to sound normal, 'Billy cut his hand and was carted off to hospital. The preceding forty-five minutes were so dull I nodded off.'

'Dear God, it's getting more like *The Archers* every week – what's the matter with you?' Sally interrupted herself to look at her friend suspiciously. 'You haven't been blubbing again, I hope?' There was a painful pause as Claire tried to regain control of her feelings to no avail.

'I miss him,' she whispered miserably. 'Oh, Sal, I loved him so much,' and she burst into uncontrollable sobbing.

Sally was apparently unmoved by this spectacle. 'Really?' she said dryly, 'I suppose it's possible to love a turdfaced piece of shit – '

'Don't speak about him like that,' protested Claire between sobs. 'He's beautiful . . .'

'Handsome is as handsome does,' observed Sally sagely, relenting and putting her arms round her friend's shoulders. 'What he did wasn't very pretty, though, was it?' she asked gently.

'No,' agreed Claire, brokenly trying to overcome her sobbing. Eventually she said, 'Sal . . .'

'I'm here.'

'Sal, I wish I could have had the baby.'

Neither of them said anything for a long while.

Claire's childhood had been almost idyllic. Generous, strong, loving parents had given her a splendid education. She had responded to her happy upbringing in kind. A hardworking, lively intelligent girl, she had done well at school, always coming among the top of her class. She was well-mannered,

16

considerate and charming, and, being an only child, learned to amuse herself. She was an avid reader and loved good music – in every way the perfect child. Until she reached her teens. Still hardworking and ambitious, but now moody, temperamental and a rebel, she flouted her parents' authority on every occasion, slamming doors, screaming at the top of her voice for no apparent reason and disappearing for days on end. On her return, she would refuse to inform them where she had been. Indeed, she hardly communicated with them at all. Her mother bore this transformation in her adored daughter with true Anglo-Saxon stoicism, was patient, kind and tried to understand. Claire's father, however, retreated, literally and metaphorically. He withdrew into a hurt silence and increasingly shut himself away in his study. Communication became a problem between all three. Claire conversed with her mother only in monosyllables, and when on rare occasions, Beatrice Jenner tried to elicit from her daughter what was troubling her, she became totally silent and would then disappear again for several days. Her mother would fret and then pretend that nothing had happened when Claire returned.

Her parents were not surprised when Claire announced that she would not be sitting her A levels, but instead was joining a group of friends on a trip to Turkey. Her mother was horrified, her father outraged, that their daughter should throw away her education and chance of university for a whim. Claire argued that a trip in a Land Rover exploring new lands would be an education in itself. But unchaperoned? There would be other girls, well, one other. And three men. But why not sit her exams and go in the summer? Because they were going now, and in any case, she didn't want to go to university. She had no desire to teach, for God's sake! Well, what did she want to do then? Beatrice made every effort to get through to her daughter. Her husband sat silently staring at the arrangement of dried flowers that occupied the hearth during the summer months.

'I want to be an actress,' Claire announced.

Both her parents were stunned. It was the first intimation they had ever had of it.

'But you know nothing about acting or the theatre, dear,' her mother had protested.

'I don't care. It's what I want to do. It's what I'm going to do.'

A strained argument followed, which continued through the evening. Eventually a compromise was reached. Claire would forgo Turkey. She would sit her exams, and her parents would pay for her to go to drama school. If she could get in, of course. Claire was jubilant. Her ruse had worked. Did they really think she would not sit her exams? She'd worked so damned hard for them. She was not about to be thwarted of the brilliant results she knew she would surely get. And she was going to drama school, a closely kept dream come true.

She had never told anyone about it, even her best friend, Debbie. Claire knew that her parents imagined that she was indulging in every vice known to man or woman when she disappeared for days on end. Nothing could have been further from the truth. She would go off into the country and hide away in a caravan belonging to Debbie's aunt. They would go for long walks, revelling in the freedom, and work quietly at their A levels. Admittedly, Claire did feel the odd pang of guilt knowing that her mother would be worried about her, but she would quell it hurriedly. She half confided her dream of being an actress to Debbie, but didn't reveal the whole truth. She casually mentioned that she might like to become a photographic model. Debbie was thrilled and lost in admiration. It sounded so glamorous and so unattainable. Claire shrugged it off as though it were unimportant, and decided not to tell anyone of her secret longing, not until it became a reality.

Claire's mother, although initially shocked by her daughter's revelation, comforted herself with the hope that perhaps all the pent-up emotion that seemed to be locked in Claire's bosom would now find an outlet. And so it proved. Claire had sailed through her auditions and been accepted at one of the leading drama colleges. And she had done well there, too, winning the Shakespeare prize at the end of her three years. It had not been easy to get work when she left, but she had managed to attract the attention of an up-and-coming young director in a workshop she'd done for schools and filmed for television. It had been just the break she needed, getting into TV and innovative theatre work simultaneously. There followed a season with one of the more prestigious repertory companies. A critic whose opinion was respected tipped her as a young actress to watch. She was on her way. And then she met Roger.

It was three days since Claire had had her abortion. She had known at the time that it was probably the only sensible course. Roger no longer loved her – if indeed he had ever loved her. She had wanted the baby for his sake. A small thought had crept into the back of her mind. She had tried to brush it away, but it kept coming back. Had she wanted the baby just to keep Roger, to make Roger love her again? If so, his reaction could hardly have been worse.

'Well, I hope you don't think it's mine,' he had said furiously when she had broken the news to him.

Claire had looked at him stunned. 'I haven't slept with

anyone else,' she had cried. 'I love you. Why should I want to fuck anyone else?'

'Oh do try to be adult, Claire,' Roger said baldly.

'What do you mean "adult"? I trust you are not trying to tell me that you have fucked someone else?'

'Well, of course I have.'

It had been said. There was a long frozen silence. She'd half suspected it for months. It wasn't much of a shock, but it was numbing nevertheless. She felt icy inside. It explained everything – why he'd been ignoring her phone calls, his behaviour on the infrequent occasions they had been together. His lovemaking had been perfunctory; expert but almost clinical. Claire sat there appalled, not looking at him for ages.

Finally she said, 'I'd better go.'

Roger had said nothing, but as she rose and picked up her things, he had fished inside his pocket and pulled out his cheque book. She had watched him, mesmerized, as he had written out a cheque for £500.

'You'd better have it terminated,' he said. He had not been able to bring himself to say the word 'abortion', she remembered. 'This should take care of it.'

He handed the cheque to her. She'd taken it automatically, folding it and putting it away in her bag, hardly realizing what she was doing. She just wanted to get out of the room, away from him. She turned to go without saying a word.

As she reached the door, he said, 'I hope you'll be all right, Claire.'

She left the flat without looking back at him. She didn't want his pity. She walked down the stairs and out of the main door in a dream. She never remembered driving away, only the pain in her chest, which was almost unbearable.

*   *   *

Sally re-entered the room bearing a tray.

'You know, darling, what you need is a job. Here, try this. It's not half bad.'

'A job? I'm not fit for work,' protested Claire feebly, shifting her limbs and hoisting herself up in the bed, to receive the soup.

'Nonsense! If you were offered a part tomorrow, you'd be off like a shot, you know you would.'

Claire took the tray, before replying, 'I suppose you're right. I don't know where I'd get the strength from, though. I feel as weak as a kitten.'

'You look a bit like one, too. All sort of fluffy and vulnerable.'

Claire laughed in spite of herself. 'I look a fright and you know it.'

'That's better,' said Sally, smiling encouragingly. 'It's so lovely to hear you laugh.' Claire turned away. 'It will get better you know. It will take time, but it will get better.' Sally laid her hands gently on top of Claire's.

'Yes, I know . . . I've been reading the book you bought yesterday. It's beautifully written.'

'I thought you'd like it.'

'Absolutely no sex or violence.'

'Precisely.'

'Makes one believe in a better world.'

'There's one out there waiting for you.'

Silence.

Finally Claire looked up and said, 'Sal, you've been wonderful to me. I'd never have got through this without you.'

'That's what friends are for,' said Sally breezily. 'Now what else are we going to watch tonight?'

'There's one of those Hollywood biblical epics on later,'

said Claire, glancing at the paper, which was amongst the reading matter strewn across the bed.

'Oh good, I love those,' said Sally gleefully. 'They're always good for a laugh and, boy, could we do with one. And then there's all those lovely hunky men wandering around in their little skirts – it'll do you good to see that there are some other good-looking men around, even if they are all in Hollywood.'

'As this movie was made in 1954, most of them will be pushing seventy,' observed Claire.

'Now, now, no ageist remarks, please. What's wrong with older men? Come to think of it, it's what you need, a nice older man to look after you. Might treat you properly.'

'Do they get any better as they get older?' asked Claire doubtfully.

'Not really,' replied Sally, who prided herself on being an authority on the sex. 'Usually a bit more reactionary. Oh, and their balls get bigger.'

'Really?' Claire giggled. 'How do you know?'

'It's a well-known fact,' said Sal airily.

'I might give it a try in that case,' replied Claire.

Sally smiled her approval. 'That's better, you're sounding a bit more like your old self.'

'I can't be my old self, not without Rog,' said Claire bleakly.

'I mean your *old* self,' Sally emphasized. 'The one you were before you met Svengali.'

Claire looked up, surprised.

'Oh yes,' Sally continued, 'you've no idea how that man dominated your life. What was the big attraction?'

Claire reflected for a moment. 'Sex – initially. It had never been so good with anyone before.'

* * *

22

That night, after Sally had gone home, Claire lay in the dark, trying to sleep. Her mind unwillingly turned to thoughts of Roger. Whatever his faults, he was a considerate and thoughtful lover. She had been astounded the first time they had been in bed together. It had been at his flat after a photo session. First he had stroked her neck and shoulders gently, and kissed her softly, running his fingers lightly down her throat to her breasts, just brushing the tips of her nipples. He had caressed her, lovingly kissing her body all over, driving her wild with anticipation. The sudden unexpected violence of his entry into her drew from her a gasping scream, which seemed to spur him on. His bottom lip glistened with lust as he thrust into her. She had become frantic, when he had suddenly withdrawn and started licking her clitoris avidly. Then sucking on it. She moaned and begged him to fuck her. His eyes had narrowed and the gleam of white, even teeth showed, an indication that he was amused by her pleading. Then he had slapped her sharply on the face, telling her to shut up. He would fuck her in his own good time.

She came to expect more shows of violence from him. On occasions, he would tie her by the wrists and ankles to the corners of the bed, then make her wait for the sublime lovemaking she knew was to follow. After a while, he would kneel astride her face and slowly push his cock into her mouth. He would bring himself almost to the point of orgasm before suddenly stopping and masturbating her until she had reached the same point.

Other times, he would be waiting for her, naked. 'Tie me up,' he would say, as she started to undress, eyeing her hungrily. She would see that his erection was already huge. He would stand obediently while she tied him with his hands behind his back to the posts at the foot of the bed. She would take her scarf and blindfold him, then spend an intensely

23

pleasurable half-hour tantalizing him. On her knees she would work her way up his legs with small kisses. As she arrived at his balls, she would see his cock jerk in anticipation of her touch. She would then leave him to wait. He would groan and beg her to continue. After a while, watching him writhe in anticipation, she would suddenly take his cock into her mouth, pushing his foreskin back with her lips. She enjoyed the power of being in control of him sexually on these occasions. After these bouts of titillation, their lovemaking would be frenetic and entirely satisfying, leaving them both exhausted.

Claire lay unblinking in the dark. He'd become bored with her. That was all. He had needed new stimulation, which she could no longer give him. She knew he had not wanted to make any sort of commitment, and had not expected any from her. The last thing he had wanted was for her to have a child. Claire wondered for the hundredth time how she had managed to get it all so wrong. She had thought he loved her. She realized now that she had mistaken lust for love. Well, she'd know better next time. Next time? How could there ever be a next time? She only wanted him. She would never be able to do all those things with anyone else. What she could not put from her mind was the thought that Roger was perhaps doing them at this moment with someone else.

Whoever she was, she couldn't possibly give him all that she, Claire, had given him. Four years was a long time. He'd soon realize his mistake. He'd start to miss her and come back to her. With this reassuring thought, Claire finally drifted off to sleep.

3

'What did you think of last night's episode?' Hugh Travis, the producer of *The McMasters*, tentatively put the question to his immediate superior, Martin Roberts. They were both seated at either side of Hugh's desk, reading through the next batch of episodes. There was a considerable pause as Martin mulled it over.

Finally he said, 'Not bad, not bad – a bit slow in places, perhaps, but on the whole, it was – er – well, it was – er –'

'Crap!' announced Larry Matthews from the doorway. Both men looked up startled. Larry swung into the room, clutching some scripts and a pair of spectacles in his hands. He closed the door behind him and flung himself into the nearest available chair. 'Unmitigated crap!' he informed the ceiling. 'Weary, flat, stale, and unprofitable,' he quoted for added effect.

The other two looked at each other. Hugh rolled his eyes heavenwards and shrugged his shoulders resignedly. He knew that Larry was right. His verdict was perhaps a little forceful, but he had a point. The series was becoming stale, predictable and – dare one even think it? – dull. Martin looked dismayed.

'Oh dear, do you think so? I thought it had moments . . .' he faltered. 'Moments of . . .'

'It had moments', interrupted Larry, 'of hitherto

unplumbed depths of dreariness.' Here he adopted an attitude of extreme languor. 'That simply dreadful scene with those two elderly juveniles droning on at each other, boring the pants off me and, I imagine, the rest of the country!'

'Who are you talking about?' asked Martin genuinely puzzled.

'I think he's referring to Geoff and Bella,' muttered Hugh. 'Droning were they? It seemed quite a lively little scene to me,' he added defensively.

'Lively? *Lively?*' Larry emitted a contemptuous snort. 'It had about as much life as last week's doughnuts!'

'Why do you refer to them as "elderly juveniles"?' persisted Martin.

Larry looked at him pityingly. 'Because you know as well as I do that they're both well into their middle years, yet they insist on prancing around like a couple of teenagers, Geoff in particular. Let's face it, the succession of prepubescent pulchritude that has passed through these portals, over the last few years to enjoy the dubious pleasure of on-screen, and more often than not off-screen, amorous activities with our leading man, simply to pander to his vanity, has completely deballsed the series.' He now had their undivided attention. 'As I remember it, you, my venerable old friend,' Larry was addressing his remarks to Hugh, 'had a humdinger of an idea back in the dark ages, seven or eight years ago. A saga centred around a family business of fine arts, antiques, and paintings, the infighting, intrigue of the international art world, sibling rivalry, the struggle for power, at the core of which was a crumbling marriage and all the tensions attendant thereon . . .'

'It was your idea, actually,' Hugh interjected mildly.

Larry glanced at Hugh affectionately. 'I seem to remember, you dear old thing, that you dreamed up this stunning scenario to provide a suitable showcase for the not inconsiderable talents of the love of your life, the then breathtakingly beautiful Bella -- am I right, or am I right?'

There was a pause as the two men regarded each other across the desk.

'Hot on the alliteration today, aren't you?' was all Hugh said.

'Aren't I though,' replied Larry equably.

Martin shuffled his feet uneasily and adjusted his position in his chair. The conversation seemed to have drifted into emotional waters and Martin was feeling like the proverbial fish. He was well aware of Hugh's abiding passion for Bella. As was Hugh's wife, Mona. She had learned to live with it. She knew that by comparison with Bella, she was ordinary, the unkind might even say plain. She also knew that Hugh would never leave her. Bella knew it, too. She had been aware from the beginning that the series was a sort of consolation prize. Hugh was giving her all that he was able.

Bella had had a drink problem for some time, ever since she had realized that her career was not going to go the way she had hoped. She had wanted to be up there alongside the greats, among the great classical actresses of her generation. That's why she had come into the profession. She was not able to put her finger on exactly what had gone wrong. But whatever it was, it had been compounded by seven years as the star of the most popular drama series of the decade, and the alcohol helped to blunt the keenness of the disappointment. She had been twice married and had had innumerable affairs, nearly always with younger men. Hugh had remained the constant element in her life, a sort of father confessor. They had long since ceased to have physical relations. For him, however, she had never ceased to hold an all-consuming fascination. He admired her undeniable talent, her husky beautifully modulated voice, her voluptuous good looks, but he loathed her drinking, not least because he knew he had contributed in part to her reliance on its dubious comfort.

'We've lost the bite this show had at the beginning. The almost unbearable tension between warring husband and wife. The will-they-won't-they-make-it situation. Everybody knows they won't because he's been floating around with a flotilla of fatuous floozies.' Larry was getting into his stride. 'And furthermore,' he continued, 'I have spent the morning wading my way through Episodes Ten and Eleven and I am now seized with an urgent desire to find a quiet corner somewhere and hang myself!'

The other two regarded him steadfastly and waited. They knew that this histrionic outburst was simply the prelude to an inspired suggestion. Larry would attack the problem in the most extreme terms and then quite casually supply the solution.

Larry Matthews's position at South Eastern Television was unique. He was ostensibly PA to Hugh Travis, and responsible for the smooth running of the studios during recording days. But he had somehow managed to engineer himself into a position immediately behind Hugh's right ear, and had a very large say in the casting, story lines and even budget allocation. He had been at drama college with Hugh twenty-five years previously, where they had become fast friends. When Hugh had reached his exalted position as Head of Series at SETV, Larry had suddenly turned up one day demanding a job. Acting, he had said, bored him. He needed a new challenge and it was absolutely certain that he, Hugh, was the man to provide it. It was true that Hugh was at that very moment in need of a personal assistant, a fact that he was quite sure Larry had somehow ferreted out for himself. They had gone off for a long luncheon together, during which

28

Larry had poured out his heart to Hugh. His personal life, he confided, was in disarray. He needed a new start in life. He begged his old friend to give it to him. He was prepared to work his balls off for the chance. Hugh knew, looking at the intelligent good-looking face, now showing signs of age, that Larry would be as good as his word. He also knew he would make an invaluable assistant. As to what personal problems Larry might have, Hugh did not know and didn't care to enquire. He had never been quite sure as to Larry's sexual predilections – he had a feeling that he had possibly had a string of attachments of both sexes, but he let that pass. He gave him a job, and after a couple of minor successes together they had thought up and put on *The McMasters*, which was, and had been from the first episode, a smash hit. Hugh regarded him now with an amused tolerance. Larry had certainly breathed life into South Eastern Television. Things were never dull when he was around.

'I take it you have a solution?' Hugh said eventually, aware that Larry was waiting for a cue.

'Of course,' replied Larry languidly. 'I've rewritten them,' and he closed his eyes, as though the exertion of his labours had been too much for him.

'I thought you might have,' said Hugh mildly.

'What's Colin going to say?' Martin looked perturbed.

'Fuck Colin,' replied Larry blithely. He opened his eyes and looked at them. 'You're the producers of the series, you're the arbiters of taste, for God's sake, and we all know that what has been served up in Episodes Ten and Eleven is nothing more or less than sentimental drivel!'

There was a longish pause, then Hugh said, 'Right! Well, we'd better hear your rewrites then.'

'I thought you'd never ask,' observed Larry dryly, as he sat up, put his half-glasses on the end of his nose and opened

29

the first script. 'That'll teach me to take holidays,' he muttered as he found the right page. 'That load of twaddle that passed for ''prime-time drama'' last night was perpetrated when I was in San Francisco, of course. Ah, here we are. Now first of all I think I should mention I've introduced two new characters – '

'You've done what?' exploded Hugh, sitting bolt upright. This time Larry had gone too far.

'Two new characters,' repeated Larry patiently.

'Without consulting me?' Hugh was outraged.

'I'm consulting you now,' said Larry, unimpressed by Hugh's outburst, 'that's why I'm here. This is the consultation.'

'Have you any idea how much two new actors will cost the series? Yes, of course you have,' said Hugh, answering his own question. 'We've been over the budget together!'

'I know exactly how much it will cost – and we solve the problem by losing two of the others.'

Throughout this exchange Martin had looked aghast and was incapable of speech.

'Who do you suggest?' asked Hugh, scarcely able to believe his ears.

'Well, the appalling Patsy for one,' Larry said, looking beadily at Hugh, whom, he noticed, had the grace to blush. 'Crotch casting never works,' Larry had stated bluntly at the time. 'Then, there's dear old Fred – he's finding the going a bit rough. We could put him out to pasture – or not have him in the series quite so often,' he added hurriedly, seeing their horrified faces. 'Oh come on, girls, we've got a hit series on our hands here, which has at least another couple of years' life in it. We've got to keep it up to scratch or, let's face it, we won't be asked back again. It'll go down the pan at the end of the season.'

There was another silence as they considered the prospect.

'All right,' said Hugh, finally. 'What's your idea? Who are these newcomers?'

Larry looked at him over the top of his spectacles. 'I want to put the cat among the pigeons,' he said quietly. 'A threat, a rival, a stunning young woman. She tries to steal Paul McMaster's clients, his business, and, finally, his heart.' There was another pause.

'I like it,' said Hugh simply. Martin nodded in agreement. Larry allowed himself a small smile. 'And the other character?' asked Hugh.

'An American,' said Larry, watching their faces closely. 'A rich American playboy with a weakness for fine art, who falls for the new girl and decides to back her financially.' And he sat back to watch their reactions. They both stared at him unblinking.

'I like that, too,' said Hugh sanguinely.

'What do you think, Marty?' demanded Larry cheekily.

'I think you'd better read us your rewrites,' was the quiet response.

'Attaboy!' said Larry enthusiastically, drawing his chair up to the table.

'And then,' said Hugh, 'we'd better draw up a shortlist of possible actresses.'

'And possible Americans,' added Martin, determined not to be left out. 'Quite a few live in this country, I believe.'

Larry delivered his final bombshell. 'I thought we might import someone from Hollywood,' he said airily. 'Shall I start reading?'

4

Geoffrey Armitage stood in the untidy rambling kitchen of his spacious home. The face that featured so effectively in *The McMasters*, making millions of female hearts beat faster every Sunday evening between 7.45 and 8.40, was at this moment gazing with unseeing eyes at the deep yellow wall in front of him. The intensity of the colour offended him to the depths of his soul.

'Why yellow?' he had asked his wife, Sukie, as he stared aghast at the deep yellow ochre walls after they had just moved in.

'It's an optimistic colour,' she had replied firmly. 'It'll be like waking up to a glorious sunrise every day.'

'No it won't, it'll be like waking up inside a fried egg every day,' he had retorted. He had worn sunglasses for a week as a mute protest. It seemed to him that the children's noise at breakfast was amplified because of the relentlessly cheerful walls. He had stated his objections on numerous occasions, but his wife was unmoved, and the walls had stayed yellow through the ensuing years. Now he was waiting for the toaster to eject its load into the immediate vicinity, which he would deftly field. The toaster was ancient and erratic, and would either emit a sort of dull phut and produce two pieces of warm bread, or, after an interminable wait, suddenly and startlingly give an abrupt click and two scorched brittle objects would catapult ceilingwards. Geoffrey had a recurring daydream. He was sitting in a small ultra-clean, high-tech, white and red kitchen. In front of him, carefully laid out on the shining white and chrome table, were a glass of freshly squeezed orange juice, a large cup of steaming, freshly ground coffee and a plate of crisp bacon rashers, a perfectly poached egg and lashings of deep beige toast sodden with butter. A slim young blonde, wearing only a plastic apron, was ministering to his every need. There were no children present. At this moment, the kitchen door burst open and Nicky, his younger son, hurtled in. At the same time the toaster sprang into life and two blackened pieces of toast sailed through the air.

'Bad luck, Dad,' said Nicky, picking one up from the floor. 'You've burned the toast again.'

'I have not burned the toast again,' his father emphasized. 'The fucking toaster has burned the toast again.'

'You shouldn't swear, Dad. Mum doesn't like it, she says you swear too much in front of us.'

'Fuck your mother,' muttered Geoff on his hands and knees, looking around for the second piece of toast.

'It would be incest,' observed Nicky knowledgeably, helping himself to a packet of Sugar Puffs from a cupboard.

'What?' said Geoff, startled, looking up abruptly and hitting his head on the table.

'Oh no,' groaned Nicky, examining a plastic container. 'There's no sugar!'

'You don't need sugar on Sugar Puffs!' said Geoff, outraged.

'Daad!' wailed his son. 'I always have sugar on them.'

'Well, you shouldn't. You'll have false teeth by the time you're twelve.'

'Mum, there's no sugar!' said Nicky, with hands

outstretched in a dramatic gesture to his mother, who had just come into the kitchen laden with a pile of dirty linen.

'Yes there is, you just haven't looked properly. Who gave that cat a piece of toast?' she asked with interest.

Geoff sighed. The second piece had landed by the Aga. Brambles, the cat, positioned himself next to it every morning to keep warm and observe the family breakfast for any stray scraps of food that might drop to the floor. He was frankly disappointed with today's offering and, after several attempts to chew his way through the outer crust, gave up, leapt up onto a worktop and settled himself comfortably next to the breadboard.

'Get off!' Geoff addressed the cat furiously. 'Honestly, Sukes, it's terribly unhygienic. That cat is encouraged to pollute our food.' The cat in question gave him a look of cold contempt, leaped down to the floor, stalked across the kitchen in high dudgeon, broke wind and made an abrupt exit through the cat flap.

'Ugh!' Nicky exclaimed in disgust. 'Brambles has farted! What a pong!'

'Nicky,' protested Sukie feebly.

Geoff decided to be firm. 'Kindly get on with your breakfast and if you can't say anything pleasant, don't say anything at all – and you don't need that.' He deftly removed the sugar packet that Sukie had obligingly found and put on the table. He crossed to the kettle, which had just boiled, and poured water onto instant coffee in a cracked mug.

'Is it a studio day?' asked Sukie. 'I've lost track.'

'No, it is not a studio day,' Geoff said with elaborate politeness. 'It is a read-through day. We are reading through the next two episodes.'

'Well, let's hope to God they're better than last Sunday's horror,' said Sukie calmly.

'Thank you for those few words of encouragement and support,' replied Geoff satirically, after a brief pause. 'I appreciate your keen interest in my work and I'm gratified to learn that you rate my talent as an actor so highly.'

'It's got nothing to do with your talent as an actor,' she retorted. 'I'm just saying that the episode was bloody awful, that's all.'

Nicky decided he could make a useful contribution to the conversation. 'Timpson Minor said it was stupid,' he said, then clapped a hand over his mouth, realizing that 'stupid' could hardly be classified as 'pleasant' and said hurriedly, 'His sister loves it. She's six.'

'That's about the age group it's aimed at,' Sukie agreed. 'And as for that bimbo what's her name, Patsy? Yes, Patsy Hall. Where on earth did they find her?'

Geoff lowered his head to hide the fact that he was blushing furiously. He had been having an intermittent fling with Patsy ever since she'd joined the series. He was aware that she was totally talentless, but she smelt, felt and tasted delightful. He decided to employ double bluff tactics.

'Oh come on, she's not that bad.'

'She's appalling.' Sukie poured herself some tea. 'She can't act, she can't move, she can't speak and, worst of all, she has absolutely no class!'

'I think she's one of Hugh's mistakes,' Geoff said lamely.

'I really think you should have a word with Hugh. He may be losing his grip.'

'Have I met him?' asked Geoff, abruptly changing the subject and addressing his son – 'this Timpson turd?'

'Geoff,' Sukie remonstrated.

'No, Dad, his parents are very rich. I'd hardly bring him back here, would I?' asked Nicky, giving his father a pitying look.

'Oh that's nice, isn't it? Are you suggesting that your home is not good enough for turdfeatures Timpson?' enquired Geoff icily.

'Geoffrey, please,' interposed Sukie.

'Dad,' said his son calmly, 'if you can't say anything pleasant, don't say anything at all.'

'I shall say what I bloody well please,' said Geoff venomously. 'You can tell Timpson Minor from me that I think he's a pain in the arse.'

'Who's a pain in the arse?' panted Ben, as he came in through the back door clad in running gear. 'Hi, Dad.'

'Hello, Ben,' said his father, surprised. Ben was fifteen and as laid-back as Nicky was energetic. 'What are you doing here?'

'I live here, remember?' replied his son easily.

'I meant, why aren't you at school, and what are you doing in your tracksuit?'

'Marathon practice,' replied Ben briefly. 'Who's a pain in the arse?'

'Ben,' said Sukie sternly.

Nicky filled him in. 'I was telling Dad that Timpson Minor thought Sunday's episode of *The Old Bastards* was stupid.'

'Nicky!'

'Well yes,' said Ben, 'but he only said that because Timpson Major said it.'

'Who the hell do these Timpsons think they are?' Geoff asked in a voice rising with sarcasm and disbelief. 'Are they experts in the field of the television dramatic critique or what?'

'No, of course not, Dad,' replied Ben equably, 'but on this point you must admit it's a fair assessment.'

'Did you see Sunday's episode?'

'No.'

'Why not?'

'I never watch it, Dad, you know that. They all watch it at school. Unfortunately.'

'I saw it,' said Sukie, still thinking of Patsy. 'It stank!'

Geoff looked stunned for a moment. Then, with all the dignity he could muster, he said, 'Did it? Did it indeed? Well, I should like to point out to you all that this stinking programme pays the mortgage, buys the food, provides for your future, supplies your sports equipment, pays for your holidays . . .'

'Feeds the cat,' Nicky suggested helpfully.

Geoff glared at him. 'Feeds the cat,' he conceded. 'Er, buys, er . . .'

'Buys Mum's clothes,' prompted Nicky, determined to help his father out.

Sukie glanced down at her fading jeans and sagging tee shirt. 'What clothes?' she asked.

'Thank you, I can manage to quote from this litany of advantages without your assistance,' Geoff remarked to Nicky. Then, turning to his wife, he said, 'Are you aware that there is a pile of dirty washing in the middle of the floor?'

Sukie regarded the offending heap with mild interest. 'Yes, as a matter of fact, I was going to ask you if you could add a laundry service to your list of things that that crass TV series makes possible?'

'Crass?' enquired Geoff politely.

'What's crass?' asked Nicky.

'Oh come on, Geoff, you must admit it *is* pretty dire.'

Geoff rose to his feet without a word and left the kitchen.

'Nice one, Mum,' observed Nicky.

'What are you going to eat, Ben?' asked his mother.

'Beans on toast,' replied Ben immediately, 'but I'll get it.'

'Can I have some?' chimed in Nicky.

Geoff reappeared carrying a script and a jacket. 'I am going

37

out now,' he announced. 'I may be some time. I am, in fact, about to make the same sort of heroic gesture as that remarkable man Captain Lawrence Oates. I am going to compromise my integrity, jeopardize my career, sacrifice my dignity – it's a form of suicide, I think you'll agree – and all for the sake of my family – to whom I am devoted – to ensure their survival. In other words, I am going to attempt a read-through of this crass, stupid, nay dire television series – which stinks and of which I am happy and proud to be the figurehead. You must excuse me – duty calls.' And so saying he opened the back door and swept out.

There was a brief silence as the little group remaining in the kitchen went about their business. Ben proceeded to heat up some baked beans and cook two perfectly golden brown pieces of toast, one for Nicky, one for himself. Sukie poured herself a second cup of tea. After a moment or two, Brambles thrust a tentative head through the cat flap. Having ascertained that the coast was clear, the rest of him followed and he walked confidently in, made straight for the breadboard and settled himself down comfortably beside it, paws tucked beneath him.

'I think you could have been a bit more circumspect about the laundry service, Mum,' Ben said.

'What's circumspect?' asked Nicky.

'Well, it is a dreadful show,' said Sukie defensively. 'It used not to be, but it's become just dull and improbable, which sounds like a paradox, I suppose . . .'

'What's a paradox?' asked Nicky.

'What it needs,' continued Sukie, 'what it really needs, is an injection of new blood, a bit of life – a new character. And to get rid of the ghastly Patsy,' she added savagely under her breath.

38

5

'They are looking for a tall blonde to play a tough business woman, owner of a rival art gallery, bent on poaching the McMasters' clientele and putting them out of business. The story line being, of course, that the two galleries eventually decide to merge and Sara Harper, that's the character, takes over joint control of the business with Paul McMaster and he falls for her, which causes all sorts of complications on the work and home front, as you can imagine. It's a great part and you're absolutely right for it, except that you're not tall and you're not blonde – hang on a minute, there's someone on the other line.'

Thus spake David Hawkins, Claire's agent. It was exactly two weeks since her abortion and Claire was at the lowest ebb of her life. She now realized that Roger was basically an egotistical cruel shit. So why, she asked herself, was there this appalling pain where she believed her heart was located. She supposed it was the rejection. Being dumped. Not wanted on voyage. Tears started to well again.

David's phone call had given her a small ray of hope. Sally had stated unequivocally that what she needed was work. It would change her whole perspective on things. A couple of weeks to recuperate – get her strength back and she'd be ready to take on the world again. Claire secretly doubted this. But right on cue, David had phoned. She hadn't heard from him in weeks and as ever, the prospect of a new challenge had thrilled her. And now she was not even being considered for a part for which she was eminently suitable because her hair was the wrong colour and her stature too short. In normal circumstances, Claire would simply have shrugged her shoulders and said 'That's showbiz'. But somehow, now, it seemed as though she wasn't good enough for Roger and she wasn't good enough for South Eastern Television either. She was inadequate on all counts.

David was speaking again. 'You still there Claire?'

'Yes. David, why does this character have to be blonde?'

'Because Bella Shand is dark, I suppose. Oh don't ask me – I shall never understand how producers' minds work. Anyway, I did point out to Martin and Hugh that you were perfect for the part in every other respect and that they ought to at least see you and let you read.'

Ah, another spark of hope.

'And what was their reaction?'

'They said that they'd think about it.'

'When was this?'

'Last week.'

'You never told me,' said Claire, thinking how much just a prospect would have helped her get through last week. But David knew nothing of recent events. She wouldn't have dreamed of telling him.

'Of course not,' replied David briskly. 'There's no point in raising your hopes until I've at least secured you an interview. When did you work with Larry Matthews?'

Claire thought hard. 'I never have,' she said eventually. 'Why?'

'He seems to know your work, that's all.'

'Oh, I remember, he came to see us in *The Rivals*, well, not me exactly, his boyfriend was in it playing Faulkland.'

40

'Ah, that would explain it. Well, anyway, they're going to see you on Thursday, eleven forty-five at their offices at Holroyd House. Do your best!'

Claire fell a thrill of excitement surge through her. 'How should I try to look?' she asked him enthusiastically.

'Tall,' David replied dryly, and hung up.

Claire laughed out loud. It was the first time she'd laughed in weeks, she realized. She had an uncanny feeling that things were going to get better. She recognized a familiar steeliness, a sense of resolve and determination coming over her. She was going to get this part. She wanted it. More than that, she needed it. It was going to be her salvation. Thursday. Today was Tuesday. That gave her a whole day to sort out something suitable to wear. She might have to borrow an item from Sally's wardrobe. She crossed to the large mirror that hung above the sofa. Dear God, she thought, I look a fright. Her face was gaunt, pale, her eyes deep and unfathomable, her hair limp and untidy. She sighed heavily and crossed back to the phone. It suddenly rang. Her heart leaped. Roger, she thought involuntarily. She picked up the receiver with trembling hands.

'Hello,' she said timidly, hardly daring to hope.

'Hi, kid, how you doing?'

It was Sal's cheery voice. Claire felt an initial shock of disappointment followed by one of relief. Of course it wasn't Roger, it was never going to be Roger again. And a bloody good thing too!

'Hi, Sal. I'm okay. No, as a matter of fact I'm more than okay. I'm seeing some producers about a job on Thursday so things are looking up.'

'Darling, that's wonderful. Can I come round tonight?'

'Well, funnily enough, I was going to ask you over. I was just about to dial your number. How did you know?'

41

'I'm clairvoyant, and one doesn't dial any more, one punches.'

'True. What time will you be here?'

'In about an hour. I'm bringing some food. You're looking a bit peaky so I'm going to cook you supper!'

'You darling.' Claire was genuinely touched. 'You couldn't possibly bring most of your wardrobe with you as well could you? God knows what I'm going to wear for this interview.'

'What's the part?'

'Oh, sort of classy ballbreaker by the sound of it.'

'I've got just the thing! See you later,' and Sally rang off.

Claire felt better than she'd done for ages. Suddenly there was real hope. She wandered slowly into her bedroom and slid back the cupboard doors. Three long peasant skirts – Roger had liked peasant skirts. A calf-length tweed skirt and matching long jacket – Roger had liked those, too. The high-necked long-sleeved velvet evening dress that Roger had chosen for her, and a cashmere stole – and several pairs of low-heeled pumps. It dawned on her that her entire wardrobe consisted not of her taste but of Roger's. She had dressed to please him. There was certainly nothing suitable for a tough aggressive business woman here.

She remembered how she used to dress before she met Roger: trousers, sweatshirts, boots; jeans, tee shirts, sneakers; very short skirts with high heels and little nipped in jackets; daringly low-cut evening dresses and anything that was either ethnic or outrageous. Individual clothes for a confident independent woman. She had worn make-up too. Sometimes lots of it. She enjoyed wearing it. Roger had somehow persuaded her that she looked better without it. The only time she got the opportunity to make up was on stage or before the cameras. That's how she'd first met Roger. In front of the camera. She'd had long hair then, too. A thick wonderful shining mane. And she'd been wearing a lot of makeup. He'd come to take her photo for a magazine article, a glossy in-depth piece featuring young actresses who had been tipped as 'the girls most likely to succeed'. It had been her only real taste of fame so far. Roger was one of the most successful photographers around, and he'd fallen for her at once, she knew that. She could tell by the way he looked at her. And by the photographs he had taken of her. Yet within a year he had persuaded her to cut off her lovely hair and divest herself of all her make-up. She stood staring at the open cupboard as she remembered. Why had he wanted to change her? It was a mystery.

She walked slowly over to the dressing-table, sat down, and opened the left-hand drawer. Yes, it was all there, her make-up box, false eyelashes, everything. Deliberately she started to apply a golden tinted foundation, not thickly but just enough to give her a tan-like glow. Next, eyeliner, flicked up at the ends to give her eyes an upward slant, her favourite exotic look. Then she outlined her lips with a lipliner, filled in her mouth with a paler lipstick, never a dark one, not for Claire. A smudge of eyeshadow, bronze blusher on the cheekbones and temples, even the chin. And finally, yes, why not? Natural-looking eyelashes, stuck right at the roots of her own, and liberally mascaraed top and bottom.

Her hair had now grown back to almost shoulder length, but was looking decidedly lifeless. She opened the other drawer and pulled out the hairpiece she had bought last year. She had suddenly been asked to play Mary Magdalene in a charity Christmas show. They couldn't afford to hire a wig for her, so she had gone out and bought one herself from a theatrical wigmakers. She had seen an advertisement announcing that they were selling off old stock. She had been thrilled with it, and had worn it a couple of times since on stage. Now she rifled around and found some hairpins. She wound small sections of her own hair on the crown of her head and secured them with hairgrips. Then she brushed the false hair vigorously and attached it to the pin curls with large hairpins. She teased her own hair back to blend in with the false piece and, hardly bearing to look at herself, sauntered into the kitchen to fill the kettle. Tea. One of her favourite indulgences.

Suddenly she remembered an old holdall in the broom cupboard in the passage. She was sure she had kept some of her old clothes there. She all but ran out of the kitchen, wrenched the cupboard door open and dragged out the case, unzipped it – and yes, it was bulging with garments. Thinking she could use them when she next decorated, she'd never thrown them out. They were mainly jeans, trousers and tops. She exclaimed with delight as she unearthed some much-loved jungle-green army fatigues. She bundled the rest back into the case and carried it lovingly into the bedroom. The kettle was boiling and she ran to make the tea, then hurried back to the bedroom and took out the fatigues. Admittedly they smelt a bit strange, but that couldn't be helped. She'd give them a good wash that night.

She tore off her blouse and ankle-length skirt, stepped into the all-in-one outfit and zipped up the front. It still fitted well. If anything it was a touch large; of course, she had lost weight recently. It needed a belt – well, at least she still had those. On a shelf in a cupboard she found her favourite. It was very wide, brown shaped leather and she fastened it around her waist with mounting excitement. Shoes – of course, trainers – she used those for rehearsals. She dug them out of the back of the wardrobe and rammed them on her feet. Then, picking up the rest of the clothes from the bed, she strode confidently back into the kitchen, opened the door of the washing machine and chucked them all in. Washing powder and softener followed, then she slammed the door and clicked the controls. She poured a large breakfast cup of tea and wandered into the sitting room. Then, and then only, did she allow herself a good look at her reflection.

To her delight and surprise Claire saw a girl she had once known smiling back at her. She all but whooped with joy. Could it be that she actually felt happy? That the awful weight of misery that she had been dragging around with her for months was beginning to lighten? The anguish of the last two weeks had been insupportable and she knew it would be a long time before that diminished. But this was the start. She surveyed herself from all angles, then sat down on the sofa to sip her tea. Perhaps some music? No, no, not music, not yet. Music stirred the emotions. No, she mustn't overreach herself. One step at a time. Practical progress first. The door bell rang. Again her heart leapt. This was ridiculous. She must learn to control herself. She put the cup down on the glass coffee table and went to the front door.

'Hello, darling. I'm a bit early. Does it matter?' Sally stood in the doorway laden with carrier bags and clothes slung over her arm. 'My God! Have I come to the wrong flat?' she exclaimed in amazement as she took in Claire's appearance.

Claire laughed. 'Do you like it?'

'Like it?' cried Sally, dropping her burdens and hugging her. 'Oh, darling, welcome back!'

'Have I really changed that much?' asked Claire, extricating herself.

Sally stood back and surveyed her. 'This is the girl I knew four years ago. You look stunning!'

Claire smiled back at her. 'I think I'm going to get better, Sal,' she said evenly.

'I know you are,' Sally replied with conviction. 'You look heaps better already, though admittedly you smell a little funny, sort of mildewy! Nothing that a drop of scent won't put right.'

Claire giggled. 'I'll go and get some.'

Sally stopped her. 'No, darling, new man, new scent,' she said firmly.

'But I haven't got a new man,' protested Claire laughingly.

'Looking like that, you soon will have,' said Sally. 'Yep, new job, new man, I'm absolutely convinced of it.'

'Yes,' said Claire doubtfully, 'but I've got to get the job first.'

'And so you shall!' said her friend with determination. 'See what I've brought you!' And she rescued the clothes from the floor where they had fallen.

'But, Sal,' protested Claire, as Sally held up a superb-looking garment, 'this is your new Italian suit!'

'That's right,' responded Sally gaily. 'It's perfect, isn't it?' And she held it up against Claire. 'This'll get you the job!'

6

She had class. Of that there was no doubt. She looked good, was in fact stunning. High cheekbones, slanting grey eyes, dark reddish brown hair and a flawless complexion. Hugh noted it all. The impeccably cut slate-grey suit. The moss agate earrings and matching ring, the dark green of which was picked up in a long narrow silk scarf hung loosely around her neck. The shoes and handbag of matching grey suede. The hair piled on top of her head. Hugh felt a surge of excitement. He had found Sara Harper.

'Excuse me a moment will you, Ms Jenner?' He rose from his seat. 'Oh, would you care to take a look at the script?' he added. 'I'm just popping down the corridor.'

'Thank you, yes, I'd love to.'

He seemed to be in a hurry, Claire thought. As soon as he had gone, she picked up the wodge of type-covered paper that he had placed in front of her. The pages were held together at the top with a single clip. 'The McMasters. Episode 10', it said on the front page, followed by a list of the producers, assistants and various other administrative personnel. She flicked through the pages, trying to find her character. She already thought of it as 'hers'. She had an idea that Hugh was impressed. He had seemed agitated. She noticed that she often had this effect on men. Ah, here it was.

Int. Sara's office.

A tall blonde woman is perched on the edge of a desk. She is speaking on the telephone. She swings a shapely leg as she talks.

SARA: I don't think I will have any difficulty in obtaining the Rembrandt sketch for you, Contessa. What are you prepared to go to – (She breaks off abruptly as her office door opens quietly.) Who the hell are you? Get out of here! (She glares at the intruder.)

PAUL: Good afternoon. Ms Harper, I presume?

SARA: Who are you and what the hell do you think you are doing in my office?

PAUL: My apologies, Ms Harper. I came to pay my respects. Well no, to be truthful, I came to size up the opposition. (He smiles charmingly.)

SARA: (Unimpressed.) Who let you in?

PAUL: I let myself in. I was hoping you wouldn't mind. (He gives her the benefit of another dazzling smile.)

SARA: Well, I do mind. Get out!

PAUL: (Taken aback.) I beg your pardon. I had no idea you'd take it so –

SARA: I said get out! (She picks a nearby ledger and flings it at him. He ducks and exits hurriedly.)

Claire smiled to herself. This was right up her street. She had to have this part. The door opened and Hugh reappeared with another man in tow, older, bald, benign-looking.

'Ah, Ms Jenner, you're still here,' he sounded relieved.

As if I'd think of going anywhere with a part like this hanging in the balance, thought Claire.

'This is Claire Jenner, Martin,' said Hugh. 'Ms Jenner, this is our producer, Martin Roberts.'

'I'm so pleased to meet you,' said Claire, rising to shake hands. Martin nodded and smiled shyly, shook her hand vigorously but did not speak. They both seemed uncertain of what to say next.

Then, seeing the script, Hugh had an inspiration. 'So, what did you think of Episode – er – Ten – is it? Yes, Episode Ten.'

'I've only just glanced at it,' replied Claire, wondering how on earth he supposed she'd had time to read it in the few minutes it had taken him to fetch Martin.

'Yes, yes, of course,' Hugh replied. 'Did you manage to find our Sara?' He spoke of the character as though she were a personal friend.

'Yes, I found her first entrance. I think it's brilliant.' Both men looked at her eagerly.

'Good, good, splendid,' said Hugh. 'And how do you feel about her?'

'I can handle her,' she replied, fingering the script for a moment, then tossing it across the desk.

'You can?' said Hugh. They were both looking at her intently.

'Oh yes, she's right up my street. Would you like me to read for you?'

'Oh no, no, good Lord, no, that won't be necessary, we know of your reputation.'

Do you? thought Claire in amazement. What reputation? She'd hardly done any television. Then she remembered. Of course, Larry Matthews – he'd obviously said nice things

49

about her Lydia Languish. 'Oh, I'm so glad,' she laughed. 'That's all right then.'

Martin had still not said a word, but was looking at her as though he wanted to drink her in. Claire didn't quite know what was expected of her. Hugh finally wound up the meeting.

'Well, thank you, Ms Jenner, for coming in to see us. We'll be speaking to your agent this afternoon.' He held out his hand. Martin followed suit. Claire, relieved that it was over, gathered her things together and took Hugh's outstretched hand.

'Thank you for seeing me,' she said charmingly. And then offered her hand to Martin. She had turned to go when the door burst open to reveal a tall blond good-looking man.

'Claire Jenner!' he proclaimed dramatically. 'What a lovely surprise. Are you leaving us?'

Claire crossed to the door, recognizing Larry Matthews at once. 'How good to see you again,' she said and meant it. 'Yes, I'm just off.'

'Then allow me to escort you to the lift.' And he took her arm and steered her out of the room and down the corridor.

'You look stunning,' he told her. 'I'm sure we'll be seeing a lot of each other.'

'I do hope so,' replied Claire fervently.

He propelled her into the lift, waving goodbye as the doors started to close. 'Have no fear,' he called out, as they shut and the lift started with a slight jolt to descend.

I think I've got it, Claire thought excitedly to herself. I think I've got it! She had driven herself to the offices and had been allowed to park briefly at the back of the building. She rescued her car, and smiled and waved cheerily at the man on the gate as she drove off. It took her some time to negotiate the London traffic. It was raining heavily and conditions were bad. She hardly noticed. All the way back, she kept saying to herself, I think I've got it, I think I've got it, hardly daring to believe it. When she finally got home an hour later, she tore up the front steps, flung herself into her flat and made straight for the telephone.

'David, David, it's me. I think I've got it!' she cried excitedly.

'Yes, they want you,' replied her agent mildly.

'How do you know?' she asked astounded.

'They rang the moment you left and offered you the part.'

'Oh God,' breathed Claire in a sort of ecstasy. 'It's a wonderful part, David, it really is.'

'Good,' said David briefly, 'then let's hope they offer you some wonderful money to go with it, which I very much doubt.'

'I don't care what they pay me,' said Claire recklessly.

'Well I do, I need the money even if you don't,' replied David tartly. Then relenting he said, 'No, seriously, Claire, I'm very pleased, you deserve it, well done!'

'Thank you,' said Claire happily. 'I won't let you down.'

'I know that,' replied David. 'You never do.' It was the nearest to a compliment she'd ever received from David, and she felt a warm glow of contentment.

He then instructed her to get pencil and paper and jot down filming dates. He told her that wardrobe and make-up would be contacting her, and to make herself available to them. And she was to present herself at the studios at the next recording a week from the day, for a make-up test.

She left an excited message on Sally's answering machine, thanking her profusely for the loan of the suit, which she was convinced got her the part.

She then phoned her mother in Wiltshire. She hadn't spoken to her in weeks. Claire had deliberately not contacted her during her recent unhappiness, not wanting to burden her and add to her own distress. Beatrice Jenner was over the moon. Inordinately proud of her beautiful daughter, she had known it would only be a matter of time before she got the break she deserved.

'Roger must be pleased,' she said happily.

The remark took Claire completely unawares. Finally she said falteringly, 'Oh, er, Roger and I are not seeing one another any more, Mum.'

'Oh dear, I am sorry, darling,' was the sympathetic response. 'When did this happen?'

'Oh, months ago. I didn't bother you with it at the time, because – well – it really wasn't important enough – we'd been building up to it for ages.' Claire was awfully afraid that she was going to cry. The sound of her mother's caring, understanding voice had brought a lump to her throat and she suddenly realized how much she had missed her.

Beatrice had heard a note of distress in her daughter's quavering voice, but kept her own counsel. She said, 'Well, darling, it's marvellous about this part. Your father will be thrilled.'

'How is he?' asked Claire, concerned.

'Not very well, darling, but this news will do him a power of good!'

After Claire had finished speaking to her mother, she felt guilty. She had not asked after her father for ages and her mother had borne the worry all alone.

It also occurred to her that she had not thought about Roger once the whole day.

7

Patsy carefully drew a dark red line around her pouting lips, then filled it in with deep pink shiny lipstick. A coat of clear lip gloss was applied and she stood back to survey the result. She was well pleased with what she saw – a startlingly pretty girl with a peaches and cream complexion, large dewy blue eyes and faintly pink blonde hair like candy floss. A voluptuous figure completed the perfection. She was perfection and she knew it. She could tell by the glances of wide-eyed disbelief she drew from males wherever she went. She was 'The McMasters' own little bit of Hollywood glitz'. That's what the *Globe* had said about her when she had first appeared in the series. She had been thrilled. It's what she wanted more than anything, to make it to Hollywood; they really appreciated her type of looks out there. So her Auntie Thelma had told her. Unfortunately, the *Globe* had followed up this eulogy the next week by dubbing her the programme's token brainless blonde bimbo with the big boobs and tiny talent. Patsy had been mortally wounded. She had a lot to learn when it came to acting, she would be the first to admit it. But then she had had no formal training, what did they expect?

Patsy had been a photographic model for nearly all her life. Her father had deserted her mother when Patsy was only four. She had not seen him since. There had been Christmas and birthday cards to begin with, but they had become sporadic and finally stopped altogether. Patsy hadn't minded a bit – she could hardly remember her father and there had been plenty of uncles to take his place. They had all spoiled her – she was, after all, such a pretty little girl. Her mother, suddenly realizing just how pretty her little girl was, enrolled her with a modelling agency. Patsy never looked back. She featured in commercials, knitting patterns, magazines and had even had a bit part in a children's TV series. Both Patsy and her mother had made a comfortable living, but her education had been sorely neglected. Patsy had no recollection of ever having read a book right through in her life.

When she was seventeen, her mother took up with someone called Bruce, who was keen for them all to go and live with him in his native Australia. But Patsy was unwilling to sacrifice what she considered to be a promising career, and to her mother's relief declined to join them. Patsy's mother was not entirely sure that Bruce's interest in Patsy's welfare was purely avuncular. Besides, Patsy was really much too pretty and only served to remind her of her own fading good looks. So Patsy was left to the mercies of Thelma, her mother's sister-in-law, who felt that her brother had neglected his own child and that she should try to make amends.

Auntie Thelma actively encouraged Patsy in her career and no one was happier than she when Patsy landed the part of Gemma, secretary to Paul McMaster in the most popular series. Admittedly, Patsy had little more to do than appear once or twice an episode with trays of coffee, or to announce the arrival of important clients, but Thelma gloried vicariously in Patsy's fame. She told her that the producers were bound to build up her part when they saw how popular she was. She was going to be a big star. Already Patsy was recognized wherever she went. She often caused quite a sensation in her local supermarket. She revelled in it. Then there was the attention she got from Geoff, who played Paul, the leading man, the star of the series. She had felt really important. He'd taken her out to dinner on a couple of occasions when they'd been on location. The affair that followed had been intermittent due to the fact that Geoff was married. Patsy didn't mind. She accepted love how and where she could find it.

She was never short of boyfriends. One of them, Stephen, had been one of the 'uncles' that had visited her mother on occasions. Now he visited Patsy and always brought presents: glamorous lingerie, expensive costume jewellery, perfume and on one glorious visit, a fox fur jacket, which she still persisted in wearing, oblivious to the critical looks of other women. His best present ever had been the little white Peugeot he'd given her for her twenty-fifth birthday. She always looked forward to his visits with breathless anticipation. Sadly, since her new-found fame, they'd become less frequent. As he patiently explained to her, if his wife found out, his visitations would have to stop altogether, and then no more treats for his baby.

Patsy resigned herself to Geoff's attentions, which paled by comparison. Somehow boxes of chocolates and bunches of flowers didn't compare favourably. Anyway she was nearly always on a diet, and the flowers died so quickly and smelt horrid. Instead, she'd asked him to persuade the scriptwriters to build up her part in the series. If he couldn't afford expensive gifts this was the least he could do for her. She wanted to be a star, she'd had a taste of fame and liked it. Now she wanted to be accepted as an actress as well, and what better way than to play opposite Geoff, a respected classical actor in his younger days? But Geoff was strangely evasive on the issue and she noticed that his attentions seemed to be less enthusiastic than before. Auntie Thelma said that publicity was the secret. Exposure. She needed to become a household word, to be in demand. Then the producers of the programme would realize what they'd got and would build her up. This was all very well, but how was it to be achieved?

Patsy surveyed herself in the long mirror in her bedroom. She smoothed her hands over her curvaceous frame. She couldn't fathom it. She'd got everything. Why couldn't they see it?

She was startled by the sound of the phone ringing. Who could that be? Maybe the studio had changed her call. She felt important as she moved slowly to the white phone by the bed. Let them wait. She picked up the telephone and put on her best telephone voice. 'Patsy Hall speaking.'

'Oh, hello, Pat. Snellor here, Tony Snellor. I'm a features writer for the *Globe*.'

'Oh yes.' Patsy was thrilled.

'We'd like to do a double-page spread on you, Miss Hall, your career, interests, boyfriend, et cetera, bit about the series – you know the sort of thing.'

'Oh yes,' she agreed eagerly, 'I do.' Patsy had had bits and pieces in the press before, but never a double-page spread. That'd make the cast sit up and take notice. 'When did you want to do it?' she asked, slightly flustered. 'I'm working all this week.'

'As soon as possible. We'd like the piece to go in on Saturday.'

'What, this Saturday?' she asked breathlessly. Her triumph was to be sooner than she thought. Their faces at the read-through on Saturday morning – thank goodness they rehearsed Saturdays. She couldn't wait!

'This could do you a lot of good, Patsy,' said Snellor, mistaking her silence for hesitation, not realizing that it took a few minutes for Patsy's brain to engage in gear.

'Oh yes, it could,' she agreed readily.

'Tomorrow looks good for me, how is it for you, Pat?'

'Patsy,' she corrected him primly. Tomorrow! Patsy was genuinely appalled. Tomorrow she was in the studio. It was impossible. Oh no, she couldn't miss this chance. It occurred to her that no one in the cast actually bought the *Globe*. Well, that didn't matter, she'd buy a copy and leave it lying around.

'Oh dear, I'm in the studio!' she wailed. 'It's the first day of Episode Nine!'

Snellor thought quickly. He was on to something here. This was a heaven-sent opportunity. This bimbo was thick as two short planks. She'd spill the beans all right. He only had to promise her blanket coverage, front-page picture, anything. And he could get the lowdown on everything that was going on behind the scenes on *The McMasters*. They'd finally get the dirt on Geoffrey Armitage. Trevor would be very pleased with him. This was going to sell a lot of papers! He kept his cool.

'What, all day?'

'Oh yes, it's my big episode! I've got quite a lot to do. They're building up my part,' she said proudly.

'How about lunch?'

'Lunch?'

'Yes, lunch. You break for lunch, don't you?' asked Snellor irritably. This girl was going to try his patience, he could tell that.

'Oh yes, I have a lunch break.'

'Good. I'll meet you for lunch in the club. Shall we say one o'clock?'

'What, tomorrow?'

'Ye-es,' said Snellor patiently. 'Tomorrow, in the club, one o'clock.'

'That'll be nice,' said Patsy, with gratification, thinking of all the envious glances she would attract.

'Yes,' agreed Snellor. 'We can have a nice little chat about things over a drink and a sandwich.'

'The food's not very good up there,' protested Patsy, thinking how much better it would be to have lunch in the canteen where everyone could see them. Most people went to the canteen on studio days. Only hardened drinkers like Bella popped up to the club for a drink at lunchtimes, and even she eschewed the smoky atmosphere on studio days. 'Couldn't we go to the canteen?'

'Can we get a drink there?' asked Snellor anxiously. He could never face an interview without a drink. Come to that, he couldn't face anything without a drink. Trevor was always nagging him about it. It was all very well for Trev. He didn't have to do the dirty work.

'Oh yes, they do wine by the glass,' Patsy assured him.

Wine! Snellor shuddered. No, it had to be vodka or this scoop would not have the impact that he knew would make Trevor's heart sing and bring his own impending promotion a little bit nearer. The truth of the matter was that Snellor was a common or garden hack and his whole ambition in life was to become a features editor. A raise in salary, a guaranteed by-line and a photograph. Respect from the boys in the Wine Press.

'The club is better, not so much noise.' Snellor decided not to give her the opportunity to argue. 'See you there then. One o'clock,' he repeated to make sure she'd got it straight.

But Patsy was not to be put off. 'I have to have my lunch,' she said truculently. 'It's my big episode.' Patsy was very fond of her food and the nervous tension of the studio day was the only legitimate excuse she had to indulge. Snellor sighed. He could never understand this preoccupation with food. His idea of lunch was a double vodka washed down with several of the same. One ate at night. Hugely. But lunchtime was drinking time.

'Look, Pat – ' Snellor began.

'Patsy,' she corrected him again.

'Patsy. I want this piece to do you justice.' This was absolutely the very last thing that Snellor wanted. 'It's not easy to be creative when both of us are stuffing our faces.' On reflection Snellor wished he'd phrased it more delicately, but he pressed on. 'It's going to be an in-depth interview – and we've got to set up a photo session this week, too,' he added to distract her attention.

'Oh right. Of course. I could manage Thursday. I've got a day off. Is that all right?' asked Patsy anxiously. She couldn't bear it if anything went wrong now.

'S'cutting it fine, but if we do them in the morning we'll probably just manage it.'

'Oh good,' Patsy breathed with relief.

'I'll get Phil onto it,' said Snellor, determined now to finish the conversation. 'Expect his call later on. See you in the club at one.' And he put down the phone.

Patsy was ecstatic. She went straight to her wardrobe, decided at one glance that she had nothing suitable to wear and spent a blissful afternoon shopping in her local boutique.

At the lunch break the next day, she could hardly contain herself.

'Aren't you coming to the canteen, love?' called out Meg, who played the wife of the McMasters' picture restorer, George, when she noticed Patsy rushing off in the opposite direction.

'No, I'm meeting a journalist in the club,' replied Patsy importantly.

'Fame at last!' muttered Simon Lavell, who played Tom McMaster, dryly under his breath as he watched the retreating figure disappear down the corridor.

Tony Snellor was ensconced at a corner table in the club,

and on his third double vodka when Patsy arrived. He waved to her in an expansive manner.

'Could you sign the gentleman in, please, miss?' said the commissionaire on the door in a sepulchral voice. 'He said he was with you.'

'Oh, yes, of course – it's Mr Snellor, isn't it?'

'Don't ask me, miss, he's your friend, not mine.' He sounded relieved.

Patsy carefully wrote in 'Mr Snellor', his first name completely eluding her. Then she sashayed over to his table, in a manner calculated to alert the attention of every susceptible male in the room. As indeed it did. Well satisfied with her entrance, Patsy seated herself and crossed her legs provocatively, exhibiting a considerable amount of thigh. Snellor was suitably impressed and mentally congratulated himself on persuading Trevor that Patsy Hall was the business.

'Did Phil ring you?' enquired Snellor, after he'd ordered a Martini and lemonade for Patsy at her request. She was so excited, she'd completely forgotten she had a big scene with Bella in the afternoon and alcohol was not conducive to concentration in a stressful situation in the studio. Patsy's mind was apt to wander at the best of times.

'Oh yes, thanks,' she said eagerly. 'He wants to do pictures of me relaxing at home.' She had been delighted with Phil's phone call, which had been fulsome to say the least. Phil had been well primed by Snellor.

'So how are you enjoying the series, Patsy?'

'It's lovely. I get to wear some really great clothes, and I love working with famous people like Bella and Geoff.' Patsy had wit enough to realize that it would be wise to keep on the right side of Bella, especially in print.

'Good, good,' said Snellor. 'Got any romance going in your

life at the moment?' He tried to twinkle at her, but it manifested itself as a leer.

Patsy giggled coyly and pretended to blush. 'Ooh no, I'm a career girl, Mr Snellor. I don't have time for romance.'

'Tony, please,' said Tony Snellor, with as much charm as he could muster. 'I find that difficult to believe, a stunning-looking girl like you – all the other ladies in the cast must have been furious when you joined the series.'

'Do you think so?' said Patsy, overcome.

'Of course. What did Bella have to say?'

Patsy giggled again. 'You'd have to ask her. She's usually up here,' she added looking around the room. 'She likes a drink or three.'

'Does she?' Tony Snellor took out his miniature tape recorder, placed it on the table between them and switched it on. Patsy turned back, disappointed that there was no sign of Bella. Snellor took a large swig of vodka. 'Tell me, Patsy, how do you get on with other members of the cast?'

Patsy pondered this for some time. She was longing to air her grievances to someone, and maybe if she said she was unhappy in public they would realize and be nicer to her.

'I wish they were nicer to me,' she whispered.

Snellor sat up. 'I can't believe they're nasty to you,' he said hopefully.

'They are sometimes. Well, not nasty, exactly. Perhaps they're just jealous, like you said.'

'I'm sure I'm right,' said Snellor. 'I bet you have trouble with that Bella, don't you? I mean, she must be worried by a younger, beautiful rival, don't you think?'

'Yes, I suppose so,' agreed Patsy, nodding her head sagely.

'You know, Patsy, I could do you a bit of good here,' said Snellor, looking at her with interest. He'd just had one of his brainwaves. They didn't happen often, but when they did, they were humdingers. 'I've been watching this series and, I must say, since you've come into it, it's perked up no end. I think you've got what it takes. But producers aren't always so quick off the mark. But if an artist is seen to be getting a lot of publicity, that means something to them. The ratings go up and they start to build up that artist's part. Soon she's taken over and become the star of the series. Do you follow me?' Snellor glanced at Patsy. Had he gone too far? No. She was gazing at him with shining eyes. He pressed home his point. 'What I'm saying here, Pat, is, you give me the stories and I'll guarantee to give you the publicity. It needn't be too obvious. Just little snippets about what's happening behind the cameras from time to time. We angle it to include a nice big picture of you. We might even put you on the cover of the colour supplement on Sunday if you come up with the right story. What do you say?'

'I think it's a wonderful idea, Tony!'

8

Full of trepidation, Claire started to get ready for her visit to the studio. It was the day of her make-up test and she was apprehensive to say the least. Her previous encounters with make-up artists had not been happy. She had only done a couple of small parts in television, and had not had the nerve to stand up for what she wanted.

'After all, Sal,' she had complained to her friend after an earlier disaster, 'I know my face better than anyone else. I know what suits me. I know how to make the best of my features. I mean, I realize I'm no beauty . . .'

'Oh, don't be ridiculous, you're gorgeous! Everyone knows that. You've just got to be firm; you're too nice, that's your trouble. Diana Barry throws brushes and things around if she doesn't get what she wants.'

Claire looked appalled. 'I couldn't possibly do that, it's just not professional,' she said primly.

'Well then, you'll just have to go on looking like the back of a number nine bus.'

'I know, I know. I just don't know how to handle those make-up girls. They're all harridans,' said Claire feelingly.

'They're just bullies,' retorted Sally, 'and like all bullies, if you stand up to them, they'll crumble.'

'I know you're right, I just don't have the guts,' Claire had replied miserably.

That was a couple of years ago, however. She had the guts now, she was tougher now – Roger had at least done that for her. She was determined not to be bullied this time into having a face that was, in her opinion, totally characterless – no eyes nor cheekbones, just lips and eyebrows. She had looked dreadful. It had destroyed her confidence and she had cried bitterly afterwards. When she had seen herself on the television, she had been enraged. Never again, she thought savagely. This was the biggest break of her career and nothing, but nothing, was going to get in the way of her success. She drove to the studio, nervous but determined to win. The more she thought of her previous humiliations, the more furious and the more resolute she became. She was determined to win the forthcoming battle. For battle there would surely be, she felt certain. By the time she arrived at the studio gates, she was trembling, whether from fear or anger she wasn't sure, but she managed a tremulous smile for the official residing on the gate.

'I am here for a make-up test for *The McMasters*,' she said, suddenly feeling a sense of belonging to something rather special.

He seemed delighted and allowed her to park in the area in the middle right outside the main building, an honour usually the preserve of the top brass of South Eastern Television. Even famous stars had been known to have been turned away from this car park. The gate attendant's power was absolute. Every visiting actor was at the mercy of his whims and moods. This unexpected favour put Claire in a buoyant mood. She parked and strode confidently into the building. There were several women officiating in the vast reception area. She approached one and was steadfastly ignored. As she turned to another, a phone rang and the receptionist picked it up and became engaged in an animated discussion. Claire addressed a third.

'My name is Claire Jenner. I am in *The McMasters* and I am here for a make-up session. Where do I go?'

'Red assembly – lower ground,' said the woman, without looking up. She seemed unimpressed, if not disinterested, by Claire's announcement.

'Thank you,' said Claire politely. She made her way to the escalator that went down to the basement, glancing as she went at the huge colour photographs that were arranged around the walls of the reception hall. There was one featuring the current cast of *The McMasters*. She would be amongst them soon, she thought to herself happily. Soon, she too would be as famous as they were. She would not be ignored by the receptionists but welcomed and made much of. At the bottom of the escalator she came to a corridor with another off it at right angles. Illuminated signs indicated 'Red Assembly' and 'Make-up Department'.

Claire could hear sounds of chatter and laughter coming from within. Her heart started to beat a little faster. She approached the door clutching her handbag and script to her, and entered. She stood there for a few moments before anyone noticed her. The make-up room was long and narrow, and the walls were hung with mirrors surrounded by fluorescent lights. The long uninterrupted worktop that went the full length of the room was covered in powder puffs, make-up brushes, jars, bottles, little round pots of pencils, sponges, combs, heated rollers and every known aid to beauty. In front of the mirrors, at regular intervals, were six chairs of the type used by dentists. Actors and actresses were sitting in these, being tended by make-up artists – Claire's harridans – who were clad in crisp pale blue overalls and seemed to be on very good terms with their victims.

A young man, nearest to the door, observed Claire's entrance through the mirror.

'Well, hello!' he said cheerily. 'Look what's just walked in, everyone.'

Claire stood uncomfortably. 'Hello,' she said, trying to overcome her shyness.

The make-up girl nearest her, who was tending the young man, turned around with no hint of welcome in her face.

'Yes?' she enquired imperiously. 'Can we help you?'

Claire took a deep breath. She knew she had to start as she meant to go on.

'I'm Claire Jenner,' she announced loudly. 'I'm playing Sara Harper – I've come for a make-up test.'

The entire room came to a stop. The rest of the make-up girls were arrested in mid-operations to stare at the interloper, whilst the cast members turned as one to eye her with ill-concealed curiosity.

'Hello, dear – very pleased to meet you,' said Meg immediately, with great warmth.

'Hello,' replied Claire gratefully. 'And I you,' and she smiled back at her.

'And a very attractive addition to the cast, if I may say so,' said the young man suavely, swivelling round in his chair to face her, stretching out his hand. 'I'm Simon Lavell, welcome aboard.' Claire took the proffered hand.

'Thank you. I'm really glad to be here,' she said trying to believe it.

'And we're very glad to have you, love,' called Reg from the far end in his homely Northern accent. He played George, the restorer in the series, and husband of the character played by Meg. 'You'll liven things up, I shouldn't wonder. Could do with a new bit of blood.'

Claire laughed, and coloured slightly.

'Hello, Claire, I'm Amy,' said a rather pretty brunette with gamine looks, laughing eyes, and hair cut in a bob with a heavy fringe. Claire remembered that Amy played Sophie Longthorn, the receptionist for the McMasters' rather grand premises.

Also sitting being made up, but too shy to speak, were Frederick Derby, an older actor in his late seventies, who supplied the aristocratic element in this very British television series, and Jason Wright. He played Billy, the boy in the workshop who was responsible for the packing of valuable items. These two turned to smile at Claire. She smiled happily back. At least they all seemed pleased enough to see her. Particularly Simon Lavell. He was still eyeing her in a critical way. The make-up girl who had greeted her so coldly now took charge of the situation.

'We're not ready for you yet – we're in the middle of a recording, you know.'

Claire blushed in spite of herself. 'I was told to be here at four thirty,' she said with as much courage as she could muster.

'By whom?' asked the termagant.

'Sonia, Sonia asked me to be here at four thirty,' insisted Claire, anger starting to rise at this public humiliation.

'She's on the floor doing Patsy's retake, wouldn't you know,' said Simon, jerking a thumb in the direction of a large monitor that was affixed to the wall about a couple of feet down from the ceiling. Everyone glanced up at the monitor. The sound had been turned off and there was indeed evidence of a retake of a scene in progress. The screen was filled with huge close-ups of Patsy Hall. Claire looked at her curiously. She had a low opinion of Patsy's acting ability, although she conceded that she was a lovely-looking girl. She seemed to be looking vacant at the moment, as though unsure of what to do next.

'Look at her,' said Simon contemptuously. 'She hasn't a bloody clue.'

Claire was astonished at this blunt dismissal of a fellow actor, but said nothing.

'Get it right, love!' he jeered at the screen, as it became apparent that the scene was being shot yet again. 'We all want to go home tonight!' The rest of the room laughed uproariously, even kind Meg and Reg. Plainly, Patsy was the company joke. Someone turned the sound up and after another attempt, Patsy got it right and the whole make-up room cheered. Except Claire, who was genuinely appalled by the goings-on.

The camera that had been trained on Patsy swerved off her and came to rest on an out-of-focus picture of the set doorway as Larry Matthews listened to instructions on his headphones from the director.

'Yes, yes, oh thank Christ,' said Larry in a relieved tone to the empty doorway. 'It's a clear everyone.'

Another cheer went up from the make-up room. Suddenly the door burst open and Bella erupted into the room.

'God give me strength!' she exclaimed, making for the nearest chair. Simon hurriedly vacated it. Bella collapsed noisily into its leather cushions.

'Where did they find her?' she said dramatically. 'They never told us about this at the Academy.'

'Of course they did. Didn't you ever do improvisation classes – where you had to make love to a lamppost?' asked Simon. 'I know we did.'

'I must have been away that day,' muttered Bella, picking up a brush and tapping furiously with it on the table. It was obvious that she was in a foul mood, the result of trying to act opposite Patsy. Simon decided to create a diversion.

'What am I thinking of? Bella, my love, you haven't met the latest addition to this remarkable series, Claire Jenner!'

Bella swivelled round in astonishment, seeing Claire for the first time. She wreathed her face in smiles.

'My dear,' she said graciously, 'how lovely. We've been so looking forward to your arrival. Welcome!' And she rose majestically from her seat to meet Claire who had moved towards her. Bella embraced her warmly, then held her at arm's length to view her the better.

'Well, this is an improvement. I'm glad to see that Hugh hasn't completely taken leave of his senses. You're much more what *The McMasters* is about – class! You are extremely welcome!' And she gave Claire's upper arm an encouraging grip, then released her, turned abruptly to the chair again and flung herself into it.

'Now, Glynis dear, what the fuck are we going to do about my face? Trying to act opposite that ghastly little tramp has completely ruined my make-up!'

The door opened again and the object of her ire wandered in disconsolately. She was followed by an attractive brunette, who was looking anxious.

'Sonia, my pet, you're late for our new member – what will she think of us?' said Simon teasingly to the late arrival.

'Oh, I'm sooo sorry,' said Sonia breathlessly to Claire.

'Please, it's all right, I think I was early,' replied Claire hurriedly, anxious to establish good relations with the woman who held her future success in her hands.

'It's just – that we got held up,' continued Sonia in a confidential undertone so that Patsy could not hear. 'But I'm ready for you now,' she added with a winning smile, guiding Claire to the chair where Jason was seated. He sprang at once to his feet.

'Hi, I'm Jason. Nice to meet you – I hope we get to do scenes together,' he said with a shy grin.

'Hello,' replied Claire, warmed by his friendly manner.

'I hope so, too.' Jason edged out of the way and Claire sat tentatively in his place and braced herself for the next encounter. Sonia stood behind her.

'I expect you do your own, don't you?' she said quietly.

'What?' said Claire, startled.

'Make-up,' replied Sonia. 'I can see you're good at it – you look lovely.'

'Oh – thank you,' said Claire, unable to believe her ears. 'Well, yes, as a matter of fact, I do.'

'You'll need a bit more base, Claire. Would you like me to do that?' enquired Sonia, smiling gently. 'Then you can do your eyes and things.'

'Yes, of course.' My luck's in, thought Claire as she gave herself over to Sonia's ministration.

'Now, what are we going to do with your hair?' running her fingers through Claire's soft reddish brown curls. 'It looks quite good tied back in the nape.'

Claire suddenly became aware that she was under scrutiny. She turned and met Patsy's hostile gaze. Sonia followed her look.

'Patsy,' she said, 'have you met Claire yet?'

'No,' said Patsy solemnly. 'Hi,' she added casually, before turning away without waiting for Claire's response.

'Take no notice of her,' whispered Sonia in her ear. 'She thinks she's the star of the show.' Claire was rattled by Patsy's evident dislike of her and thought privately that if she had made an ally in Sonia then Patsy was decidedly an enemy.

9

It was ten o'clock on another blindingly hot day in Bel Air – a misnomer if ever there was one, the only air worth breathing being of the conditioned variety. Somewhere a telephone was ringing. Jim Dutton stirred from the mists of a drug-induced sleep. He moved his head and opened one eye blearily. He became aware that he was not alone. A very young girl with red hair of an impossible hue was sprawled on her stomach across the pillow next to him. Another girl, a blonde of the type known as 'platinum', lolled over his loins, her mouth half open near his flaccid cock. They were both sound asleep, the blonde obviously having abandoned her attempt to arouse his flagging ardour mid-operations. The redhead's breath smelled appalling. The phone continued to ring. Where the fuck was Consuela? The number of phone calls and possible job offers he'd missed through that goddamn broad not answering the goddamn phone . . . then he remembered he'd had to dismiss Consuela the previous week. Hell! It had come to something when he couldn't even afford a goddamn housekeeper. Something had to break soon. What the fuck did his goddamn agent think she was doing?

He crawled across the redhead, who moaned and rolled over onto her back, displaying a pair of enormous breasts. This had the effect of giving him an instant hard-on, which almost distracted him from his mission. The phone rang relentlessly; it obviously intended to go on ringing until someone answered it. He glanced hungrily at the huge nipples. 'Later, later,' he muttered, and staggered across the room. He always kept the bedroom phone on the table by the window. It was the only way he could be certain of making an early morning call at the studio. He had to be sure of actually getting out of bed.

'Yeah,' he said huskily into the mouthpiece of the onyx and gilt turn-of-the-century-type telephone.

'Hi, sweetie,' said a cheery voice on the other end. It was Meriel his goddamn agent! 'I was beginning to think you'd died on me, honeybunch.' She sounded in high good humour.

'Likewise,' growled Jim. 'I haven't heard from you in months!'

'Jimbo, that is such a lie. If you're alluding to the Universal project, we are pushing as hard as we dare at this point in time. Now, concerning the Golden Globe Awards – '

'Holy shit!' intoned Jim. 'Have you any idea what time I hit the sack?'

But Meriel was questioning him closely on his activities at the awards ceremony. Had he interacted with the right people? Meriel started giving him a list of the casting directors who apparently had been impressed by his appearance. Jim caught sight of his reflection in the huge mirror that served as the bed head.

'Jeez,' he muttered to himself as he gazed longingly at the recumbent beauty on the bed, 'I'm standing here completely nude with an erection like the Empire State Building and my asshole of an agent, who can't get me an interview much less a screen test, is giving me the third degree on last night's guest list.' He started to work his foreskin up and down his penis automatically. If only Meriel would get off the goddamn phone he could get down to the biggest pair of tits he'd seen in a long time. He groaned involuntarily.

'What was that, honeypie?' queried Meriel.

'Uh, nothin', it's okay – uh, say Meriel, can any of this wait? I'm kind of busy right now.'

'Oh sure thing, sugar – oh, just one thing, though, there's these two British-type guys – want to sign you up for a TV series.' Was this broad raving or what?

'A British TV series? They only ever get shown on HBO, Meriel!'

But Meriel was unimpressed by his reaction. 'Think about it, Jimbo. There's not a lot of work around right now and there's a lot of talent chasing what there is.'

Meriel knew how slim the chance was that Jim would get the Universal movie. It would go to Kurt Russell or Patrick Swayze for sure. Unless they got a better offer – and then Jim would be up against the two-dozen others in his own league.

'You'll be getting a call from them any time – I gave them your number – they're flying over to see you in the next couple of days.'

I do not believe I'm having this conversation, Jim thought wildly. One day I'm being tipped as the hottest thing to come out of Hollywood since Kevin Costner and the next I'm on a meteoric ride to obscurity in a British TV series. This cannot be for real.

Jim was good-looking, even by Hollywood standards – but apart from possessing a physique that could have passed muster as a quarter back with the Miami Dolphins, Jim's main asset was a gentle, sensitive, little-boy-lost expression that seemed constantly to assail his features. Women were bowled over by it. So were female casting directors (who, although technically women, were in fact a breed apart).

Producers, on the other hand, seemed strangely resistant. Once it had dawned on Jim that his boyish charm and devastating good looks could be used to get what he wanted, he used them mercilessly. He had been discovered by his agent, Meriel Brooks, playing Chance Wayne in a production of Tennessee Williams's *Sweet Bird of Youth* at the Pasadena Playhouse. She had got him a small but regular part in a daytime soap series and he had bedded her out of gratitude. This in fact had not been necessary so far as Meriel was concerned. Her job was the motivating factor in her life, that and the antiques that graced her lovely West Hollywood apartment, and her plastic surgeon's bills that were extortionate. But she had accepted Jim's offer without any fuss. It had only happened once and they had been firm friends ever since.

She had introduced him to the Hollywood social scene. They had breakfasted at the Beverly Hills Hotel, lunched at Le Dôme, dined at the Ivy, been to countless premieres, awards ceremonies and charity galas and benefits. The Hollywood élite had welcomed them. The champagne had flowed and the cocaine had drifted. Jim had launched himself into a full and varied sex life. Women flung themselves at him and he had lost count of the number of girls he had bedded.

Meriel had finally got him the lead in a fairly awful but enormously popular life guard series, which required him to do little more than sprint across the sand of Malibu plunging at least once an episode into the pounding surf to rescue a damsel in distress or preferably a small boy or dog. Sometimes all three. The distressed damsels were invariably of a curvaceous and pneumatic build and inevitably found their way into Jim's super kingsize bed. After two seasons, the series had been dropped and so had the monthly pay cheques. Jim had lived well beyond his means and funds were now seriously low. He knew he would shortly have to give up his rented villa and move to something smaller and cheaper in downtown Hollywood. He couldn't bear to contemplate the thought. He revelled in this life style. True, Meriel had managed to get him a couple of guest roles in other popular TV programmes, but with success as a TV star went the usual trappings – the personal manager, the publicist, the accountant, the attorney, the Armani suits, the Gucci accessories, the status car, the housekeeper, the pool attendant, the gardener, the coke snorting . . . the coke snorting, that along with Consuela would have to go – unless, of course, he could get the Universal picture – that would solve everything. He was in with a chance, of that there was no doubt. He would have to clean up his act, of course. The girls would have to go, so would the booze and the coke – while he was making the picture – but, boy, what a time he would have afterwards.

'Okay, okay, Meriel, don't worry, doll, I can handle it.' He stalled trying to get rid of her. His cock was getting bigger all the time and he felt ready to explode.

He finally put down the phone and hurled himself onto the bed. In no time he was ensconced in a sort of demi-paradise, happily sucking on the glorious breasts, his cock in turn being sucked by the soft lips of the platinum blonde. He was only dimly aware of an impending phone call, which might transform his whole life.

10

It was very early and bitterly cold. Claire shivered involuntarily as she dressed for her first day's location filming in her tiny hotel room. She had driven down the previous night, arriving outside Maidstone around nine. The small hotel boasted only three stars and seemed deserted.

'They've all gone out to eat,' confided the receptionist. Then, seeing Claire's slightly forlorn look, she added, 'They asked for you when they got in from the day's shoot,' airing her recently acquired knowledge of TV terminology.

'That was nice of them,' said Claire, considerably cheered. She had hoped to break the ice before the morning's work by briefly socializing with her fellow actors. An exchange of pleasantries over a night cap with Geoffrey Armitage would have calmed her nerves before having to play her first scene opposite him on the morrow. She had developed quite a crush on him after seeing him as Berowne in *Love's Labour's Lost* at Stratford when she was a schoolgirl. And now here she was – playing his rival and new romantic interest. It seemed extraordinary that she was to play opposite him. She was apprehensive yet exhilarated by the prospect.

'And Mr Dudley was with them,' volunteered the girl as an afterthought.

'Oh yes, he's the director. Well, thanks. I think I'll go to bed now, I have an early start in the morning.'

'The others are in the bar if you want to join them,' the girl volunteered.

'What others?' asked Claire doubtfully.

'I don't know who they are. I didn't recognize any of them'.

'They'll be the technicians – you know, the film crew.'

'Oh yes,' said the girl, losing all interest. 'Would you like an alarm call?'

'Yes please, five forty-five, and could I have some tea as well?'

'Certainly, madam, and a morning paper?'

'No thanks, I've got quite enough to worry about with the script.'

'You're the new romantic interest, aren't you?' queried the receptionist, who had kept a close eye on the free publicity in the tabloids.

'Yes, that's right,' replied Claire, pleased to be recognized.

'I hope it goes well for you.'

'Thanks. I need a good night's sleep to cope with it!'

She had, in fact, slept fitfully; she put it down to nerves. She was, she now realized, very nervous. She was shivering with apprehension as well as cold. After she had dressed in trousers, polo-neck sweater and boots, she scraped her hair back and fastened it with an elastic band. She looked at herself in the mirror. Pale, too pale. Never mind, the make-up would soon put that right.

There was a tap at the door – the chambermaid, a very young girl, with a tray of tea. Claire thanked her and poured herself some tea, warming her hands around the cup between sips. She listened to the news on the radio and went through the lines in her script over and over again. She had several scenes to film, all set in and around an auction room. There was quite a lot of dialogue and she was determined to be word-perfect on every occasion.

At 6.35, she put on her quilted waterproof coat, assembled her handbag, script and small holdall and, donning a pair of huge sunglasses, grabbed her room key and went downstairs. In the lobby she found Sonia waiting smilingly for her. They exchanged greetings and were shortly joined by Terri, the very pretty dark floor assistant. It was her job to make sure that everyone was in the right place at the right time, whether on location or in the studio. She greeted Claire with a cheery, 'Hi, I'm Terri. Everything okay?'

'Yes thanks, I'm fine,' replied Claire, feeling anything but. The lobby was beginning to fill with people.

'Glad to see you've got something warm on – you're going to need it!' Terri added. She herself was clad in ski wear. 'I've got thermals on underneath,' she confided. 'Don't worry, wardrobe will provide you with some.'

'I'm very glad,' smiled Claire with feeling.

'Bus is here,' called out someone.

Claire gradually began to realize as several other people, men and women of all ages, climbed into the minibus with her, that her companions were extras, crowd artistes who had been requisitioned to supply the background action in the day's filming. She smiled at them in a friendly fashion and greeted them shyly. They responded in like manner. She wondered if they knew that this was her first day. Terri stood by the driver and counted the heads of her charges.

'Are we all here?' she called out anxiously.

Claire was about to tell her that Sonia and the rest of the make-up girls were not present, when she saw them getting into a car that had drawn up alongside and was being driven by the dreaded Glynis. Claire thought it strange that she had been bundled in with the extras – not that she was in any way snobbish, she had simply hoped for a car to take her and her fellow actors to the location. She studied her call sheet more closely. She appeared to be the only actor called early. The men were not called until 8.30. Terri came and plonked herself in the vacant seat next to Claire.

'You could have followed us in your own car if you'd wanted to,' she said, as if reading Claire's thoughts. 'It means you can get away quickly when we've finished. The others like to dash straight back to London on the motorway.'

'Oh yes, of course. Well, I'll probably do that next time. I need to find my way around first,' said Claire.

'You'll be all right,' said Terri reassuringly. 'They're not a bad bunch.'

The bus rumbled away in the first light of day and, twenty minutes later, pulled up in the car park of the grounds of a large country house. The doors swung open and it disgorged its passengers.

'I'll take you straight to make-up,' announced Terri, giving Claire no choice in the matter.

They picked their way across the potholes in the car park to one of several caravans whose interiors were aglow. There were other vehicles, the wardrobe department and the caterers were housed in caravans, whilst the sound and elecs had smaller vehicles. Several members of the crew had already arrived in their cars. All had converged on the catering van, which was dispensing hot bacon and egg rolls and porridge. There were trestle tables where people could help themselves to cereal and toast and coffee or tea.

Claire mounted the steps of the make-up caravan and blinked in the fluorescent-lit interior. Sonia was already there, busy laying out her equipment. She smiled when she saw Claire and gestured for her to seat herself. The make-up caravan was especially equipped for the purpose. It was a smaller replica of the make-up room at the television studios, but with only three mirrors and three dentist's chairs. Sonia's place was in the middle and Claire was soon swathed in a make-up cape and had given herself over to Sonia's ministrations. Less than an hour later, she was transformed. Her hair had been curled. Her skin glowed in spite of the make-up, and her eyes were luminous. She was looking the way she knew suited her best and she felt happy and confident.

She was next conducted by Terri to the wardrobe caravan, where she shivered in spite of the electric blow heater that was blasting through its interior. She donned the thermal underwear, and then put on a pale pink suit and fedora. She had exchanged her thick socks for glossy tights and her sneakers for a classy neutral three-quarter-heel Italian pump. She had only just managed to get herself ready when Terri appeared at the door. 'You're wanted on set,' she said peremptorily. 'Now,' she added with a shrug, raising her eyebrows in a don't-ask-me-I'm-just-the-office-boy sort of look. Claire sat gingerly in a waiting car, which Terri herself drove up the winding drive to the house. Glances of admiration and approval from the film crew followed her as she was led by Terri around technical equipment and into a small reception hall where a camera had been set up. The director, Scott Dudley, a diminutive but attractive middle-aged man with a lively expression and a shock of iron-grey hair, was sipping coffee and deep in conversation with a pretty, plump blonde girl. Terri brought her charge into Scott's eyeline. They both turned to view the newcomer.

'Good morning,' said Scott, in what Claire could only describe later to Sally as a provocative way. 'Well, you're an improvement on the general standard of pulchritude in this god-forsaken series!'

Claire blushed under her make-up. She noticed that it was mainly men of a certain age and older that treated her as a sex object.

80

'How do you do, Mr Dudley?' she countered politely.

'Know your lines, do you?' asked Scott bluntly, ignoring her solicitude.

'Of course,' replied Claire hotly. It was one thing to be subjected to mild sexist chat, she was used to that, but to impugn her professionalism as an actress was not to be tolerated.

'Okay, okay,' he said easily, 'keep your hair on. It looks very nice by the way – doesn't it, Pam?' He threw the observation in the direction of the blonde.

'Yes, lovely,' said she.

'Pam's my number one – can't move an inch without her,' he said, giving Pam's bottom a playful squeeze. Pam seemed to have no objection to being treated so familiarly, merely giggling.

'Had breakfast?' asked Scott.

'Er – no,' said Claire.

'Should do – we've got a tough day ahead.' And so saying, he turned abruptly away to address a remark to a large burly man whom Claire soon realized was the lighting cameraman. She turned around to discover that Terri had disappeared and left her to her own devices. To cover her confusion, she started to devote her attention to the script, which she was clutching. Scott's remarks had rattled her.

'Care to go over some lines?' said a deep, smooth, charming voice. Claire's heart fluttered and she looked up into the quizzically smiling face of Geoffrey Armitage. His look of amusement turned to one of intense admiration as their eyes met. 'I am enchanted to meet you, Miss Jenner. Please forgive the casual approach, I've tried to attract your attention for some time. You seemed to be engrossed in the script so I thought I'd try that avenue.'

Claire hardly heard what he said. The rest of the room

seemed to have floated away and she had the absurd notion that she believed in love at first sight. Or was it lust. Certainly, the way Geoffrey was looking at her was lustful and yet she thought she detected a softness in that look, a sort of yearning, regret. She couldn't fathom it, yet she felt utterly bewitched.

'We're ready for you, children. Ah, I see you've met.' Scott's cheery voice broke the spell. 'Walk this way, please,' and he guided them to a doorway that had lights trained on it.

'Right, now, Geoff, you enter on action across to the table here.'

'What table?'

'We'll put one there.'

'Table coming in!' yelled someone.

'Not now, not now,' said Scott impatiently, 'we don't need it on this shot. So, in you come, Geoff.'

Geoff obliged. He crossed to the centre of the room and mimed putting his auction programme on the imaginary table.

'All right, darling!' called out Scott. Claire, waiting behind the door, was too nervous to bridle at the familiarity. 'And – cue,' said Scott. Claire entered. 'And pause by the door, look at him intently, then as he starts to go – start to go Geoff' – Geoffrey obliged – 'then you, darling, you say your first line from the doorway, then come to him – and cue.'

Claire did as she was bid. She played the dialogue that followed well and she knew it. She had energy and intelligence and the scene, short though it was, worked beautifully.

'Good stuff,' said Scott in a surprised voice, when the rehearsal was over. 'We'll go for one.'

'Make-up checks!' called out one of the floor assistants, Brian.

'What for?' demanded Scott. 'They haven't done anything yet.'

82

'Forget it,' amended Brian, as Sonia and Glynis were about to dart in. But Glynis was not to be deterred.

'Do you mind?' she said with heavy irony to Scott. 'I need to check my artiste.'

'Funny how you're never around when we need you,' muttered Scott to the camera crew, 'usually around tea break.'

Claire was relieved that Glynis, who as make-up supervisor deemed it beneath her to attend to anyone but the stars of the show, was not her make-up artist. She was disappointed that Larry was not part of this team for her debut, but he was on the next episode and she would probably have got her confidence by then. They did the take.

'Print it,' said Scott with satisfaction.

Geoff took advantage of the situation. 'I'm going to enjoy our scenes together,' he murmured quietly, looking deep into Claire's eyes as he spoke.

Claire felt herself go weak at the knees.

There followed close-ups of each of them. Then a shot of Claire leaving the building amongst a crowd of milling extras, and getting into her car. Then a shot of her arriving. Then a shot of Geoff watching her departure from the door. Then Claire driving away. By the time this sequence was completed, it was almost lunchtime.

'Everyone back at one forty-five to do the auction scene,' called out Brian loudly. 'And that means *everyone*,' he yelled to the crowd of extras who were making a beeline for the catering van.

'Can I get you something?' said Geoff, clasping Claire by the elbow and steering her away from the crowd. 'Let's go to the caravan – oh yes, they've actually provided the actors with a sort of green room,' he said, seeing Claire's look of surprise. 'It was Bella's doing – she insisted – went to Hugh

83

and beat him up, verbally, until he gave in. Have you met Bella, by the way?'

'Oh yes.'

'Then I'm sure you get the picture.' He settled her in the actors' caravan and then set off in search of food.

Over lunch he chatted to her easily. He had a fund of amusing stories from his days at Stratford, and told them with relish. Claire found herself giggling continuously and at one point was actually convulsed with laughter. Afterwards, they walked together to the make-up caravan, to be made presentable for the next shot. Claire felt she'd known him all her life.

The whole of the afternoon was taken up with shooting the scene in the auction room. They were separated then, being rivals in the bidding for a rare painting by a minor Italian master. But Claire was acutely aware of Geoff's unabashed gaze of admiration and he was attentive and solicitous of her wellbeing whenever they were allowed to relax off-set between setups.

By the end of the day, Claire knew without a doubt that unless she was very careful there was a very great danger of her falling for Geoffrey Armitage. He had a reputation as a charming seducer and she now knew why. She also knew that he intended her for his next victim.

11

It was in fact Larry who had suggested Jim Dutton. Far from being immune to 'crap TV' as he had so contemptuously labelled it, Larry made a point of watching just about everything that was shown on television. It was his contribution to his job. He saw it as his duty to be informed on what the public wanted, who and what was popular, and to try to analyse that tantalizingly elusive quality that makes a person or a programme irresistibly watchable. In America it was known as the 'Q' factor. American TV researchers devoted hours of every day and days of every year to unravelling this mystery. A cross section of the citizens of the United States of America would be closeted in small viewing rooms with screens upon which were flashed mug shots of actors and actresses – some well known – some famous – some completely unknown. The captive audience was then instructed to press buttons to indicate its preference – and hey presto, another TV star would be born! Larry preferred to call it the 'Ikon' factor – the deliberate manufacture of a popular idol. It was the job he coveted most – Warwick the King Maker, the power behind the throne.

It was he who had put Claire's name on the list of potential recruits for *The McMasters*. She and the glamorous American import would boost the ratings, so ensuring Martin's, Hugh's and his own tenure at the studios for at least a further two terms.

He had been idly flicking through innumerable channels on American TV whilst visiting some old friends in San Francisco, when his gaze had alighted on the undeniably attractive form of Jim Dutton. All his life a connoisseur of male pulchritude, Larry was impressed. Jim was almost impossibly good-looking and possessed a fine physique. Larry had happened to catch an episode in which Jim had been given a couple of emotional scenes, which he had handled well, not indulging in the usual Hollywood sentimentality. And he brought a wry humour to the part, which lifted the dialogue out of the prosaic and mundane.

After seeing the episode, Larry had contacted Meriel Brooks and requested photos of Jim. Her office had obliged, sending a selection, plus a curriculum vitae. Larry had returned home triumphantly after his vacation and had awaited his chance. At precisely the right moment, he had burst into Hugh's office brandishing the pictures aloft.

'There's our new leading man!' he had cried dramatically as he slung them onto Hugh's desk.

Hugh had been startled but impressed. 'What makes you think we can afford him?' he had asked after surveying the array of male loveliness in silence.

'He needs a job,' replied Larry promptly. 'He can't afford to haggle.'

'He certainly looks good,' murmured Hugh doubtfully. 'Can he act?'

'Well, admittedly, I haven't seen his King Lear, but he's certainly up to the standard of this series,' retorted Larry waspishly.

Hugh ignored this – he was used to Larry's jibes. In any case, he had no illusions about the quality of programme he was producing. Of its own genre, as a drama series, it was top of the league, but it wasn't exactly Shakespeare.

After a few further moments spent sifting through the pictures in silence, Hugh picked up a phone and said, 'Deirdre, has Martin gone to lunch yet? . . . Good. Ask him to pop in here for a moment, will you?'

'I knew you'd go for him,' smiled Larry smugly. 'Any chance of a coffee?'

'Oh, and Deirdre, could you pop up to the canteen? . . . There's a dear . . . Yes, sandwiches and coffee for three.'

'A working lunch? I like your style,' said Larry happily.

A few seconds later, Martin's head appeared around the door. 'What am I missing? And why am I being denied my lunch break, not to mention my lunch?' he demanded cheerfully.

'Here's metal more attractive,' said Larry enigmatically. He liked to quote at will from plays, just to make sure that no one forgot his theatrical pedigree. Martin had an idea that this was from *Hamlet* but as his only previous encounter with the play had been as one of The Watch at his prep school, he could not think immediately of a suitable response. Instead, he contented himself with, 'Well, it had better be good – I'm starving.'

'Then feast your eyes on this!' said Larry, with a grand gesture towards the photographs strewn over the desk.

'Good Lord!' exclaimed Martin in amazement. 'Who on earth is this?'

Larry sighed dramatically. 'Is that really all you can say?' he asked despairingly. 'This, my dear Martin, is none other than our new leading man – and, you must admit, he's got what it takes.'

'Has he?' asked Martin, scrutinizing the photos more closely.

'My dear,' Larry explained patiently, 'this bimbo has

survived the rigours of the ''Q'' factor and come out smiling.
This is one tough baby.'

'What the hell is he talking about?' Martin turned to Hugh
for an explanation.

'I think he means that Jim Dutton – for this is he – has
got what is known as sex appeal – he has ''it'' and ''it'' is
the missing element in the series and, er, Jim is going to, er
– supply – er ''it''.'

'Oh well, I suppose he knows best,' said Martin dubiously.

Meanwhile Larry was dancing around the room. 'Loves,
I'm just going to pop to my office. Shan't be a minute. You
can start without me, I'll soon catch you up.' And he
disappeared through the door.

'You're way ahead of me,' muttered Martin, when he had
gone. Still riffling through the photos in disbelief, he said
curiously, 'Tell me, Hugh, how did Larry come to get this
job?'

'We were at drama school together,' replied Hugh
promptly.

'Oh yes, of course – was he any good?'

'What, Larry, as an actor? Oh yes, very good. A bit flash
for my liking, mind you, but yes, he was good.'

'I sometimes wish he'd go back to it,' said Martin with
feeling.

'Oh come on, he's very good at his job,' said Hugh stoutly.
'He has a good instinct when it comes to casting. Look at
Claire Jenner – she was his idea, remember.'

'Yes, but this, this – chap, can he act?' Martin queried
darkly.

'According to Larry, good enough for *The McMasters* at any
rate.'

'Charming.'

'I make a point of being charming whenever possible,' said

Larry, re-entering bearing a briefcase. 'Well, have you cast him?'

Hugh smiled indulgently. 'Give us a chance, boyo.' Martin seated himself, stretched out his legs and surveyed his feet critically. Larry wondered idly why such a large proportion of television producers wore socks with sandals. Deplorable taste. 'I think I should like to meet this chap before making a decision,' said Martin eventually.

'Well, you can't,' said Larry bluntly. 'He's in Los Angeles. I tell you what, though, it just so happens that I have with me an episode of *Beach Guardians.*'

At this point there was a muffled sound outside the door. Larry opened it to reveal Deirdre, bearing a tray of refreshments.

'Greetings, Deirdre,' cried Larry happily. 'You have appeared at an opportune moment in the history of television drama.'

'Oh yes,' said Deirdre doubtfully, as she carefully set down her burden.

Larry grabbed a sandwich and said, 'Have you ever seen *Beach Guardians?*'

'I never miss it,' replied Deirdre firmly.

Even Larry was taken aback at this. 'Why ever not?' he asked, sandwich poised midair.

'Cos of Mike Murphy. He's gorgeous, I'm mad about him,' said Deirdre, at 35 a confirmed virgin.

'I rest my case,' said Larry, triumphantly turning to the others with an expansive gesture. 'Coffee anyone?'

Deirdre beat a hasty retreat before she was asked something she couldn't answer.

'You will be rewarded in a future life,' Larry called after her, 'or possibly next week when I buy you a drink in the club!' But she had gone, the prospect of drinking publicly with

Larry being more than she could bear to contemplate. 'So there you have it,' he said, turning back to Hugh and Martin 'straight from the mouth of the lovely Deirdre. What judgement, what discernment. Do tuck in, these sarnies are not half bad.'

They ate, and eventually Martin said, 'Larry?'

'Hello.'

'Larry, who is Mike Murphy?'

'I was wondering when you were going to ask me that – and I must say, it has taken you an unconscionable time. Mike Murphy is the hero of *Beach Guardians*, a load of old twaddle if ever I saw it, and is played by, of course, none other than our hero, Jim Dutton, and I think that this may be a suitable moment for me to introduce him to you.'

Jamming his third sandwich between his teeth so as to leave his hands free, Larry clicked open the briefcase and produced a video cassette. In practically every producer's office there is a television and VCR machine for this very purpose. He inserted the cassette into the recorder and all three settled down to watch a slice of American beach life.

'This'll make your hair stand on end,' said Larry happily. 'Well, what's left of it,' he added hurriedly, with a glance at Martin's almost bald pate. 'Enjoy!'

12

It was like the first day at school, Claire thought. The same nerves, apprehension, shyness, awkward introductions. Not knowing one's way around. Unfamiliar surroundings – well, not quite in this case. She'd worked at South Eastern Television before, but only briefly. And although she had now met most of the regular cast of *The McMasters*, she still felt a stranger. Gathering up her script and handbag from beside her in the car, she made her way with some trepidation through the revolving doors at the front of the building. She glanced at the board opposite the reception desk behind which sat a security guard.

'Morning, miss. Lovely day, innit? What show you on, then, the *Ronny Lee Spectacular*?'

Claire bridled. Did she really look like a dancer? she thought haughtily. Then she remembered that dancers were invariably young and very attractive, and decided to feel flattered.

'No,' she smiled indulgently, still scanning the board for the relevant information, 'I'm on *The McMasters*.'

'Sixth floor, miss,' said the guard promptly.

'Oh yes, I see. Her eye had just alighted on the name. 'Which room?' she asked, turning back to him.

'Both rooms, miss. It's a big production, lots of sets – you'll see. What are you playing then?'

'Oh, I'm the new girl,' said Claire shyly.

'You'll find them in the canteen, I shouldn't wonder – seventh floor.'

'Thank you, thank you,' said Claire gratefully.

She crossed to the lift, got in and was about to press the button, when she was joined by an elegant, well-known actress in her forties, Patricia Morgan. Claire gave her a slight smile, but the older woman merely looked at Claire coldly and pressed the button herself and the lift started up. It went straight up to the fifth floor. The doors opened and several people got in, all talking avidly. Claire did not recognize any of them and deduced correctly that they were production staff. The lift doors opened at the seventh floor and a pungent aroma of bacon and eggs wafted past. Everyone piled out and made their way in the direction from whence it came. As she reached the canteen, the smell increased in intensity and a low buzz of chatter could be heard. She followed her companions from the lift into the room, which was large, with dozens of tables. Huge picture windows looked out over the West London skyline. She joined the queue for breakfast, but at the hot food section she decided she couldn't face anything cooked, and opted instead for a glass of orange juice and a yoghurt.

'That's not going to last you till lunchtime,' observed a charming voice behind her.

Her heart stood still. Geoffrey Armitage. She glanced up, blushing prettily in spite of herself. 'I – I never eat breakfast,' she stammered, wondering why her normal sense of composure seemed suddenly to have deserted her.

Geoff ignored her reply. 'Do you like Dvořák?' he asked.

Claire was startled. 'Well, yes, as a matter of fact I do,' she admitted truthfully. 'In fact, I love him.' She felt she had gone too far.

Geoff, however, looked at her with unabashed admiraticn. 'How bloody fantastic,' he said happily.

'I've just been listening to him on the radio,' Claire ventured.

Geoffrey grabbed her wrist impulsively. 'Did you hear the Serenade in D? So did I.' They had reached the checkout counter and Claire nearly spilled the contents of her tray. 'Jenny,' said Geoff, 'I'm paying for these.'

'Oh no, please,' Claire protested.

'Don't worry, you'll have plenty of opportunities to return the compliment,' said Geoff, twinkling at her.

Claire was enchanted. She felt her heart fluttering delightfully. She really would have to watch her step, she reflected. She'd heard of Geoff's reputation, she knew he was married. No married men – that was rule number one. Married men were out. A mug's game, Sal always said and, God knows, Sal should know, thought Claire remembering her friend's ongoing romance with Bill, her airline pilot. For years that had been giving Sally torment. He'd said initially that he would leave his wife. They always say that, Sal had said. But of course he hadn't. They never do, Sal had said. Sally seemed to spend her life by the phone, waiting on the off chance of a sudden call from Bill to say he was on his way. Sal would immediately go into overdrive, rush round, preparing herself and the meal. Sometimes he would turn up. And sometimes he wouldn't. Sally became resigned to the situation. It suited her, she said. She had her relationship. And she had her independence. Yes, it suited her very nicely. 'Well, it wouldn't suit me,' Claire had declared emphatically. No, absolutely no married men, not in any circumstances.

'You're looking quite gorgeous, you know,' said Geoff the married man. The tribute was sincere and completely unexpected. It was ages since anyone had complimented her on her appearance. No, that wasn't true. Larry Matthews had, and so had Sal. By anyone, of course, she meant Roger. Bloody Roger – why did he have to keep intruding on her thoughts? There was a wound situated somewhere in the centre of her chest that was probed anew each time she thought of him.

'Shall we sit over here?' asked Geoff, indicating a table in the corner.

'Where are the others?' asked Claire doubtfully, glancing across at a nearby table at which were seated a couple of members of the cast. She didn't want to isolate herself from the rest of them, although she had to admit she was flattered by Geoff's attention.

'Oh don't worry about them. You'll be seeing enough of them for at least another two years.'

'And you,' Claire pointed out the flaw in his argument. 'I'll be seeing you for the next two years as well,' she added, rather wishing she hadn't been so blunt.

But Geoff was quick to take the advantage. 'I very much hope so.' He looked her straight in the eyes with unmistakable intensity. Claire once again felt a sensation of dizziness. She was being chatted up, she knew, and she liked it. It made her feel attractive, desirable again. It was a good feeling. She obediently followed him and sat apart from the others.

'Well, you certainly didn't waste any time, I see,' remarked Simon Lavell archly, as he passed them bearing a tray. Geoff, however, seemed immune to his taunts.

'Ms Jenner is the prettiest girl in the room. It is only natural that I should ask her to join me for breakfast,' he said blithely.

Patsy Hall, standing in the breakfast queue, caught sight of the intimate twosome and fumed quietly. She was furious about Claire. She had expected to become the new star of the series, firmly convinced that her blonde prettiness and undeniably wonderful figure would be enough to rocket her to stardom. Gradually, the various members of the cast drifted in and smiled and waved at Geoff and Claire but went to adjoining tables. Then Bella Shand arrived and made straight for their table.

'Has no one warned you about our Geoffrey?' she asked plonking her tray down. 'Watch him, he'll be after you. Geoff, you have no right to monopolize our newest cast member. I'm sure she'd much rather mingle with the others than have you breathing down her cleavage,' and she pulled up a chair and sat down heavily.

'I hope you're not going to eat all that,' said Geoff, eyeing her laden plate, completely unperturbed by her remarks. 'Isn't it about time for the annual diet?'

Bella, in her turn, ignored him and glanced at Claire and then back at Patsy, who was scowling as she paid for her breakfast. 'Well, I must say, Geoff, your taste has improved – oh, am I in the way?' she added, observing Geoff's unabashed look of admiration as he gazed at Claire, seemingly oblivious to Bella's comments. Claire felt herself blushing furiously.

'What about Mahler?' he asked.

'Mahler is wonderful,' replied Claire, laughing.

Bella made an explosive sound. 'Hah! More your line than Guns and Roses or Prince, eh, luvvy?' And she patted Geoff's hand reassuringly.

'May I join you?' asked Scott Dudley, sitting down without waiting for a reply. 'Come on, Pam, pull up a chair, there's plenty of room.' There wasn't, but everyone moved around until Pam had managed to squeeze herself in.

'Filming looks good,' he continued to Geoff. 'She comes

over well, your new leading lady.' He indicated Claire with a nod of his head.

Geoff glanced apprehensively at Bella who had bridled on hearing Claire thus described. 'I'm not surprised,' he replied. 'I enjoyed doing the scenes.'

Scott caught sight of Patsy at a nearby table. 'God, have we still got that ghastly little tart with us? I may have to go to the loo during her scenes.' Claire felt as though she was in the lion's den, this was undoubtedly the top table, but she wasn't sure that to find herself at it on the first day of rehearsal was a good beginning.

'Don't worry, darling, she's hardly got anything to do in this episode,' said Bella comfortingly, referring to Patsy.

'Yes,' agreed Scott, 'and what she does have won't be on camera.'

'You're the director,' Bella beamed at him happily. Then there was silence for a few minutes. They all tucked happily into their breakfast, Bella regaling them with details of a play she'd seen the night before. 'Oh God, is it time to go down?' she said, glancing at her watch and making a great show of rushing to finish her scrambled eggs.

'Take it easy, plenty of time,' said Scott, leaning back in his chair and fondling Pam's thigh.

But Bella was adamant. 'Must set the new girl a good example,' and she rose majestically, picked up her coffee and made for the door. 'See you down there,' she called back. The other members of the cast, observing Bella's exit, hurriedly started to gather their things and follow her. Bella had made her point. She was still the leading lady and intended to remain so.

In the rehearsal rooms, Claire found herself seated in the middle of a huge table, next to Geoff. He had insisted. The read-through was always something of an ordeal, as not only were the regular members of the cast there, twelve or so in number, but also the visiting artistes and the heads of the various technical departments. Larry started the rehearsal.

'You'll find rewrites on the table in front of you. Please put them into your scripts before we begin,' he called out. This was easier said than done and Claire spent several anxious moments trying to find the appropriate place in her script to insert the new pages.

'Everyone ready?' asked Scott finally, glancing around the room. Larry caught Claire's eye and flashed her an encouraging smile. She felt considerably heartened.

They started reading, Pam timing the scenes. As Claire's first entrance approached, she felt her apprehension mount. Her lungs felt constricted and she could hear her heart pounding, but when her turn came, she spoke up with a clear, energetic confidence and she could sense that she was the object of several pairs of eyes.

'Get out of my office or I'll send for the security guards!' she thundered at Geoff in the first encounter. They had read the scene well. She finished it and glanced up to see Larry grinning at her approvingly. Her only other scene in the episode had already been shot in the pre-filming, so she had no more to read. When it was all over there was a general air of satisfaction. It was obvious that everyone was pleased with the improvement of the quality of the writing and story content.

'Very good, dear,' said Bella graciously to Claire afterwards. 'You're going to be an asset to this series.' Even Bella could see that the series could only be improved by this very necessary injection of new life and she let her professionalism override her jealousy.

'You were just terrific,' whispered Geoff, squeezing Claire's arm. 'We're going to have a ball playing opposite

'Holy cow!' observed Jim with feeling, and put down the phone. Well, he'd taken her at her word. He had been primed. He was ready. He was shit-hot. All they had to do was to come and get him.

The sky had remained cloudless for months as was its custom in Los Angeles, though to be sure there was often a pall of smog hanging over the city, but the penetrating Californian sun would inevitably manage to burn its way through. Today, however, the weather had broken and Beverly Hills was enjoying its first torrential rain for a year. The sidewalks were inches deep in water. The rain streamed along the guttering and gushed down the sides of the ochre painted buildings. Jim observed it with mixed reactions. Good for the garden, no doubt. Save the slog of watering the lush dark green subtropical bushes, which thrived in this climate, and which he'd had to do himself since his lack of funds had obliged him to dispense with the services of the Spanish boy who normally fulfilled this function. But he hadn't counted on it. He wasn't prepared for this. He regarded it as ominous, an omen, and not a propitious one at that. It unsettled him. He had an uneasy feeling that a change was about to take place. He'd worked for this, he'd planned it all in his imagination. He'd seen himself strolling in for his interviews, fit and tanned, immaculately dressed in his Armani suit, with the sleeves rolled up just enough to reveal the smooth, tanned wrists. The silk shirt unbuttoned just enough to disclose a hint of muscular bronzed torso. The Italian shoes he'd got on a flying visit to Dallas at the fabulous shopping mall there. The blond hair carefully streaked to appear sun-kissed. The discreetly applied mascara. The whole effect was stunning. This carefully manufactured casually glamorous look was calculated to be just sufficiently tousled and rumpled by the drive to the casting offices along Sepulveda Boulevard – the hair slightly disturbed by the light breeze from the walk from the car park to the main door of the steel and glass front entrance, aided by a hand carelessly run through the golden locks on arrival, – to suggest having tried hard enough to impress, but not too hard.

But now he had to brave the elements. Now it would be a mad dash from the parking lot to the building, he would get drenched en route and arrive looking dishevelled. He supposed he could take an umbrella. An umbrella? He wasn't even sure he had one. They were always provided on location on the rare occasions when they became necessary. Which wasn't often because at the first drop of rain, shooting would invariably be abandoned and the entire unit would move back to the studio to film an indoor scene instead. Anyway, he could hardly arrive with an umbrella, even if he could find one. It would totally destroy his image. Perhaps it would be better to ring for a cab, then at least he could be driven up to the front entrance. Yeah, that was better. But there wasn't too much time between interviews and he had no idea how long the first one would take. Nope, a cab was no good either. There was only one thing for it, he would have to hire a chauffeur-driven limousine for the whole day. It would cost him and would impress no one other than the security guards on the door, but what the hell – this was important. He phoned up several firms and found one for $250 for the day.

He felt good as the limo sped off Doheny Drive, swishing through the rain-drenched streets. He stared listlessly out at the huge billboards advertising Michael Douglas's latest movie. And Kevin Costner's. He should be up there with them. What the hell had gone wrong? He shook himself impatiently. This was the sort of thinking that made his friends tell him that he had an attitude problem. Positive thinking was the answer. Any moment now he would be up there. It was all a matter of timing. He became momentarily despondent again as he remembered that the two roles he was being seen for were hardly the sort of thing that either Douglas or Costner would consider doing, being of a commercial populist nature, but he rose above it. He'd probably get the art movie. It would lead to something. He'd be noticed, acclaimed even. He'd turn in a riveting performance, a sort of cross between Jack Nicholson and Nick Nolte. These two had long been his heroes. They exactly mirrored his own dual personality. One day he would cultivate Nicholson's manic charm, another, Nolte's brooding danger. Yes, he had it all – plus, he was better-looking than either of them. Thus buoyed up, he sank back into the luxury of the limo and gave his thoughts up to a delicious reverie of the adulation and praise that would be heaped upon him once his talent was recognized.

Jim was the son of theatrical parents. His mother had been Barbara Dutton, a darling of 1950s B-movies. She had starred in any number of black-and-white crime thrillers and had graduated to support roles in big Technicolor epics. She had never quite made the big time, but had been a respected actress. She had married a good-looking small-time actor who had taken to drink in a big way, unable to cope with his wife's continued success and greater earnings potential. Bill Crawley, Jim's father, had died from alcoholism when Jim was fourteen. His mother never recovered, but struggled on for several years. But the parts became fewer as she got older, and she finally took an overdose of barbiturates on a lonely New Year's Eve, shortly before her fiftieth birthday.

Jim was devastated and blamed himself for not seeing enough of her, for not taking care of her. He had inherited his father's good looks – and, unfortunately, his taste for drink – and his mother's talents, and he was determined to be a success for her sake. This was uppermost in his mind as the limo pulled up outside a large office block, a considerable way from the centre of the city.

'Come around in about thirty-five minutes,' Jim instructed the driver. 'You can park up in back,' he yelled, but the limo had turned onto the freeway, the driver intent on a late breakfast at the local diner. Jim fervently hoped he would materialize again in time for the next appointment. He sighed and, considerably flustered, hurried inside. The security guard regarded him bleakly. He didn't wait for Jim to give his name, but jerked a thumb in the direction of the elevator.

'Sixth floor,' he intoned.

Jim nodded, thanked him briefly and made his way along the marble hall. He had hoped the elevator would have a mirror in it, but he was out of luck.

On the sixth floor, he found himself in a large reception area. The place was packed. There were actors and actresses of almost every type and age. There were numerous imitation leather sofas and chairs dotted around, nearly all occupied. He stood for a moment perplexed.

'Yup, this is the place,' a distinguished-looking elderly actor said dryly, observing his hesitation.

'Thanks,' replied Jim with genuine gratitude.

'My wife enjoyed your series,' continued the greyhaired one, obviously keen to talk.

'Thanks,' said Jim again, absently.

This was a general audition. What the hell was Meriel thinking of, sending him here?

He was about to turn around and go in search of a telephone to give her a piece of his mind when the older actor, who looked very familiar, spoke again. 'You'd better report to her,' he said, indicating a large blonde in her forties who was presiding over a reception desk at the end of the room. 'Go on,' he urged, determined to be helpful, 'or you'll miss your turn.'

Summoning up what was left of his dignity, Jim approached the desk. The blonde looked at him malevolently.

'You got your sides?' she demanded abruptly.

'Pardon me?' enquired Jim, wondering whether he had heard correctly.

'Your *sides*,' she emphasized loudly, 'you gottem?'

Jeez! What the fuck was going on here? Meriel had said nothing about pages of script, or sides, as they were called in America. He'd assumed he would be one of maybe six carefully selected names who would be seen at discreet intervals during the day. He had anticipated offering generously to read a page or two of dialogue, but only if the interview was going badly and only as a last resort. And here he was amongst a crowd of nobodies, being treated like a bit part player.

He gripped the edge of the desk and said quietly but firmly, 'No, I do not have my sides. I was not sent any sides. My name is Jim Dutton and I'm here to see Mr Goldstein.'

'Oh my Gad,' she drawled. 'We don't have any spares – we used 'em all up. You'll have to wait till someone comes outta there.' She jerked her head towards the door of an inner office.

'That's quite all right' said Jim with elaborate politeness through gritted teeth. 'If you'd be kind enough to tell Mr Goldstein that Mr Dutton is here?'

She ignored this request. 'You'll have to sit and wait your turn,' she said briefly.

Jim again contemplated turning on his heel and leaving, but remembered his dwindling bank balance and, swallowing his pride, quickly sought out a vacant seat and sat seething, privately planning a suitable revenge for Meriel.

104

After a few moments, a young girl with curly nut-brown hair emerged from the inner office. She looked flushed and her eyes glowed. Well, she's been a hit, thought Jim enviously. A well-preserved middle-aged man with an obvious toupee went in next. He came out again almost immediately. He was followed by a not so young actress, very thin with hollow cheeks and huge eyes, an ingénue type but well into her late thirties, Jim guessed. She didn't last long either. It was the turn of the silverhaired actor next. His stay was also brief. But he came out smiling broadly.

'A mere formality,' he called out happily to Jim as he went to the elevator. 'Hope you do as well,' and he waved cheerily.

By this time Jim was angry. He was the star of a fucking TV series, for Christ's sake.

Finally the blonde gorgon behind the desk nodded in his direction. 'They'll see you now,' she snapped. Jim wondered idly why she had to be so thoroughly unpleasant. Was it that she sensed the unease and tension in the air. He was certainly feeling uneasy and, boy, was he tense. Meriel was going to have some explaining to do. He entered the inner sanctum.

There were three people seated behind a large table, one of them an attractive brunette in her early forties. He paused momentarily at the door, leaning seductively against it as he closed it behind him, and gave her the benefit of a half-raised eyebrow, a quizzical amused glance, followed by a dazzling smile. She eyed him coldly.

'Hi, Jim, take a seat.' A large rangy man of fifty or thereabouts indicated the hot seat opposite them. He spoke with an easy familiarity although Jim and he had never met before.

'Hi,' said Jim with considerable energy in response, flashing the beacon-like smile at random around the room, and lowering himself into the chair in a manner that suggested he could only just accommodate his balls in his pants. The female remained unimpressed.

'Okay, Jim, it's all yours,' the man continued without bothering to introduce the others, pushing a few pages of script towards him. 'Francie tells me we're fresh outta sides – it seems you were overlooked. How are you on dialogue at sight?'

'On dialogue, I total,' said Jim leaning back in the chair and shooting the woman another of his famous seductive looks, calculated to melt a prospective fuck at fifty paces. Not this one. She regarded him with ill-concealed hostility. He gave it up and picked up the script.

'Go for it, Jim.'

Jim went for it. He gave it all he had. The tall man who was conducting the interview, whom he supposed to be the director, Leslie Newton, read with him. The woman he guessed was the casting director, Lee Travis. The third occupant was short, fat and bald, with keen sharp brown eyes, the archetypal film mogul. Goldstein, who else? Jim read well, his classes at the Theatre Studio had paid off. When he had finished, he slung the script onto the table with a gesture he later realized could easily have been interpreted as defiant, where he had intended confidence.

Lee Travis bridled and finally spoke in a rather pleasant husky voice, the pleasantness somewhat marred on this occasion by the iciness of her tone. 'How's your British accent?'

Jim was surprised, he had no idea that the role was British. 'I can handle British,' he replied casually.

'Let's hear it,' she said.

Jim was startled. 'Er, oh righty, er, yeah, okay, let's see now.' He dredged through his memory and finally came up with a piece of Shakespeare from a play he'd done during his spell at the Pasadena Playhouse. '*Let me play the fool: With mirth and laughter let old wrinkles come, And let my liver rather heat with wine Than my heart cool with mortifying groans. Why should a man –* '

'Fine. Okay. Thanks,' she interrupted him.

He stopped and looked. 'I'm sorry. Is there something wrong?'

'No, it's fine – you're not what we're looking for. Thanks for coming in.'

Jim was stunned. The interview was over. He never knew how, but somehow he found himself back in the reception. He made his way to the lobby. His driver was as good as his word and was waiting for him outside. Jim wandered out oblivious of the rain and flung himself into the back of the car in a sort of stupor. The car pulled away.

'Where to?' asked the smiling driver.

Jim hardly heard him. He'd been humiliated. He'd been dismissed and he hadn't got the part.

14

Claire's one scene in the studio recording had gone brilliantly. She had brought a new dynamic energy to the scene. She was aware of it herself. The company were enthusiastic in their support for her. Even Bella, who regarded *The McMasters* as her own property, was forced to admit grudgingly that the injection of energy, beauty and the indefinable air of class that Claire had in abundance would do the series nothing but good.

Patsy, however, was mortified. She had earmarked the role of younger leading player in the series for herself. She was totally unaware that her acting ability was minimal and she never really seemed at ease on screen, and believed herself to be 'a cross between Sarah bloody Bernhardt and Eleonora fucking Duse', to quote Bella. Bella could see no good reason for Patsy to be in the series at all – she was of the generation of actors who believed that performances came first – looks were a bonus. Bella had been a beautiful girl, having the same kind of classy good looks and talent that made Claire so watchable, and she was still stunning to look at. Patsy, although only dimly aware of their disapproval, put it down to jealousy. The extraordinary fact was that Patsy was popular with the audience, who seemed not to notice her lack of acting talent.

'Nothing succeeds like mediocrity,' Bella had observed sagely. 'The great unwashed', referring to the lower echelons of the viewing public, 'cannot bear to be confronted by anything that makes them feel inadequate. But show them Miss Pea-brain lisping her way inaccurately through yet another scene of misstressed syllables and they are perfectly happy. "I could do better than that," they think, and how bloody right they are!'

Claire quickly became popular with the cast. She was always word-perfect in her lines and played the scenes with energy and style. Larry Matthews watched her progress with ill-concealed pride and approval. The showing of her first episode was greeted with acclaim by the TV critics, who stated unequivocally that the series was long overdue for an injection of someone who could act. Bella fumed secretly over this, but laughed it off in front of the cast. Larry instructed the scriptwriters to write in bigger and better scenes for Claire. Bella noted this and kept her own counsel. She knew in her heart it was the best thing for the series. *The McMasters* had shot up in the ratings again and had found a new burst of national popularity. But it was a bitter pill to swallow. Claire had deserved her place, there was no doubt about it.

Geoff did not lose any time in consolidating his position as Claire's prospective lover. He renewed his attentions ever more ardently. He pursued her relentlessly. Claire had to admit she found it highly flattering, all the more so after the traumatic rejection by Roger. Geoff made it quite plain that he regarded her as the most intelligent, witty and desirable woman he had ever met. She was not to know that he had acquired this technique after many years of practice. He was now ready for his latest kill.

There was another bout of filming due to take place in and around Petworth, and many of the company were encamped in a nearby country hotel. Geoff, Claire, Simon and Patsy were amongst those taking part. Geoff was determined to seduce Claire and had offered her a lift. At first Claire had declined, saying she had a perfectly good vehicle of her own, but then, as luck would have it, the little car developed engine trouble and she had to go into rehearsals by tube.

'Should have got a Japanese bus,' remarked Bella unsympathetically.

'I prefer Swedish models myself,' said Simon knowledgeably.

'Well, you would,' retorted Bella. She was in a foul mood, Claire's popularity was beginning to irk her and she had just seen the script for the last two episodes of this series.

'Have you seen what those hen-brains have given me to do in Twelve and Thirteen? I could phone it in – no filming again either. Dear God, why don't they just bundle me into a truck and send me off to the home for exhausted donkeys or whatever it is. I've become redundant!'

'Don't worry, love,' said Meg soothingly. 'They'll write you up again, I'm sure.'

Bella glared at her. 'I should like to remind you that Episode Thirteen is the last one in this series,' she said cuttingly. 'Fuck me, even the appalling Patsy has only marginally less to do than I have – God, she really is thick you know . . .'

'Patsy Hall is the most stupid female in Europe,' observed Simon calmly.

'You can say that again,' said Bella, 'only don't, she's just come into the room and she'll take it as a compliment.'

That was two weeks ago and Bella was not amongst those present in the hotel bar, but was drowning her sorrows elsewhere. The cast had all drifted in one by one to the bar, joining each other at a low table that abutted to a large comfortable sofa and was surrounded by plush armchairs. Claire had been coerced into accepting Geoff's lift and they had chatted happily about the series all the way down. The journey had been a mere forty-five minutes and they had arrived at their destination at the cocktail hour.

'You're dining with me, of course,' said Geoff as they checked in at the desk.

'Am I?' she smiled happily.

'Eight o'clock suit you?' he asked as he signed his name with a flourish.

'Oh yes, fine,' she replied, a little dazed at the speed and ease with which he made the assignation.

'Good,' he said, taking the proffered key from the concierge. 'See you in the bar for an apéritif at a quarter to,' and he headed for the stairs.

The hotel was an old coaching inn with an abundance of exposed beams and bulging walls. Claire was delighted to find that her room boasted a four-poster. She looked forward to sinking into its depths protected by the drapes and hangings. She went into the luxurious little bathroom and gazed at herself in the mirror. She decided she was looking a lot better than she had for a long time. How her life had changed. A mere few weeks ago she had almost given up. She had been in despair, and now here she was, a successful actress in the most popular TV series, and being courted by one of the most attractive men on television. It was unbelievable, but wonderful.

She had a shower and liberally doused herself with an expensive scented body spray, which she kept for special occasions. She put on some black underwear and wriggled into a simple little black dress. Glossy black stockings and plain black suede high heels completed the outfit. She turned her head upside down and brushed her hair vigorously, then tossed it back as she came the right way up again. This had the effect of sending her hair into a cloudlike halo around her face, which had a pleasant glow of pink from being the wrong way up. Her sparkling eyes matched the diamanté earrings that she clipped on and the rhinestone ring she slipped on her finger. A final spray of her favourite perfume and she was ready. She picked up a small black suede bag and almost waltzed out of the room.

Geoff was waiting for her in the bar. He rose to his feet as he saw her. I just love the civilities of life, she thought.

'The arrival of the Queen of Sheba no less,' he greeted her, grinning boyishly. She knew it was charming flattery, but she didn't care. It was so wonderfully romantic.

'Why thank you, slave,' she retorted, equally charmingly.

'Oh dear,' he said, indicating a chair for her, 'is that my role for tonight? I was rather hoping it might be Solomon.'

She laughed. 'Then you'll have to acquire a little more dignity, sir.'

'I'll do my best,' he replied, assuming a serious countenance. 'What will you drink, my dear?'

'Gin and it, please.'

'What a sweet old-fashioned thing you are,' he observed in Coward-like clipped tones. He repeated the order to the waiter, who was hovering nearby, adding a vodka and tonic for himself. He sat gazing at her with undisguised admiration. She felt herself blushing and averted her eyes.

'I have a feeling tonight is going to be rather special,' he said quietly after a moment.

She still couldn't look at him. They sat in silence for a while. She felt she should say something but she didn't want to break the spell. Geoff was not the least disturbed by the silence. He'd noted in the past that this quiet approach had the effect of disarming his prospective victims.

Eventually the waiter returned with their drinks. Geoffrey gave his room number and signed for them. Claire made a small noise of protest, but Geoff said firmly, 'My shout.' After the waiter had gone he added, 'And the dinner's on me – it was, after all, my idea. What's the matter?' he asked, smiling engagingly. 'Afraid you'll have to sing for your supper?'

Claire smiled. 'No, of course not.'

'Let me assure you, my dear Ms Jenner, I shan't ask you to do anything you don't want to. I just want us to have a cosy little intimate supper – by candlelight, of course – and talk and laugh over old times.'

'We haven't had any old times,' Claire countered, laughing.

'Yes, we have. We just haven't had them together, that's all. I thought we could compare experiences. Could be fun, don't you think?'

'Well, yes,' she agreed lamely. It seemed that however she retaliated, he managed to score over her and wrong-foot her. It continued in this vein throughout supper. Claire found herself laughing a lot.

Then, towards the end of the evening, he took her hand in his and, gazing earnestly into her eyes, said, 'I've changed my mind. You've utterly bewitched me. Do you think it would be possible for me to come to your room later?'

Claire was dumbfounded. She just looked at him without saying a word. The question had caught her completely off guard as Geoff had intended it to. They had been gossiping about Bella and Hugh.

He saw her reaction and said, 'Just for a night cap.'

'Oh come on,' said Claire scornfully amused.

'I'm sorry, have I said something untoward?' asked Geoff, raising an eyebrow.

'Well,' said Claire disparagingly, 'it's such a cliché, isn't it? I mean, it's like asking someone up for a coffee or to see your etchings.'

As usual Geoffrey was more than a match for her: 'Time-honoured chat-up line – what's wrong with that? Miss Jenner, I am, I admit, trying to chat you up. You are the most beautiful, most talented and most adorable girl I have ever met and I would very much like to take you to bed.'

Claire held her breath for a moment, then let out a gasp of astonishment. 'You really do take the biscuit. You're what my mother would call the pink limit!' she said.

'Your mother sounds like a sweet old-fashioned thing, too. Tell me about her.'

'All right,' she said, then went for the jugular: 'I will if you'll tell me about your wife.'

'Phew!' he said, collapsing back in his chair. 'You know how to get a guy where it hurts. All right – here goes. I am locked in a boring mundane marriage with a lovely girl who deserves something better than me. She is devoted to our two sons, who are both delightful, and, bless her, she has lost all interest in the physical side of our relationship. I love her dearly, but only as one might love a slightly irritating sister or aunt. I have high hopes of her taking a young lover 'ere long, if, indeed, she has not already done so. It would explain the disdain with which she regards any attempt on my part to renew conjugal relations. My offspring, as I have said, are a delight in every way and treat me like shit. Also featured in this perfectly normal ménage is a cat called Brambles, who is possessed of a singularly malevolent disposition and who, unhappily, has only a tenuous grip on his anal expellations. There, has that answered your question? And now let's hear about your doubtless enchanting mother.'

'She might be a gorgon, for all you know,' said Claire, who had listened to Geoff's monologue with amusement.

'She couldn't possibly be anything quite so Greek when she has such an enchanting daughter – cue!' he commanded.

Claire found herself describing her adorable mother and her ailing, elderly, father.

'I, too, have an adoring mother. We have so much in common,' he said. 'Shall we continue this fascinating discussion in the privacy of your four-poster?'

Claire thought, what the hell, what harm can it do? – he's almost certainly bound to be a wonderful lover.

Geoff signed for the meal and escorted her out of the restaurant. They had to go through the bar to get to the staircase. The other members of the cast and crew were all sitting there, having just returned from a Chinese meal outing.

'Oh, so there you are,' called out Simon meaningfully.

'You missed a lovely meal,' said Pam, who was more than slightly pissed.

'Oh no we didn't. It was delicious, thank you,' replied Geoff breezily.

'Night cap?' asked Scott, who had his hand on Pam's thigh.

'No thanks,' said Geoff, 'going to look at the jokes.' He was referring to his script. 'Big scenes tomorrow. Want to be at my peak.'

'Then we should have shot them fifteen years ago,' rejoined Scott dryly.

Everyone laughed, it was seldom that anyone other than Bella scored over Geoff.

He, however, was sanguine. 'I'll get you for that,' he said easily.

'Oh no you won't,' said Scott. 'I'm the one calling the shots, remember.'

Everyone laughed again. Claire took advantage of the diversion to make an exit.

'Good night, everyone.' She waved.

'You know your call?' asked Terri anxiously.

'Six thirty in make-up,' confirmed Claire. 'Don't worry,

I'll be there,' and she made for the stairs. Geoff stayed on chatting for a while.

'Oh come on, one little drink won't hurt you,' said Scott, winking in the direction of Claire's retreating figure.

'You've twisted my arm,' said Geoff. Patsy had said nothing but sat looking daggers at Geoff. He blithely ignored her.

After a little more banter and a brandy, Geoff excused himself and went off to his room. Waiting for him was a tray containing champagne in a bucket of ice and two flute glasses. He had ordered them before going down to dinner. He went into the bathroom, cleaned his teeth, loosened his tie, splashed on more aftershave, and, with the champagne in one hand and the glasses in the other, left his room, whistling quietly to himself.

Patsy, under the pretence of going to the loo, had crept upstairs intent on confronting Geoffrey in his room and creating a scene. But first she had gone to her room to freshen up and check her make-up. She emerged at the exact moment that Geoff arrived at Claire's door and knocked. It was opened and he went in. Patsy felt a knife of jealousy twist in her gut and she retreated. She stood panting with fury, then remembered the lustful glances of one of the technicians downstairs. Well, it was going to be his lucky night. She'd make Geoff pay for this betrayal. She checked her appearance for the twentieth time that night and went downstairs again to proposition Garry, the undeniably very attractive boy who worked in the sound department.

Meanwhile Geoff and Claire were sipping champagne, gazing deep into each other's eyes.

'Well, this is it,' said Geoff, 'the moment of truth has arrived.'

'Yes,' agreed Claire quietly. 'I think I should tell you,

Geoff, that I had an abortion not so long ago. I'm not sure that I'm up to any of this.'

There was a horrified pause. Geoff had not been expecting this. But he took it in his stride.

'You poor darling,' he said with genuine sympathy. 'Listen, I've got a good idea. Why don't we pile into that four-poster and I'll give you a lovely cuddle and make it all better. No, really,' he added, seeing her expression. 'I mean it. Just a cuddle, nothing more.'

Five minutes later they were in bed and Geoff was caressing her and cooing over her, making soothing sounds, stroking her head and hair, trying to reassure her. Claire submitted to his embrace. In no time at all his hands had wandered to her breasts and with a groan of pleasure he bent his head to suck at her nipples. It was Claire's turn to groan. She let her hand find his erect cock and started stroking it. Then lust got the better of her and she squirmed down the bed and took it into her mouth – it tasted delicious. She suddenly felt wild with passion and, pulling herself up, she straddled him and guided his penis into her. She found herself taking control of the situation and started to ride him frantically. He craned his head up to suck at her breasts. They clutched at each other and fucked as though their lives depended on it. They both realized that they needed something from each other and each was determined to satisfy in return. They kissed long and deep. Claire could feel Geoff's sweat, damp on her own body. She had forgotten how wonderful making love could be. And she really felt as though she was making love, not just fucking. He was a tender, attentive, considerate lover and made sure she was approaching her climax before even thinking of coming himself. They came together, pulsatingly. It was a glorious sensation. Claire could not remember it being this good with Roger. She was surprised that she even managed to think that while it was happening, but she did. She felt as though she had exorcised Roger for good.

They fell back exhausted into the downy depths of the four-poster and slept soundly. Claire awoke early the next morning. She remembered she had an early make-up call. She turned her head on the pillow to look at Geoff. He, accustomed also to early film calls, was already awake, gazing at her.

'I think I'm in love,' he said.

15

The producer's run was a phenomenon peculiar to recorded television. Claire, having spent most of her career working in the theatre up to this point, found it an alarming experience. Each episode was of fifty minutes' duration, and consisted of a mixture of scenes recorded in the studio and sections shot on film, sometimes interior, but mostly exterior on location. *The McMasters* being concerned with the antique business, the filming block, which took place in summer, was located in and around famous antique fairs up and down the country, some actual, some fictional. There were also forays into London, in and around Belgravia and Mayfair, for exterior shots, which were always fraught, the camera crew and actors having to contend with horrific traffic conditions and congested London streets. These locations were universally loathed, as it nearly always seemed to be raining or cold or both, but, for the sake of continuity, adequate cover could not be worn.

The main bulk of each episode, however, was recorded in the studio. The routine was the same each time. The episode would be rehearsed for just over a week in the rehearsal room in London. The cast was then able to become acquainted with the dialogue and the director with his camera shots. Then the cast would do a run through of the show for the technicians. This enabled the lighting and cameramen to judge the positions of the cameras and light. Bella always claimed that this particular ritual was a total waste of time as they never put them in the right place anyway.

Then, on the day before going in front of the cameras in the studio, the producer, the executive producer and their acolytes would appear and the cast would then be required to give a performance for their benefit. After a producer's run, whole scenes had been known to be cut or severely trimmed, usually on the pretext that the show was over-running. But too often the cast subsequently discovered that this was not the case – it was simply that the offending scene was considered too indulgent, or too boring or too off the wall, only to be replaced eventually by an equally indulgent or boring wodge of filming. These wodges were never off the wall: interminable shots or stock footage of exterior scenes – a car making its way slowly through London traffic – a panning shot of scenic sameness and unoriginality guaranteed, in Bella's opinion, to send the impatient viewer switching channels in a fury of frustration. So, as no one wished to have their scenes cut, all the acting stops were pulled out. Concentration was of the utmost as distractions abounded. The result was that the tension in the rehearsal room immediately before and during one of these runs was at breaking point. Everyone was nervous. Even the old hands who pretended they weren't.

The relief when it was over was enormous, but there was still the producer's verdict to be announced. Notes were given as in the theatre. These were comments on individual performances and requests for alterations in dialogue or interpretation. These notes were observed by most, but ignored by the very experienced like Bella and Geoff, who claimed to be the best judges of their own performances. If the producer's wishes were continually flouted, the unwary actor would find himself saying the offending speech whilst

120

the camera was firmly trained on his protagonist in the scene. There was an ongoing battle of wits between actors and directors. The actors had some justification, as most directors were inept and had worked out their camera scripts long before seeing what the actors had to offer. These were treated with contempt by the actors. The standard of scriptwriting, too, varied enormously and the rare combination of good script and good lighting, cameraman and good director was greeted with jubilant expectancy by the actors.

It was normal practice for the producer, director and scriptwriters to get into a huddle in the rehearsal room after a producer's run, sending the cast off to the canteen to await their verdict. Like naughty schoolchildren, Claire thought, waiting for their form marks. Bella voiced the general opinion in her own down-to-earth way. 'One is forever being judged in this fucking profession,' she said loudly to no one in particular. The entire cast was seated in the canteen at adjoining tables, as was their wont on these occasions, as if by banding together they found some sort of collective strength to combat the criticisms they knew were to follow. Bella warmed to her theme.

'I mean, what the fuck are we doing, sitting here like a plate of prunes, whilst those morons pass judgement on our efforts? Dear God, they wouldn't know an actor from a hole in the ground,' she said heatedly, letting her glance rest momentarily on Patsy, who, digging into a plate of overcooked lasagne, was blissfully unaware of Bella's meaning.

'You're right,' agreed Geoff who always knew a cue when he heard one. 'Did I really slog my guts out at Stratford all those years, learning my trade, to end up trying to invest this load of bullshit with life?'

The entire cast groaned in unison; they'd heard this one before.

'Dahling', drawled Bella reprovingly, 'I trust you did not "learn your trade at Stratford". One hopes that you'd at least mastered the preliminaries in, where was it – Frinton? Awfully hard on the world tourist trade to go all that way and pay all that money to be treated to a postulant Prince Hal or a novitiate Navarre.' She mentioned two of Geoff's more notable successes.

'Cow!' observed Geoff good-naturedly.

'I mean, it never stops,' Bella continued undeterred. 'We're judged if we're good enough to go to drama school – ' another dig at Patsy – 'then we're judged if we're good enough to get a part – continuously, and even when we've made it and proved ourselves, we're judged on every bloody role by a bunch of embittered, uninformed hacks who claim to be critics, who also, as it so often transpires, wouldn't know an actor from a hole in the ground, or indeed a play for that matter. How else do you account for the eulogy accorded Georgie Trevellian in *The Woman who Screamed*?' Her venom was now directed at her old rival. She and Georgie had shared billing, dressing rooms and even boyfriends at the Birmingham Repertory Company. Georgie had made a name for herself in esoteric Beckettian-type plays on the fringe, whilst Bella had spent the last seven years demeaning herself (so she thought) in *The McMasters*, which had brought her fame, but not the acting accolades for which her soul yearned.

'I saw her in that – I thought she was awful,' Reg volunteered helpfully.

Bella's humour improved. 'That doesn't surprise me,' she replied sunnily. 'She's basically an ensemble actress.'

'I wonder what they'll have to say today,' interrupted Meg, trying to change the subject.

'Your scenes went down well,' Bella remarked chummily to Claire. 'It's nice to know that the cretinous Colin can write decent stuff when he puts what passes for his mind to it.'

Bella was far too experienced an actress to let her true feelings be known to a younger rival, instead giving vent to her spleen on the unfortunate Colin. Everyone at the table knew that the dialogue had improved because Claire had provided the inspiration. Bella knew it, too, and was consumed with jealousy.

'Well, if they cut one word of Claire's stuff, I personally will be livid,' she stated emphatically.

Again, everyone at the table knew she meant exactly the opposite. Even as she spoke, Larry was seen approaching their section bearing a polystyrene cup of coffee and an enigmatic expression.

'You're looking smug, Larry, what's the SP?' asked Meg happily. She was content with her lot in the series. Regular money, a bit of fame and good company — what actress could ask for more?

'Yes,' agreed Bella tartly. 'You've got a sort of "I-know-something-you-don't-know" look about you, which is decidedly infuriating.'

'And so I do,' conceded Larry, with a self-satisfied smile as he pulled up a chair from a nearby table and attempted to squeeze himself in between Claire and Reg. They obligingly shifted their chairs to accommodate him. 'But I've been sworn to secrecy by "them",' he added darkly, 'so you'll have to guess.' Larry had a foot firmly entrenched in both camps, but his allegiance came down on the side of the actors — being an ex-actor himself. He had an abundance of charm and a whiplash tongue that kept the studio running like clockwork, and made him universally loved and feared in equal measure.

'We're coming off at the end of this season,' said Reg promptly, exhibiting the actor's ever-present insecurity.

'Nope,' said Larry.

123

'They've got more sense,' scoffed Bella.

'They're going to repeat all the previous series,' suggested Meg hopefully. She was laughed down unanimously.

'We're going to the Caribbean on location,' said Jason.

'In a series about antiques?' replied Larry scornfully.

'Oh no, of course not.' Jason retired crushed.

'Well, two of the characters could go there on holiday – a honeymoon or something,' said Patsy stoutly, coming to Jason's defence.

'Right up your street that, isn't it, dear?' retorted Larry waspishly.

'Are they going to write in a new character?' asked Claire quietly, hoping in her heart that they were. She found her personal success exhilarating, but knew that it had cost her the friendship of many of the cast.

'Got it in one!' exclaimed Larry admiringly. Claire was living up to his expectations. Her professionalism – the way she always knew her lines, the way she always looked stunning and the integrity and truthfulness that she brought to the scenes – won his applause. He also admired her brand of ballsy, gutsy acting.

'Another one!' gasped Bella incredulously, seeing her part diminishing even further. 'Not another woman, I hope!'

'No,' said Larry, relishing his role as Nemesis. 'Another man.'

'Oh,' said Geoff, alarmed.

'A man in his thirties.'

'Ah,' said Geoff, relieved that his position as patriarch was not to be threatened.

'To play opposite Claire,' Larry continued, placing an affectionate arm around Claire's shoulders.

'Me?' said Claire, astounded.

'Settle, petal,' said Larry patting her reassuringly. 'Yes,

124

you. A lovely hunky American, all of your very own, you lucky girl you!'

There was a stunned silence, broken finally by Patsy and Jason speaking in unison. 'American?'

'Yep,' said Larry, thoroughly enjoying the sensation he had created.

'Good God!' said Bella. 'They must be getting desperate!' Everyone laughed.

'Why do you say hunky?' enquired Patsy, wide-eyed and not a little jealous. What had Claire got that made her so exceptional? Well, never mind, she'd soon have this new man panting after her and get her part written up. They'd soon see that a glamorous American required an equally glamorous female to play opposite him. Yes, they would soon realize their mistake. 'Do you know who he is?' she asked, trying to conceal her disappointment.

'Certainly I do,' said Larry.

'But you're not going to tell,' said Reg, who knew Larry's methods.

'Certainly I'm not,' replied Larry. 'My lips are sealed.'

'No they're not, you've told us everything except his name,' retorted Reg.

Larry shrugged, as though the subject had suddenly lost its appeal. 'You wouldn't know him,' he said dismissively.

'How do you know?'

'Cos I assume that you've all got better taste than to watch the sort of crap television he appears in. Well, Patsy might know him,' he added as an afterthought.

'What's he been in?' Patsy asked breathlessly, oblivious to the insult.

'Oh some sort of life style, surfing thing – you know beachboy stuff, bristling with blonde bimbos – of both sexes,' replied Larry airily.

'Not Jim Dutton!' shrieked Patsy.

The rest of the cast squealed in unison and pretended to swoon, sending her up mercilessly and causing the rest of the canteen occupants to cast surprised glances of disapproval in their direction. They cared not. *The McMasters* cast were a law unto themselves. They were the most popular TV series in the country and let no one forget it.

'Jim who?' asked Meg.

'Never heard of him,' snorted Geoff contemptuously.

'He's the latest hot tip for the Hollywood big time,' said Patsy knowledgeably. They all hooted with laughter again. It began to dawn on Patsy that she was not being taken seriously. 'What's so funny about that?' she asked haughtily. Nobody bothered to reply.

'Well, that's nice for you, dearest chuck,' observed Geoff tauntingly to Claire. 'A lovely piece of Hollywood beefcake to play opposite – that should liven things up!'

'Yes,' agreed Claire doubtfully, not knowing whether to feel pleased or insulted.

'Anyway, who the fuck is Jim Dutton?' demanded Bella furiously.

16

'Mr Snellor?'

'Speaking.'

'It's Patsy Hall, Mr Snellor.'

'Oh, hello, Patsy. I thought you'd died on me.'

'I'm awfully sorry, it's been a big episode for me, you see. I had a scene with Geoff and one with Simon – I had to tell him about the new – '

'Yes, yes, Pat, cut the crap – I mean, er – don't spoil it for me, I'll watch on Sunday. What's the SP?'

'What?'

'The latest, what's the latest on the set – behind the scenes, I mean?'

'Well, I think you're right, Mr Snellor. I think they're building up my part. I've got three scenes next week. Oh, and I thought the pictures were just great, Mr Snellor. My Auntie Thelma said I looked really lovely.'

Snellor groaned. He had an appalling hangover and Trevor Grantly, his boss, had already given him an earful that morning. He wanted the dirt on *The McMasters*. Now. Preferably sooner. The mindless meandering of the blonde bimbo with the big knockers did not constitute front-page banner headlines. Nobody was interested in Bella Shand's minor alcoholic misdemeanours. What the readers wanted to know was who was getting a leg over and over whom were they getting it. Were they going to have to print endless spreads of the dimwit with the admittedly sizeable Charlies – there were plenty more where she came from, Trevor reminded him – or was he, Snellor, finally going to pull his finger out and come up with a really hot story? Snellor had assured him that he was teetering on the verge of something big, he could smell it.

If there was one feature on Tony Snellor's otherwise repulsive physiognomy that Trevor found tolerable, it was his nose. It led a life entirely of its own devising and seemed to operate quite independently of its owner. At least this was Trevor's private opinion, since, as his colleague was more or less permanently inebriated, he could find no other logical explanation. This remarkable nose cost the newspaper group some £35,000 per annum before expenses and on occasions Trevor had to admit that it had been worth it.

But times were hard, they were in the throes of a fucking recession for Christ's sake. They had to get the dirt on TV's most popular soap before their rivals, or he, Snellor, would be all washed up. Down the plughole. Tony Snellor, who had a keen ear for a metaphor, would have appreciated Trevor's clever use of the device if he hadn't had such a headache. However, he managed to jot it down in his notepad on returning to his office, resolving to use it in his piece on *The McMasters*. It irked him that he was never allowed to give full vent to his creative flow and had to write in clichés to satisfy his editor. He had, in fact, been on the point of ringing Patsy to gee her along when her phone call came through. And now here she was drivelling on about some bloody relative or other. He had somehow to get her featherbrain to settle for two seconds and persuade her to part with the vital information he was quite sure she was concealing.

'Great, Pat, great. The pics were terrif, weren't they? The

ed is keen to use some more – there's even better shots of you. The picture desk is saving the really good ones for the big story. Come on now, let's have something really hot for this Sunday.' There was a pause as Patsy thought hard. She bitterly resented Claire. She'd come into the series and looked all set to take over. Geoff was mad about her, anyone could see that. The double humiliation of the scene at the hotel and the one on set had rankled badly. Patsy was not bright, but she had a certain native cunning, and it was telling her that if the world, and in particular Geoff's wife, knew about his obsession with Claire, not only would the romance be finished but, she happily surmised, Claire's stint on the series also.

Tony Snellor said irritably, 'Hello, hello, Pat, are you still there? I've got a deadline to meet, you know.'

'It's Patsy – I hate Pat', she said haughtily. 'You put Pat in the paper, too. Auntie didn't like that. She says I should complain, that it was important for my career.' Snellor clutched his throbbing head in disbelief. Career!? This little tart was definitely one sandwich short of a picnic! 'The thing is, Tony,' she decided that the enormity of the revelation would justify the use of his Christian name, 'the fact of the matter is, that I do have something very private to reveal.'

I won't hold my breath, thought Snellor to himself. 'Oh yeah, let's have it then.' He resigned himself to yet another hot tip about a future development in the already unbelievably tedious plot.

'Are you ready?' she queried. 'Have you got a pen ready?'

'Yeah, I've got a pen ready,' replied Snellor wearily. There were times, he reflected, when he seriously began to wonder if he wouldn't rather have dealings with one of those flat-chested serious actresses. At that moment his eye caught the day's curvaceous page-three exhibit. He felt a minor stirring in his loins as he gazed reverently at the magnificent breasts with erect nipples therein displayed and changed his mind.

'Well,' said Patsy slowly, 'I have definite information that Geoffrey Armitage and Claire Jenner are – you know – having it off.'

Snellor gasped and dropped his pen. 'Claire Jenner, the new girl?' he asked in disbelief.

'Yes, that's right.'

'And Geoff Armitage?' He could hardly believe his luck.

'Yes,' said Patsy bitterly.

'Are you sure?'

'Course I'm sure.'

'How do you know?'

'Cos I saw him go into her bedroom at half past twelve – at night – didn't I? He was carrying champagne – and two glasses,' she added for effect.

Snellor's muzziness suddenly cleared as a surge of adrenaline made its way to his fuddled brain. He retrieved the pen and started scribbling frantically. 'Tell me more,' he commanded.

'That's all I know,' said Patsy lamely.

'Oh come on, you must have seen them together,' he almost snapped.

'Well, they were all over each other the next day – it was disgusting – and him a married man, too,' she added piously.

'Yes, he's married, isn't he?' said Snellor, who knew perfectly well that he was.

'Oh yes,' said Patsy with satisfaction.

'And he's got two kids?'

'Er, yes.' Patsy had always conveniently managed to put Sukie and the children to the back of her mind when engaged in intimate relations with Geoff.

Snellor was all intent concentration. 'What do the other

actors think?' he asked. Patsy remembered the looks of cynical amusement on their faces, and Bella's cryptic remark, and decided to interpret them in her own way.

'Naturally they're shocked – well, it's not nice, is it? I mean, he's supposed to set an example to the rest of us – to the nation, isn't he?'

My God, thought Snellor, she thinks she's working with the Royal Family! 'So, can you sum up your feelings in your own words, Pat – er Patsy?'

'Oh no,' objected Patsy, 'you promised me – anno – annom, er – you know.'

'Anonymity,' Snellor amended. 'Yes, of course. I just thought you might be able to give me some idea, you know – a quote or two from the other members of the cast.'

'Oh no, I can't do that, they'd know who it was, and you promised me anonymity – you did,' she insisted.

'Okay, okay.' Snellor was prepared to concede any point now. 'So, when did all this start?'

'Their first day of rehearsals.' Patsy's tone was contemptuous. 'She never left him alone – oh no, of course, before that – Glynis said she was after him on the filming – '

'Who's Glynis?' interrupted Snellor.

'One of the make-up girls – she saw it all. She's a real homebreaker, that Claire Jenner.'

Snellor's nose was starting to tell him that Patsy's comments were not entirely disinterested. He had a sneaking suspicion that Patsy was holding a candle for Geoff herself. Was it possible that she might have been involved too at some point? If so, this story could only get better and better. Yes, he'd have to string Patsy along for a while yet, at least until he'd got the full story. He could always tackle the Don Juan angle later. He'd need a follow-up.

'How can you be absolutely sure it was Claire Jenner's

room he went into?' He must get his facts straight. Trevor always came down like a ton of bricks on sloppy research.

'Cos he was chatting her up in the bar earlier, they arranged it. I heard him.'

'Ah, so it was the other way round – he was after her?' Tony had suspected as much. Patsy bit her lip.

'Well, she didn't exactly play hard to get, did she?' she said, unable to keep the bitterness out of her voice. She was remembering how easily she, Patsy, had succumbed to Geoff's advances. It was his voice that had done it. It was just like being in a black-and-white movie – the sort they showed on Sunday afternoons. So romantic. He'd given her the works – candlelit dinner, soft music – it had been wonderful. She'd said to him, she remembered, how wonderful it would be if they could play love scenes together on screen and he'd promised to mention it to Hugh. He never had, of course. He hadn't meant a word of it. None of it. Well, now he was going to be sorry that he'd betrayed her. He'd be sorry all right.

'Well, thanks, Pat – sy. My editor will be really pleased with the help you've given us. It'll boost your ratings, too.'

When Patsy put down the receiver, she found she was trembling. This surprised her. She decided she needed a fag and a drink to steady her nerves. She hurried over to the shelf with the mirror tiles behind it, on which stood the drink and glasses. She poured herself quite a stiff gin and tonic and went over to the overmantel mirror to check her appearance. She was startled to note that the girl peering out at her was really quite plain, ugly even. This caused her to down her drink hurriedly and pour herself another. She devoted the rest of the evening to getting drunk and listening to golden oldies and finally went to bed and cried herself to sleep.

Tony Snellor, meanwhile, had hurriedly cobbled together a story, partly from what Patsy had told him, but mostly from what his nose had guessed. He typed it up on the word processor under the headline, 'Soap Star In Hot Water'. Then he rushed along to Trevor's office and burst in, without waiting for his knock to be answered. Trevor, a keep-fit fanatic, was in the middle of doing forty press-ups.

'Trev, Trev, I've got, I've got it.'

'Thirty-five, oof, thirty-six, oof, thirty-seven, oof – '

'Sunday's front page! "Soap Star In Hot Water" – '

'Thirty-eight – oof.'

' "Geoffrey Armitage, balding star of super soap series, *The McMasters*, will find himself in hot water today – " '

'Thirty-nine – oof.'

'Trev! Listen – this is it!'

'Forty – oof – oof – oof – What the fuck is that load of rubbish you've just written? – oof.' Trevor Grantley sat winded on the floor and glared balefully at his over-excited underling. Snellor, who was used to Trevor's scathing sarcasm, merely handed his boss the story he'd just written and collapsed into the nearest chair to await the verdict. Trevor started reading, emitting a low whistle as he did.

When he'd finished, he said, 'The story's a beaut. This is the business all right. So, she finally came through, Little Miss Muff and Tits, did she? Okay. I'll get the picture desk onto it. We need big pics of Geoff and the Jenner bint. This can fill the front page – you rewrite the copy – the analogy's crap. And leave the headlines to the pros, will you? How often do I have to tell you?'

'But, Trev, you – '

'Listen, sunshine, just stick to the facts – she's young and sexy, he's married and over the hill. Follow up with the betrayed wife's reaction in Monday's edition. I'll put Stella

17

'I want a word with you, my sweet!'

Bella stood in the open doorway of Hugh's office, arms akimbo, eyes flashing. It occurred to Hugh, startled as he was from perusing Episodes 11 and 12, that she bore an uncanny resemblance to an avenging Valkyrie about to embark on a hell-raising mission. In short, he did not like what he saw.

'Good God, Bella, I thought you'd gone home hours ago,' he said, surprised.

'Home! Home!' snarled Bella, her voice rising. 'I won't have a home to go to soon! What the fuck are you trying to do to me?' She staggered into the room and leaned her weight on the desk, glaring at him menacingly. The office was not a large one and it now seemed to Hugh that it was entirely filled by Bella's presence.

'You've been drinking,' he observed mildly. 'I suppose you've just come from the pub.'

'Well, what of it? Is it any of your fucking business what I do with my leisure hours?'

'No, of course not,' replied Hugh wearily. 'It's just that as the leading lady of this series, it might be advisable to set a better example to some of the younger members.' It sounded pompous, and he knew it. It also provided Bella with exactly the cue she needed.

'Leading lady! Leading lady! You call the one paltry scene

and pathetic dialogue I've had in the last three episodes material worthy of a leading lady? I'm a supporting artiste, ducky.' She spat the words out. 'A bit part player! And I'd like to know what the fuck you're going to do about it!'

Hugh looked her squarely in the eye. 'Sit down, Bella, and let's talk this thing over,' he said firmly.

'I don't want to sit down, I've never wanted to sit down less in my life!' she shouted.

Hugh passed a hand wearily over his forehead. 'Bella,' he began, 'you've been doing this series now for . . .' Bella seized the moment.

'I should like to remind you that without me there wouldn't be a series.' Her tone had now become low and intense. 'This series was created for me – '

Hugh looked up sharply. 'For you and Geoff,' he corrected.

'For ME!' Bella insisted. 'For me. You created it for me, you know you did. But now it appears that I'm no longer needed. You've found metal more attractive.'

Everyone on this bloody series seems to have done *Hamlet* at some point in their careers, thought Hugh irritably.

But now Bella was starting to become tearful. 'Don't try to deny it, you loved me then.' Hugh groaned inwardly. Bella started sobbing. 'And now some chit of a girl has taken it all away from me. Well, if that's the case, go ahead, make her the star, let her have the series, but without me; because I have no intention of staying anywhere I'm not wanted.' Bella collapsed into the chair and started crying freely. 'You wanted me once,' she said pathetically.

Hugh looked away embarrassed. Yes, he had loved her once, he had admired her robust lust for life and her integrity as an actress, her classy looks, but he had loathed her drinking habits. It was after one such drunken hysterical scene as this that he knew he would never leave Mona, who was unexciting by comparison, but with whom he could enjoy uninterrupted periods of peace and harmony. Bella sobbed noisily for some time.

Eventually, during a lull, Hugh said, choosing his words carefully, 'You're quite wrong, you know. You are a wonderful actress and you've made this series what it is. People watch it because of you.'

Bella looked up, her eyes brimming with tears, grateful, as all actresses are, for a scrap of comfort, an acknowledgement of her talent.

'But you know as well as I do that with an ongoing saga such as this, there is only so much that can happen to any one character. New story lines have to be introduced. New characters have to be found to provide these story lines. Claire has not taken these away from you. You are, and always will be, number one, both with Martin and myself and the public.' Hugh knew that what he was saying was not strictly true, but he could see that Bella was believing it. She wanted to believe it. Hugh pressed home his point. 'It's just that it's Claire's turn for the moment. Everyone has to have a turn. You remember Geoff's cancer scare story line – '

'But that involved me,' Bella interrupted tearfully.

'Yes, I know.' Hugh's tone was firm. 'And we are going to involve you again – '

'But you've got this American star to play opposite her,' Bella protested brokenly.

Damn Larry, thought Hugh. Why can't he keep his big mouth shut?

'He's supposed to be young and glamorous, so he's hardly likely to get involved with me, is he?'

Bella's voice was becoming self-pitying, but, even as she spoke, an idea was beginning to form in Hugh's mind. Yes, why not? Older woman, younger man, bring the rivalry that exists off-screen into the story line. Give the two women bitchy scenes to play together – young glamorous man caught between. He momentarily ignored Bella as he started to jot down ideas on the back of the script in front of him.

'Well, that's where you're wrong again,' Hugh said, without looking up. 'We were planning some extremely good scenes for you, but of course I can understand your feelings. It's hard on you at the moment. You haven't had much to do recently. But I had thought that, being the professional that you are, you would be generous enough to take a back seat for the sake of the series. No, I know,' he held up his hand to silence her as she was about to protest again, 'I do see your point of view, believe me, and if you really feel that you want to leave us, Martin and I will not stand in your way.' He had called her bluff.

She stopped crying abruptly. To say that she was shocked would have been putting it mildly. She was horrified. With many actors who find popular fame overnight, it often goes to their heads; they start to believe their own publicity. The scriptwriters find writing for actors' own personalities rewarding and it is sometimes difficult to separate fact from fiction. She stared at him, hardly daring to believe her ears.

'You want me to leave?' she said at last, incredulously.

'No, of course not. You said you wanted to leave – and you know, Bella, you always get your own way,' Hugh added with a wry smile. He knew he had won.

'Oh, darling,' Bella started crying again, 'you know how much I've always loved you – as if I'd ever let you down – I was just terribly hurt, that's all.' She rose unsteadily to her feet and made her way around the desk to Hugh. Wiping her eyes with the back of her hand, she plonked herself onto his lap and enveloped him in her arms. Hugh turned his head to avoid her breath, which was truly awful, and Bella's kiss landed by his ear. 'Have you really got lovely scenes for me, baby?' she crooned.

'Oh yes,' replied Hugh truthfully. 'They're going to be humdingers.'

Bella nestled contentedly into his chest. 'Oh, lovely – you are a darling baby.'

Hugh sat there trapped, he was awfully afraid that she was going to fall asleep on him. After a minute or two he said, 'Come on, it's time you went home. Upsadaisy.'

'Where we going?'

'I'm going to drive you home,' said Hugh firmly.

'Oh good. We going to bed?'

Hugh hoisted her to her feet and manoeuvred her with some difficulty to the door. He had no intention of going to bed with her.

'No,' he said, 'I'm going to drive you to your house, then I'm going to drive me to my house and write you lots of lovely scenes. That's even better, isn't it?'

'Yes, lovely,' Bella agreed happily.

18

It had all the appearance of being a perfectly normal Sunday. Sukie was pottering about downstairs in the kitchen, enjoying an early morning cup of tea. Ben was in his room, working on a complicated problem on his computer. Nicky was pestering him to play a Nintendo game, and could be heard wandering restlessly about the house. Geoff was dozing fitfully, trying to enjoy his day off. Sukie could hear the sounds of distant shouts of fury from Ben as Nicky disturbed his concentration.

Damn, she thought, they would wake Geoff and there would be her lovely Sunday morning gone. He'd get up all grumpy and she'd have to coax him out of his mood.

She heard the thud of the Sunday newspapers as they landed on the front doormat. Sukie rose and wandered into the hall. How she loathed the ritual of the Sunday newspapers. Her husband had steadfastly ignored her for years, devoting the entire day to wading through them surrounded by a sea of newsprint. Her only chance of getting to see them at all now was before he was up. She clutched them to her and crept back to the kitchen, then strewed them at random across the scrubbed deal table to compare headlines. She usually managed to read the front pages of most of them, and get a brief glimpse of the theatrical notices in a couple of the arts sections, before Geoff would appear, demand a cup of tea and then commandeer them, stomp off gruffly to the living room with the papers tucked firmly under his arm. As though they were his personal possessions, thought Sukie crossly. He was always gruff when she had managed to sneak a look at them first, because he preferred them in their virginal pristine state. This proprietorial high-handedness infuriated her. It had almost caused a divorce in the early days when she had refused to pander to his whims.

Brambles had noticed her re-entry into the kitchen, and had risen from the windowsill, arching his back and stretching first his front and then his back legs in an almost impossible arabesque. Then he jumped down and started sniffing disdainfully around his food dishes. They were all empty. He leapt up onto the table and sat squarely in the middle of the papers she was reading.

'Oh really,' said Sukie irritably. Brambles put a pathetic paw up to her cheek. 'Yes, all right, all right, I'll get you some breakfast!'

If it wasn't one thing it was another. She rose. Brambles acknowledged her efforts with a strange sound that was a cross between a miaow and an abrupt purr. They both went to the cupboard. It was entirely empty. 'Damn!' she said aloud. Well, that was definitely her Sunday morning ruined. She was wearing her 'sloppies', as she called them – sort of long johns under her dressing-gown. She scribbled a note: *Gone to corner shop. Fresh out of cat food. Back in 5 mins – Sukie/Mum*.

She exchanged the dressing-gown for a green waxed raincoat, thrust her feet into some green wellingtons and, grabbing her purse and car keys from the dresser, she left quietly by the kitchen door, which abutted on the garage. She glimpsed Brambles's expression of impotent fury as he watched her departure.

Her whole life was bound by the wishes and whims of others, who for some reason seemed to be entirely dependent on her. There were times when she regretted deeply her decision to abandon her career to look after Geoff and have his children. She'd been a promising actress, she knew that and she'd loved it. Oh well, those days were over, no sense in looking back. She turned all this over in her mind as she drove to the corner shop, then parked recklessly on the double yellow lines right outside. It was Sunday, who cared?

She dashed into the shop, went straight to the shelf where she knew the cat food was stacked, and grabbed half a dozen tins of Brambles's favourite. She suddenly decided to treat herself to a glossy interior design magazine. Yes, why not? – she'd lost all chance of seeing the newspapers now. She turned to the newsagent section of the shop, her eye raked along the shelves and then she froze appalled in her tracks.

On the front page of one of the more lurid tabloids was a large colour photograph of Geoff and beside it was one of Claire Jenner, the girl she knew was the new up-and-coming star of the series. The headlines read, *McMASTERS STARS SECRET STEAMY LOVE AFFAIR SHOCK*. Sukie's heart started pounding so loudly she thought the other customers must hear it. At the same time, she felt sure she was going to faint. She closed her eyes and tried to regain control of her senses. Then she opened them and glanced quickly around the shop to see if anyone had noticed. The other customers all seemed preoccupied with their own purchases. She looked down again. There were only two copies of the paper left. So the whole of the neighbourhood had seen it by now. She picked up both copies and, trying to appear nonchalant, took them and the cans of meat to the counter.

'Just these, thank you, Betty,' she said with as much normality as she could muster. She was aware that she was starting to shake.

'Morning, Mrs Armitage, going to be a nice one, I dare say.'

142

'Yes,' replied Sukie doubtfully. She fumbled in her purse for the change and after a muttered 'thanks' got out of the shop as quickly as she could. Obviously Betty hasn't seen the paper yet. But doubtless Stan, Betty's other half, was even now poring over the article in their flat above the shop.

Sukie flung herself into the car and roared away. She couldn't think. She daren't think. She parked the car back in the garage, then she scurried into the kitchen apprehensively. No. No one was down yet. She threw one of the papers into the dustbin, then rammed the other into the pocket of her mac. With trembling hands she started to open a can of meat, whilst Brambles, blissfully unaware of her agitation, rubbed himself against her legs. She slammed the dish down on the floor and automatically filled a bowl of milk and one of water, then crept up the stairs to her sewing room. Her sanctum sanctorum, as Geoff always called it. She locked the door and, taking the paper from her pocket, she sat on the window seat and opened it, her heart still thumping. She prayed fervently that she had been mistaken, that it was some other member of the cast, that they had simply used his picture because he was the star of the show. She read the headlines again and again, trying to make sense of them. But there was more.

> Geoff Armitage, 47, the paunchy star of The McMasters, TV's top-rated soap, is secretly dating busty sexpot Claire Jenner, alias Sara Harper. Their steamy off-set affair has shocked fellow cast members as balding Geoff, who plays the randy Paul McMaster in the series, is married with two kids.

Sukie lowered the paper and gazed with unseeing eyes into the garden. It couldn't be true. It couldn't. She became aware that somewhere in the house a telephone was ringing. Then it stopped.

143

'Mum!' yelled Nicky. 'Mu-um! It's for you!'

Sukie shoved the paper back into her pocket. 'Coming,' she called out huskily.

She unlocked her door. She could hear Nicky in the hall saying, 'She's just coming.'

'Who is it?' she said to him in a stage whisper from the top of the stairs.

Nicky shrugged. 'It's a woman. She says she wants to speak to you.'

Sukie started to descend the stairs. She could smell the aroma of cooking coming from the kitchen.

'What's going on?' demanded Geoff from the landing. 'Can't you boys let me have at least one decent lie in? Is that too much to ask?'

Sukie took the phone from Nicky. 'Hello?'

'Is that Mrs Armitage?' said a charming voice. Too charming.

'Yes,' said Sukie, suddenly wary.

'Ah, Mrs Armitage, I dare say you have seen the article in today's *Globe* – I was wondering if you had any comment.'

Sukie was stunned, but only for a moment. 'Go to hell!' she said hoarsely, losing control and slamming the phone back on the receiver.

Geoff was nearly at the bottom of the stairs. 'What on earth's the matter with you?' he said with an astounded look at his wife. 'Who was that on the phone?'

In reply, Sukie pulled out the crumpled newspaper from her pocket and thrust it at him. Then, starting to sob, she ran past him, up the stairs and flung herself into the sanctuary again. Closing the door, she stood with her back against it and burst into tears. The phone started ringing again.

'What's the matter with Mum, Dad?' said Nicky, wide-

144

eyed. But Geoff was gazing in horror at the front page of the *Sunday Globe*.

'Dad?' insisted Nicky.

'Go and eat your breakfast,' said Geoff abruptly. He picked up the telephone. 'Yes?' he rasped. Then: 'Who is this?' Then he too slammed the receiver down. He switched on the answering machine and strode into the kitchen where Ben was idly frying eggs.

'Who the hell turned the answering machine off?' he bellowed. Both boys stared at their father, who appeared to have taken leave of his senses.

'I did, Dad,' said Ben in an awed voice.

'Who asked you to?'

'N – n – n – no one, Dad. As we were all up . . . I thought . . . '

'Well, in future kindly mind your own business. This happens to be my house and it is my answering machine and you will not interfere with things that do not belong to you. Is that understood?' His voice had risen to a shout.

'Yes, Dad.' Both boys spoke in unison in subdued voices.

Geoffrey turned on his heel and left the kitchen. He went straight to his study. Once alone, he opened the newspaper and stared at the front page. Then he collapsed slowly into a chair. 'Dear God,' he muttered. Then he put his head into his hands. 'Dear God in heaven.'

19

Sally stood in her small garden flat, the phone clamped to her ear. 'Come on, come on, for God's sake answer,' she muttered under her breath. In her other hand was the copy of the *Sunday Globe* with its lurid headline. 'Where the hell are you, Claire? Please answer the phone!'

She had been trying intermittently to reach her friend from the moment she had seen the newspaper. Sally, as was her custom, had strolled down to the newsagent's early in the morning to pick up a selection of 'heavies'. She did this every Sunday. She never bought the trashy papers. Her great Sunday treat was to have breakfast in her little 'conservatory', as she called the glazed lean-to that abutted against the back wall, encompassing the French windows, and where she could sit in all weathers and enjoy the tiny back garden. She would lounge in her favourite wicker chair, propped up with cushions, sipping a cup of Earl Grey tea, dipping her toast into her soft-boiled egg and doing all the crosswords. The radio would be playing quietly in the background, the best china would be out and she would tackle the crosswords one after the other. Crosswords, like clothes, were Sal's passion. Today, however, the serious newspapers lay untouched in a folded heap on the floor where Sal had flung them as she had come in. She had seen Claire's picture the moment she entered the paper shop. She had bought the paper, appalled by the headline, and had purchased her usual order, then had run all the way home.

Why the hell wasn't Claire responding? She always left the answering machine on when she went out – why did she have to forget today of all days? Suddenly the phone was picked up.

'Hello.'

'Oh thank God, Claire.'

'Hi, Sal darling, how lovely to hear your voice!'

'Never mind that, where have you been, in God's name?'

'Sorry, love,' replied Claire, oblivious to the terse note in Sally's voice. 'I've had the most gorgeous walk all the way along the tow path, right down to Ham House and back again.'

'What on earth time did you get up?'

'I haven't really been to bed – well, I have, but I couldn't sleep – I sat up most of the night reading. Geoff wrote me reams and reams of the most beautiful letter. Oh, Sal, I've never been so happy. Do you know, I really believe I'm in love for the first time in my life. He's just the most divine man I've ever met – '

'Darling, he's married.' There was a small silence.

'Yes, I know, it's a bugger, isn't it?' said Claire drolly.

'How did you leave things between you and Geoff?' Sally, for once, was at a loss to know how to break the news to her friend. Claire seemed so happy, she couldn't bear to spoil it. 'You know what I mean, how did you leave it?' repeated Sally.

'Well, we're just going to see how things go – you know. Sal, he seems to be crazy about me. I must say it's rather pleasant – and I'm certainly mad about him.'

'Did he say anything about leaving his wife for you?'

'Good God, darling, it's rather early days, don't you think?

147

He says he thinks I'm the most wonderful woman he's ever met, though.'

There was another pause, then Sally said quietly, 'I don't think I'd care to be his wife.'

Claire said eventually, 'Well, she doesn't know about us yet – I rather wish she did actually.'

'How do you think she will react when she finds out?' asked Sally.

'I do wish you'd stop putting such a damper on things. He's not in love with her any more. He said so. He loves her, of course, but they don't sleep together. Anyway, she doesn't know about us yet.'

'She will do by now.'

'What do you mean?'

'You obviously haven't seen the *Globe* today?'

'The *Globe*?' asked Claire amazed. 'Of course not, I never buy it – I didn't think you did.'

'I don't. Claire darling, I'm afraid I've got some bad news. I hate to do this when you sound so happy, but you have to be prepared. They're bound to get on to you –'

'Who? Sal, what's happened? What are you talking about?' Claire emerged abruptly from her euphoria.

'Darling, it's in the papers.'

'What is?'

'You and Geoff. It's on the front page of the *Globe*.'

There was a long pause, then Claire said slowly, 'I don't believe you.'

'I'm sorry, Clairey, but it's true. Oh God, it's ghastly – what are we going to do?' and to her horror Sally found herself weeping.

'Oh, Sal, come on, it's all right. Don't cry – please. I'm sure it'll be okay. What does it say?'

Sally was stunned by Claire's calm reaction and stopped

crying abruptly. 'You sound very sanguine about it, I must say.'

'What does it say?' insisted Claire.

'It's hideous – it's so cheap and vulgar. Shall I bring it round?'

'No, it's all right, I'll go out and buy it. I couldn't be bothered with the papers today – it's all been so blissful. I'll pop out and get it now.'

Sally was genuinely shocked. 'Did you hear what I said?' she asked incredulously. 'It's all over the front page – your affair with Geoff – there are pictures of both of you. It mentions his wife and children – it's horrendous.'

'Well, as you say, she'll know now, won't she?'

'I don't like to hear you like this,' said Sally quietly. 'Have you forgotten what you went through just a few weeks ago?'

'No, of course I haven't. It was the worst thing that ever happened to me – you know that – but I have to survive, Sal – and I've come through, mainly thanks to you. I think I'm a different person now because of that dreadful experience. Nothing can ever be quite so bad again. I'm a new woman. I've got a wonderful job, I've found a wonderful man. So what if it is all over the newspapers – it'll just boost the ratings and save Geoff the trouble of breaking the news to his wife.'

Sally sank slowly into the nearest chair, still holding the phone to her ear. She was genuinely shocked at the change in her friend. 'Don't you feel anything at all for his wife and those two boys?' she asked in an awed voice.

'Of course, but that's his problem, not mine,' replied Claire pragmatically.

'But it's because of you that they're splayed all over the front of that ghastly rag,' suggested Sally.

149

'No,' Claire corrected her promptly. 'It's because of him – he's the one with the responsibilities, not me.'

'You're described as a homebreaker,' said Sally shakily.

'If that marriage had been happy and secure, it wouldn't be possible to break it up,' replied Claire with conviction. 'Surely you can see that, Sal?'

'Yes, I suppose you're right,' replied Sally doubtfully. 'So what are you going to do?'

'Nothing, absolutely nothing. Wait for developments – what else can I do?'

'But what can you say to the press? They're bound to come looking for you.'

'I shan't say anything to them. They'll make it up anyway, you know what they're like. But, how the hell did they find out?'

'That's what's been worrying me. You must have been awfully indiscreet, Claire. Didn't it occur to you that someone might notice and tip them off?'

'No, it didn't, and if it had've done, I shouldn't have minded. I can't seem to make you understand, Sal. You think I'm a green girl, don't you? In love with a married man who's never going to have the courage to leave his wife. Well, maybe that's true and maybe this is the best thing that could have happened. This way, Geoff, with whom I happen to be besotted, but whose weaknesses I recognize, is forced into a corner. He has to face the matter out. He's been cheating on his wife – well, better she finds out sooner rather than later. I admit I wouldn't care to be in her shoes, but then maybe she hasn't loved him enough these last few years.'

'And the children?' asked Sally timidly.

'You're just being sentimental, I can hear it in your voice.'

'I can't help it,' said Sally, her voice wavering. 'I can't bear to hear you sounding so hard. It's not like you.'

'No,' said Claire harshly, 'you just can't bear to hear me sounding on top. Be honest, you rang me today hoping that when you broke this news to me I would dissolve into hysterical tears, and you would then – such is your tender, compassionate nature, Sal – be round here quick as a bunny to pick up the pieces. Because, basically, you need to be needed. That's what you get off on. You wanted me to need you, didn't you?'

Tears had started to well up in Sal's eyes again. 'No,' she said in a voice choked with emotion. 'No, I just wanted to help you in what I thought would be a difficult situation. You're my friend. That's what friends are for,' and she sobbed down the phone in spite of herself.

'And now it looks like it's me who's having to comfort you. Don't cry, Sal. You know how I appreciate all you've done for me. I'd never have come through it without you. But all I'm doing is paying you the compliment of being utterly honest with you. Of course I hate the tawdriness of it all and I don't like the idea of the children being dragged into it – although Ben, the eldest, is already fifteen, you know.'

'And he has to go to school,' Sally blurted out, 'and face his friends. Have you thought of that? No, of course not – you're too bloody selfish.'

'Sal, please don't be mad at me. Try to understand.'

'Oh I understand all right – and I'm not mad at you – I am deeply, deeply sorry for you. Roger has a lot to answer for.'

'Roger? What the hell has that blot on the landscape got to do with this?'

'He's changed you – his treatment of you has hardened you. You're not the lovely, generous girl I used to know. You're all bitter inside and it's horrid.'

'I'm being realistic, that's all, Sal. All I'm saying is that this so-called revelation is a good thing. It gets everything out into the open. No one's pretending any more, and if it means that Geoff and his wife – '

'Sukie, her name is,' Sal interrupted. 'Let's call her by her name, shall we? As we're being honest and realistic here. You were saying, his wife – Sukie.'

'I was going to say that if it means that they split up, then that suits me fine. It's also better for everyone in the long run. No one wants to prolong the agony.'

'I don't think I want to continue this conversation,' Sally said suddenly. 'You can ring me when you've come to your senses.' And she put down the phone, curled up in the chair and cried her eyes out.

20

Ben and Nicky had eaten their breakfast conversing in hushed whispers. The phone had rung several times during the morning, but the answering machine had been left switched on and nobody returned the calls. This was frustrating for Ben who had promised to call his girlfriend, Karen, to confirm a visit to the cinema that afternoon. Now she would assume that he'd changed his mind. It really was too bad.

It was only after realizing that he would get into further trouble if he didn't wash up the breakfast things that the mystery of the morning's dramatic events was revealed. Nicky had taken himself off to the living room where he was watching television with the sound turned down low. Ben had the kitchen to himself. He was about to wash the frying pan, when he remembered his mother's strict instructions as to the disposal of grease. It was when he was trying to remove the congealed fat from the pan into the dustbin that he noticed the copy of the *Sunday Globe*, new and unread where Sukie had hastily thrust it.

He surmised it had been delivered in error and that his mother had thrown it away in disgust. He turned it over curiously – there was bound to be something juicy on the front page. Then he gawped. There was a picture of his father under the shrieking headlines. In horrified fascination, he read the article. He felt a rush of emotion and a red flush suffused his features. He forgot the pan and the washing up, flung down the paper and rushed up the stairs two steps at a time. He hammered on his mother's door.

'Mum, Mum, let me in,' he sobbed.

'The door's open,' Sukie said quietly.

He went in. His mother was sitting quietly on the window seat, still in her mac and gum boots. One look at his face told her that he knew everything. She looked up at him in mute helplessness. Her face was swollen with crying and she was twisting and wringing her hands in anguish. With a strangled sob, he threw himself on his knees by her side, flung his arms around her waist and held her tightly.

From his study, Geoff had heard his son's headlong rush up the stairs and his stifled cry. After a while, when nothing further happened, he emerged from the room, looking strained and dishevelled. He heard subdued sounds coming from the living room and went slowly to investigate. He found his younger son engrossed in *Prince Valiant*, a film that had transported him from the present mystifying unpleasantness and uncertainties into a cartoon world where young boys were heroes and good always triumphed over evil. Nicky started as his father entered the room.

'That's all right, take no notice of me,' said Geoff reassuringly.

'You don't mind, Dad?' asked Nicky apprehensively.

'Not at all. Is it good?' enquired Geoff.

'Yeah, Dad, brilliant!' Geoff seated himself beside his son on the sofa and they both watched intently for a moment. 'Great, isn't it, Dad,' observed Nicky happily. It was the first time his father had ever watched anything like this with him.

'Well, it might be if I could hear it,' said Geoff. 'Can we have the sound up a bit?' Nicky obliged with the remote control unit.

After a while he said, 'Dad, what's wrong with Mum?'

'She's not very well at the moment, old son,' said Geoff, ruffling the boy's hair.

'What's wrong with her?' Geoff did not reply.

The two of them continued to watch television for the rest of the morning, mainly in silence, punctuated only by the odd exclamation of terror or delight from Nicky.

At around two o'clock, Nicky suddenly said, 'Dad, are we having lunch today? I'm starving!' It had occurred to his young mind that all was not as it should be, his mother being unwell had disrupted the day's routine severely.

'I'll rustle something up for us,' said Geoff reluctantly, unwilling to leave the comparative safety of Nicky's company and face the world outside. As he left the room he caught sight of his reflection in a large mirror. It seemed to him that he looked like a drowning man.

In the kitchen the first thing that he noticed was the open dustbin and the newspaper lying abandoned on the floor. He picked it up, tore it into several pieces, and screwed up the remains, ferociously throwing them amongst the rest of the rubbish and slamming on the lid. He rummaged around the cupboards and finally managed to produce beefburgers and baked beans and Coca Cola. He also found some ice cream in the freezer. Nicky was enchanted.

'Cor, my favourite, Dad,' he enthused.

They ate their meal in silence, eyes still glued to the television set. When they had finished their repast, which in Geoff's opinion had been a meagre replacement for the Sunday roast, Nicky took advantage of his father's sudden passion for his company and suggested football in the park. Geoff groaned inwardly, but figured that anything was better than having to face his wife's agonized face. They arranged to change into appropriate sporting gear and meet in the hall in five minutes. Nicky got there first and was happily bouncing a football around on his knees when Geoff descended the staircase, clad in a tracksuit and track shoes. Suddenly, there was a large rap at the front door.

'Who on earth can that be?' said Geoff, startled.

'Probably Karen.'

'Who's Karen?'

'Ben's girlfriend,' said Nicky contemptuously.

'Well, this is a most inappropriate moment,' said Geoff irritably. 'She might at least have phoned.'

'Ben was supposed to call her, but the answer machine has been on all morning, remember?'

'Well she had no business coming around here uninvited.' Geoff was rattled. The tension in the house had now become tangible. He opened the door. A woman whom he had never seen before was standing outside. 'Yes?' said Geoff sharply. 'Can I help you?'

As he spoke, a man appeared from nowhere with something bulky concealed under his coat.

'Mr Armitage, I'm Stella Glennister. I represent the *Globe* newspaper. We were wondering if you would care to give us a statement.'

Geoff bundled Nicky back inside the hall, before turning back to her. 'Good God, haven't you people done enough damage for one day?' he said in a low urgent voice.

'Perhaps we could speak to Mrs Armitage?' Miss Glennister was not to be put off so easily.

'No! You cannot speak to anyone!' said Geoff intensely. 'Now go away and leave us alone!'

The man raised his camera and aimed. Geoffrey shielded his face and slammed the door. He found Nicky wide-eyed in the hall.

'Who was that, Dad?'

156

'Never you mind.'

'Was it the FBI, Dad?'

'Oh don't be so ridiculous, Nick. We're not in America.'

Nicky watched in dismay as Geoff strode past him into the kitchen. 'Dad, aren't we going to play football after all?'

'Yes we are!' replied Geoff determinedly. 'Come on!' Geoff snatched the car keys from the dresser where Sukie had flung them down earlier. Nicky hurried after him, out through the back door.

Slamming the door behind them, Geoff grabbed his son by the hand and pulled him into the garage, threw open the door of the car and thrust him inside. Nicky was by now of the opinion that this was proving to be the best day of his life so far. Geoff started up the engine. Sukie, in her hurry, had left the garage door open, so he was able to drive straight out. He was dimly aware of two people running to a car parked outside the house. They wouldn't dare, he thought, they wouldn't dare. He drove as fast as he could, which was not fast enough.

'Dad, we're being followed,' observed Nicky calmly, after a few minutes.

'I know,' said Geoff grimly, then in a flash of inspiration added, 'I'm going to try to lose them, hold tight!'

Nicky's eyes were on stalks as he held on to the edge of his seat and watched his father weave in and out of the steadily moving Sunday traffic, then suddenly cut down a side street and double back along a parallel road.

'Hey, hot stuff, man!' said Nicky admiringly, in the American accent he usually reserved for his more intimate cronies at school.

They finally arrived at the park after a dizzying conducted tour of the neighbourhood, and spent an energetic hour dribbling and tackling and taking it in turns to be in goal. Geoff enjoyed himself more than he had anticipated. He was certainly out of condition and he had ruined a perfectly good tracksuit, the one he normally kept for rehearsals. But he felt refreshed and invigorated, and able to face Sukie again. They drove sedately back to the house and parked carefully in the garage. Ben was waiting for them in the kitchen.

'Hey, Benjie, you'll never guess what – we were in a car chase! It was really wicked. We won, didn't we, Dad? We outwitted the villains! Where's Mum? Is supper ready? I'm about to collapse from hunger!'

'Go and change, Nicky,' said his father firmly, 'quietly. Have a wash and brush your hair and come downstairs quietly – and I don't want any noise.'

'Okay, Dad.'

As soon as he'd gone Geoff said, 'Sorry about all that stuff earlier, Ben.'

'That's okay,' said Ben briefly, turning away and busying himself with the stove.

'What are you up to?' enquired Geoff, knowing that he had just been snubbed.

'I'm cooking supper. It's what we should have had for lunch.'

'I didn't know you could cook,' said Geoff with interest.

'I can do a bit,' said Ben modestly. 'I'm not as good as Mum, of course, but I'm not bad.'

'How is your mother?' asked Geoff quietly, after a pause.

'She's asleep,' said Ben, not turning round. 'She said she had a headache so I made her a cup of tea and gave her some pills. She thought they were painkillers, but I gave her two of her sleeping pills. It's all right,' he countered, hearing his father start to protest, 'they are only mild. I thought it was

158

the kindest thing to do.' There was a long silence. 'She was in a bad way,' Ben said eventually.

'Yes,' said his father, 'I dare say she was.'

21

When Claire finished speaking to Sally, her mind was turbulent with emotions. She felt elated yet disturbed. It was out! She knew she should feel dismayed, appalled even. But she didn't. She was thrilled. She had to admit it. She was aware that she should feel sympathy and concern for the blight that had fallen upon the Armitage family. Their lives were irrevocably changed; whatever the outcome of events, things would never be the same again. But she found it difficult to feel anything for them. She was secretly pleased with the disclosure – Geoff would have to face it now.

All the same, there was something she didn't like in the sensation she was experiencing. It smacked of revenge and that was an emotion of which she had never approved. But it was there. She thought a moment. Revenge for what and against whom? She had a sneaking suspicion it was something to do with Roger. Yes, a feeling of justice having been done. It was quite irrational, of course – why should Geoff be called to account for Roger's misdeeds? She imagined that it was some sort of basic survival instinct. She had to come through, whatever the cost to others.

She didn't want to read the paper, she had no wish to be confronted by the unpleasantness. No, she wouldn't buy it. It was bound to be sordid, she didn't want actually to see the havoc she had wrought. But then again, why should she take the blame? He had pursued her. Relentlessly. He had known the risk he was taking. It occurred to her that it was a risk he'd taken before, but she persuaded herself that this time he really was in love. And surely love was worth a sacrifice? He would have to sacrifice his wife and his family. For her. She, Claire Jenner, was worth that sacrifice. She thought of Roger seeing the ghastly headlines. He would realize how very quickly she had got over him, how little their relationship had meant. Well, serve him right, that would teach him to go round messing up other people's lives. It would also teach Geoff that one couldn't fool around with other women without paying the price. Perhaps, after all, she just wanted revenge on the whole male sex. Whatever the reason, she felt a grim satisfaction at the turn of events. Sally didn't approve, that was certain. Well that couldn't be helped. Sally would have to get used to the new tougher Claire.

She wondered if Geoff would ring. Surely he would, somehow? She tried to imagine the scene now being enacted in the Armitage household, but she shrank involuntarily from it. She wondered what to do with her day. She was loath to waste her precious Sunday off, hanging around, waiting for Geoff to ring. One thing the Roger débâcle had taught her was to give up waiting for phone calls that never came. She had had very little sleep and the long early morning walk had exhausted her. She mooched around for a while, made herself some percolated coffee, sat moodily drinking it in the kitchen, decided to treat herself to a fry-up and spent the next twenty minutes cooking and eating it. It tasted delicious and she rounded it off with toast and marmalade and more coffee.

Replete and unrepentant, she wandered into the living room and switched on the television. She wished now that she had not been quite so hard on Sal. Perhaps she should ring her back and apologize. There was an arts programme on TV about the Ludlow Festival. She became interested, her parents lived near Ludlow and there were lovely shots of the surrounding countryside.

Her parents! A wave of shock horror ran through her. Dear God! What if they saw the *Sunday Globe*? Oh but how ridiculous, her mother hardly knew of the *Globe*'s existence. She was unlikely to see it, as they had the Sunday papers delivered and the *Sunday Globe* was hardly likely to be amongst them. So unless some well-meaning friend or relative saw it and rang up to offer Beatrice, her mother, sympathy, it was highly unlikely. It was in any case a one-day sensation. These days, stories like this came and went overnight. The phone rang suddenly. Claire jumped. Please God, no.

'Hello, Claire?' No, it couldn't be, not Roger.

'Hello,' she said timidly. She didn't believe this.

'Claire, it's me. Hello, baby, how are ya?'

'Roger, is that really you?'

'Yeah, you bet. Miss me?'

She felt a sense of outrage rising within her. 'Roger, what the hell do you want?'

'Hey, babe, that's not a very warm welcome.'

She really could not believe this was happening. 'Well, what the hell do you expect? What do you want?' she repeated, now furious. How dare he!

'Okay, okay, sweetheart. Don't jump down my throat. I just wanted to congratulate you on your comet-like rise to stardom and', he added cheekily, 'your exposé today with your New Man. Hey, I bet he isn't so hot in bed as me, though, huh?'

'Fuck off, Roger,' said Claire abruptly in disgust, and put down the phone for the second time that morning.

She found that she was trembling. She had spoken to Roger. Roger had actually phoned her. Why? The answer came to her in a flash. He was jealous! Of course. Also for the second time that morning she felt a sensation of elation. Revenge was sweet after all. She fetched herself another cup of coffee, then put her feet up on the sofa, nestling into the cushions at her head. She flicked through the channels on the television and found a programme on Vasco da Gama. She supposed that she was watching an education slot since the narration was informative but dull and slightly patronizing. She started to drift off to sleep, her coffee untouched on the sofa table.

She had no idea how long she slept – she realized later it must have been about an hour – before she was awoken suddenly by a loud banging on the front door. Startled, she wrenched herself awake and sat up. She had just been having a lovely golden dream, taking afternoon tea with her mother in her parents' garden. Geoff had been there, lying in a hammock, seemingly very much at home. She forced herself off the sofa and, trembling with the suddenness of her waking, tried to pull her wits together. She staggered to the front door. Perhaps it was Sal. She was now feeling really remorseful about their conversation and would welcome her with open arms. She opened the door with a look of expectancy on her face. There was a strange woman standing there.

'Yes?' asked Claire, visibly disappointed. Obviously someone collecting for charity.

'Miss Jenner?'

Claire was surprised and genuinely puzzled. 'Yes?'

'May I come in?' enquired the other politely.

Claire's warning instincts, numbed by sleep, rushed to the surface. 'Who are you?'

'My name is Stella Glennister. I represent the *Globe* newspaper, and I'd love to talk to you about the revelation in today's edition. Have you seen it?'

163

Claire was dumbfounded. 'How did you know where I lived?' she asked lamely.

'You're a celebrity, Miss Jenner,' said Stella smoothly. 'Your activities are of great interest to the general public, naturally we are aware of the location of your home.' Claire was flattered in spite of herself. 'I want to do a sympathetic piece, Miss Jenner,' Stella continued, seizing the moment. 'It would be tastefully written and benefit the series' popularity and yours enormously.'

Claire looked her up and down. Well spoken, soberly dressed, hair tied back, she was leaning heavily on a stick, her right ankle bandaged. Claire wondered idly if she had sustained the injury in a scuffle with an unsuspecting victim.

'I've already spoken to Mr Armitage,' Stella continued. Claire felt herself reddening. Stella noticed the flush and pressed home her advantage. 'As you must know, he is going to patch things up with his wife.' Claire felt a wave of shock shudder through her. 'They have two children, but, of course, you know that, and I was wondering how you felt, knowing you're going to have to continue working with him. It's going to be difficult for you, I imagine.' Her tone was soft, full of womanly concern.

'How did you find out about us?' Claire asked abruptly. She hadn't intended to ask the question, it seemed to rise unbidden to her lips.

Stella grabbed at it. 'Ah, so you admit it is true?'

Claire bit her lip. 'I didn't say that.'

'But you do have a close relationship – I must say it's hardly surprising, the chemistry between you works wonderfully well on-screen. You've certainly made that series your own, Miss Jenner.'

'We have a very good working relationship,' Claire agreed.

'Are you saying there is nothing of a more intimate nature

164

between you?' Claire flushed again. 'Could we perhaps have a little chat. I really would like to write this from a sympathetic angle,' Stella persisted. 'I mean,' she added, seeing Claire's hesitation, 'I'm sure you'd like us to get the facts straight.'

Claire was torn. She knew instinctively that Geoff would loathe her to speak to the press, but, on the other hand, she wanted to make a good impression. This was possibly an opportunity for her to get considerable press coverage for herself. Why should she worry about Geoff and his bloody family? She had a chance here to make a name for herself.

'Miss Jenner,' stated Stella firmly, 'you know that we're going to write the story anyway. I'm giving you a chance here to tell your side of it.' There was a steely edge to her voice.

'And if I don't?' asked Claire evenly. Had Geoff really made peace with Sukie already. She doubted it. Marital infidelity and its consequences were not something that could be dealt with in a couple of hours on a Sunday morning. She seriously doubted the veracity of Stella's statement. 'And if I don't?'

'Then, I shall be obliged to recount the facts as they were told to me by my source.'

Claire started. 'Source? What source? How did you find out about us?'

Stella merely smiled enigmatically. 'You were hardly discreet, Miss Jenner.'

Claire's mind flashed back to Geoff's overt behaviour in the canteen, at rehearsals, during filming, and at the hotel. They'd been seen by dozens of people. But had anyone actually seen Geoff entering her room? No member of the company had any tangible proof of his infidelity. It was pure guesswork. Obviously a casual employee at South Eastern Television had noticed something and had decided to earn himself or herself a quick buck by phoning their suspicions to the *Globe* office. This, doubtless followed up by clever questioning of the more ingenuous members of the cast – the company was always giving interviews to the press, organized by the studio – was enough for them to go on, she surmised. Claire came to a decision.

'I have nothing to say to you, Ms Glennister,' she said firmly. 'Good afternoon.'

Stella's eyes narrowed perceptively. 'You may regret your decision, Miss Jenner.'

'I doubt it,' snapped Claire. She had suddenly gone from the defence to being on the attack and it felt better. She heard a car door slam and a man approached them from the road. Now what? she thought.

'Miss Jenner,' he asked politely, 'may I take a photograph?' Without waiting for a reply he whipped out a camera and suited the action to the word.

Claire was not quick enough. She turned her head and ducked back inside the door and slammed it in their faces, but the photo had been taken. She ran into the kitchen, shaking, aware that she had not handled the interview well. After a moment the letter box flap banged and she heard something drop onto the floor. She hurried back. An envelope was lying there. She picked it up with trembling hands and opened it. It read: *Dear Miss Jenner, Thank you for talking to me this afternoon. If you change your mind, I can be reached on the following numbers.* Office and home numbers were then quoted. *I hope you will reconsider. As I have said, I would like to give you a chance to tell your side of the matter. The story is known and won't go away, sincerely Stella Glennister.*

Claire screwed up the note and flung it into the bin, then had second thoughts and rescued it, smoothed it out and put it carefully away in her carved wooden box where she kept things that were important. She might need it, she reflected.

She went to the bedroom window, which faced onto the street, and peered out from behind the curtains. Their car was still parked there. They were lying in wait, she realized. She was imprisoned.

She spent a restless afternoon trying to watch an old movie on television. The day wore on. There was no word from Geoff. At six o'clock she toyed with the idea of getting herself something to eat. She was not hungry, but she had to do something, for God's sake. She got up from the sofa and went into the bedroom to check the window again. The phone rang, breaking the silence. Geoff! she thought, her heart pounding. Oh God, what would he say? She picked up the receiver with unsteady hands and heard her mother's tremulous tones.

'Claire darling, is that you?'

'Hello, B,' she said as cheerfully as she could.

'Darling,' continued her mother in worried tones, 'darling, we've had a telephone call from some newspaper. They were asking about you.' Her mother's voice started to shake. She sounded as if she were trying not to cry. 'Claire darling, is something wrong? I must know.'

Claire felt hot tears course down her cheeks. She made a supreme effort to control herself. 'Don't worry, Mummsy, it's okay. Everything's fine – usual ghastly press gossip, that's all. Don't even give it another thought.' She did her best to sound unconcerned.

Bastards! she thought savagely. Fucking bastards!

22

It was Monday morning and still Geoff had not seen Sukie. He had risen early after an alcohol-induced sleep on the sofa in his study, and had made the boys breakfast, instructing them not to disturb their mother. He had waved them off, urging them to leave by the back gate and go through the cuttings to the station. He fed Brambles and did the washing up. Then he prepared scrambled eggs, toast, coffee and orange juice, laid it out on a silver tray and, bracing himself for an ordeal, took it up to his wife.

He knocked tentatively on the door. To his surprise her 'come in' sounded strong and firm. Even more surprising when he entered, she was up and dressed and appeared to be packing. At least, that was his first impression, since there were two suitcases on the bed and she was neatly folding garments and placing them inside.

'What are you doing?' he asked, astounded.

'I'm packing. What does it look like?' she answered curtly.

'I've brought you some breakfast,' he said lamely.

'How very civil of you, but strange as it may seem, I don't seem to have any appetite.'

'Sukie,' Geoff stood transfixed, still holding the tray.

'Correct,' she retorted, employing a favourite riposte of Nicky's.

'Sukes, those are my clothes that you're packing.'

'Well, naturally, since you're the one who's leaving.'

Geoff was unable to speak. He had not expected this. He stood watching her for some time before he finally said, 'You're chucking me out?'

'Of course, what did you expect?'

Silence.

Then: 'I thought you might be prepared to listen to what I have to say first.' He had not dared to move.

She stopped what she was doing and snorted contemptuously, 'I've been listening to what you have had to say for years. On stage and off. Every nuance, every inflection, every carefully modulated vowel sound, every vocal trick in the book. I know them all – by rote!'

Geoff hadn't seen her like this before. She seemed to be possessed. She suddenly looked up at him, the light of battle in her eye.

'I suppose you imagine that I haven't known about your tawdry little affairs, your sordid little carryings on. Yes –' as she saw him start – 'you may well look guilty. Right at the beginning, when I was pregnant with Ben, there was the dancer, Ann De Vere or De Vain, whatever she called herself. Then Liz Gascoigne, Barbara Charteris and Sophie Langton. Then, let me see –' she started to tick them off on her fingers – 'Maxine Marshall, Colleen Donnelly the Celtic beauty, you remember, Victoria Bannerman, Doreen whatsherface and Sandra thingummy something or other. And last, but not least, the ghastly Patsy Hall. That's not counting the ones I don't know about, and, of course, Miss Jenner, isn't it?'

Geoff was staring at her in disbelief. All these years he thought he'd got away with it – and all the time she'd known.

'Well, I've had enough!' Sukie suddenly shouted at him.

'I've bloody well had enough! This time you've gone too far!' In one stride she was in front of him and with an abrupt movement of her arm she brought her hand up under the tray and sent it hurtling to the ceiling. Toast, coffee, marmalade, scrambled egg, orange juice and coffee went flying in all directions. The tray clattered to the floor while Sukie stood there breathing hard. 'I've put up with the misery, the insults, the deep, deep, hurt all this time for the sake of the boys. But this final insult, this public humiliation, I will not take!' She glared at him for a moment, then went back to the packing. 'I'm nearly done. I want you out of here today, before the boys get back from school. I don't give a damn where you go or with whom. I shall be in touch with Gordon Nelson, my solicitor, this morning. Don't worry, I'm not going to take you to the cleaners financially. All I want is not ever to have to see you again. And providing I don't tune in at seven forty-five on Sunday evenings, I don't suppose I shall!' She had filled one case and was snapping it shut. She swung it onto the floor. 'Oh yes, and you'll have to order a taxi to take you wherever you're going. I shall need the car. I'm going to get a job!' She disappeared into the door that led to the ensuite bathroom.

Geoff, completely at a loss as to what to do next, collapsed quietly onto the end of the bed and tried to marshal his thoughts.

Sukie reappeared shortly with his shaving equipment and various toiletries. She rammed them into the waterproof pockets around the sides of the second case. Finally, she took his silk dressing-gown from the hook on the door, flung it in and zipped up the case. She glanced at her watch.

'Right, you've got at least four hours before you have to be at rehearsals. That gives you time to pack your books, cassettes, CDs, camera equipment and personal belongings.

170

You'll find a number of cardboard boxes in the garage. As soon as you know where you're going to be, I shall arrange for another taxi to collect them and your pictures and theatrical memorabilia and deliver them to you. Any queries or communication can be made through Gordon Nelson. I am going to ring him now to give him my instructions. Regarding the boys, you may see them, of course, but not here. I shall also be filing for a divorce.' So saying, she lifted the case off the bed and after placing it next to the other on the floor, left the room.

Geoff was too stunned to move. He heard her go down the stairs and make the phone call. He could hear her speaking to her solicitor. Still he could not move.

She called up the stairs, 'He can see me in an hour – I'm off to town – I suggest you get cracking!'

After a few minutes, he heard the front door slam, followed by the sound of the car starting up and roaring away. How long he sat there he never knew. He thought vaguely that he ought to clear up the mess on the floor. He was dimly aware that there were bits of scrambled egg on the bed and that the orange juice was staining the carpet. What did it matter? His life was in ruins. Sukie didn't want him any more. He had to go. But where? He'd lived here with Sukie for the last ten years. They'd had a flat in Fulham before that. Not nearly big enough for them and two children. But this was a family home. He'd never thought of leaving it. Well, not yet anyway. He'd had an idea that he and Sukie might retire to Wiltshire or somewhere someday. Retire! Actors didn't retire! They couldn't afford to retire. But to leave home today, now, it was unthinkable. Gwen, his mother, used to say, 'It's always darkest before the dawn.' But where would he be by dawn tomorrow? It all seemed so bleak. Well, at least he'd be able to see Claire.

23

Geoff drove to the rehearsal rooms in a sort of trance. Everything seemed unreal. He had no memory of actually getting there. He just arrived. He realized that he had been negotiating the traffic jams, roadworks, malfunctioning traffic lights, everything on automatic pilot. The whole thing felt like a bad dream. His nerve endings seemed to be standing out proud from his skin. He was numb with shock. He didn't want to think about anything. The boot of his car was crammed with stuff. The two large suitcases that Sukie had packed were on the back seat. There were pictures, tapes, video cassettes, CDs, books filling up every available corner in the car. There was a portable TV on the passenger seat covered with a long waxed raincoat. His golf clubs were propped up in the well of the seat. This was a mistake, he discovered, as they kept lurching towards the gear lever. He could hardly see out of the rear window and the car felt as heavy as his heart. This surprised him. The number of times he had thought about leaving Sukie in the past – for her sake as much as his, he'd always persuaded himself. He had imagined that he would feel elated, light-hearted, youthful and free again. Now, instead, he was incapable of feeling anything. He pulled up outside the rehearsal building and parked. He got his script from underneath a pile of sports jackets and tee shirts that Sukie had overlooked and walked into the reception area to the sound of the usual cheery greeting from the security guards. The smile flashed in reply would, he knew full well, look more like a ghastly leer. He stood statue-like in the lift. Someone asked him which floor he wanted, but oblivious to the query, he then found himself walking willy-nilly in the direction of the canteen. In a half mesmeric state, he went and bought coffee.

'Aren't you eating anything, love?' enquired the ever-concerned Meg.

Geoff looked startled. 'Is it lunchtime?' he asked, amazed.

Meg looked at him with worried eyes. 'Don't let them get to you,' she whispered sympathetically – 'it'll all work out, you see.'

'Thanks, Meg, you are a darling. I'm fine really, just not hungry, that's all.' Geoff tried to inject a sort of bonhomie into his voice but didn't quite pull it off.

There was no sign of Claire. He suddenly remembered she wasn't called for the afternoon. She'd already done her scene with Simon that morning. He was down to work with Bella, and Meg was doing several scenes with Reg. Patsy was called, however, but not until 3.30. Meg was chattering away, but he had no idea what she was saying and didn't bother to listen. He sat at the table, gazing into the middle distance. He'd left home. He had been cast adrift. He felt rootless, a displaced person, he was being buffeted about like a piece of tumbleweed. Bella loomed onto the horizon.

'What's the matter with you?' she asked immediately as she plonked herself down beside him. 'Not letting those stupid bastards get to you, I hope.'

So everyone knows, Geoff thought.

'I thought you never read the tabloids,' he said rather tersely.

'Don't be silly, darling, I had Hugh on the blower first thing in the morning asking me why I'd spoken to them. Is he really so naive as to imagine that I'd actually exchange two words with those moronic guttersnipes! I told him, I said, Hugh, you loathesome little prick, you're a dickhead – which I admit is tautological, but it seemed to sum him up at the time – I said, I have absolutely no idea that anything so utterly meaningful and serious had been going on between you. Well, yes, I knew you were flirting with her and all that, but I thought you were still pursuing the appalling Patsy – although how you could bring yourself to even contemplate getting to grips with someone who has not even one iota of ability is beyond me. But that's men for you. Anyway, I said, try not to be more of a prat than you actually are, Hugh darling. No one from the *Globe* has asked my opinion and I certainly wouldn't give it to them if they had, though I must say, Geoffrey, it looks as though you've blown it this time. How's Sukes taking it?'

'Badly,' said Geoff. 'She's thrown me out.'

Bella whistled. 'Can't say I blame her – I wouldn't put up with it – well, I didn't,' she added, reflecting momentarily on her two failed marriages. 'So, what are you going to do?' For once she was genuinely concerned. She and Geoff exchanged a continuous barrage of banter, but *au fond* she had a great affection for him.

'See if Claire will put me up for a while.'

'And then you'll panic and try to go back to Sukie and then Claire will be upset and then you'll be upset because everyone else is. Oh God, can I really live through all of this?' said Bella dramatically, clutching at her brow.

Geoff managed a half-smile and said, 'I'm going down to the rehearsal room to look at my scenes.'

Bella put her hand on his arm. 'Don't worry, darling, we're all rooting for you, you know.'

Geoff pressed her hand with his in a gesture of gratitude. 'Bless you, Bella, you're a trouper.'

'So are you, old love – don't forget that,' she murmured.

Thus encouraged, afternoon rehearsals passed off without incident. Patsy was rather bright-eyed and jumpy. She had taken note of Geoff's overladen car and drove herself mad all afternoon wondering what he was up to. He steadfastly ignored her; he couldn't cope with that situation as well.

Claire, meanwhile, had had a fairly uncomfortable morning of it. She had endured endless good-humoured ragging from Simon, who had labelled her The Scarlet Woman. Amy had been kind and had smiled at her encouragingly at various moments throughout the rehearsal.

'Simon,' Claire had drawn him to one side during a coffee break, 'how do you think they found out?'

'Haven't a clue. Have we a mole in the cast, do you suppose?' he said darkly, looking around furtively.

'I just can't think how they found out,' she repeated in worried tones.

'Listen, forget about it. There are a million ways – a receptionist or a waiter at the hotel earning themselves a quick fifty pounds perhaps. The thing is, it's done. You've just got to keep a low profile now, that's all. They'll pester you for a while, then they'll get bored and it will be someone else's turn. Just concentrate on the work, that's what you're here for – the rest will take care of itself.'

Claire looked at him with gratitude and a new appreciation. Simon might indulge in slightly irritating banter most of the time, but his heart was certainly in the right place, she decided.

Apprehensive all morning, Claire toyed with the idea of hanging around until after lunch to see Geoff, then decided against it. He had not rung her – who could guess what

176

horrors had been happening at the Armitage house? She suddenly felt panicky. It had all gone wrong. He would have promised Sukie never to see her again. Well, he wouldn't be able to keep that promise – he would have to see her, of course; they had scenes together but the thought of being close to him and his not wanting her any more was unbearable.

As soon as she had finished her scenes, she scuttled off home. Now she really didn't want to see him, she didn't want to see the embarrassment in his eyes as he was unable to meet her gaze, or the guilt on his face if he did. She drove straight past her front door just to ascertain whether or not the press were still lurking there. All was normal, however, and indeed there had been no sign of them that morning, much to Claire's relief. Now she rushed in and double-locked the door behind her. Having made some tea, she went straight to the phone.

'Hello, Sal?' she said when the switchboard put her through. 'Listen, darling, I'm fearfully sorry about yesterday. I was in a bit of a state, you know.'

Sally's voice sounded relieved on the other end. 'That's all right, Clairey. I knew that you were having a bad time. I'm glad you feel better.'

'It's just that I've been a bit jumpy recently. I suppose I must be in love,' and she laughed rather hollowly.

Sally hesitated before saying, 'Have you heard from him?' The question hung in the air for a moment.

'No.'

'I see.'

'It's a bit worrying really.'

'Darling, think about it. Things cannot be too good at home, he must be having a hell of a time there. Didn't you see him at rehearsals?'

'No,' replied Claire. 'We had different calls. He wasn't due to do his scenes till – well, now, really. I didn't hang around.'

'Do you want me to come over after work?'

'You are a doll. No, I'm all right. I've got to face this on my own. The press has gone, at any rate.'

'The press?'

'They tried to worm their way into my flat yesterday and then sat outside for ages when I wouldn't let them in. I hope they've lost interest as I didn't play ball.'

'Don't you believe it – now's when they start to play dirty, so be warned.'

'Right.'

'What are you going to do this afternoon?'

'Have a massive clear up – this place looks like a tip – then learn some lines, and get an early night. I'm feeling a bit bushed actually.'

'Good idea. Regroup your forces, gird your loins or whatever, ready for the next onslaught.'

'Sal?'

'Still here.'

'What do you think he'll do?'

'That, my dear Watson, depends entirely on what she does.'

'Yes, I suppose you're right.'

'I just know I wouldn't care to be a member of that household right now – not even the cat. They pick up on these things, you know.'

'How did you know they had a cat?'

'Saw a charming family picture of the Armitages At Home. Cat was amongst those present, centre stage but livid.'

'Oh God,' said Claire miserably, 'I feel terrible.'

'Well, don't,' said Sal sensibly.

'Sal, listen, I'll phone you tomorrow and apprise you of developments.'

'I can't wait – tara.'

Claire felt better after she'd put the phone down. She had hated quarrelling with Sally. She tried desperately to put Geoff at the back of her mind while doing her chores. She then had a long soak in the bath, washed her hair and slipped into her towelling robe. She was all fresh, glowing and pink from her bath. The robe was long and apricot in colour and her brown curls were piled on top of her head with tendrils damp around her neck. Suddenly there was a loud rap at the door. She started. Dear God, the press, she thought, they're back. She stood still, her heart pounding. Then she crept into the bedroom and peered out from behind the curtains at the window.

Geoff! He was standing on the front step. There was another loud knock. Shaking and trembling, she flew to the front door, fumbled with the lock and wrenched it open. Geoff was smiling at her, surrounded by suitcases and paraphernalia.

He gave her a sheepish look. 'Hello, darling. Can I come in?'

24

Jim had fared no better with his second interview than he had
with his first. He'd managed to get across the valley on time
and had met what he later described to Meriel as a 'screwball'.
The guy was nuts, he said, and had treated Jim with ill-
concealed contempt. The 'art' movie had a plot that was a
hotch-potch of explicit sex and excessive violence, and Jim
had been revolted by the stage directions. He wouldn't have
wanted to do it if he'd got it – if he hadn't worked for ten
years . . . if he was down to his last dime. He'd arrived home
to find several further demands waiting for him for unpaid
bills, and when Meriel had renewed her assault on him about
the British TV series he'd reluctantly agreed. At least it would
get him out of the country and the IRN off his back. He was
between a rock and a hard place, and he had nowhere else
to go.

'So, do we have a deal?' Meriel asked him impatiently.

'Yup, we have a deal.'

'That's my boy!'

He'd been to a real estate agent and leased his house to
a visiting Japanese film producer anxious to break into the
Hollywood scene.

'Write me, Jimbo,' said Meriel, who had suddenly gone
sentimental on him when he rang to say goodbye.

'Surely, honey,' he replied, feeling rather alone.

South Eastern Television had grudgingly agreed to a club-class air ticket, and a charmingly pretty air stewardess from Florida, called Sherri, had managed to get him upgraded to first. Jim had indulged in a delightful flirtation with her all the way over and she'd given him her phone number in London. She did this trip regularly, it transpired, and stayed with a girlfriend in Earls Court on stopovers. He promised to contact her. On arrival at Heathrow, feeling a little jaded and travel weary, he'd been surprised to find a reception committee awaiting him. The tabloid press was out in force and he found he was a star again. In the States his show had been cut, and, as he hardly ever went out in public, apart from awards ceremonies and premieres, he was unprepared for the hordes of women of all ages that were lined up in the public concourse to greet him as he came out of the exit. The place was in uproar. Jim was surprised, pleased and flattered. Maybe the old Brits were not going to be so bad after all.

A chauffeur holding a card aloft that bore the legend *Dutton. SE TV* caught his eye. Obviously this guy was not a devotee of the series.

'Hi,' he called good-naturedly, across the divide. 'I think you're looking for me.'

'Thank you, sir,' replied the driver deferentially. 'This way, please.'

Jim struggled through the crowd, who were ecstatic at getting so close to their idol. Jim certainly made a pretty impressive figure. Tall, bronzed, muscular, with amused, quizzical, pale blue eyes and a dazzling smile, his blond streaked hair glinting as the flashbulbs popped, he was every inch a popular movie star. The girls surged around him, squealing and squeaking with delight as he made his way laughing through them. He signed countless autographs, shook extended hands and submitted to the embraces of the more daring with good-humoured grace. Finally, accompanied by the tolerantly patient and slightly bemused chauffeur, he made the exit and sought the refuge of the limousine that was awaiting him. It had been Larry's idea to provide a vintage Panther de Ville saloon. It was a good publicity gimmick and Jim was enchanted.

'Hey, this is really wild,' he'd observed as he settled back into the plush leather upholstery. 'I feel like I'm in *The Great Gatsby*.' The girls all peered at him through the tinted windows and a patrolling policeman had to all but prise them away so that the vehicle could glide on its way. The sizeable boot would not begin to accommodate the numerous pieces of matching leather luggage Jim had deemed it necessary to bring with him, and a taxi had to be hurriedly summoned to accompany them to the little Georgian house that had been rented for him in the fashionable part of Shepherd's Bush bordering onto Notting Hill. It was in a tree-lined avenue, had a small walled garden and a sheltered patio and was beautifully furnished with modern classical furniture and antiques and good paintings.

'Kinda quaint,' was how Jim summed it up to Meriel, when he checked in with her to assure her of his safe arrival.

He was, in fact, extremely pleased with his new home. It was both cosy and airy, charming, comfortable and very convenient for the studios and the rehearsal rooms. Rehearsals for the camera were an unknown luxury for Jim and he would find it difficult to get used to them, but he had a feeling he was going to be happy in London, England. Sure there was no pool, but at least there was a Jacuzzi, jet shower and a waste disposal unit, none of which he had expected, having been warned by some of his New York friends that the amenities in Britain were primitive.

182

South Eastern Television had timed his arrival with consideration, to give him time to recover from his jet lag and acclimatize himself before having to get on another plane – for Amsterdam. He was due to film his first scenes in an hotel there, on the canals and at the Rijksmuseum. He had been provided with scripts, which were waiting for him on the hall console table on his arrival. He noticed that his scenes – only two or three per episode – were quite spikey and unsentimental. Most of them were opposite a girl called Claire Jenner. He wondered if she'd be his type. He reflected wryly that most women on the whole were his type. Jim hardly ever experienced rejection. Women threw themselves at him; he wondered idly if British women would be the same. He had hardly unpacked and settled himself in when the phone rang. He picked it up.

'Yup,' he said cheerily. He was feeling reasonably optimistic about this whole venture. A cultured English voice spoke.

'Good afternoon. Mr Dutton, I presume?'

'Sure as hell is.'

'Jim – may I call you Jim? We haven't met, but I've seen you so often and I'm such an ardent admirer of yours that I feel sure we're going to be firm friends. My name is Larry Matthews. I'm the PA/floor manager/part-time script editor/assistant producer and general factotum on *The McMasters*. Welcome to England. I hope you are as comfortable as can be expected?'

'Gee, thanks, Larry. Pleased to make your acquaintance. Hey, tell me, where can I get something to eat around here?'

'Do you like French cooking?'

'Er, is there a local diner?'

'Lovey, you're not on Santa Monica Boulevard now, you know. You'll have to try and mix with the natives. You will,

183

however, find a goodish McDonalds, if you're really desperate. Otherwise I suggest you pop along to the local supermarket and rustle something up for yourself. There's one just around the corner.'

'Rightee, I might just give that a try. When do I get to meet you guys?'

'My goodness, you are keen – I should take advantage of the lull before the storm if I were you.'

'Are you serious?'

'Deadly serious. You may not have to go leaping in and out of the surf, baby, but, I should remind you, we are not renowned for the clemency of our weather, and even if it pisses down – we shoot. Hopefully Amsterdam will be kind to us. How is your Dutch by the way?'

'Dutch?'

'I jest, everyone but everyone in Holland speaks English – sorry American.'

'Is that right? Listen, er, Larry – this Claire Jenner, is she okay?'

'Forget it,' advised Larry, who was *au fait* with American TV stars and their proprietorial air with their female co-stars. 'She's spoken for.'

'How's that?'

'She's, er – living, sort of – with the, er, one of the actors in the series. Don't worry, there's plenty of other crumpet hanging about the set to amuse you.'

'Pardon me?'

'Girls, lots of them, pretty ones.'

'You on the level?'

'Absolutely. Listen, you gorgeous hunk of manhood you –' This guy has to be a fag, Jim thought to himself – 'get a nosebag on –'

'Pardon me?'

'Get yourself something to eat. I can recommend the Pomme d'Or. You're a European now, you know.'

'Hey, that's really neat.' Jim was pleased. 'Sounds like you guys are going to make me really welcome here – I like that.'

'Can't wait,' said Larry dryly. He had a feeling that Jim was going to be the second kick up the arse that season for the series.

Jim decided to try the French restaurant. He found the number in the directory and such was his confidence, booked a table for two for eight o'clock. Then he fished out Sherri's number from the inside breast pocket of his beige antelope jacket. She had, it transpired, just showered and dressed and was wondering what on earth to do with her evening. Half an hour later she was getting out of the taxi and ringing Jim's front door bell.

'Hey, you're my first guest!' he greeted her ebulliently, as he looked her up and down with undisguised admiration.

'I'm quite sure I won't be your last,' she drawled. She looked delicious. A very pretty, all American apple-pie girl with the obligatory suntan that distinguishes most air hostesses and bouncy streaked blonde hair that almost matched Jim's own. He showed her around the little eighteenth-century house. She expressed her approval, deemed it 'adorable' and 'cute'. It was a pleasant evening and Sherri persuaded him to walk to the restaurant.

'You know this place?' asked Jim surprised.

'Why yes, I've passed it several times on my way into the airport,' she said hurriedly. The truth was that Sherri had spent many a pleasant evening in there with rich Americans that she'd met on the flight.

Jim and Sherri spent an entirely delightful evening, regaling each other with tales of their respective home towns, he filling her in on his life as a beach bum, as he put it, on his TV series in the States. Later that night they were back in Jim's house in Jim's bedroom. Jim Dutton may have come to Britain, may have acquired honorary European status, but that night he was back on home territory.

25

By the time Sukie got back from the solicitors, all evidence
of Geoff had been expunged from the house. She had stopped
off at a couple of rather expensive stores and bought herself
two new outfits. She had also booked an appointment at the
local up-market hairdressing and beauty salon. She was going
to have a manicure and pedicure, a session of sun-bed
treatments and her rather ordinary dark brown hair cut and
hennaed. She had also bought some new scent and some
rather frothy underwear. She arrived home feeling elated. She
had even stopped off at the fishmonger's section of the
supermarket and purchased Brambles some fresh fish. After
the emotional rigours of the weekend, which had disturbed
him profoundly, this unexpected treat had the effect of driving
him into a sort of feline frenzy of delight. He could hardly
eat for purring.

The house was silent on her return, but this was not unusual
as the boys were always at school at this time of the day, and
Geoff often away rehearsing or filming. No, there was nothing
different about a silent house. What was different – and it
struck her as soon as she entered – were the numerous spaces
and empty hooks on the walls where Geoff's pictures had
hung. The watercolour of him as Malvolio, which had greeted
her in the hall, was missing. The shelves in the study were
almost bare. The absence of his hi-fi, portable TV, cassettes

and CDs left great gaping holes and the place had the air of a city that had been sacked.

A sudden panic seized her. She darted into the hall and looked in the understairs cupboard. Yes, he'd taken his golf clubs. She ran upstairs. His wardrobe and drawers were empty, even the airing cupboard had not escaped the pillage. She gasped. He'd taken towels, sheets, pillowcases, a hot-water bottle and the electric blanket. She felt decidedly shaky. It seemed he'd taken her at her word. He'd left nothing to chance. He obviously had no intention of ever returning to her. Well, she didn't bloody want him to, the bastard. She remembered the sympathetic glances she'd received in the shops and a fresh wave of humiliation and misery swept over her. The full horror of the sham of the marriage that she had been living for the last, at least, twelve years had not yet sunk in. She felt in a heightened unnatural state – sort of empty inside, she decided.

Now she sat at her kitchen table watching the cat devouring the fish, which smelt revolting, but the animal was happy. She gained a grain of comfort from that. There was also a great deal of satisfaction to be had from the way she had dealt with the crisis. Promptly and effectively. She wasn't going to be one of those wives who wilt about, suffering, while their spouses blithely continue their lives as though nothing had happened, only superficially mortified and full of remorse until the next time, she thought bitterly. No, she'd done the only possible thing: chucked him out. It would, in any case, be quite pleasant to have the place to herself for a change. She might even move, sell, and take the boys to the country. She loved the country – she quite relished the idea of starting up a whole new life of being independent again. Ben was very mature already and she could easily send Nicky off to her sister's. Nan had two children of her own, the same age as

Nicky, and he would love the companionship. I'm being selfish, she thought guiltily. Just for a change I'm putting myself first.

But how on earth was she going to manage without Geoff? She could not even contemplate life without him, pompous, arrogant, selfish, lying bastard, that he was. The boys always helped her in the house – he never did.

She glanced round the kitchen. What a revolting colour! Time for a change there as well. Blue would be nice, Dutch blue, to go with the blue and white china. Brambles had finished his feast and was attending to his toilette, washing and rewashing his face with his paws. She smiled at him as she caught his golden eyes when he paused momentarily, but he only gazed back expressionlessly before abruptly continuing his labours. She rose from the table and crossed to the phone, which hung on the wall. After checking a list of numbers that was pinned up on the cork board next to it, she dialled and waited. She got through to an answering machine.

'Hello, Ted, this is Sukie Armitage,' she hesitated slightly as she spoke her name. Armitage – she wasn't Armitage any more, she'd just applied for a divorce. She was going to reassume her maiden name from now on. She'd explain it to Ted when she saw him. 'Um, listen, Ted, I wonder if you're busy at the moment, well, in the next week or so, because I'd love you to come and paint the kitchen for me – a sort of lovely deep seventeenth-century Dutch blue – if you know what I mean. Oh, and the bedroom as well.' Yes, why not? She couldn't bear the thought of sleeping in the room she'd shared with Geoff during the ten years they'd lived in this house. 'I thought it would be nice to have the bedroom done sort of apricot and peach. White is so cold. Do you think you could manage to fit me in soon? Please ring me back when you get in.'

She replaced the receiver and started unpacking the shopping that she had dumped on the kitchen table – the usual groceries that she'd picked up in the supermarket. Sausages and mash for the boys' supper – she stopped – no, this was a special occasion. She remembered that she and Geoff had arranged to give Hugh and Mona supper the day after tomorrow. She went to the freezer and extracted the king-sized prawns she'd bought for the occasion. She also took out the Black Forest gâteau. The boys would love this. She put them on the worktop to defrost and found some rice in the cupboard. They were all going to celebrate. She would make prawn risotto for them all. She went to the phone again and rang Mona.

'Mona, it's Sukie.'

'Oh, my dear.' Mona's tone was full of compassion. 'I've been so worried about you. I didn't like to ring as I thought you and Geoff would probably be sorting things out – I didn't want to pry – you understand.'

'Absolutely, darling, don't worry, it's all okay. I've chucked him out.'

There was a longish pause before Mona said, 'That's very brave of you, Sukes.' Sukie knew full well that Mona was wishing she'd had the courage to do the same to Hugh when she found out about his affair with Bella. Mona had lived with the hurt and humiliation for years now. It had become part of her life.

'Thank you, darling, but it had to be done. I'm not like you, you know, stoic and all that. It isn't in my nature to be patrician. I'm actually phoning to say the supper's off. I've sorted him out, as you put it – I now need to sort out myself.'

'What are you going to do?' asked Mona.

'I'm not sure – get a job if I can. I'm suing for a divorce. There's only so much humiliation one can take.'

190

'I know,' agreed Mona quietly.

'At least yours hasn't been public – national news,' said Sukie.

'No,' replied her friend. 'Sukie, I may be able to help you with the job idea. Give me a couple of days to make a few calls, but I've heard of something that might suit you – you may be the very person they're looking for.'

Sukie's heart leaped. 'Who? What?'

'I won't say any more until I've spoken to them. Where's Geoff gone? Do you know?'

'No, and I don't care. To the latest conquest, I suppose.'

'I doubt that very much,' said Mona. 'She's a very independent girl.'

Sukie winced. 'I don't really want to discuss her, if you don't mind.'

'No, of course not, sorry,' said Mona hurriedly. 'Well look, darling, I'll be back to you as soon as I've made some enquiries, but I have high hopes of success.'

'Bless you, Mona, you're a darling. Love to Hugh – bye.'

Sukie put the phone down with a mixture of emotions flooding through her. The mention of Claire had been like a knife twisting in her gut, but she was all the more determined to make a new life for herself. She picked up the remainder of her shopping from the kitchen table and took it upstairs. She unfolded the two outfits she had bought and hung them lovingly in her wardrobe. They were beautiful, and perfect for a job interview. She felt a surge of excitement. It was rather disconcerting, this strange succession of differing emotions. But she felt more alive than she'd done for years.

Back downstairs, she switched on the radio. Geoff had hated music playing during mealtimes. Well, now she could listen to it whenever she felt like it. She chuckled to herself; she felt like a naughty little schoolgirl. She started to prepare the meal and laid the table. The best china and silver would be suitable, she decided, to celebrate her first day of freedom for sixteen years. She cast her mind back, she'd given up a promising career as an actress for Geoff. She started to quote some lines that came to her quite suddenly. '*Love is blind, and lovers cannot see the pretty follies that themselves commit.*' Jessica in *The Merchant of Venice*. Geoff had been playing Lorenzo opposite her. That's how they had met and fallen in love, in rep. She sighed. She'd enjoyed acting, she'd loved the camaraderie, the companionship, being with other people all bent on a common pursuit – the getting on of a show. She'd missed it desperately at first, then Ben had come along and followed by Nicky to occupy her time fully. She had chummed up with Mona when Geoff first landed the part in the series. But she had to admit that, being at heart a gregarious girl, she'd missed the involvement of a company and had endured many lonely moments when her husband had been away filming. Now all that was going to change. And soon. She was about to rejoin the human race. By five o'clock, when the boys returned, supper was ready.

'Something smells good,' observed Nicky, wrinkling his nose in anticipation. 'Wish that was for us.'

'You having a dinner party, Mum?' asked Ben, surveying the scene with some amazement. 'This is a new departure, you don't usually eat in the kitchen.'

'Yes, we are having a dinner party and you're invited, and yes, this delicious aroma is indeed for you.'

'Oh God, it's not your birthday, is it?' asked Ben, horrified.

'Oh no!' said Nicky, clapping his hands over his mouth in even more horror.

'But it's not for another three weeks yet, is it?' said Ben.

'You're absolutely right,' said his mother. 'We're celebrating your father's departure.'

They both stood there dumbstruck. Eventually Ben said, 'Is that because of the papers, Mum?'

Sukie nodded.

'Oh yes, I know all about that,' said Nicky knowledgeably. 'Dad's been messing around with some girl on the series.'

Sukie looked at him. 'How did you know that?' she asked.

'They're all talking about it at school,' replied Nicky airily.

Sukie hung her head. 'Oh God,' she said miserably. 'I'm sorry you've had to put up with that.'

'Oh no problem, Mum,' said Nicky. 'It's happened to dozens of the boys at school. Ours is the only one in the paper, though,' he added proudly.

'Oh, darling,' said Sukie and rushed across to hug him.

They had a surprisingly jolly meal. Both boys tucked into the food with gusto. The only comment on the novel situation that evening came from Nicky. 'It's fun without Dad, isn't it?'

The next day a phone call came from Mona.

'Sukes, how would you feel about being an assistant casting director?'

'What?'

'I mean it. A girlfriend of mine, Anthea, has had complications with her pregnancy and has had to bow out suddenly on a big movie. They need someone bright, intelligent who knows the business backwards and asked me if I knew of anyone.'

'You're kidding. They'll need someone with experience – I don't have any.'

'Sukes, if you were given a script now, could you cast it?'

'Well yes, of course I could, standing on my head.'

'Well then –'

'But –'

'Don't worry, I told them you'd been casting some characters in *The McMasters*.'

'You didn't!' Sukie was genuinely shocked. 'But that isn't true.'

'Yes, it is – you suggested Jason and Meg and several others.'

'Well, yes, but only because I'd seen them in something on television.'

'There you are then. Anyway, it's too late – I've already got you an interview – tomorrow morning, noon, Soho – can you make it?'

'You bet.'

'Good, get a pen, I'll give you the address.'

26

Claire pulled Geoff inside and flung her arms around him. He submitted to her embrace, then eased himself away.

'I'll get my things in. I think we'd better attend to the mundane things of life before we give way to the celestial,' he said, disentangling himself gently. She helped him carry the piles of belongings in and dumped them in the hall. 'I hope you don't mind. I'm afraid there's rather a lot,' he said more than once as they staggered in and out laden with books. He seemed changed, different in some way. She could not quite pin it down. Certainly more subdued, as though he were in a dream.

She brushed the thought aside and said, 'You finish here, I'll make you some tea.'

'I'd love a Scotch, if you've got it.'

'Oh yes, of course,' she replied half apologetically. 'You must need it.' The whole situation seemed unreal and unnatural, with an undercurrent of charged emotion. She hurried into the sitting room, thanking whatever gods who suddenly seemed to be smiling on her that she had done such a thorough job of the housework that afternoon. She was trembling slightly, she realized, and decided she probably needed a Scotch herself. She heard Geoff shut the front door and find his way along the passage to her.

'This is rather nice, I must say,' he said, gazing around

appreciatively at her little sitting room, which was indeed charming and was a sharp contrast to his own comfortable but shabby room at home, which bore all too clearly the marks of family occupation.

'Do sit down,' said Claire rather more formally than she intended. She had longed for Geoff to visit her in her abode, but had never dreamed it would be in these traumatic circumstances. 'Here you are,' she said, handing him a drink. He had flung himself on the little cream sofa. She took her own drink and sat herself down in the matching armchair opposite him.

'Cheers,' he said, raising his glass. She followed suit and they both gulped down a draught.

Then she asked tentatively, 'Are you all right?' sensing that he was anything but.

Geoffrey examined the bottom of the whisky glass thoughtfully, then said with an abrupt bitter laugh, 'She's thrown me out!'

Claire's heart tightened. She would have preferred that he had left of his own volition. 'I'm sorry,' she said with genuine concern.

'Don't be,' he replied shortly. 'I deserve it.'

Claire said nothing, but twisted her glass round and around in her hands. There was silence for a while, then Geoff took another swig of his drink.

'Pretty bloody, wasn't it, the "revelation"?' He emphasized the word satirically.

'Yes,' agreed Claire quietly. There was another pause.

Then he said, 'Come and give us a cuddle then.' She leapt up immediately and rushed over to him. He took her in his arms. 'Kiss it and make it better,' he said huskily.

Claire lay down on top of him and gave him a long, deep kiss. He slipped his hand inside her towelling robe and felt the silky smoothness of her shoulder, then let his hand travel down to her breast. Her nipple became erect in response. He pulled at it gently with his fingers. She let out a gasp. Then she raised herself up over him, letting her robe slip from her shoulders. He groaned with pleasure at the sight of her glorious breasts. She leant over him and guided her nipple into his mouth. He sucked hard, then he pulled away the robe and eased himself down the sofa. She straddled his face as his tongue found her clitoris, teasing her by licking it lightly, then he plunged his tongue into the moist, warm opening of her cunt. She moaned, and let him continue for a while, luxuriating in the ecstasy of it. Then she got off him and, kneeling by the side of the sofa, she kissed him again passionately, tasting the musky juices of her cunt in his mouth. She unzipped his flies and prised his cock out from his pants. He abruptly turned her round so that she was on all fours on the floor. Still fully dressed, with just his cock sticking out from his trousers, he mounted her, pumping in and out frantically, grabbing her hips and pulling her onto him.

'I adore fucking you,' he whispered urgently, as he bent down over her caressing her breasts and tweaking her nipples. He was unable to control his climax and came suddenly and violently.

'I'm sorry, I just couldn't hold back any longer,' he said afterwards, masturbating her to orgasm. 'I am sorry,' he repeated, as they lay side by side on the floor – 'it's all been such a ghastly strain these last two days.'

'I know,' she whispered. 'I'm sorry too, it's all my fault.'

'What do you mean?' he jerked his head up to look at her. 'Why is it your fault?'

Claire was surprised at the suddenness of his reaction.

'Well,' she replied naively, 'if you hadn't started an affair with me, you'd still be a happily married man.'

Geoff laughed grimly. 'I suppose I should have known I'd be found out sooner or later. I'm afraid you are not the first, my darling – but you must have known that?' he added, seeing Claire's look of startled dismay.

She felt as though a knife had just gone through her. After the romance, this wanton cruelty was hard to take.

'Yes, of course,' she said hurriedly, covering her hurt. 'Would you like another drink?'

'Yes please, and I'm ready for my supper now too, please, miss.'

'Oh, right – oh dear, I'm not sure what I've got in, but I'll find something.'

'Of course you will,' said Geoff good-humouredly. He used to regular meals always on the table at his behest. He would invariably ring Sukie to tell her what time he would be back so that this arrangement could continue satisfactorily. He was perfectly confident that things of a domestic nature would proceed in the normal fashion with Claire. 'Oh and, darling,' he called out after her, 'there's some washing that needs doing.'

Claire stopped in her tracks, then slowly retraced her steps.

'What's the matter?' asked Geoff, seeing the look on her face.

'Where are they?'

'In one of those cases – the green one, I think.'

Claire looked at him steadily. 'Then I suggest you get unpacked whilst I'm making supper – then you can do the wash while we're eating.' Geoff stared at her open-mouthed.

She started to go out but turned back again. 'And you'll find the iron under the sink and the ironing board in the cupboard in the hall.' She went into the kitchen.

Geoff was stunned. He had never in his entire life done his own washing and had only twice tried to iron his shirts, on the two occasions when Sukie had been in hospital having the boys. On each occasion he had abandoned the attempt and cajoled the cleaning lady into doing it for him. He realized that fucking on a regular basis was not going to be the only change in his life. He downed the rest of his whisky and helped himself to another. He could hear Claire in the kitchen banging about with the saucepans and rifling through cupboards. He went into the hall, grabbed two of the suitcases and took them into the bedroom. It was very feminine and pretty, a baroque flavour in the decor. Decidedly sexy he decided, as he noted the drapes around the bed. This relationship would certainly have its plus side, but what of his other creature comforts? He would miss those. Well, Sukie would have less to do – just the boys to cope with. A spasm of pain seized him as he thought of the boys sitting down to supper, wondering where he was.

'Help yourself to more Scotch,' Claire called from the kitchen.

Geoff went to obey instantly. He was a hardened Scotch drinker, but was now beginning to feel slightly drunk. He supposed the shock of recent events, plus the fact that he had not eaten anything all day, had produced this effect. He then continued unpacking the dirty shirts, socks and pants and carried them to the kitchen. Claire smiled to herself as she watched him pile them into the washing machine.

'I wouldn't put the coloured things in with the white ones,' she observed quietly as she grated some cheese, 'otherwise everything will go a sort of dirty pink or bluey grey.'

'Oh right,' said Geoff, removing the crisp white shirt, which in Claire's opinion didn't need washing at all. Obviously Sukie's standards differed greatly from hers.

'How do you work this thing?' asked Geoff puzzled, trying to read the instructions on the front of the washing machine. Claire left what she was doing to show him.

Geoff was impressed. He'd decided long ago that washing machines held some esoteric mystery that was completely beyond him. He came and put his arms around her from behind and kissed her neck.

'I think you're wonderful,' he murmured.

'I hope you like macaroni cheese, it's all I've got.'

'It's my favourite,' he replied truthfully.

'Rather ordinary, I'm afraid,' she continued happily enjoying his attentions, 'but I have a rather good Medoc, which I've been saving for a special occasion.'

'This is the one – pretty special, I'd say.'

They sat happily eating the macaroni cheese accompanied by a tomato and basil salad, washed down by the red wine. They went to bed early, mildly drunk and completely happy, and lay in Claire's large bed half shielded by the drapes from the half-tester. They drifted happily off to sleep in each other's arms.

Claire had a habit of leaving the bedroom windows wide open and the curtains undrawn. From the security of her bed, she liked to look at the trees on the opposite side of the road waving in the breeze. Tonight was no exception. They had been asleep for about an hour when Claire opened her eyes. She suddenly became aware that the room was flooded with a bright light. Moonlight? No, it was far too bright. A streetlight? No, there wasn't one that near. She sat up in bed. What could it be? An accident? A police car? Murder investigation? Her imagination ran riot. She glanced at Geoff, sound asleep. Quietly, she slid out of the bed so as not to disturb him, tiptoed to the window and peered cautiously out. She recoiled in horror, half blinded by the glare of an arc lamp that was trained on her window. She ran back to the bed.

'Geoff, Geoff,' she whispered urgently in his ear. 'Geoff, for God's sake wake up.'

Geoff stirred. 'Um, what is it, darling – are you all right?' he mumbled trying to stroke her.

'Geoff, listen. Don't say anything – they've got a light trained on this window.' Geoff was suddenly awake.

'What?'

'Ssh!' she said frantically in a stage whisper. 'Don't say anything – they may have sound equipment.'

Geoff was now wide awake. 'What the hell are you talking about?' he whispered back. Claire was trembling.

'They're out there, they must have got cameras with telephoto lenses,' she said in awed tones.

'Jesus Christ, I don't believe this.' Geoff got out of bed.

'Don't let them see you.'

Geoff crouched down on the floor and pulled his dressing-gown down from the foot of the bed. He wrapped it around him and, crouching, on all fours, got to the door. She heard him go to the kitchen, at the back of the flat. She sat on the bed shivering. She could hear him telephoning the police. He seemed to be arguing with them. She, too, sneaked out, grabbing her towelling robe and keeping down. Once outside in the passage, she ran to the sanctuary of the kitchen. Geoff, looking angry and tousled, was just putting the phone down.

'I had some trouble making them believe me,' he said harshly. 'As those bastards are not in the garden, technically they're not on private property, so they're not trespassing. I said what about invasion of privacy? They said the law was not specific on that point – remember the Royal Family. He thinks they can move them on for disturbing the peace and creating a public nuisance – they're sending a squad car.'

He slumped heavily into the nearest chair and ran his hands through his hair.

Claire looked at him with wide eyes. 'I just can't believe this is happening,' she said. Geoff looked up at her. 'This, apparently, is the price you have to pay for the privilege of entertaining the public. You're not allowed any free time. You have to entertain them off-screen as well as on.'

27

'They're back,' Geoff announced grimly, as he came into the kitchen where Claire was doing his morning toast for him.

'Oh no!'

'I'm afraid so. Thursday, you see, they want to get something in for the Sunday editions. Sell a lot of copies. Wrest the *Chronicle* readers away with another nice juicy headline.'

'It's beastly,' said Claire with feeling.

'People will be people.' Geoff was sounding decidedly irritable. Claire was worried. The week had been fairly euphoric. It had been lovely going into rehearsals together. Claire would dash out in the lunch hour and buy the essentials for their day-to-day existence. Geoff would stop off on the way home and pick up something special from the delicatessen and they would prepare the meal together, then sit and eat it by candlelight. He said he'd never been so happy. But she could sense an unease; she wondered if he was truly happy. Every now and then she caught a faraway look in his eyes.

'What time are you on today?' he asked abruptly.

'Ten thirty,' she replied, handing him the toast. 'You're not called till this afternoon, are you?'

'No.' He seemed detached.

'Are you all right?' she asked him for the twentieth time that week. 'If we just ignore them – I mean, we've got to leave separately anyway – they'll see me go, they won't hang around for you.'

'No, you're probably right.'

Claire gave it up. It was hateful having one's every movement charted. He was likely to remain recalcitrant for the rest of the day. What she really needed was encouragement, strength and support, and particularly optimism. Geoff had said nothing about either his wife or the boys all week. It was as though they had ceased to exist. She was quite sure he had been thinking of them and she wished he had confided in her. But, it was early days yet, she decided. She devoured her own toast, washed it down with some orange juice, glancing at her script as she did. 'I'm off to Amsterdam next week, you know,' she said.

'So you are,' he said looking up. 'That'll be nice for you.'

'I wish you were coming,' she said wistfully. He didn't reply. He had that distant look in his eyes again. She rose abruptly and went to put the finishing touches to her make-up, then returned to pick up her handbag and script, and bent down to kiss him.

'See you later,' she said. 'I'm off to brave the barbarians at the gate.'

'Good luck,' he replied, giving her a quick kiss.

Claire left the kitchen and went into the hall. She opened the front door and boldly marched out to the car. Immediately, three car doors slammed as their occupants saw her approach. She got straight into her car and started up the engine.

'Miss Jenner.'

'Claire.'

'Could we have a quick word?'

'Just a quick photo, Claire.'

She ignored them and drove quickly away. They took the photos anyway. She didn't care, she was not afraid of them any more. They had done their worst and Geoffrey had come to her. So in a way they'd done her a good turn.

Rehearsals seemed to drag on that morning. At twelve o'clock, Karen from the wardrobe department arrived and stood smiling at Claire from the door. Claire suddenly remembered that she had to go shopping with her for the Amsterdam trip – she'd forgotten all about it. Geoff's sudden arrival and their little idyll together had driven all other thoughts out of her head. As soon as she had finished rehearsals, she and Karen went off in a taxi to Harrods. They were taken up to a small, private area just off one of the main fashion floors and given coffee and biscuits. There was a selection of outfits already hanging from a rail, which Karen had chosen on an earlier recce. Claire was impressed with Karen's choice. She tried on one or two dresses and a little linen suit. These were put to one side as reserves. Then Claire and Karen, accompanied by a senior female employee, went around the store choosing further outfits. Trousers, tops, skirts, jackets, a couple of cocktail dresses, even several pairs of shoes and some handbags, all were noted to be sent up from the various departments and deposited in the intimate little fitting room.

Claire felt rather rich and powerful wandering around, picking out garments. It was really most entertaining. She forgot all about the press and the fact that she would probably have to see them on her return home. After trying on what seemed like innumerable outfits, Claire chose a cream silk suit with a very short skirt and a very long jacket; a deep plum chiffon cocktail dress; a black and tan and cream dogtooth check jacket with long tan skirt and tan suede boots. A pair of sage slacks with matching silk shirt and a long, loose cardigan with an enormous wide belt of olive and silver completed the selection. Claire was enchanted with them all. They were intended for the Amsterdam filming, and she was pleased that she was going to look her best for the glamorous new male American import.

Their purchases made, Claire and Karen returned by taxi to the rehearsal rooms. It had gone 6.30 by then. Claire checked the car park to see if she could see Geoff's car, but there was no sign. She hurried to her car and, waving farewell to Karen, drove off.

It took the best part of an hour to get home in the rush hour traffic. She parked and realized that Geoff's car was not there. Surprised, she was just about to get out, when she remembered the press. There were a couple of suspicious-looking people sitting in their cars. Of course, Geoff hadn't been able to face them. Well, she could hardly blame him. She wasn't looking forward to the mad dash for the front door herself, and then the intrusive hammering and almost proprietorial knock that invariably followed. She sat there for a while, wondering whether to go to look for Geoff. He was probably in the nearest pub. She revved up again and shot away to the Duke of Marlborough, which was the nearest. No, he wasn't there. She went on to the Queen's Head, the Royal Oak and the Leather Bottle. In each one she strode confidently in, looked around and, finding no sign of him, came straight out again. Where the hell could he be? Perhaps he'd gone to Hugh and Mona's. Of course, that was it. He couldn't face sitting inside waiting for her with the reptiles outside and had gone to Hugh's place. There would be a message for her in the flat.

She drove home again. The other cars had gone. She

chuckled. They obviously thought she'd gone out for the evening and had given up. Well, that was something. She parked happily and, humming to herself, she ran up the steps and let herself in. Unconcernedly, she slung her script and handbag down in the hall. She desperately needed a cup of tea – Harrods had been great fun, but exhausting. Still humming she went into the kitchen. Yes, there it was – an envelope propped up on the kitchen table, simply addressed 'Claire'. Geoffrey wrote good letters, they were always romantic, witty and full of idiotic anecdotes. She resolved to make the tea first and save this one until she was sitting down and drinking the much-needed restorative. She switched on the radio; they were playing Mahler's Fifth Symphony – glorious, one of Geoff's favourites. She made a cup of Earl Grey and sat at the table, took a sip, then picked up the envelope and opened it. It read:

My darling. I don't know how to begin to write this, it is the hardest missive I have ever had to pen. And to you of all creatures who least deserves it. First of all I must thank you for giving me the most beautiful week of my life. A brief moment in time but a lifetime of happiness. I was making a grab at youth, I suppose, I should have known that it was impossible to find peace at my age. The fact of the matter is, I have a wife and family whom I love – that cannot change. You must know that I love you, too. It is for this reason that I have gone home. After a week of torment I have decided that that is where my true happiness lies. It will be difficult for us to continue to play opposite each other in the circumstances, so I shall have a word with Hugh and ask him to alter the story line to include alternative romantic involvements for each of us. Try to forgive me, my darling, if you can. I know I will have hurt you dreadfully – please try to understand my actions. I cannot live with myself knowing the

*pain I am causing my dear ones. I remember my mother telling
me it is impossible to find happiness at the expense of someone
else's. And now I am giving you pain, too – the thought of
your unhappiness reading this letter is intolerable to me. However,
there are only two episodes left in this series and you are off
to Amsterdam next week. A change of scene will help the wounds
to heal. I just pray you will be strong. One day you will get
over it and in time may learn to forgive me. I will love you
always – Geoffrey.*

She sat staring at the letter, stunned for a moment. Then,
with a contemptuous snort of disbelief, she abruptly crumpled
it up and threw it across the room with as much force as she
could muster. Then she sat back in her chair and roared with
laughter. The letter was a joke – she'd never read anything
like it in her life. She picked it up again and uncrumpled it,
then crossed to the phone on the wall.

'Sal?' she said, when it was answered, 'do you want a really
good laugh? Then listen to this – you will not believe this.'
And she read out the letter with satirical venom.

Sally was appalled. 'That letter would be obscene if it wasn't
so funny, not to say pathetic,' she gasped eventually.

'I knew you'd appreciate it – good, isn't it?'

'Purple prose doesn't begin to describe it. I particularly like
the way he's going to deprive you of your best scenes in the
series under the guise of saving you the pain of working with
him – great!'

'Yes, I thought that would appeal to you. I rather like the
introduction of the mother figure as a touch of pathos.'

'Yes, so did I – I think you should send it to the British
Museum for the benefit of students in the year 3000 – the
habits of late twentieth-century Caucasian male. What are
you going to do?'

'Get on to Hugh pretty damn quick and make sure I don't lose any of my scenes.'

'That's my girl!'

'Apart from that, maintain a calm exterior and dignified silence and behave as though I hadn't even noticed his absence.'

28

Peckham was depressing in the rain. It was depressing any time. Sean paused momentarily from flexing his pectorals. No, that wasn't strictly true. It was only really depressing when he was out of work. Like now. How long had it been? Too long. Nine months, to be precise. He inhaled deeply and recommenced his exercise routine. What the hell was he doing this for? He was keeping himself in trim, and fit and ready, above all ready, for when the call came, as it surely must. Soon. Well, at least he was doing something, which was more than his bloody agent obviously was!

He exhaled savagely. He couldn't remember when he had last been for a job – yes he could, four months ago – four months and what had it been? The cattle market, a line up of exploitable flesh. He was one of fifteen young men all different physical types, all being considered as potential purveyors of the ideal boy-next-door look guaranteed to set females hearts fluttering – all in the cause of a unisex shampoo. The clients obviously had no idea what they wanted. That is why the casting director had chosen at random a cross section of good-looking young men in their late twenties. Sean glanced at himself in the mirror as he remembered this. He was good-looking, there was no doubt about that. He always worked out in front of the mirror, it gave him encouragement to see his muscles slowly but surely being toned. Then he would do his voice exercises. After five minutes or so of these there would invariably be banging from the flat below and a negro voice would bellow, 'What de hell d'ya think ya doin' up dere, man? You wake up d'baby. Cut that out there, man!' Well, *she* certainly doesn't need voice lessons Sean would think, and fifteen minutes later he'd be washed and changed and on his way to Tottenham Court Road to the Theatre Centre where, with a bit of luck, he might be in time for a voice class – or possibly there would be one in the afternoon. In any event, he would be bound to bump into some mates and although it would cost him money that he didn't really have, anything was better than the soul-destroying boredom of working alone, day after day. Today was such a day. He shared his tiny flat with a couple of girls, both secretaries. They had advertised in the local paper shop for a third party and had been dubious at first about a man. But Sean had turned in a good performance and they had both come under the spell of his undeniable charm and good looks. He hadn't fancied either of them, although neither was unattractive. 'No sex appeal,' he'd explained to his mate Henry. 'Absolutely no chemical reaction whatsoever, Hen. Zero rating in the physical stakes.'

Henry was deeply envious of Sean's domestic situation. Being of an undecided sexual persuasion himself, he was convinced that his dilemma could be resolved for him if he was, as he put it, 'locked up night after night with two predatory females, who would doubtless force me into sexual submission and sort me out.'

'Good God, they're not predatory, Hen, they're nice sensible girls with very clean habits – too clean actually. I get nagged half to death if I so much as leave a mug unwashed in the sink. It does have its drawbacks, this integration of the sexes on a non-emotional level.'

Actually the arrangement suited him beautifully. Both girls were out all day except for weekends, when Sean would meet up with Henry in Clapham, where his friend shared a basement flat with his twin sister, Georgina. They were inseparable. Boarding school had parted them and they had both pined and were joyously reunited in their late teens. Sean thought privately that therein lay the root of Henry's sexual ambivalence. But all three got on famously and Georgina would be content to work in the flat with her radio on when the two boys when out on a Saturday night to the cinema or to queue for standby tickets at the National Theatre. The twins' parents were wealthy and indulged their offspring's artistic aspirations. Henry would never be a great actor, but his amiable disposition, shambling gait and slightly podgy honest face – 'like a dear old moth-eaten teddy bear,' one of the girls at drama college had said – had already landed him some supporting roles in TV and films. It was at drama college where the two had met, at the Academy. Georgie, on the other hand, was studying to be a fashion designer and the flat was always hung about with swathes of fabric that she had dyed, and sketches of her embryonic work. Sean had secretly wished that they would ask him to share the flat with them, but the offer never came. Which was a pity, he reflected for the umpteenth time, as he slammed the main door of the tiny Edwardian villa and trudged off down a street full of identical Edwardian villas. He preferred the more rarefied air of Clapham Common to the cosmopolitan tawdriness of Peckham.

Four months since he'd had an interview for anything. Nine months since he'd worked. He was utterly broke, couldn't afford to go to the Theatre Centre, but he must do his vocal exercises somewhere. He'd tried them on the nearest bit of common land, but passers-by gave him funny looks, children jeered and dogs barked hysterically at him. Hen always paid for him at the National Theatre – insisted on paying – it gave him pleasure, he said. Why should his friend deny him the pleasure of giving pleasure? Sean became used to the situation, but every now and then it irked him. He was beginning to think he'd never work again.

He wondered if he should make the journey to Fulham instead, and confront his agent, Jan Hunter, in her lair. She was a rather formidable female in her forties. Sean had a healthy respect for her talent, energy and somewhat waspish tongue. He knew that if anyone could get him work, she could. He glanced at his reflection in a shop window as he passed. He enjoyed looking at himself and did so at every opportunity. Girlfriends, of whom there had been many, accused him of being vain. Well, why not? He was good to look at – tall, slim, grey-green eyes, dark curling hair and a dazzling smile. He should have got that commercial, he thought as he surveyed his Adonis-like features reflected in the window. The rejection still rankled. Not that he particularly wanted to be seen looking like a drowned rat and then a raving poofter by the entire nation for God knows how long, but he could have done with the money. No, he wouldn't go to see Jan today. It would only depress him further. She wouldn't have any hope to offer him and, in any case, she hated her clients popping in unexpectedly, especially when she didn't have even a sniff of work for them.

'How can I be expected to get work, if I'm not sent for interviews?' he would complain to Hen. 'If only I could get an audition, I'd get the part.'

'What with the whole of London up as competition? You'd be lucky,' Henry had retorted ruthlessly.

'Thanks for your confidence in my ability,' Sean had said in injured tones.

'Well, you do whinge on, it's so boring.'

Sean had said nothing further on the subject, and instead had poured out his complaints to the sympathetic ears of his two female flatmates, Judy and Melanie. He had been too proud to do this up until now, pretending all the time that work was just around the corner, that he was being considered for a major movie or TV series and then, when neither of these materialized, that he had been pipped at the post by a well-known actor. But as the months passed, and he was reduced to whatever part-time work he could get locally, he found the charade more and more difficult to keep up. He started blaming his agent for his lack of acting work and the two girls listened attentively and tried to offer reassurance.

No, he couldn't face Jan today. For one thing, he was looking too scruffy. He glanced down at his fading denim jeans, torn fashionably at the knees, his overwashed tee shirt and worn leather jacket. His training shoes were filthy and splitting everywhere. He quite liked looking this way, but he knew that she did not approve – although, he thought bitterly, it might make her realize what desperate straits I'm in. But he'd left a message on the answering machine so she knew where to find him if she needed him. Fat chance!

Three-quarters of an hour later, he strolled into the Theatre Centre, having first adjusted his one luxury, the very expensive sunglasses he'd treated himself to with the spoils of the last job.

The place was buzzing with activity. Everyone was out of work, it seemed. The café, which served a constant stream of light refreshments, was bursting at the seams with people. To his chagrin, his entrance went almost unnoticed, although he stood in the doorway surveying the scene for a few moments before threading his way through the thronging tables.

He was paying for a cup of coffee when he felt a hand

clapped on his shoulder and heard a voice that had the faintest twang of a transatlantic accent say, 'Just the man I need. How are you? What are you up to right now?'

'Hi,' said Sean, surprised, turning around awkwardly and racking his brains for his assailant's name. It came to him just in time. 'Oh, hi, Mike, good to see you.'

'Come on, come and sit down, we need to talk, man.' Sean winced at the sixties' familiarity, as he followed the older man to one of the only two vacant tables.

'You're looking great,' observed Mike easily, as soon as they were seated. 'What are you on?'

'Don't be daft,' replied Sean, grinning in an embarrassed way.

Mike ignored the remark. 'What are you up to?' It was the question all out-of-work actors dreaded most.

'Oh you know, this and that,' replied Sean airily. 'Waiting to hear about a TV series actually.' It was a lie and they both knew it.

Mike called his bluff. 'Wow, that's too bad. I could use your type of actor right now. Great part, too – right up your street –'

'When exactly is it?' Sean butted in just a shade too quickly.

They had met originally at the Academy when Mike had come in to direct an Arthur Miller play and they had got on well. Mike recognized Sean's talent and raw sexual energy; Sean had sized Mike up as a bit of a bullshit merchant, although a talented one. He might have guessed that it takes one to know one and that Mike saw right through his act. He had also timed his enquiry carefully. He knew that Sean desperately needed work and as the job he was offering was a splendid part, but with very little money, he knew that he was in with a chance of getting a splendid actor.

'As of now,' said Mike in reply to Sean's question.

'Who's dropped out?' asked Sean cynically.

'Listen, kiddo, I wanted you originally – as I say, it's your kind of part – but the word was out that you were busy.'

'Who said so? Not my agent surely?'

'Do me a favour, I don't talk to agents – they give me all kinds of grief. No, you know, just people around here seem to think you were up for some big TV or something, so I didn't bother to call you.'

Curses, thought Sean. Serves me right for shooting my mouth off.

'Anyways,' Mike continued, 'when Julian dropped out, I thought, I know just the nuthead for this job. I didn't have your number so I moseyed in here in case you showed. Or I thought maybe your mate Hen might be on the premises – you still hang out with Hen?'

Sean winced again at this extraordinary hippy-like jargon. Whatever sort of books did Mike read? What movies did he see? He seemed to have come to a grinding halt twenty-five years ago. He even dressed like it – faded jeans, long hair tied back in a pony tail, shirt open almost to the navel revealing a strange hieroglyphic device on a chain and a fair amount of middle-aged torso. Sean liked him though, in spite of his slightly off-the-wall philosophies and self-consciously anarchic ideas. He was always exciting to work with – a challenge. And what Sean needed at this moment was a challenge.

'Oh yes, Hen and I are still good mates.'

'He's a weirdo,' remarked Mike dispassionately.

Talk about the pot calling the kettle black, thought Sean to himself, but all he said was, 'He's all right, is Hen.'

Mike ignored this. 'So, you interested in this part or not?'

'Well, tell me about it, what's it like? What is it?'

Mike looked at Sean's eager face and knew he had hooked

216

him. 'It's your birthday and Christmas all rolled into one, mate. Just wait till you see it.' Mike was enjoying himself.

'When can I read it?' asked Sean, waxing more enthusiastic by the minute.

'Read it? Roll on, mate. You start rehearsals at two-thirty this afternoon.'

29

Sukie, with her swinging, silky, newly dark red hair, her lightly tanned body, her beautifully manicured nails and her delicious little linen suit in blue with matching pumps and shoulder bag, almost danced her way along the streets of Soho. She not only had a job, but she had been given her first assignment. The interview had been a mere formality. Her new bosses had been more than satisfied with her and, alarmingly, seemed to be under the impression that she had cast *The McMasters* personally and single-handedly, the only really unfortunate moment during the whole proceedings being when Diana, the head of the agency, congratulated her on casting Claire Jenner, the brilliant new girl in the series, and having the imagination to engage Jim Dutton, the American beefcake import from the American surf series. Sukie was quite overcome with embarrassment when these were mentioned, which they quite naturally interpreted as modesty, she deduced. Larry had obviously had a hand in all this. It was Larry who had cast Claire. Well, maybe he had done her a good turn after all. She should have left Geoff years ago. In her heart of hearts she knew that her relationship with him was a convenient habit. Well, she was out of it all now. She would resolutely put the pain and humiliation behind her. She knew from various girlfriends who'd been through the same situation that she would experience terrible withdrawal symptoms and appallingly diverse emotions. All had unequivocally recommended an affair with a younger man. Good for her ego. Make her feel young and desirable again. She actually quite fancied the idea. But that could wait. Now she was starting a whole new life, she was going to be financially independent again, her own woman, and here she was on the first leg of it.

They'd signed her up straight away, asked her if she could start immediately. She'd spent the afternoon learning the ropes in her new office. She was glad she'd found out about word processors and computers. She'd picked that up from her sons. The fax machine seemed simple enough, but what was really glamorous was that she had a secretary who dealt with most of the paperwork in any case. She felt strangely disoriented. The dizzying speed with which her life had changed over the last forty-eight hours had sent her spinning like a top. It was, it had to be admitted, exhilarating – especially as it was combined with the emptiness in her stomach.

Her step was light as she made her way to the underground. She was taking a tube to Fulham – the Arts Community Centre, wherever that was. There was an actress there who had attracted a lot of attention in her previous play and she was a possible candidate for the film she had been recruited to cast – the life story of Vasco da Gama. It was all tremendously exciting. She felt more alive than she had done for years. As she hopped on and off tubes, changing at Embankment, she thought briefly of the boys and smiled as she imagined them coping on their own. She'd rung earlier and left a message on the answering machine telling them where the food was, as if Ben needed telling – he'd be in his element, in charge of Nicky and the household. She had reminded Nicky to feed Brambles – Nicky would love it. He

219

would do his favourite trick of opening two tins and carefully putting half the contents of each into the same bowl with accompanying crunchy bits. He maintained that it made it more interesting for Brambles, like meat and two veg. The boys would be all right, she knew that much, relishing having the house to themselves – suddenly being deprived of both their parents, she realized. Well, that's the way things were going to be from now on.

She started to wonder what Geoff was doing and then hurriedly shut her mind to it. Geoff was no longer part of her life. He'd chosen to disregard her feelings and wellbeing, he'd chosen his path – so let him continue along it. It was not her business any more. She found herself at Fulham Broadway and got out, wondering as to the exact location of the theatre. She noticed several hand-printed fly posters for the production, then a hand-painted sign with an arrow indicating the direction in which the theatre lay. She followed the instructions and found herself entering what appeared to be a sort of community centre, Victorian externally with 1950s interior and additions. She went in and approached a girl selling tickets at the small card table that served as a box office.

'Just one, please.' Usually, agents and casting directors had seats reserved in advance, but this was a very casual arrangement. 'Is there a bar here?'

The girl, who reminded Sukie of the sort of girl she'd been herself in the 1960s, pale and dressed entirely in drab black, with long pale brown hair braided intricately with raffia, replied, 'There's a place where you can get coffee.' She spoke without much enthusiasm. 'Through there,' and she indicated some half-glazed swing doors.

Sukie thanked her and pushed through the doors to find a rather shabby area with plastic tables and chairs. There were quite a few people there already. Tea and coffee urns stood on the counter of a bar-like area, several cartons of milk and a large chipped glass bowl of white sugar, polystyrene cups and plastic spoons completed the picture. It was all very basic. For some reason, Sukie felt in urgent need of a large Scotch. She stood there undecided for a moment. There was a quarter of an hour to go before the performance started.

'There's a pub just across the road,' said a young man who was operating the urns and taking the money. It was as though he'd read her thoughts. 'I'm afraid we don't have a licence yet.'

Sukie smiled. 'Thanks,' she said, 'I'll have some tea later.' She hurried across the road into a very noisy gin palace. It was the sort of pub she loathed, but she needed that drink. As she sipped it thankfully, it suddenly occurred to her that she was probably suffering from delayed shock. She stood there thoughtfully, looking around her unseeing. She was in a strange new world – well, it was the same old world, of course, it was just that she was alone in it. She gulped down the rest of the whisky and, feeling suitably fortified, went back to the theatre.

I mustn't make a habit of this, she thought. I don't want to be one of those women who takes to the bottle when her husband takes a mistress or leaves her for a younger woman, or simply spends all his waking hours at the golf club. No, she was different; she was going to enjoy her new-found freedom.

She accepted a cast list from the girl on the door. The raked auditorium led down to an acting space that was no more than the size of a pocket handkerchief. Well, it was certainly intimate. The lights went down and, feeling decidedly cosy and warmed by the alcohol, she settled down to watch the performance.

Desire was a sort of English version of *A Streetcar Named Desire*, inasmuch as the plot was similar: a slightly unbalanced girl fled home from a violent, unhappy marriage, only to find it was a case of the frying pan into the fire, since there was a dangerously brooding Kowalski-type young man lodging with her family, the sexual tension between the two being apparent from the moment they met. It was an interesting little piece and the girl was certainly excellent. But, what really caught Sukie's eye was the young man's performance, which was mesmeric. He was tall, well built with dark good looks and piercing grey-green eyes. He was an extremely dangerous and magnetic young actor. For the most part he gave a still panther-like performance, but erupted violently every now and then. At the interval, Sukie could not wait to look at her programme. Sean Mallin. She hadn't come across him before, and yet he seemed familiar. Perhaps she had seen him after all, or perhaps he simply reminded her of someone else. The boy had talent. She had to cast him in this movie, but as what? All the male parts were cast. Well, she'd just have to keep an eye open for something stunning for him in her next project.

She'd already got the bug, she realized. It was thrilling. She also realized that of course it was the sense of power it gave her, having the ability to give someone the chance they'd always dreamed of. Someone who deserved it. She was hardly aware of the plot in the second half. She never took her eyes off him. He was riveting, there was no doubt about it.

Afterwards, she went to the little coffee bar again and spoke to the man there.

'That was a splendid show,' she said with genuine warmth. She had already deduced that he had something to do with the running of the place.

'Thanks – early days yet here,' he said, jerking his head

222

in the general direction of the auditorium, 'but we're doing well with this one – profit share, of course, but that's not unusual these days in fringe ventures.'

'I thought the young man was very good,' she said with feeling.

'Sean? Yeah, talented lad, doesn't work though – they don't appreciate looks in this country. Are you in the business?'

'Oh yes,' said Sukie, ready with her stock reply – I used to be, now I'm just married to someone who is an actor. Then she suddenly remembered. 'Yes, I'm a casting director, I used to be an actress.'

'Ah, so you're on the prowl for new talent – well, you've certainly come to the right place. And here's the boy himself,' he added. Sukie turned around and found herself looking straight into the piercing grey-green eyes. For a moment she was quite overcome, then she pulled herself together.

'I thought you were tremendous,' she said easily, holding out her hand. He took it and looked deep into her eyes.

'Thank you, you're very kind.'

'I'm Sukie – ' she hesitated, then said – 'Marlow.' It was years since she'd introduced herself thus. She'd taken her mother's maiden name as her stage name, it having a more romantic ring to it in her opinion than Wilson, which was her real name.

'Hello, Sukie Marlow, are you an actress? The name sounds familiar.' It was the first time anyone had said that to her in years; she felt absurdly flattered.

'I used to be – I'm now a casting director.' She tried to sound casual.

His eyes widened. 'Freelance?'

'With an agency. At the moment we're working with Minotaur Productions.'

223

He gave a long low whistle. 'Are you casting the Vasco da Gama movie?' he asked, impressed. Sukie laughed.

'Yes, I am. You obviously know all about it.'

'Lots of my mates have been up for it,' he said, sounding slightly bitter.

'Why haven't you?' she asked. 'I've only just come on to it. You should have been seen. Mind you, they're getting lots of actors from the Continent. It's on location in Spain and Italy mainly.'

'Yup, that's the trouble, I look too exotic — or at least so I've been told.'

'You look fine to me — and you're a fine actor. I shall look out for something for you.'

She knew she'd overstepped the bounds of professional etiquette, but she didn't care — she'd meant it. He gazed at her in admiration. She felt herself blushing slightly. It was a long time since she'd flirted with a young man and she had to say the experience was extremely pleasurable. But she'd gone far enough. She made her excuses and left, leaving him looking thoughtfully after her. She went home in a whirl of excitement and mixed emotions.

Ben had put Nicky to bed, but was waiting up for her.

'Had a good day, Mum?' He looked up from the Stephen King book he was reading.

'Absolutely terrific,' she replied, throwing down her bag.

'What's the new job like?'

'Oh Ben, it's wonderful. It's all right, darling, I shan't have to leave you every night — it's just that I've been thrown in at the deep end.'

'Best way to start, Mum. You're looking good on it,' observed her eldest son, revelling in his new role as head of the household.

The next day, Sukie bounced into the office.

'Drama!' announced Diana as she entered. 'We've lost an actor!'

'What? Who?' said Sukie, immediately on the alert.

'Can you believe this – boy gets a chance like this and has to go and play bloody rugger. I don't think he's got an unbroken bone left in his body.'

'Which boy?'

'John de Stefano.'

'No!'

'Oh yes. We are now minus Vasco da Gama aged twenty-six.'

Sukie thought hard for a moment. 'We're not, you know,' she said. 'I know the very actor for the job.'

30

Getting Sean for the part of the young Vasco da Gama had
not been as easy as Sukie had anticipated. The photographs,
videos, CVs had all to be obtained from his agent's office.
Jan Hunter, sensing a killing in the air, was obliging yet cagey
about his availability. A West End transfer was a possibility.
The fringe show had been a hit, he was being considered for
a major TV series, etc. The man was in demand. Yes, he
would be available to meet the American producers and they
did realize, didn't they, that he had received stunning notices
for his role in *Desire*? This, of course, was all to make Sukie
believe that he was worth more money than they actually
wanted to pay.

Sukie discovered to her surprise that she was more than
equal to the occasion. Yes, she did appreciate Sean's talent,
but Jan should remember that she, Sukie, had seen the play
and, good though it was, she thought it unlikely to transfer
without any stars in the present climate. And Jan did realize,
didn't she, that this was the opportunity of a lifetime? Any
young actor would be fortunate indeed to land a part in what
was, after all, set to be the major movie of the year, and not
only any part, but a leading role, and perhaps she, Jan, would
like to get her skates on and bike the stuff around to the office
as they would, of course, be seeing other possibilities. Jan
immediately came forth with at least three other actors she

226

wanted them to consider for the part. Sukie was beginning to get impatient. For God's sake, she wanted Sean to get the part, but the American money would need persuading. Was there anything other than an episode of *Casualty* on video? Yes, it transpired, one of *The Bill*, but he played a green-horn policeman in that and it seemed hardly suitable. There was something from *Robin of Sherwood*, but that was not recent. 'Send it,' commanded Sukie imperiously. And have Sean at the ready for an interview/video test, probably early next week. Jan capitulated. Sukie wondered if she dared ring Sean at home. It wasn't usually done, although she had known it happen. She asked Jan for his home number in case of costume fittings, etc. Jan obliged. Once she had got rid of her, Sukie rang Sean.

'Hi.'

'Oh hello, Sean. It's Sukie Marlow here. Perhaps you remember, we met last night when I caught your performance at the Community Arts Centre.'

'How could I forget? My God, it didn't take you long to find me something – I'm impressed!'

Sukie realized immediately that he was treating her like he might treat any casual acquaintance, certainly not with the deference normally accorded a casting director.

'Well, it's a long shot, you know. I mean, I know you're perfect for the part, but we have to contend with the Americans. That's why I'm ringing. You know how little imagination they have. I want you to come to meet them looking as much like the part as possible. Don't shave, don't cut your hair, and make it look as curly as you can, and if you would wear some sort of Harrison Ford-like garment, I'd be grateful.'

Sean laughed. 'Fear not,' he said. 'I appreciate your concern, Ms Marlow, but I have to keep my designer stubble

227

for this part I'm playing at the moment. You may recall I wear my hair greased back for Stan. It's actually quite long, and curls quite naturally with a little help from others, as Algy would say.'

It was Sukie's turn to laugh. 'Great,' she said. 'Oh yes, and I'm sending a script over. Be ready to come to meet them early next week.'

'When does the filming start?'

'Next month.'

'For how long?'

'Twelve weeks.'

'Oh boy!'

'It's the sort of opportunity you deserve. I'm just trying to do everything I can to help you get it.'

Sean mentally blessed whatever benign power it was who was looking down on him so favourably when he had suddenly decided to go to the Theatre Centre that rainy day.

'Ms Marlow, I really do appreciate what you're doing for me – thank you. What's the part like?'

'Sort of Harrison Ford, really, and, please, call me Sukie.'

'Okay, Sukie, thank you, and I'll do my best.'

'I know you will.'

The photos, CVs, video cassettes and all other relevant information had finally arrived and the script was biked off to Sean's little flat in Peckham, with strict instructions to the rider to hand it over personally. At 5.30 that afternoon the calls started coming through from Los Angeles, and Sukie faced her first real test. She sold Sean with as much verve and whole-hearted determination as she could muster. Diana had given her a big buildup as the hottest casting director in town, if not Europe. Sukie thought, not for the first time that day, how the whole of the entertainment business, certainly the film world, ran almost exclusively on bullshit.

Finally she had it all organized. The producers had agreed to see Sean and possible test him. Jan Hunter had been persuaded to be reasonable about securing his release from the play should it become necessary. Sean had been instructed how to dress and behave for the interview. All he had to do now was a show at night at the Community Arts Centre, and work on the film script for the interview. The girl in the play opposite him had been completely overlooked.

Sukie sat back in her chair, contemplating her success. It wasn't bad for two days in the office, she reflected. She gathered up her things and left the building. She was tired, it had all been quite a strain and so rushed. She was glad to find a seat on the train. When she got home, she found the boys already in the middle of their supper.

'That looks good. Is that one of your specials, Ben?'

'Yes, and there's plenty left for you, Mum.'

'We saved it for you,' volunteered Nicky, 'because it was so bloody good.'

'Nicky,' admonished Sukie laughingly. 'Well, thank you both, it's jolly nice of you to be so thoughtful.'

'It's only what you used to do for us,' said Ben simply.

'I must say,' said Sukie, as she accepted the plate of vegetable and cheese bake that Ben had placed in front of her, 'I must say, you seem to be coping very well with your altered circumstances. I'm very grateful to you both for reacting so splendidly.'

'Oh that's okay.' Nicky took it upon himself to be spokesman. 'We like it better without Dad. There's a better atmosphere.'

Sukie faltered slightly in lifting her fork to her mouth. She knew that she had helped in creating that earlier tense atmosphere.

They chatted happily, she telling them about the movie and

229

they bringing her up to date about their doings at school. It was a heart-warming time for Sukie. For in spite of her new-found freedom and independence, and her exciting new career, she knew there was a great gaping, aching void of a wound somewhere in the region of her chest and it was going to take some time for it to heal over.

She read Nicky a story that night whilst Ben went off to do his homework, then pottered happily about the kitchen. Suddenly she heard a noise in the garage. She froze. The kitchen back door was open, she was well aware. What a fool she was! Why the hell was she so casual about it, and what was she doing leaving her children alone at the mercy of any passing madman? All these thoughts rushed through her head as she waited like a trapped animal. The back door opened quietly.

'Geoff!' She almost burst with a mixture of abject terror that had suddenly become relief. Then disbelief took over. 'Geoff! What the hell are you doing here?'

'Hello, darling. I'm back.'

Sukie stared at him. 'What?'

'I've come home,' he said. 'If you'll have me,' he added lamely.

He stood gazing at her soulfully from the doorway. Sukie stared at him transfixed. They stayed looking at each other for a moment. Then the strain of the last few days, the deep hurt, humiliation, the exhilaration, the strange euphoria of mixed emotions suddenly came to a head and erupted.

'How dare you come here? Home? What do you mean, home? This is no longer your home, you forfeited all rights you had to calling it home! You've systematically abused it and me for years. It was just a place where you lived! From whence you could conduct operations! HQ! A home is a place where people live and trust each other. Live in harmony, together, in warmth and mutual support. Face life together. There's a code of behaviour, a set of rules, which I adhered to and you didn't. You cheated on me, you lied to me, you made a fool of me – oh yes you did, you deceived me year in, year out. You broke all the rules and the price you have to pay is that you can no longer call this your home. You don't belong here any more. We don't want you . . . This is not . . . your . . . home.'

The pent-up emotions finally became too much for Sukie and she started to sob hysterically. Geoff was by her side in an instant. He took her in his arms and held her there tightly.

'I'm sorry. Oh, Sukes, I'm so sorry. I've been a complete and utter bastard. I've ruined your life – and the boys – I just wish to God you could forgive me.'

Sukie continued to cry in his arms. He let her sob her heart out. Eventually, as her grief subsided, he stroked her head, trying to soothe her. Then he led her to a chair and sat her down. He made her a cup of tea and put the cup in front of her. Sukie smiled up at him weakly.

'I take sugar,' she said.

'Good God, do you?' said Geoff, amazed, and went to the wrong cupboard.

'It's in the canister on the top over there,' she said, half laughing.

He brought it to her and sat down opposite her, looking concerned.

'What do you say, Sukes? Can you forgive me?'

Sukie turned her tear-filled eyes on him.

'Of course I can. It takes two people to make a marriage, you know. There must have been something I wasn't giving you that made you turn to those other women. Maybe it was my preoccupation with the boys, maybe you could sense my resentment about giving up my career for you, who knows?'

231

Geoff stared at her astounded. He had no idea that she had been harbouring such thoughts. 'Your career? Why didn't you mention it? I would have been only too happy for you to continue acting.'

'Would you?' asked Sukie wryly. 'Anyway, darling, as I say, it takes two to make a relationship and I am quite prepared to accept my half of the blame.'

'I think you're wonderful,' said Geoff, with genuine admiration. 'It'll be better this time, you'll see. I'm a completely reformed character,' and he took her hand in his and stroked it.

Sukie shook her head slowly. 'You don't understand, do you?' she asked gently. 'There's nothing left, darling. Oh some happy innocent memories, yes – a sort of comfortable domesticity, of course – but I would never be able to trust you again. I can never forget that for years you lied to me. Our marriage was a sham, I will never be able to forget that. Yes, I can forgive you because basically I think you can't help yourself. I feel sorry for you, I suppose – but I certainly don't want to live with you any more. In the few days I've had on my own, I've tasted freedom for the first time for years. I've managed to get myself a job, which I'm enjoying enormously. I even flirted with a young man yesterday, mild by your standards, of course, but thrilling in its own way. The boys are fine. It's lovely having them to myself and watching them cope so well with the situation. In fact, all in all, life is much better without you. Oh yes, of course I will miss you. A lot. But I'll get over it. I don't need any more of the deep hurt and humiliation you've meted out to me over the years. I've got out and I'm staying out. Thank you for the comfort just now. I'd like to look upon it as a gesture of friendship for old times' sake. And now, I'd like you to go before Ben comes down. He's upstairs doing his homework. He's enjoying being the head of the household – the "man" about the place. I don't want to spoil that. Goodbye, Geoff.'

She had spoken in quiet gentle tones throughout. Now she rose with a calm dignity and went across to the back door, which she held open for him. Unable to speak, Geoff slowly got up. At the door he paused momentarily and looked at her with unutterable sadness, then left quietly. Sukie shut the door and locked it. Once in the security of the garage, Geoff leaned against the breeze-block wall and wept silently. Then he got into his car and drove away.

31

For just about the first time in his life, Geoffrey Armitage was at a loss to know how to deal with a situation. It had never occurred to him that Sukie would not want him back. He was utterly convinced that she had thrown him out in a fit of outrage and anger – understandably, he was prepared to concede, but they had had rows before and she'd always capitulated.

He had felt disoriented at Claire's. It was lovely to see her, be with her, certainly make love to her. But it wasn't home. It was unfamiliar. The sights, sounds, smells and atmosphere were strange. He missed the boys, even the bloody cat, for God's sake. But most of all he missed Sukie. Her easy-going, rather laid-back approach to the everyday things of life. Claire was temperamental, edgy, you never quite knew where you were with her – but with dear old Sukes – yes, he missed the burnt toast, the pile of washing in the middle of the kitchen floor, the hideous yellow of the walls . . . The walls, he suddenly realized, had had something different about them. They were still yellow in places, but patchy, areas had been replastered, lining paper had been scraped away as though in preparation. My God, she was having the place redecorated. It was sacrilege – she was destroying their home. No, he thought miserably, he had destroyed it. It was his doing. He'd had the best wife in the world and he had simply not realized it.

When she flung herself into his arms sobbing, he had not been surprised. That was exactly how he had expected her to react. He had thought that she would simply take him back into her heart and her bed, and their life would continue in the comfortable way it had done for the last sixteen years. It was hard on Claire, of course, as it had been hard on Patsy, but they were young. Heartbreak was part of the process of growing up. Married men having affairs with young girls was an everyday occurrence. They would get over it – in time. But for Sukie to tell him calmly and quietly that their life was over was unthinkable. He had fondly supposed that when he took her at her word and removed all his stuff, that after a few days she would be devastated and regret her hasty actions. At first he had liked the romantic buzz moving into Claire's place had given him, but he had known in his heart of hearts that it was temporary – that it would only be a matter of days before Sukie begged him to return to her.

A growing conviction came upon him that maybe Sukie was suffering from some sort of midlife crisis. She had certainly not seemed herself. All that talk of flirting with young men – well, he'd just have to give her time. Give it a week, she'd come to her senses. What on earth would the boys think? He wished he'd seen them, at least. He would have explained the situation to them, might even have enlisted their aid in persuading their mother to go on those hormone tablets, or whatever they were. He'd deliberately taken all his stuff as she had instructed, mainly to give her a shock. Of course, he reflected, the publicity was awful, but it happened all the time in their profession. It was an occupational hazard, and he'd come prepared to lie until he was blue in the face about it: a flirtation – infatuation: the girl had fantasized about him; someone had got the wrong end of the stick, had misinterpreted innocent actions; the papers were always doing this sort of thing and sometimes they got it completely wrong. There were endless ways of getting around Sukie and he'd been ready to try all of them. When he'd crawled back to her, he was going to pretend he'd spent the week with Hugh and Mona – they'd back him up – and if she found out the truth then he'd simply say that the time with Claire had been disastrous and only made him realize what a fool he'd been and how much he loved Sukie and what a wonderful woman his wife was. But he had not had the opportunity, and here he was out on his ear.

His belongings, of course, were all still at Claire's. Claire was there, doubtless sobbing heartbrokenly into her pillow. He was sorry to have made her unhappy – she was a lovely girl, talented, beautiful, classy, eminently desirable and, dear God, he was going to have to play scenes opposite her. He would have to get hold of Hugh – the situation would be intolerable. All these thoughts spun through his mind in a haphazard fashion as he was driving along aimlessly after leaving Sukie in the kitchen. He had heard her lock the door after him. The tears continued to course down his cheeks. He realized there was only one thing to be done. He'd made his bed, he'd have to lie on it. Well, Claire was a delightful girl. He'd get used to her somewhat spartan routine in time. He supposed he'd better telephone her first, give her a chance to get herself ready for him – as she would be so overjoyed she wouldn't want him to see her all swollen-eyed.

He spotted a telephone kiosk at the side of the road and pulled over. It was a phonecard machine. That was all right, he always kept one about his person so that he could phone Sukie from the rehearsal rooms or studios. It was starting to rain heavily. He dashed out of the car and into the booth. He took his diary out of his jacket pocket and found Claire's number. He heard the phone ring. It was picked up.

236

'Yes?' said a rather terse voice.

'Hello, darling, it's me – Geoff.'

'Yes, I know. All your stuff's here – I'm sending it around tomorrow, okay? I'm really not up to it tonight.'

'Claire darling.' There was a pause.

'What?'

'Darling, I'm coming round now.'

'Jesus Christ, surely you can wait twelve hours? I'm just getting it sorted . . .'

'Claire, my darling, listen, I'm coming back to you . . . that is, if you'll have me,' and Geoff gave a little chuckle, as though amused by his own witticism. There was a stunned silence.

'Claire? Claire darling, are you there?'

'Yes, of course I'm bloody well here. You are joking, I trust?' she said slowly.

Geoff laughed. 'I knew you wouldn't believe it. Yes, my beautiful girl, I'm all yours. I'm on my way round, but I thought I'd better call you first. Thought you'd like to be prepared for me.'

'Oh, how considerate. Look, excuse me if I've got this all wrong, but I was under the impression that you were, or should be, at this very moment, enjoying an ecstatic reunion with your long-suffering wife – ' She sounded cold, remote.

He interrupted her: 'What a fool I've been.' He tried to sound humble.

'Yes, you certainly have.' She was icy now – he had not expected this. He was prepared for tears of gratitude. Instead he was getting a passable impersonation of Snow White's stepmother. He wasn't having much luck with women today, he reflected.

'You sound awfully cross,' he said in a mock serious voice.

'I hope you'll be in a better mood when I arrive,' and he chuckled good-naturedly.

'You come near this flat and I'll call the police,' she spat venomously.

'Darling, please don't be so melodramatic. I'm not going to hurt you – I'm coming back to you. Don't you want me back?' What on earth was the matter with the female sex? They'd all taken leave of their senses.

'Who the hell do you think you are?' Claire had a sympathetic, captive audience of one in the shape of Sal, who had turned up and was helping her pack Geoff's things in black polythene sacks. 'Some sort of latterday bloody Jove, rampaging around, seducing all and sundry and abandoning them at will? You seem to have forgotten, you left me a long, and if I may say so, extremely turgid letter that frankly would have been better suited to the pages of a cheap novella.' Sally was nodding her head vigorously and giving Claire the thumbs up sign. 'You informed me that you loved your wife and were returning to the bosom of your family. After sixteen years of marriage, this is only natural and perfectly understandable and, of course, I realized you must do what you feel is right and proper. I respected that position. I have already spoken to Hugh and he has absolutely no intention of altering the scripts. So we will have to play the scenes opposite each other to the height of our histrionic skills. There will be absolutely no contact between us off set, other than that necessitated by the normal civilities of life. I am putting all of your belongings into a taxi first thing tomorrow morning. I'm off to Amsterdam shortly, where I intend to have the time of my life. Please do not telephone me again.' Claire put down the phone to a rapturous round of applause from Sal.

Geoff started to protest, then realized that she'd cut him off. He stood in the phone box stunned. He couldn't fathom it. In the old days he'd have had both of them eating out of his hand. He shook his head bewildered. He was losing his touch. What on earth was he to do now? He'd got to go somewhere. He needed, desperately needed, the comfort of a soft, feminine body next to his. A beautiful woman to explore and delight him, sweet smelling and compliant.

Patsy! Of course, the ever-obliging Patsy. He looked up her number, and then realized the units on his card were all used up. Damn! Oh well, never mind, he'd just risk it and turn up at her flat. She would welcome him at any rate, although, with the way his luck was running at the moment, he wasn't going to count on it. He got back into the car and started to drive towards Patsy's place. She lived on the other side of London. He sighed. He'd have to get some more petrol.

By the time he'd filled up, and stopped off to have a drink to fortify himself against the double rejection he'd just experienced, it was getting late. He arrived at Patsy's rather tawdry little place in Archway at getting on for midnight. She opened the door, deliciously clad in a negligée. She was in the middle of doing her nails.

'Oh, it's you,' she said surprised.

'Well, who else could it be?' asked Geoff, genuinely puzzled.

Patsy giggled. 'I do have other admirers, you know,' she said coquettishly. 'Mind my nails, they're still wet.'

'Do you?' said Geoffrey, shocked. 'I thought you were my girl.'

'Well, you haven't been treating me very well just lately, have you. You can't expect me just to sit at home and do nothing with my evenings.'

'I'm sorry, baby,' Geoff crooned, taking her in his arms.

'Mind my nails,' Patsy repeated crossly.

'Sorry. Listen, my adorable little darling, it's been hell for me, too, having to cope with temperamental, inexperienced new actresses, but Hugh made me promise to make things easy for Claire – it's important for the series you see.'

Patsy looked at him with wide eyes. 'But I should be playing opposite you. Why aren't I playing that part?'

'Because, sweetheart,' said Geoff desperately searching around in his befuddled mind for a plausible excuse, 'you're far too young and pretty for a silly old fool like me, they need a more m –' He was about to say mature and then realized she might misinterpret that – 'an older, less glamorous person than you. The public wouldn't accept us, now would they? We've broken all the rules, haven't we? Aren't we naughty?'

Patsy giggled again happily in his arms. 'I suppose you know best,' she said a little sulkily, 'but you did say before that we were going to have scenes together.'

'And so we shall, my darling, so we shall. And guess what, we're starting right now – I've left my wife, I'm all yours.'

32

Claire stood by the tree-lined canal in the Herenstraat. It was
a perfect day and Amsterdam was looking its best in the May
sunshine. She gazed in mute admiration at the imposing
seventeenth-century architecture, the lovely tall red brick
façades with their prettily sculpted tops of scooped out and
rounded baroque brickwork, decorated with white stonework
scrolls and globes; the numerous heavy wooden doors painted
a lovely deep, deep dark green, shutters and railings often
picked out in the same colour; cobblestones underfoot, the
sun glinting on the canals and on the glass tops of the river
boats that plied their busy trade up and down the waterways,
crammed with sightseers. Claire was enchanted with the place.
It was her first visit. There was a sense of being in a fantasy.

Her rejection by Geoff so soon after Roger's betrayal had
not hit her as hard as she had expected. She was badly hurt,
yes, but in a funny sort of way she was not surprised. Maybe
it was because she had never really believed the reality of his
arrival in the first place. The whole idyll had a dreamlike
quality and she had been only too aware of the faraway look
in his eyes. All the time he had been there, she now reflected,
she had half known it was all too good to be true, and here
she was, feeling raw but still alive, standing in the centre of
a foreign city, the centre of attention herself, superbly dressed,
coiffured and made-up, and by her side, one of the most

attractive men in the world. Passers-by and tourists alike had stopped in curious little knots to watch the filming.

Claire glanced up at Jim. He was quite breathtakingly handsome, dressed in superbly cut Armani casuals, his honey-coloured hair blowing slightly in the gentle breeze. He was wearing a considerable amount of tan make-up on his face and eye shadow, eyeliner and mascara on his eyes. How good men look in make-up, Claire thought. Geoff had looked the same on that first day's filming – she checked her thoughts abruptly.

She had given herself a good talking to. If anything was to come out of this second disastrous love affair, it was that she must learn something from it. She must learn to cope with the anguish of rejection. Perhaps there was something in herself that attracted, even invited, men to walk all over her – a deep-seated lack of self-worth perhaps. She had made a resolution to treat herself with respect, to love herself, to realize fully that she was a worthwhile human being. A talented, lovable girl, worthy of being treated as such. But first she had to believe it herself.

Sally had given her quite a stern lecture after this latest débâcle, had told her categorically that she was well out of it and she pitied the poor wife who had got this apology for a man back in her life again, just as she was tasting the first delights of a doubtless footloose and fancy-free existence. Not giving the girl a fair chance, Sally had observed dryly. A week of freedom hardly seemed a fair exchange for years of relentless infidelity. Sally was unremitting in her condemnation of the whole episode and strongly advised Claire to cancel and proceed, the whole affair being so absurdly brief as barely to warrant serious consideration, and certainly no tears were to be spilt.

Claire, for her part, wanted desperately to put the whole

sorry business behind her, but knew she was going to have to find the courage of at least six strong men to be able to cope with seeing Geoff every day for the remainder of the series, and play scenes opposite him. She had been true to her word. She had rung her agent, David, who had been surprisingly sympathetic about the whole matter, and had promised to speak to Hugh on her behalf to make sure the scripts were not altered. She was determined to rise above the situation. She recognized that her relationship with Geoff was possibly an infatuation whilst she was still trying to get over Roger. On the rebound. She kept trying to rationalize it, to play it down, to make it seem less important than it was. She had been flattered, that was all. He was very handsome, talented and charming. 'And the most notorious womanizer in the business,' Sally had pointed out ruthlessly.

'Sal, why didn't you warn me?' Claire had wailed when her friend had come over to help her pack Geoff's belongings.

'I did,' replied Sally unkindly, 'but you had become temporarily afflicted with selective hearing.'

Now Claire sighed heavily. What a complete mess the whole thing had been.

'Would you care to run some dialogue?' The husky American tone in her ear brought her back to the present with a bump.

'Yes, I'd love to,' she said, smiling willingly up at her handsome escort.

Jim was a great deal taller than Claire and he had to lean down to mutter in her ear. The crew were putting the finishing lighting adjustments to the scene that they were about to shoot. The director for this location, Douglas Jones, was to be seen chatting to the owner of one of the canal boats by the bridge, which was to be featured in the next setup. Jim took her arm and guided her away from the main activity. Steve, the lighting cameraman, noted their absence. He had been gazing at them down the viewfinder of the camera. Now, instead of asking them to stay so he could carefully light their features for the take, he instructed the camera grip to stand in for Jim and Terri to take Claire's place. Jim was blissfully unaware of the fact that British television finances did not run to the luxury of stand-ins for their leading artists. Steve, a man of easy-going temperament, knew better than to point it out. He could add the finishing touches during the final rehearsals. Jim led Claire a few yards away to the protection of a tree.

'It's gorgeous here, don't you think?' she asked him, looking around her entranced.

'Certainly is. Tell me, would you care to join me for supper this evening after we wrap? I'm told there's a hell of an Indonesian place here on Singel.'

'That's not far from here,' said Claire, marvelling at the ease with which Jim had sussed out somewhere to eat within a few hours of being in the place and being on the point of acquiring a partner to accompany him.

'Okay then, I'll pick you up in the lobby an hour after we finish, what d'ya think?'

'Well,' said Claire, feeling slightly railroaded, 'that's very kind of you. Shall we rehearse?' She neatly avoided answering.

'Okay, shoot!' They ran through the scene several times until they were both word-perfect and at ease with the dialogue.

'We're ready for you,' called out Dougy's assistant.

Claire and Jim came to stand on their marks, which were little pieces of coloured tape stuck to the cobblestones. They rehearsed the scene several times, then decided to go for a take. Jim immediately demanded a mirror in true Hollywood leading-man fashion. Sonia obliged, then handed the mirror to Claire so that she could check her make-up. Claire applied another coat of pale peach lipstick and they were ready to shoot.

'Quiet, please, everyone.'

'Turn over.'

'Sound running.'

'And – action!'

Claire and Jim played the scene well. They made a handsome couple and both were good at their jobs, Claire with her energy and sexy grittiness, Jim with his quiet American boyish charm. Once the scene was over, Larry Matthews suddenly appeared.

'We could do a remake of *Gone With the Wind*. You're dynamite together, you two – just been watching you on the scanner,' he said in answer to Claire's startled look. 'You look sensational and the chemistry between the two of you was burning up the cables!' he enthused.

Claire, blushing, was thrilled. She was glad to be thought a match for such a glamorous co-star.

'So that's why you weren't on the Norwich trip,' said Garry, Patsy's conquest of the sound department. 'Making sure you were on this one.'

Larry rounded on him. He didn't tolerate cheekiness from underlings easily. 'I'm here to make sure our new star is well looked after – and pretty young men like you should think twice before they speak or they're liable to get their bottoms smacked. Some of them already have, of course,' he added dryly, giving Garry a meaningful look. Everyone laughed uproariously and Garry busied himself with his sound equipment, rewinding the tape and looking suitably embarrassed. He put on the headcans and listened to the recorded dialogue.

'Sound is okay,' he said, finally, removing the earphones. 'We should do a wild track of background noise, though.'

'I'm so relieved that your peccadillo hasn't affected your work,' observed Larry with high sarcasm. There was more general laughter, but Garry refused to be distracted.

'Quiet for a wild track,' he called out.

'Quiet everyone, please!' yelled Dougy's assistant. 'Don't move – no talking, silence means SILENCE – THANK YOU.'

They all stood in utter quiet whilst Garry and his assistant recorded the rustling of leaves in the trees, the odd bird cry, the murmur of tourists' chatter, the muted engine of the canal boat and the splash of the water slapping against the banks of the canal and sides of passing craft.

When they had finished, Jim, astounded, said, 'Aren't you guys going to do close shots?'

'Don't worry, luvvy,' said Larry. 'Dougy will see you all right, won't you, petal? You'll make sure we capture Mr Dutton's handsome, chiselled features in close-up, won't you, Douglas?'

Dougy, unperturbed at being addressed thus, nodded assent. He was a man of few words, preferring instead to get on with the job, and was renowned for long, complicated shots without a cut and getting the filming in under schedule and under budget. He was also a prodigious drinker, but this did not seem to affect his work.

'Tracking two shot down to water's edge, close in on dialogue, back to two shot taking view onto boat, camera follows you as boat pulls away.'

'Got you,' said Jim, catching on quickly and thinking how different working methods were with the Brits. For a start they actually rehearsed. It was all so easy-going and unrushed and rather pleasant. So different from the frenetic factory-like conditions in which his series had been filmed.

He looked at Claire. About as different as anything he'd

come across at home. She was, he noted with approval, a natural beauty. The nearest he'd seen to her sort of looks was Jacqueline Bisset, whom he'd admired from afar. After the plastic starlets he'd been bedding for the past few years, Claire's loveliness was refreshing. Her nose, teeth, breasts and hair all seemed real. Her skin glowed and was of the Celtic type, liberally scattered with freckles. But the main attraction for him was her undeniable class – her accent fascinated him – and he was determined to get her into bed as soon as possible.

The rest of the day's shoot went off smoothly enough – they managed to cram in two other locations that afternoon. Lunch had been taken al fresco at a local restaurant. This made a delightful change from the usual film catering firms who were engaged and who could differ in quality from the very excellent to the very indifferent. It was a heavy schedule for both Claire and Jim as they were in virtually every setup. They finished at about 6.30, when the two actors were released, the film crew staying on briefly to pick up stock shots of the city and canals. As they entered the foyer of the Amstel Hotel, Larry waved at them from afar. He was seated on a high stool at the bar.

'Greetings!' he called out cheerily. 'I've booked us all in for supper at the De Boerderij – meet here at seven forty-five!'

'Lovely,' Claire called back, with a wave.

'Great,' said Jim with slightly less enthusiasm. He had been planning a tête-à-tête this evening with the lovely Miss Jenner, introducing her to Indonesian cuisine, and then with who knew what delights to follow. They separated to go to their own rooms and Claire had a much-needed relaxing bath. It had been a long day and her feet were sore from standing around in high heels. But she had put in a good day's work and she had sensed that Dougy, although saying little, was pleased.

Larry had been shrewd in his choice of venue. He had also saved Claire from becoming just another feather in Jim's cap – or, as he might have put it, another notch on his gun. The restaurant was a lovely, old-fashioned place, which reminded Claire of the film sets in *The Prisoner of Zenda*, and the food, which had to her mind a Germanic flavour, was delicious. Just about everyone from the crew was there and it was a jolly chummy evening. She felt that she belonged, and that people liked her. It was a start, she reflected, to her recovery from the recent disappointment.

Jim was immensely attentive, he sat opposite her and gave her his almost undivided attention for the whole of dinner. After the meal, they all decided to walk back to the hotel, it being a lovely evening. Jim took advantage of the situation to take her hand in his, and they sauntered along happily. Someone had the idea of a visit to the red light district. There were squeals of delight from the make-up department and they duly set off in that direction.

Claire was fascinated. She had never seen anything quite so blatant and yet so mysterious – women actually sitting in windows so that they could be seen. A man viewing a woman would then approach the door and she would rather reluctantly, it seemed to Claire, drag herself to her feet and go to greet him. Many of the windows were empty, for obvious reasons. All the sex shops seemed to be open, even though it was late at night, and there were many strip shows and live sex acts advertised. She and Jim had become separated from the others slightly. He suddenly pulled her inside the doorway.

'Let's catch one,' he whispered urgently in her ear.

'What!' said Claire, genuinely shocked.

'Come on.' And Jim pulled her down the stairs.

Before she knew where she was, she was entering the darkened world and pulsating music of her first live sex show.

33

They descended the worn-carpeted stairs in a dull yellowy orange glow, just light enough to avoid falling over. The sinister-looking man at the bottom of the staircase stopped them and muttered something unintelligible, taking a close look at Claire.

'It's okay, pal, she's with me. She's over age,' Jim said, taking out a handful of dollars. 'How much?'

'Fifty,' said the man, eyeing the dollars hungrily.

'I'll give you thirty,' said Jim blithely, obviously used to this sort of negotiation. The man shrugged his shoulders in a resigned fashion and gestured for them to follow him. The pulsating music grew louder as the man held back some curtains, and they went through into what appeared to be a small auditorium.

At first it seemed to be pitch black, then they were aware of a strange bluish light on the stage – in the centre of which Claire could discern moving figures. At first she couldn't quite make out what was happening. They seemed to be slowly dancing and gyrating. It was only after she and Jim had sat down that she realized fully what was going on. To her horror, Jim took her right down to the front. One thing was for sure, she could not see clearly and she could hardly believe what she could see.

A girl and three men were involved in the performance.

The girl was lying on a bed, writhing around as, one by one, the men lay on top of her, seeming to penetrate her, but Claire felt sure that it was simulated. Then with a great show of strength, one of the men pushed the others off and appeared to go down on her, then seemed to fuck her. One of the other men started to play with her breasts and the third with himself. The whole thing had a slightly comic air, mainly because of the bad acting, but then gradually Claire found her feelings changing. The scenario went on for a while, then the music changed and the girl sat on the edge of the bed and a man stood either side of her. She took a cock in each hand and sucked first one then the other and finally both at the same time. The third man was kneeling down in front of her during all this, supposedly sucking her labia. The girl then knelt on the floor on all fours, one of the men looked as though he was mounting her, one of the others was ramming his cock in her mouth and the third was lying under her and sucking at her tits. It was all curiously unsexy, as it was quite obvious that they were all pretending to enjoy it. It was very dark and impossible to see anything very clearly. The rhythm of the music changed abruptly again and they all changed their positions.

Claire glanced covertly at Jim. He was watching, his mouth apart and his eyes half closed. He became aware of her look and took her hand in his and held it for a while, then he quite deliberately placed it between his thighs. The bulge in his trousers was enormous and rock hard. Claire hardly dared breathe. She had never done anything so intimate with any-one she'd only just met in her life before. She had also never been to a live sex show before. Jim gently rubbed her hand over his cock, she felt a thrill of pleasure course through her. God, what was he doing? She had hardly even exchanged pleasantries with this man. She made a small impatient movement as though to leave.

Jim, misunderstanding, inclined his head towards her and whispered, 'Yuh, come on, let's get out of here.'

He took her hand and they left silently and quickly. Once outside the fresh evening air seemed sweet and wholesome. Jim never spoke a word as he hurried her back to the hotel. Once there, he strode up to the concierge's desk and demanded both their keys. Then taking her by the elbow, he steered her towards the lift.

'Your place or mine?' he muttered.

Claire said nothing, but just looked at him with huge eyes. The lift stopped at the fourth floor. They both got out. Again Jim grabbed her hand and almost hauled her along to his room. He inserted the plastic card that served for a key, opened the door, drew her inside and closed it behind them. Then he suddenly swooped down, picked her up in his arms and carried her to the bed. He slung her down upon it, not roughly, but certainly not gently, then tore off his jacket, tie and shirt. Claire gasped audibly. She had never been at such close quarters with so perfect a male torso. Sun-bronzed rippling muscles met her startled gaze and she mentally decided to abandon herself to what looked like being a very exciting night. He had eased himself on top of her and had straightaway pulled down the top of her dress and was sucking hungrily at her breasts. She felt helpless in the face of this display of unbridled lust. He started working his way down her body now, alternately kissing and sucking at her stomach, her hips, pulling the dress away, then easing his tongue inside her pants. She was glad she'd put on stockings – the sort that stayed up on their own – at least he didn't have to contend with tights. He pulled her pants off and, taking the lips of her vagina in his fingers, started to lick and tease her clitoris. She was almost beside herself with pleasure. His tongue was now probing her vagina. She felt she was going

251

to climax and was clutching at the covers of the bed in a frenzy, tossing her head from side to side.

He got off the bed abruptly and undid his belt, then unzipped his trousers. He pushed his shoes off without bothering to undo them. Then yanked off his socks. He did all this in the manner of a slow striptease. Then he let his trousers drop to the floor. She watched lustfully, as, looking at her, he started to rub the enormous swelling in his underpants, then very slowly he eased out what seemed to Claire the biggest penis she'd ever seen. It was erect, almost clamped to his stomach, his balls too seemed very large and hung down.

'Come and get me,' he said softly.

She needed no second bidding. She crawled down the bed and took the enormous shaft in her mouth, cupping the silky smooth balls in her hands as she did so. She heard him gasp and groan as her tongue explored the velvety smoothness of the helmet of his cock, then suddenly, she sucked hard at it. He pushed her head down with force to make her take more and more of it into her mouth. Then he pulled her off and, picking her up again, made her straddle her legs around him as he eased himself into her. Claire almost screamed as he did so. Then he carried her about the room as she rode his cock. They landed on the bed and she sat on top of him like a little girl having a pee, she always thought, and watched while his huge stalk went in and out of her cunt. She could feel the sharpness of him about to come as he released juices that drove her wild with desire. He turned her over and pushed her legs together under him so that she could feel his large satin-smooth balls rubbing against her thighs. It wasn't until he was on the point of orgasm that he kissed her. Her hand flew down to her clitoris, as she realized he was about to come, and she brought herself to the point of climax at the same time as he. They exploded together. He shot his load into her, while she had spasm after spasm of ecstasy, even after he had finished and was lying, spent, on top of her. She could hardly move or breathe, but she was satisfied.

She felt herself drifting off into sleep. She could feel the dampness of his sweat on her chest. They both slept soundly for what seemed like ages, but was in reality only about twenty minutes. On waking, he opened one eye and looked at her. She smiled back at him.

'Welcome to Europe, Mr Dutton.'

'You're really something, you know that?'

'I assume that's a compliment,' she replied.

'Hey, I'm thirsty. Let's see what's to drink in the mini bar.' And he climbed off her and, with his cock still incredibly erect, sauntered over to the other side of the room.

'Champagne,' he said gleefully, holding up two half-bottles. Claire's mind went fleetingly back to the last time she'd had champagne in an hotel bedroom. 'Lovely,' was all she said, however. He went into the bathroom and she could hear him pissing. Then he turned the taps of the bath on.

'I'm going to take a soak, will you join me?' She started to pull herself together. 'There's glasses in back of the cupboard,' he called out. After a moment Claire eased herself off the bed and went over to the cupboard. 'There are robes hanging on the door,' he added. Claire did as she was bid and carried the glasses and the luxurious towelling robes into the bathroom. He grinned up at her as he swished herbal gel around in the water. 'Champagne in the tub – beats the shit out of Barny's Diner.'

Claire assumed that this was the American equivalent of Joe's Café, so she smiled her agreement and delicately put a toe in the water. Then she climbed in and immersed herself in the steaming foam.

'Come on in, the water's lovely,' she said softly. He opened the champagne and filled the two glasses, carefully setting them down on the floor whilst he lowered himself gingerly into the bath. Then he leaned over and handed her a glass. They both slid down until just their shoulders were above the foam and lay there, luxuriating in the cleansing comforting warmth, sipping their drinks and gazing into each other's eyes.

'This is a bit of all right,' said Claire eventually, reluctant to break the silence but feeling that she must.

'How's that?'

'Paradise,' she said by way of explanation. 'Thank you, Mr Dutton, for my treat. It's not every day that I get to see a live sex show followed by another live sex show, you know.'

'You're really neat, you know that?' he said, grinning charmingly.

'It's the first time I've ever been to one of those.'

'You're kidding! You on the level?'

'Absolutely – was it any good? As you obviously know about these things.'

'About average, I'd say – but, gee, did it make me horny.'

'Yes, I noticed. That was a really lovely fuck, thank you.'

'My pleasure, ma'am.'

He took one of her feet in his hands and started to massage it. They stayed a long time in the bath, taking it in turns to wash each other, gently, Claire wonderingly running her hands over the hard muscled body. Eventually, they emerged, completely relaxed and happy, and wrapped themselves in the towelling robes.

'You gonna stay here?' Jim questioned her.

Claire shook her head. 'No, I'd better not. It's sweet of you, but we've got another tough day ahead of us tomorrow

and I shall sleep more soundly on my own – and so will you,'
she added.

'Okay,' said Jim easily.

'See you tomorrow,' said Claire blowing him a kiss.

'Surely,' said Jim pursing his lips at her.

She picked up her clothes and bag, and quietly left his room.
She scuttled along the corridor to her own suite and slipped
in. She had no idea as to Jim's marital status, personal affairs,
in fact knew very little about him at all. But one thing she
was sure about: charming and handsome though undoubtedly
he was, she was not about to fall for him. She thought this
as she snuggled down into her extremely comfortable bed.
He was a superb lover, too. Better than Geoff. She was
surprised to find herself smiling in the dark. Yes, Jim Dutton
had purged her of her physical longing for Geoff in the same
way that Geoff had rid her of her obsession with Roger. Well,
she wasn't about to become obsessed with Jim. She was going
to keep herself free and independent and, above all, available.

34

At 12.30 on the dot, Sean presented himself at the reception area at Diana de Charteris Casting Services. The girl on the desk was impressed. He was as good-looking as any of the models she had seen, but with an undefinable something that said 'actor'. A sort of quirky air of insecurity tempered with a defiant arrogance. A charismatic sexuality. A physical awareness and mental alertness. This one had it all and was tall, dark and handsome to boot. He flashed the girl a charming grin. She was enchanted. After a morning spent dealing with two harassed Americans, one loud and aggressive, the other loud and neurotic, who kept her busy with constant demands for food and drink of, to her mind, an outlandish nature – the pastrami on rye with dill pickle she could just about manage, thanks to the delicatessen on Old Compton Street, and she had had to make it herself – but where on earth was she to get a pineapple and coconut milk shake? In desperation she rang up Fortnum and Mason for this exotic drink and the iced cream of broccoli soup they also wanted. She had had to track down a video camera team, as the Americans had only just decided that they would, after all, test Sean, having stated categorically that they wouldn't. It had taken all of Sukie's powers of persuasion and patience. They had been all for hiring a little-known American actor, and at one point, in a bizarre set of coincidences, even Jim

Dutton's name had been bandied about, Diana having to explain that Sukie had already cast him in *The McMasters*. Then there was some chat of buying him out of the series. Finally they were talked into trying Sean.

'This guy had sure better be something special,' Bernard de Angelo, the elder of the two partners, had announced grimly.

'Oh but he is, I know you'll think so,' Sukie had gushed, hoping to God they could see what she saw.

Sean was instructed to wait in the reception area and flung himself into the plush cream leather and chrome chair. The receptionist, Linda, rang through to Sukie.

'Right,' she said. She put down the phone and, smiling at him winningly, held out some pages of a script. 'Ms Marlow says can you look at pages seventy-seven to seventy-nine.'

'I've already been given a scene,' said Sean, startled. 'I've learned it,' and he pulled out some battered sheets of typewritten dialogue from his back pocket.

'Yes, she knows that, but they want you to do this scene as well,' and she handed it to him as she came over to the desk. He took it back to the seat and immediately buried himself in the contents.

'It's all right, they probably won't expect you to know it,' said Linda, glancing at him anxiously as he started committing the dialogue to memory.

'My dear, er – I'm sorry I didn't catch your name,' he looked at her queryingly.

'Linda.'

'My dear Linda, if you would give me leave for a few moments, I shall be word-perfect. You see, what you don't quite appreciate is that I have every intention of walking out of here today with this part under my belt, so to speak.' And he gave her the benefit of another dazzling smile, then returned to his study. Linda retired, suitably impressed.

After about ten minutes, one of the doors opened and Sukie came out almost furtively, and said to him in a hushed whisper, 'I'm terribly sorry to keep you waiting. It shouldn't be long now. How are you getting on with the other pages?'

'Oh that's okay, I know them,' said Sean, who had risen to greet Sukie.

She gave him a glance of approval. 'Well done,' she said, looking him up and down. 'And you look wonderful – absolutely perfect.'

'So do you,' replied Sean disarmingly. Sukie laughed and retreated to the comparative safety of the main office. Linda gasped audibly at his effrontery.

He turned to her. 'They're building up my entrance nicely – wouldn't you say?'

'They always do that,' observed Linda knowledgeably. 'It makes them feel powerful – gives them the edge – don't let it affect you,' she added with concern.

She had taken quite a shine to this brash yet charming young man who was the most attractive male she'd seen in months. And God knows, there'd been enough of them coming through those doors. But this one had got something, she just hoped he wasn't too cheeky for his own good. Linda was a very pretty girl, with long ash-blonde hair and sparkling blue eyes. She attracted a lot of attention from the various actors who came in and out of the offices. But Sean's mind was on other things. The part. And Sukie. They were inexorably bound together – the way she had recognized his talents, had immediately put herself on the line, taken a chance on him. He knew how much she was risking for him. And she was an undeniably pretty woman. The pert features

258

and swinging silky red hair, trim figure and wonderful legs. He'd noticed the legs the other night.

Today she was dressed in the palest pink light wool suit with a very short skirt and a deep plunge neckline. High heels and a discreet glitter of diamanté at the ears and wrists completed the outfit. She had dressed unashamedly for the Americans. It was a showier look than she would normally assume, but she felt she needed to dress up for the occasion, she needed to pull this one off. She was going out on a limb.

Linda would normally have held considerable attraction for Sean, she was just his type – pretty enough for a dalliance, but no danger of getting involved. He had had a string of girlfriends, but had not had a serious involvement for a couple of years; the last one had become too heavy for him. Women didn't seem to understand. His career had to come first. It was his whole life. There was no room for emotional entanglements. But Sukie was different. For one thing she was older, considerably older, he imagined. At least ten to fifteen years, he guessed. And she seemed to care as much about his ambitions and aims as he did, and was prepared to devote herself wholeheartedly to them. The girls in his life so far had seemed intent only on getting him to make some sort of ghastly commitment, wanting to settle down with him and chain him to a mortgage and a family. It was all too horrible even to contemplate. He wondered idly what Sukie's personal situation was. He knew one thing for sure: if this job worked out, even if it didn't, he was going to ask her out. As a way of saying thank you. The calculating side of him also recognized that there would be a distinct advantage in having his own tame casting director. Not a bad move.

The door opened again and Sukie reappeared and came over to him.

'They're ready for you. I'm sorry it's taken so long. Just be your own charming self and it'll work out.'

Feeling a strange mixture of confidence and apprehension, Sean followed her into the main office. It was a large room panelled in light oak, which lent a period feel to it and made Sean feel thoroughly at home. The two Americans looked up expectantly as Sukie ushered Sean in. Bernard de Angelo was seated at a huge desk – to Sean's mind, the archetypal Hollywood film producer, small, stocky, Italianate, with bright humorous keen brown eyes. Deek Bradford was standing with his back to the window, an air of ill-concealed neurosis about him. He was younger, tall with thinning hair and gold-rimmed spectacles. Sean thought fleetingly that Diana de Charteris Casting Services should take them both on their books – they could get a lot of work playing Hollywood film producers.

'This is Sean Mallin, gentlemen,' Sukie said with the air of a conjurer producing a rabbit out of a hat. 'Sean, may I introduce the producers of *Vasco*, Mr de Angelo and Mr Bradford.'

There was a momentary pause while they all registered each other. What the two Americans saw surprised them: a tall, extremely good-looking young man in his early thirties, well built, with regular tanned features and just enough designer stubble on his chin, and dark, slightly curling hair, which was long by today's fashion standards, but perfect for the fifteenth century. He was wearing tight black leather trousers tucked into black boots and a denim shirt, opened enough to expose a fair amount of smooth tanned chest. The sleeves of the shirt were pushed up to show strong tanned wrists. He grinned boyishly as he approached them, his smile lighting up his handsome features. This was his stock in trade. He had perfected it over the years, ever since it had dawned on him

260

that he had been blessed with more than ordinary good looks. First he would give the unwary stranger the benefit of his brooding, smouldering handsome features, then he would break into a sudden smile. His face would utterly transform, his eyes would twinkle mischievously. His even white teeth gleaming against his tan. It worked now.

'Hey!' said Bernard de Angelo, impressed.

'Hi!' said Deek Bradford, his neurosis subsiding momentarily in the general radiance of Sean's smile.

They all shook hands and then Sukie directed Sean to a captain's chair in the middle of the room. He sat down easily, with one leg propped up on the other thigh, one thumb hooked in his belt, the other languidly resting on the arm of the chair. It was a studied, posed nonchalance and they liked it.

De Angelo opened the proceedings. 'You know about this little movie of ours?' he queried ironically, although he knew full well that the question was unnecessary. The entire world knew about the massive undertaking, it was a global event. Sean appreciated the irony – it was a commodity that few Americans possessed.

'I've heard it's terrific,' he enthused.

'Have you now? Well the budget's certainly terrific.' It was obvious that the money was Bernard de Angelo's chief concern. Deek Bradford adjusted his position to get a better view of Sean. De Angelo continued, 'You've gotten a look at the dialogue, Sukie here tells me.'

'Oh yes, I think it's wonderful.'

'You do? Well now, ain't that something – you think the dialogue's okay. Deek, what did I tell you?' he yelled triumphantly across at Bradford, although the latter had obviously heard for himself.

'What height are you?' asked Bradford abruptly.

'Six foot one.'

'What's the problem?' growled de Angelo. 'He's Costner-type height – looks like the Dalton guy with maybe a natz of Brosnan, who gives a shit?'

But Bradford was not to be distracted. 'Could you read something?'

Sean immediately got up. 'Of course.'

'I like his style,' said de Angelo approvingly, from the depths of the desk, picking up a cigar. Sean grinned again. A cigar! It was too good to be true.

'Wait,' said Bradford imperiously. 'We'd better get the video team in.'

'Hey, give the guy a break, will ya?' said de Angelo, puffing on his cigar.

'That's fine by me,' said Sean. 'Let me do it for the cameras, that way you don't have to sit through it twice.'

'I like his style,' repeated de Angelo to himself.

Sukie dashed into an adjoining room to fetch the camera operator. Sean glanced at his two interrogators, but they were preoccupied with their thoughts. The brief hiatus gave Sean a chance to collect his thoughts. Sukie came back in followed by a man carrying a video camera and another with a pup, a small lamp on a stand. They set themselves up immediately opposite Sean as Sukie directed.

'We need lines off,' said the older man.

'That's all right, Mr de Angelo, I'll do them, I have a script,' said Sukie eagerly.

'You wanna part in this movie, too, kid?' joked the boss.

'Doesn't everyone?' she laughed back.

'What da ya mean? Everyone's in it. The folks in this room are the only goddamn people in Europe that I haven't cast.' Everyone laughed dutifully.

Sukie found the page and took up a position next to the

camera, the time-honoured film-making tradition for a close-up.

'Running,' said the cameraman.

'Action!' barked de Angelo.

Sukie nodded to Sean and they launched into a scene between the hero and villain. All Sukie's past acting experience came back to her. She played the scene for all she was worth, knowing that the more Sean had to act opposite, the better he would be. The dialogue crackled. It went well, they both knew it.

'Cut!' said the self-appointed director. 'And print! – you both got the part.'

Deek Bradford was looking relaxed for the first time since he'd arrived in England.

'I don't need to see any more,' said de Angelo, leaning back in his chair. 'Call his agent and talk money – and –' he jabbed the air in Sean's direction with the cigar – 'I want you dirt cheap, okay? You're a terrific-looking guy and you're loaded with talent, but that don't mean I'm going to pay you any more. I'm giving you a hell of a break. We are talking international stardom here. You read me?'

'Yes, sir,' said Sean, who could hardly believe what was happening.

'You're just what we're looking for,' agreed Bradford quietly.

'Okay – that's it – get the guy a costume and let's see him on set in,' de Angelo glanced at his watch, 'five days from now – okay? Vamoose, scatter!' They took him at his word and all left the office hurriedly.

Once outside Sean turned to Sukie. 'Is he serious? Is this really happening?'

Sukie was jumping up and down. 'You did it! You did it!' She turned to Linda. 'He got it!' she cried happily.

263

'Oh wow!' Linda was genuinely thrilled. 'That's wonderful.' They both embraced Sean. Then Sukie pulled herself together.

'Right, now I've got work to attend to – plane tickets, hotel reservations, your agent to talk money to, costume fittings – keep yourself available, don't go anywhere,' she commanded.

'What about the play?' asked Sean anxiously. 'I hate letting them down.'

'How much longer did you say you had to run?'

'Just to the end of this week.'

'Then you can do it.'

'But there was talk of a transfer.'

Sukie gave him an old-fashioned look. 'If they've got any sense, they'll hang on for the transfer till the movie's released. You'll be a star then – they'll pack the place out! Don't worry, I'll sort it all out. Just don't go anywhere other than the theatre.'

'All right,' he agreed, 'but only on one condition.'

'I beg your pardon?'

'That you'll have dinner with me tonight after the show.' Sukie beamed at him. Linda pretended to get on with urgent paperwork. 'Will you?' he pleaded.

'Thank you, but I can't – truthfully,' she replied, remembering Ben and Nicky at home; she must see them tonight. 'But what I will do is join you for lunch in a couple of days when I've talked to your agent and organized everything. That way we can combine business with pleasure.'

'You're on,' said Sean delightedly.

35

Geoff awoke to find himself gazing blearily into the beady eye of a floppy pink animal of unidentifiable strain. He hurriedly shut his eyes tight, hoping that the nightmare would dissolve in due course. He could hear the murmur of someone speaking quietly somewhere – a woman's voice. He had no idea where he was. There was a strange, sickly sweet perfume wafting about the airways. Where the hell was he? What day was it? Did he have to go to work? He had an idea that it might be Sunday, he also had a vague memory that Sundays hadn't been too good of late. He resolved to sleep through this one. The murmuring voice continued. Geoff tentatively opened an eye again. Yes, the ghastly pink thing was still there. Gradually his eyes closed, and the low hum of the voice in the distance lulled him to sleep.

Patsy was in the living room. It was indeed Sunday morning and Tony Snellor, confident of finding Patsy at home, had rung early to find out what the latest was, and to get something set up for the following week. As usual, Snellor's nose was on overdrive and was telling him that something was afoot. There was a story lurking round the immediate vicinity of the set of *The McMasters*. Patsy was behaving peculiarly. She was covering for someone, he felt quite sure.

'It's very good of you, Tone, to take so much trouble over me,' she cooed.

'We think you deserve a break, Pat love. How's it coming along?'

'Well,' said Patsy, suddenly lowering her voice even further, 'they haven't built up my part like you said they would.'

'Give it time, Pat, give it time. Have you got someone with you?' he asked abruptly.

'I actually had a scene cut in the last episode,' she persisted bitterly.

'Your boyfriend with you for Sunday, all nice and cosy? Remind me of his name again.'

'I don't have a boyfriend, well not on a regular basis, at any rate.'

'Why are we whispering then?'

'I've got someone staying with me,' said Patsy, suddenly finding her wits.

'Oh,' said Snellor, disappointed. 'Any more on the Claire Jenner/Geoff Armitage front? They still shacked up together in leafy Kingston?'

But the cutting of the scene, her best one, still rankled with Patsy. 'But you said you would make me more popular.'

'Pat, Patsy, listen, we've had dozens of letters in – the readers all love you – they want more pictures – they can't get enough of you. Now when can you do them – on set this time, please – when would be best?'

'It was my best scene,' said Patsy, aggrieved, 'and they don't let people on the set – only the official photographer.'

Snellor capitulated. 'Tell you what, Pat, how does five thousand pounds sound to you?'

'What do you mean?'

'Look, Pat, it takes time to build up a following and sometimes longer for the nobs to realize it. Sorry about your scene – they'll catch on soon. In the meantime, I'm offering you a nice fat consolation prize – five thousand smackers. Think about it – think about all the snazzy little outfits you could buy with that.'

Five thousand pounds! She realized that it was the equivalent of payment for several episodes.

Snellor took advantage of the lull in proceedings. 'We were thinking of a sort of weekly column – you know – general goings-on on and off the set. The readers would love it – snippets of gossip, possible story lines and developments – we could even ask the viewers what they think. You may be sure they'll vote you in. We could gear it to give you a boost, you know: "And when will the voluptuous, talented Miss Hall get her big break? This stunning actress deserves better – scriptwriters take note".'

'Ooo!' Patsy gasped.

'That's right,' urged Snellor, feeling that at long last he was getting somewhere. It had actually been Trevor's idea, prompted by Snellor – 'She's sitting on something red hot, Trev, I know it.'

'Please, no filth,' Trevor had held up a deprecating hand. 'The readers don't want filth, just good old-fashioned dirty innuendo,' and he had chuckled to himself.

As always Snellor felt he'd missed something. Trev had the effect of always making him feel a couple of beats behind. He'd got to crack this one. For once, Trevor came to his rescue.

'We'll pay her,' he snapped. 'I can't take much more of this Saturday morning spread of Miss Busty Blonde Bombshell Bimbo nonsense. My wife's beginning to smell a rat. We've got to have a story to back it up. She's making us look foolish. Offer her a couple of thousand – you can go to five if she's prepared to dig the dirt, and I mean all of the dirt.'

Patsy agreed to think about it. She had been anxious to get Snellor off the phone. Now that she knew they were prepared to pay her, she knew the ball was in her court. And the idea of all that money to spend on herself was irresistible.

She put down the phone and tiptoed back to the bedroom. Geoff was sound asleep in the bed, surrounded by her toy animals. How sweet, she thought, he was actually embracing Lucky, her pink llama.

She left the room quietly and went to the bathroom, where she applied the considerable amount of make-up that she wore all the time, including in bed, but which had become streaked and patchy after the exhausting lovemaking in which she and Geoff had engaged the previous night.

The odd thing was, she thought to herself as she started to repair the damage, she found the whole proceedings rather distasteful. She knew that something must have gone wrong with Geoff and Claire and she hated being a replacement. Her native cunning told her that Geoff was only using her, and she suspected that both Sukie and Claire had thrown him out.

There was, to be sure, a certain satisfaction, and not just a physical one, to be gained from knowing that he still found her desirable. But she also knew that most men found her so. Bedding Garry from the sound department had whetted her appetite for young men and lovemaking with Geoff had confirmed that. First of all, he had trouble getting an erection. He had said he thought he was becoming impotent, but then spent most of the rest of the night proving he wasn't. Also, she was thinking longingly of Jim Dutton's superb physique, so taut and compact in contrast with Geoff's out-of-condition, flabby torso, and potbelly. She was beginning to realize, in her own dim way, that Jim had been brought into the series as a new leading man – a contemporary sex symbol. Geoff had had his day and would become a sort of patriarchal figure. Patriarchal was not what Patsy was thinking, as she was not familiar with the word. Older man of the series was nearer the mark. No, she decided, as she carefully applied her eyelashes, she and Jim would make a perfectly glamorous couple, and with that five thousand pounds she would be able to buy a wardrobe suitable for her new status. She cleaned her teeth and doused herself liberally with perfume for the third time that morning. Yes, it was Jim Dutton for her, but she was going to make certain that Geoff Armitage knew what he was missing. She completed her toilette and wafted back into the bedroom. Geoff stirred and blearily opened his eyes. His silver hair was dishevelled and sticking out all over the place. He pulled himself up on one elbow exposing his sagging chest muscles and potbelly. Ugh, she thought, he looks so old! She said in a whining tone, 'Ooo careful, you're hurting Lucky.' Geoff's elbow had inadvertently lodged in Lucky's pink fluffy gut.

'Oh God,' groaned Geoff, wrenching the unfortunate creature out from under his arm and flinging it across the room.

'Oh nooo!' cried Patsy in dismay. She rushed across to rescue Lucky where he had fallen. 'Oh, poor baby,' she crooned, as she cradled him in her arms. 'It's all right, darling. Mummy's here, all better now.'

Geoff groaned again loudly and collapsed back on to the bed. 'What day is it, and what the fuck is the time?' he asked in muffled tones from the depths of the pillows. He had identified the pungent sweet aroma as emanating from Patsy herself – how could he ever have been deluded into thinking it was attractive.

Patsy, still clutching the llama, looked at him dispassionately. 'It's Sunday and it's ten o'clock. I think it's time you went home. Your wife will be wondering where you are.' It was a stab in the back and she intended it to be. She could put up with an inadequate lover but wanton cruelty to her beloved toy pets she would not tolerate.

Geoff suddenly sat up and cried out. He had a terrible hangover. He had been steadily drinking through the evening without realizing it. He grabbed the numerous other toys that all but obliterated the pillows and hurled them in all directions in mute rage.

Patsy became hysterical. 'Get out! You monster!'

Geoff flung himself out of bed, grabbed his clothes from the chair and started pulling them on. Patsy, crying, was scrambling about the room rescuing her animals.

'Poor babies,' she sobbed.

Geoff turned on her. 'You stupid little bitch,' he snarled. 'Why don't you grow up? I suppose you imagine that this simpering little girl act you've perfected is irresistible, don't you? Well, it's not, let me tell you – there are real women out there, or hadn't you noticed, you pathetic little bimbo?'

Patsy stood there, tears streaming down her face, clutching her toys to her ample bosom.

'Just because you couldn't get it up last night, you take it out on poor, innocent little creatures. I call that pathetic – oh, and I know you only came here because Sukie and Claire wouldn't have you. Yes, that's right, isn't it?' as she saw his reaction. 'Well, I don't want somebody else's leftovers, thank you very much – I'm going to find myself a real man, if you must know!'

'Good luck!' said Geoffrey tersely. 'You're going to need one to look after you because you're sure as hell not going to be able to support yourself, not on your minimal talent.'

Patsy stared at him. 'What do you mean?' she gasped.

Geoff picked up his mackintosh and the briefcase containing his script and made for the door.

'My dear,' he said turning and giving his best Gary

Essendine from *Present Laughter*, 'my dear girl, you've about as much acting ability as the Pope's left buttock!' And he swept out, slamming the door behind him.

Patsy stood transfixed for a moment, then she sprang into action. She made for the telephone and rifled through the address book with the white leather cover tooled in gold that resided permanently beside it. She found Tony Snellor's home phone number that he'd left her in case of anything 'cropping up'. His wife, Mary, answered the phone.

'Oh hello, dear. Tony? Oh yes, he's here, you've just caught him before the pubs open, hang on,' she said in a long-suffering voice. Snellor came to the telephone.

'Anthony Snellor here.'

'Hello, Tony, it's Patsy Hall. Listen, I've thought over your offer, and I find it most acceptable. Give me a week and I'll tell you everything you want to know. I can meet you as per arrangement on Friday for lunch, and I'm going to let you have all the information you want – all of it.'

36

It was strange, Claire reflected, sitting nonchalantly in the back of the studio car, next to one of the most handsome and desirable men in the world as though they were mere acquaintances – no one would have believed that intimacy had taken place between them. To be sure, Jim's compact muscular bulk occupied a considerable amount of the back seat and his strong thighs, the shape of the muscles clearly visible beneath his beautifully cut stone-coloured slacks, occasionally brushed against Claire's dainty knee as the car lurched around corners. She was, however, very aware of his physical nearness. The faint musk tang of his aftershave, the animal smell of his leather jacket were all potent reminders of the lustful evening they had spent together. She felt a stirring in the region of her loins as the memory flooded back to her. She glanced at him sideways to see if he had noticed anything. She found him gazing at her steadily. She blushed.

'Am I right or am I right?' he asked quietly, giving her an amused grin.

She giggled. 'I thought the filming went well, didn't you?'

'Sure thing – slow as hell, though.'

'Slow?' she asked incredulously. 'We fairly whipped through that scene in the Rijksmuseum.'

'That's because we had the goddamn officials breathing

down our necks. Listen, honey, we could have gotten two segments of *Beach Guardians* in the can in the time it took us to rehearse one scene of this baby. No, I'm just kidding,' he smiled, seeing her expression. 'It's just that we never ever get around to rehearsing for TV in the States. Haven't you noticed how spontaneous my show is?'

'Oh yes – very,' lied Claire. She had never actually seen a single episode of Jim's series.

'Well, that's because we never rehearse, we just shoot it. I hope these boys know what they're doing.'

'Of course they do.' Claire was defensive. 'I thought the scene in the hotel bar went very well.'

'I thought the one in the hotel bedroom went even better,' he countered.

Claire glanced at the driver to see if he had heard. He appeared to be oblivious.

'Yes, I liked that one, too,' she said airily, playing the game.

'I would have liked a retake or two,' said Jim running his hand surreptitiously along her thigh.

Claire thought fast. 'Oh, I was pleased with the way things went,' she said as levelly as she could, 'but I'm looking forward to doing other scenes with you.'

'Perhaps we should rehearse right now,' he suggested with a gleam in his eye.

'What now?'

'Back at my place. There'll be new dialogue waiting for me, we could run through a couple of scenes.' There was no mistaking his intentions.

'I need to get home, I really do – just to sort things out, you know?' she said hesitantly.

'Okay, I read you. How's about if I drop by later?'

Claire could think of no good reason why not. She also

reckoned that Jim was enough of a gentleman to take no for an answer if it came to it.

'I know, why don't you come over for tea – a real English tea. I'll do you cucumber sandwiches and sponge cake and crumpets and Earl Grey tea. I'll get my friend Sally over to meet you. It'll be fun and then we can read the script to her, she's a good audience.'

'Hey, that sounds really neat. I appreciate your hospitality. You better give me your address.'

Claire felt sure that the chauffeur's ears were on fire but she didn't care. She tore a page out of her Filofax and wrote her address and telephone number on it.

'What time shall I come around?' he asked.

'Tea-time, of course – four o'clock, when else?'

'You're on.'

'Excuse me, sir, around here somewhere, isn't it?' the chauffeur interrupted deferentially.

'Oh yeah, thanks – er – up this boulevard, er, then just past the condominium block – pardon me, have I said something amusing?' he asked as Claire giggled.

'Not at all,' she said apologetically, 'but this is a street, possibly an avenue and that is a block of flats.'

'You don't say,' said Jim wonderingly. 'I wonder how long it will take me to pick up British-style talk. Okay, kid, see yah,' and Jim prepared to get out of the car as the driver pulled up outside his little house.

'It looks very pretty,' said Claire peering out of the car window.

'So do you, kid,' said Jim, suddenly kissing her on the lips. He tasted fresh and sweet, a man who didn't smoke, she realized – a failing of both Roger and Geoffrey. It was the first time she'd noticed – probably because of the hectic nature of the lovemaking that night. She waved goodbye

274

to him as he picked up his luggage and went indoors.

'Where to now, miss?' asked the driver.

'Kingston, near the park gate, please.'

'Very good, miss.' They drove on in silence. 'Seems a nice gentleman,' the driver observed after a while, as they bowled along towards Hammersmith.

Claire became immediately convinced that he was in the pay of the press and refused to be drawn. She just smiled and muttered, 'Yes. Could you possibly go by some shops – I need to pick up a few things?'

He obliged and they drove on without any further exchanges until he pulled up outside a little parade where he could park at the top of Richmond Hill. She hopped out and soon came back laden with purchases. As they sped off, she looked apprehensively out of the windows for any signs of press cars – but could see nothing suspicious. Clutching her shopping and followed by the driver with her luggage, she made her front door without incident. She tipped him, went to put on the kettle, then she phoned Sally and left a message on the answering machine.

'Hi, Sal. I'm home. Come over to tea as soon as you get in. I want you to meet Jim Dutton, he's really hunky.'

That should do it, she thought to herself.

She made tea, unpacked her case and then the shopping. She smiled at the thought of giving Jim English tea, quite a sedate contrast to the night of uninhibited lovemaking they'd been through together. She spent the next hour carefully making delicate thin cucumber sandwiches and laid them out on the best china. She put a lace cloth on the kitchen table – it would be more fun, less formal in the kitchen, she decided. Out came the silver teapot, milk jug and sugar bowl bequeathed to her by her maternal grandmother. She found, to her great delight, sugar lumps in one of the cupboards.

She also discovered some sugar tongs and suddenly remembered sets of small silver knives and apostle teaspoons. She chuckled happily at the thought of Jim coping with this dainty arrangement.

Three-thirty – just enough time to wash and change. She would put on her long white summer dress, the one she'd worn in Greece when she and Roger had been there together two years ago. It was May now, but there was an early heatwave in progress. She went to the bedroom window and opened it. Then she remembered the press, and peered out. But all was quiet and there were no extraneous cars lurking. She padded into the bathroom and had a cat wash and splashed cologne over herself liberally, then returned to the bedroom where she slipped into the charming white gown. She brushed her hair vigorously and let it fly around her face in a cloud.

There was a rap at the door.

He's early, thought Claire, glancing at the little silver watch on her wrist. Well, that's understandable, he would have no idea how long it would take to get here. There was another rap.

'Okay, okay, I'm coming. My, we are impatient, aren't we?' She ran to the door. 'Good God, Roger!'

'Yes, it's Good God Roger,' he affirmed cheekily. He was standing there, brazenly grinning at her, clad as usual in tight jeans and shirt open to the waist. His hair was far too long and looked dreadfully old-fashioned and he had a look on his face that she couldn't fathom and certainly didn't relish.

'What on earth are you doing here?' she asked bluntly.

'Well, I don't call that much of a welcome. Aren't you going to ask me in?'

She didn't move. 'I said, what do you want?'

'A little chat for old time's sake,' he said easily.

'It isn't convenient – I'm expecting some people over.'

'Oooh, is it a party? How jolly. Can't I stay and join in the fun?'

'You're not invited,' she said icily.

'Oh come on, Clairey, loosen up. I've got some photos to show you, that's all.'

'I don't want to see any photos, thank you,' she said firmly.

'You'll want to see these,' he said brandishing a large envelope and suddenly pushing her into the hall, slamming the door behind them.

Claire yelled, 'What the bloody hell do you think you're doing?'

'Come on, be a good girl, don't make it difficult – look,' he said, pulling out the photos and waving them in front of her face.

She gasped; they were nude shots of her. She remembered they'd taken them in one of their many hectic lovemaking sessions. Roger featured in some of them, but mainly they were of Claire in varying degrees of undress, even bondage.

'Jesus,' she gasped.

'I doubt if he can help you,' he muttered, grabbing hold of her and dragging her into the bedroom.

'What the fuck do you want?' she screamed at him. He pushed her down onto the bed violently and started to unbutton his flies.

'I want it to be like it was, Clairey, you and me making violent love together,' he murmured urgently.

'No!' she yelled. He hit her hard across the face, she could see his erection getting larger as he did so. She screamed again. He pulled up her dress and tore at her panties. She screamed again. He hit her again, harder. She started to cry.

'No, please, please, don't, please,' she begged him.

'That's what I like to hear. You beg, baby, go on, beg,' and again he hit her. She started yelling in earnest and frantically tried to throw him off her. But he was too strong and pulled her hands back onto the bed and started to try to thrust his cock into her. Her one thought was that if he succeeded, she might become pregnant again and she fought desperately to prevent him. She kept on screaming – surely someone would hear her. The window was open – where were the press when she needed them?

Suddenly she became aware that someone else was in the room. And equally suddenly it was all over. Roger was dragged off her and she heard the sound of the smacking of fists into flesh. She pulled herself up and her astounded gaze saw Jim, who had Roger by the throat and seemed to be shaking the life out of him.

'What the hell do you think you're doing, buddy?'

He let go of him and then grabbed what he could of his shirt collar and delivered a massive right punch to Roger's jaw. Roger crashed to the floor. Claire scrambled off the bed.

'You okay?' asked Jim casually.

'Oh yes,' breathed Claire, 'God, thank heavens you arrived when you did.' Roger stirred on the floor.

'Hey, asshole, who told you to wake up?' and Jim thumped him again. 'Where's his motor?' he asked curtly.

Claire ran to the front door and peeped outside. 'That's it, there,' she cried gesturing to a black Mercedes convertible.

Jim had followed her into the hall. Now he turned and went back into the bedroom. He yanked Roger up off the ground and carried him out in a fireman's lift. A car pulled up opposite and Sally got out. She stood watching amazed at the little scene being enacted. Jim was virtually tipping Roger into the car. Sally ran across the road.

'Hey, did I miss something?' she asked, wide-eyed.

'Nice motor – shitty guy,' said Jim, by way of explanation.

'Come on in,' said Claire urgently from the doorway.

'I'm Sally, Claire's mentor and confidante,' said Sally, extending a hand.

Jim kissed it. 'It's my pleasure, ma'am,' he said. Then examining his own knuckles ruefully, he added, 'Do you think you could kiss this for me?' He gave her the benefit of his famous dazzling grin. Sally almost fainted.

'I think I'll have to have some tea first,' she said weakly.

'Come on in, for Christ's sakes. If the press are around they'll be having a field day.' They both went indoors and into the kitchen.

'Tea won't be a moment,' said Claire, looking flushed and rumpled.

'What on earth have you been up to? Oh sorry, silly question,' said Sally, looking embarrassed.

'Oh nothing like that, well, not with Jim anyway.' They sat down at the kitchen table.

'Do you take milk in your tea, Sir Lancelot?' Claire asked Jim.

'I'm not sure. Back home I drink coffee.'

'Was it my vivid imagination or was that the dreaded Roger that I saw being emptied into that rather smart vehicle?' asked Sally with interest. 'Could you pass the sugar, please, Jim? – thanks.'

'Yes, that was Roger all right,' replied Claire, 'and if it hadn't been for my knight in shining armour here I might not have lived to tell the tale – although, come to think of it, you were pretty punctual yourself, Sal.'

'What happened? Be brief and succinct if you can, as I'm keen to sample a crumpet.'

'Try a cucumber sandwich, they're delish – Roger was trying to rape me.'

'I don't believe it!'

'You better believe it,' said Claire with feeling. She

279

suddenly remembered the photographs. 'Excuse me a minute,' she said, getting up from the table. She dashed into the bedroom. The photos were on the floor and had gone unnoticed in the scuffle. She hurriedly picked them up and rammed them into a drawer. Then she saw her watch lying on the pillow.

'It's all right, I found it – I thought he had broken it,' she said, returning, holding the watch aloft.

'Dear God, he might have killed you,' Sally said explosively. 'What on earth possessed him to behave like that?'

'Who is this bum, anyway?' asked Jim, tucking into cucumber sandwiches with relish. Claire shot Sally a warning glance.

'Oh, just some creep that's been after me for years,' she replied airily. 'Don't eat those too quickly, you'll get indigestion. More tea anyone?'

'You've just been the victim of an intended rape and here we are having tea as though nothing has happened,' said Jim, shaking his head incredulously. 'Now I really believe I'm in England.' Later on, when had excused himself to go to the bathroom, Claire told Sally about the photographs.

'What are they like?' asked Sally.

'Dodgy.'

'How dodgy?'

'Seriously dodgy. If the press got hold of them, or even got to know about them – well –'

Sally whistled. 'It's a bloody good job he left them behind then, isn't it?'

'He's got the negatives,' said Claire heavily.

'Oh no!'

'Well, they're not in the envelope, so he must have.'

'What are we going to do?'

'We?' asked Claire surprised.

'Of course we. We've got to get them back somehow.'

'Easier said than done,' said Claire grimly.

'Let's ask Sir Galahad what he thinks. He saved someone from disaster every week in his series. He's obviously finding *The McMasters* a bit tame.'

'Hey, girls, what say we all catch a movie tonight?' asked Jim reappearing. Jim's idea of paradise was a night on the town with a stunning-looking girl on each arm, whom he would then take back to his place and bed. Claire read his thoughts.

'Forget it, Jimbo. Movie fine, anything else – a no go area.'

Sally laughed nervously. 'Er – no, not really my scene, sorry. And there's my boyfriend – '

'Bring him along – let's have a foursome.' Jim was getting enthusiastic.

'Thanks, but no thanks,' said Sally very firmly. 'Listen, Claire, if you're going to be all right I'll be toddling along now. Oh God, do you think Roger's still out there?'

'Nope,' said Jim. 'I checked it out. I guess he did a runner some time back. Well, sorry you can't make it tonight. Maybe another time . . .' He looked at Sally's pert little figure regretfully.

'Yes – maybe. Bye, darling, take care,' she said, giving Claire a meaningful glance.

Claire laughed. 'Don't worry – I'll give you a ring. Bye,' she said gaily as she saw Sally out. She came back to the kitchen.

'Now, Mr Dutton, I have another favour to ask you.'

'You got it,' said Jim happily.

37

Diana de Charteris was more than impressed with Sukie's find.

'That boy really is something! Where's he been hiding himself all this time?' she asked. 'He looks sensational.'

'I think that's been his problem,' observed Sukie sagely. 'That type of romantic good looks aren't appreciated in this country, but he can act – I can tell you that. He's terrific.'

'Well, the Americans were over the moon. I've never heard such euphoria at a video showing of all things. He photographs like a dream – and all that sexual energy! What a coup, my dear, on your first assignment for us too! I shall have to watch my step or you'll be taking over the agency!'

'Not bad, is it?' Sukie laughed happily. She had been thrilled to bits and had regaled her children with tales of her triumph.

'I wish you'd cast us in it, Mum,' Nicky had sighed enviously. 'I'd like to go on a big galleon. I could be a cabin boy!'

'So you could,' agreed Sukie, 'but, in any case, if I get to visit the set and it's during your holidays, you can come with me.' She secretly planned to take them anyway.

'Oh wow!' shouted Nicky, hurling a packet of fish fingers into the air. He ran to catch them, but missed and they landed in the middle of the cat's food bowls, upsetting the water and causing Brambles to run for cover.

'Now look what you've done,' said Ben crossly, assuming responsibility for keeping an eye on Nicky's behaviour. 'Go on, clear it up.'

'Oh God,' said Nicky wearily, 'why can't I learn to control myself?' Sukie hid her smile and let them get on with it.

Sean had rung her secretary that afternoon and arranged to take Sukie to lunch the following day. The venue was a surprise, but she was to meet him outside the office building and she was to wear jeans, please. Sukie was intrigued and not a little excited. She took a change of clothes into the office with her the next day and managed to leave early, having spent the morning dealing with the mundane matters connected with getting Sean out to Spain on the appropriate day, fully equipped with costumes, hotel accommodation, passport, plane tickets, his medical examination for insurance purposes, and an up-to-date script. It had taken all of the previous afternoon and that morning to get even the basics sorted out. Although she was still waiting to hear back from Jan Hunter on the billing, she knew full well that that particular call would not be forthcoming until late in the afternoon. This would give the agent the upper hand, leaving it late enough in the day to try to force the issue.

Sukie made her excuses and left the office. She was clad in stone-washed grey jeans with an off-white tee shirt, leather bomber jacket and white trainers. Her coppery hair was flying free as she carried her grey denim shoulder bag. She came almost running out of the heavy tinted glass doors of the main entrance to the building. Sean gazed at her in admiration, she looked about twenty-eight.

'Am I late?' she exclaimed as she ran towards him.

'On the contrary, Ms Marlow, you have perfect timing. So far as my life is concerned, that is.'

283

Sukie laughed happily. 'You're not looking so bad yourself,' she parried.

He was actually looking gorgeous, she decided, although perhaps exhibiting rather more of his firm tanned chest than was comfortable for her equilibrium. He was wearing a very faded red shirt, the sleeves of which were rolled up above his elbows. His jeans were black and at his waist was an exotic Mexican-type belt of pink, red, mauve and grey stripes that slotted through the waist, tied in front and hung down. On his feet were much-worn black beach shoes and he was carrying a purple rucksack over one shoulder. The whole effect was gypsyish and, to Sukie's mind, highly dangerous. This young man seemed to grow more and more attractive to her with each encounter.

'Why thank you, ma'am.' He bowed his head graciously, grabbed hold of her hand and pulled her along the square, cutting down the back streets of Soho until they reached Piccadilly Circus.

'Why are we going so fast?' she asked.

'Because life is so short and I have to leave you so soon to go to Spain.'

Sukie felt suddenly light-headed. He was flirting outrageously with her and yet she did not care.

He grinned at her. 'Sounds like I'm going off to fight in the Spanish Civil War, doesn't it?'

Sukie was enchanted by him. She felt she was living for the first time in years. They reached Green Park and ran across the busy road. He led her to a relatively secluded spot by some trees and took off his rucksack.

'Hang on,' he commanded. 'Don't move, I'm about to demonstrate my Walter Raleigh,' and he pulled out a rolled up waterproof sheet and spread it out carefully on the grass. He indicated for her to sit down. 'Ma'am,' he said solemnly.

284

Sukie knelt down obediently, wondering what on earth the boys would say if they could see her now. At that moment, a crocodile of schoolboys was passing at some distance away, laughing and chattering. How dreadful if it had been Nicky's school! She hugged herself with a mixture of terror and delight.

'You okay?' Sean glanced at her. 'Not cold are you?'

'Not at all. It's a beautiful day.'

'It certainly is,' he agreed, crouching on his haunches and looking into her eyes. A shiver of excitement went through her. 'Are you sure you're not cold?' he asked anxiously.

'Just apprehensive,' she said looking back at him squarely.

'Not about us, I hope?' Sukie was beginning to feel panicky inside. He was rushing things a bit wasn't he? He saw her expression. 'I have a feeling, that's all,' he said, as if he could read her thoughts. 'It's all meant, you know, you turning up in my life at exactly the right moment.'

In her heart, Sukie had wondered at the extraordinary timing of events herself. Now she looked down at the daisies peeping out under the edge of the ground sheet.

'You don't know anything about me – I mean my personal circumstances,' she murmured. He was still looking at her.

'You're not wearing a wedding ring, but I think you're married all the same.' She looked up at the retreating figures of the little boys. He followed her gaze. 'You have children?' he asked.

'Two. One fifteen, the other eleven – and yes, I am married, but I am in the process of divorcing my husband.'

'Well, isn't that convenient?' he smiled at her. 'Sorry, I don't mean to be facetious – it must be horrid for you,' and he busied himself unpacking the rucksack. He produced two Tupperware boxes and a Thermos flask, a green and white check tablecloth and two matching napkins. In one tub was

285

a silver foil package that proved to contain brown smoked salmon sandwiches with lemon. In the other were raspberries. Red pepper and plastic spoons were also produced and a screw-top plastic bottle of cream. The Thermos flask was unscrewed and the contents poured into two plastic beakers.

'Cheers,' said Sean holding his mug aloft. 'Here's to our mutual triumph.'

'I'll drink to that!' she said, relieved that the proceedings had taken on a more practical tone. She was surprised to find that she was drinking a Pimms No.1.

He smiled ruefully. 'Yes, sorry, pre-mixed and no trimmings. Not very glamorous, I'm afraid, but you just wait till I get my first pay cheque for the movie. Then I'm going to take you to the Ritz for a proper assignation.'

'You really don't have to – I'm so pleased you got the job – that's enough gratification in itself. I'm just doing my job.'

'Don't you like your lunch?' he asked, pretending to be hurt.

'It's the best meal I've ever had,' she said – well, it was almost true – actually, Ben's vegetable and cheese bake was the best. She had been so proud of her son's doing it off his own bat – but this came a pretty close second. She bit into the sandwich, it was tangy and delicious.

'Not bad, huh?' He was watching her with appreciation.

'It's very sweet of you to go to so much trouble on my behalf,' she said evenly.

'Just returning the compliment,' he said munching on his sandwich. Maybe he was just indulging in an outrageous flirtation after all.

'You must admit,' she persisted, 'this is an unusual scenario we have here.'

'Not at all. Lots of my mates take casting directors out to

lunch – usually at Le Meridien, or Joe Allen – not many of then pull the *déjeuner sur l'herbe* stunt.'

Sukie had an uncanny feeling that he was lulling her into a false sense of security. 'Oh, I'd much rather do this than any of the others,' she said hurriedly – 'although, I dare say, you should be putting yourself about – so that all your future employers can take a look at this new young lion.'

'Plenty of time for that when I get back, covered in glory and medals. Will you be able to get out to location at all?'

'Not officially perhaps, but I may snatch a long weekend. My youngest, Nicky, is desperate to board a galleon.'

'That will be fun,' said Sean, again looking at her a little too candidly for her comfort. He took her hand and kissed it lightly. 'Do try.'

She felt she couldn't let the incident pass unremarked. 'Mr Mallin, I think you are exceeding the bounds of our professional relationship.'

He took another bite of his sandwich. 'I know, I'm dreadful, aren't I? But how else am I to get our acquaintance onto a more familiar footing, tell me that?'

'I'm not sure that it should be,' she faltered.

'Why not? I'm a man, you're a woman, I'm unattached, you are filing for a divorce, you say –'

'I have two children –' she interrupted him.

'And I have a hi-fi, a room full of books and some cricket gear – oh, and a live yoghurt culture called Boris.' Sukie laughed. 'Don't mock – I can't leave him for too long. He's probably wondering where I am at this very moment.'

'Don't you have anyone at home to keep an eye on him for you?' she asked, her eyes twinkling.

'Aha, so you are interested in my personal arrangements.'

Sukie blushed.

287

'All right, all right,' she conceded, 'but there's no need to crow.'

He took both her hands in his. 'Right, so now we know where we are, next question.' Sukie looked at him alarmed. 'Please, please will you come away with me for a night of unbridled passion so that I can show my appreciation by making wonderful, wonderful love to you. I can promise you it will be the best ever – I am the world's most thoughtful and considerate lover and I'm just crazy about you.'

Sukie gasped in astonishment. 'You're just crazy!' she laughed. 'This film has gone completely to your head, and you've totally lost touch with reality.'

'Exactly! You are one hundred per cent right. It's a fairy tale – a fantastical time, so let's live it to the hilt. Come on, what do you say?' He was gazing at her with shining excited eyes.

She suddenly thought of all those wasted years with Geoffrey, all the romance and excitement he'd had without her. A wave of deep hurt, resentment and anger swept over her. She made up her mind.

'Listen,' she said, 'I'm going back to the office now, and I'm going to make two phone calls. One to my friend Mona to ask her to babysit for me on Friday night, and one to the most wonderful place in Sussex where we can stay for the night. You don't leave till Sunday and I'll be back in time to give my undivided attention to my son's maths prep on Saturday. We'll have one night of paradise, as you suggest, as a special treat to ourselves. What do you say?' She threw the question back at him.

'I say that you are the most wonderful woman I have ever met,' said Sean happily.

38

When Geoff walked out on Patsy, his exit may have had a theatrical ring about it, it was certainly executed with aplomb and bravura, but the moment he was on the other side of the door the act stopped. It occurred to him that Patsy was the third woman he'd split up from in four days. Even he could recognize that he was in a bad way. He was like a drowning man clutching at straws. He had no idea what to do or where to go. He seemed to be completely unwanted. It had come as quite a shock to his system. He was now at sea, adrift, the turmoil within him made him feel alternately that he was going to burst his rib cage, then it set him reeling. He quite suddenly had a desperate longing to see his mother. Without more ado, he left the block of flats, got into his car and set off for the motorway. He had no idea what he was going to do next, but he felt sure that she would be able to advise him, console him. He had lost his sense of direction, yet whichever way he thought about it, he kept coming back to Sukie. He needed her desperately. He felt he was going to cry again, but determinedly fought back the tears. He'd behaved dreadfully to her. He'd behaved dreadfully to Patsy, too; her tear-stained little face kept coming back to him – Sukie's sobbing in his arms in their kitchen – Claire's icy tones on the phone – he'd behaved appallingly to them all. He gripped the steering wheel, pulling over into the fast lane.

Suddenly there was a blaring of horns and squealing of tyres. He came to with a jolt. He realized that he'd lost concentration – that he'd neglected to look in his rear-view mirror and had pulled out without checking the oncoming traffic. He had narrowly missed a collision. He held up a hand by way of apology to the other driver, who was gesticulating aggressively at him and mouthing what Geoff took to be obscenities through the windscreen. Geoff once again waved an apologetic hand and pulled over into the slow lane, then onto the hard shoulder, where he stopped the car and sat trembling. He stayed there for several minutes before he was able to summon up the courage to start off again. He drove slowly and carefully all the way to Oxfordshire.

About an hour and three-quarters later he turned off the A34 down a narrow leafy country lane, then left at a little crossroads and along a track that served as the drive to the fourteenth-century cottage sitting in the middle of its own grounds of just under two acres.

Gwen Armitage was in the garden, digging, as Geoff pulled up outside. Now in her late seventies, she was a redoubtable widow of enormous energy and spirit.

'Well, this is a surprise! Don't bother to ring and let me know you're coming, will you?' she greeted him cheerily.

'Sorry, Ma. It was a spur of the moment thing – I was passing through.'

'On the way to where, pray?' she asked him suspiciously, as they kissed each other. She didn't miss a trick. Geoff ignored the question.

'What are you up to?' he asked instead.

'Preparing the ground for my seedlings,' she replied removing her gardening gloves. 'Let's go in, I'll get you some tea and you can tell me all about it.'

Geoff laughed lightly – there was nothing he could keep from his mother.

'Ma, could I possibly stay here tonight, do you think? We could go out for supper in Woodstock.'

'What's the matter with my cooking? Of course you can stay. I assume that Sukie and the boys will not be bringing up the rear,' she said airily, as she led the way into the house.

The side door led directly into the kitchen. There was the familiar smell of home-baked bread and stewed apple, which seemed to pervade the air permanently. Gwen removed her wellington boots and padded in her stockinged feet over to the Aga where she put the kettle on the hob.

'Sit down,' she commanded. 'You look ghastly – all fagged out.' Geoff obediently sat at the square scrubbed deal kitchen table. 'Have you eaten?' she asked sternly. Geoff shook his head. 'Well, you're in luck – I've got some apple pie left over, I made it yesterday for lunch. The Major came over. Beef sandwich do you?'

Geoff smiled. 'You really ought to put that poor man out of his misery – oh yes please, lovely. Really, Mater, why don't you marry the old bugger – he'd love it?'

'Yes,' replied Gwen grimly, 'I dare say he would, but I certainly wouldn't. Do you think I want a man under my feet all the time? I have a very pleasant life here, thank you. Do you suppose I want cigar ends all over my sitting room and false teeth that don't belong to me by my bed?'

'I just worry about you being lonely, that's all.'

'Lonely? I have my writing, you forget, and Sylvia pops in every day, or we eat at her house, and then there's my voluntary work.'

'Oh, I know you lead a very full life – I was just thinking it would be nice for you to have a man about the place, that's

291

all.' His mother stopped in the middle of buttering the bread and looked at him beadily.

'It's unbelievable, you men still think that no woman's life is complete unless there is one of you attached to her in some way.' She waved the knife at him. 'You've still got a lot to learn, my lad – that kettle's taking an eternity to boil.'

Geoff stared at the table in front of him. 'I think I'm beginning to find that out,' he said slowly. 'I don't seem to be able to handle them any more, women, that is.'

'I wasn't aware that there was a plurality of females in your life.' There was a silence. 'Oh dear, have you been up to no good?' she asked finally, going to the larder that abutted on the kitchen and emerging carrying the remains of some roast beef in one hand and an apple pie in the other. 'You are a foolish boy. What's happened – she's thrown you out, I suppose?' she said unsympathetically.

'They all have,' he said, putting his elbows on the table and propping up his aching head.

'All?' She stopped in her tracks and looked at him astonished. 'How many did you have on the go, for God's sake?'

'Three, counting Sukie.'

Gwen digested the information, then went to the worktop and started slicing the beef and salad. She slapped the pieces of beef onto the bread and reached over to a shelf to extract the mustard. She started to plaster it on.

'Go easy on the mustard, Mater,' he said, eyeing the process dubiously.

She ignored him and squashed the slices of bread together, then cut them into quarters and, shoving them on a side plate, brought it over to the table and banged it down in front of him.

'Don't be cross with me, Ma.' He looked up pleadingly.

She fetched the tea pot and crossed to the Aga. 'What

sort of a monster have I reared?' she muttered to herself.

'I thought you'd have seen it in the papers – it was all over last Sunday's *Globe*.'

'Ah, that would explain it,' she said, her face clearing as she warmed the teapot. 'Sylvia did mutter darkly about something. She said they were printing their usual filth and lies – you don't suppose I read that trash do you?'

She made the tea. Geoff wolfed down the sandwiches. He couldn't remember when he'd last eaten. She cut a chunk of apple pie and put it in a bowl.

'It hasn't taken away your appetite, I see,' she observed dryly, as she placed the pie in front of him. 'Do you want cream with that?'

'No, I'll have it as it is – it looks good.'

'It is good, bloody good, more than you deserve.' She sat down opposite him and folded her hands on the table. 'So, what are you going to do?'

'That's what I've come to ask you – you haven't got a spoon, have you?'

'Yes, of course I have, but your appalling news has put it quite out of my head.' She went and got one from the drawer. 'So that's what this charming little filial gesture is all about is it? And I thought you'd come to see your poor old mother, see how she's getting on.' She sat down again.

Geoff extended a hand and put it on hers. 'Of course I've come to see you, Ma; you know I love to see you – it's just that I thought you might be able to help. I just don't know what to do,' he finished miserably.

'Give the apple pie a go.' He did so obediently. 'So Sukes has taken it badly? I can't say I blame her.'

'You could say that. She chucked me out the next day, went and got herself a job and is having a wonderful time flirting with men half her age.'

Gwen sat back in her chair. 'Good for her!' she cried approvingly. 'What's sauce for the goose is sauce for the gander. I always said that girl was much too good for you!'

'Mother!'

'Well I did. She should never have given up her career, she was a fine actress. You shouldn't have made her do that.'

'I did not! What do you mean?' he burst out.

'You got her pregnant practically as soon as you looked at her,' said Gwen calmly.

'Well, of course, I thought that's what she wanted.'

'It was what you wanted — her needs never came into it,' his mother observed darkly.

Geoff stared at her astounded. 'Do you really believe that?' he asked slowly.

'Yes. I'm afraid I didn't bring you up very well. I think it was the war that did it — and your father not being well. You saw me having to attend to his every need and want and thought you fancied a bit of it yourself. Maybe I didn't provide a very stable home for you.'

But Geoff would have none of it. 'I had a wonderful home and a marvellous education — and I know the sacrifices you had to make to provide me with them,' he added.

Gwen thought for a moment. 'You were an only child, of course. I expect we spoiled you — didn't mean to — we just doted on you, that's all.'

There was another considerable pause then Geoff said, 'I think I've lost her.'

'Yes, I dare say you have. How are the boys?'

'Never better — they seem to be thriving on the situation.'

'Tell Sukie to send them here for the summer hols, they'll have a whale of a time.'

'I daren't speak to her at the moment.'

Gwen looked at her son sympathetically. 'All right, I'll ring her – things will get better, you know. You're just experiencing some sort of midlife crisis, that's all.'

'I don't know what to do or where to go,' he said bleakly.

'Get yourself a flat on your own, you've got a lot of thinking to do. Sort yourself out. Take stock.'

'Yes,' he said slowly, mulling it over. 'I suppose I could manage on my own, although I haven't had to for ages – I haven't been completely alone since my drama school days.'

'Well, try the bachelor life for a bit. Try celibacy – it would do you a lot of good. You need a fallow period, give yourself a chance to get used to things. Take a break. You're looking terrible – I'm surprised any woman will look at you at the moment.'

'Well, that's the trouble, they won't. I used to charm the birds out of the trees – not any more.'

'Leave the women alone for a change. Who are these other women anyway? They must be something pretty extraordinary to make you stray.'

'Claire Jenner –'

'Oh, is she the new girl? I think she's lovely – very talented and very beautiful. Oh well, at least you've got good taste. And the other?'

There was a pause.

'Patsy – Patsy Hall – she plays my secretary,' he said shamefacedly.

'Oh my God,' said Gwen, dropping the teacosy. 'For heaven's sake, what on earth's the matter with you?'

Geoff looked at her bleakly. 'I don't know – I just don't know. I don't seem to be able to help myself.'

39

There were white peacocks strutting about the lawn. The ramparts of an ancient castle, long since in ruins having fallen into decay from Henry VIII's time, stood silhouetted against the fading light of an early summer sky. A frog plopped in and out among the water lilies in the pond and reddish golden goldfish could be discerned swimming in a desultory fashion under the water, enjoying the last warmth of the fading sun. Sukie and Sean sat by the lily pond enjoying pre-supper drinks.

'This is paradise,' murmured Sukie as she took in the setting – the sleepy castle, which had been converted into a high-class hotel, the quiet chatter of their fellow guests, the haphazard flight of an occasional bat, and the fathomless eyes of the handsome young man sitting opposite her.

On her return to the office two days ago, she had made two phone calls to set the plan in motion, then had finished the paraphernalia connected with Sean's departure and had dashed out to buy herself a cocktail outfit. She had spent far too much money, but the thought of Geoff's dalliances over the years and the amount he must have spent indulging them made her reckless. She bought a midnight-blue velvet suit with a short dress and a short-sleeved jacket. In her wardrobe she found a pair of pewter-coloured very high-heeled evening shoes with matching bag, which she'd worn for an awards ceremony and had never seen since. Some pewter and rhinestone earrings and bracelet, which had graced the same occasion, and her new frothy underwear, plus some shiny stockings completed the outfit. She searched out her overnight bag. Mona had been kind and was only too happy to keep an eye on the boys, although Ben was more than capable – but Sukie wanted to be doubly certain. She was feeling guilty and felt sure that unless someone was in the house, God would in some way punish her for her errant behaviour. The matter had been carefully put to Ben, however, who took it as a personal insult. She persuaded him that it was Mona who needed a change of scene and as the latter was hot stuff in the mathematical department and would be able to discuss his maths prep with him at some length, the arrangement was decided. Brambles, who barely acknowledged her existence these days and had transferred his allegiance wholeheartedly to Nicky, who returned the adoration two-fold, was not at all put out. Mona herself was delighted, never having been blessed with children herself, she looked forward to the event with keen anticipation.

'Do come in. What can I get you to drink?' had been Ben's opening conversational gambit on her arrival. She had been enchanted.

'This is Brambles,' Nicky had announced entering the room clutching an initially surprised and thereafter apoplectic bundle of fur. 'He's all right except he farts a lot.' Sukie smiled to herself as she thought of her two such disparate offspring entertaining her long-standing friend.

'What are you thinking?' said Sean.

'Sorry, just remembering something the boys said this evening, that's all.'

'How have they taken the divorce?' he asked gently.

She sighed. 'They've been very good, even the publicity doesn't seem to have upset them unduly.'

'Publicity?'

Sukie became flustered. 'Yes, er, it was in the papers – you won't have seen it.' Sean noticed her discomfiture and leaned over to rest his hand on hers.

'I'm sorry, that was very clumsy of me. I didn't mean to pry.'

'No, it's all right. Well, you'll find out sooner or later I dare say. My estranged husband is Geoffrey Armitage, of *McMasters* fame.'

'Good lord, really? I sort of know him – well, not exactly, I was in an episode of that once, ages ago, when it first started. I played an art student.'

'So that's where I've seen you before,' said Sukie triumphantly.

'Well,' said Sean, slightly offended, 'I have done other things on television, you know.'

'Oh I know you have,' she hastily reassured him.

'So, let me see, you gave up a promising career to become the wife of TV's most attractive man and bear his children, am I right?'

'Yes, you're right – I wasn't a bad little actress either.'

'I can vouch for that. Your reading the other day was hot stuff – that's why I got the part you know, it's all down to you.'

'Nonsense, you were stunning!'

'But you helped – it was having you to act opposite that really clinched it.'

'All right, I'll accept the compliment gracefully,' she smiled, 'but I could never have done it without you.' Sean burst out laughing.

A waiter approached them. 'Would you care to order now, madam, sir?'

'Yes, thank you,' said Sean accepting the menu.

'Can I get you another apéritif?' the waiter asked.

'No,' said Sukie making the decision for them both, 'we'll wait until the meal.'

'Very good, madam, sir. I'll be back in a moment to take your order.' The waiter left them discreetly.

'It's all so civilized,' said Sean, deep in the menu. 'Knocks Peckham into a cocked hat, I can tell you.'

Sukie giggled. 'I'm going to have two starters, if that's all right with you?'

'Anything you do is all right with me,' he said looking up over the menu to gaze at her sexily.

Sukie knew that if she'd been standing up, she'd have gone weak at the knees. Instead, she felt her stomach turn over several times in the most alarming manner. What was worse, there was a faint stirring in her loins. She felt quite light-headed. She had long since abandoned the idea of romance re-entering her life, and this unexpected adventure had left her breathless – but she was determined to enjoy it to the full. She hardly dared think of what might happen after dinner.

'Well?' asked Sean, glancing at her queryingly, 'what are you having?'

'Er, oh, curried melon, to start with, then Insalata Tricolore.'

'Hardly substantial,' he remarked.

'I like to go to bed on an empty stomach,' she said boldly.

Sean looked at her and groaned slightly. 'There speaks a woman of the world – how right you are. I shall confine myself to the poached salmon and I may join you in the curried melon, attempting a combination of the hot, tangy, smooth and refreshing.'

'Yes, indeed,' said Sukie, hardly daring to look at him.

Eventually the waiter returned and took their orders. They spent a further ten minutes basking in the quiet of the gloaming, then were ushered in to their table in the very formal dining room, where they ate for the most part in silence, just gazing at each other in mute anticipation by the light of candles. They drank hock, which was suitably fruity and had the effect of making Sukie throw any caution she might have had left to the winds, and cast all inhibitions aside. They firmly refused puddings and coffee, Sean asserting that they could always avail themselves of room service later on if they became desperately hungry, which he admitted was unlikely, but they might indulge in a night cap. After dinner they wandered into the rapidly darkening garden. Sean took her hand and they went quietly in search of the peacocks. One was clearly visible on account of its colour. It was standing silently by a rhododendron bush. The others had already turned in for the night, and were settling down to roost in their pen. They crept around to have a look at them. The birds twitched their heads, suddenly alert at the unexpected intrusion.

'It's okay, old fellow. We're just two incredible romantics come to say good night, that's all. Sorry if we disturbed you. Doesn't look too comfortable on that perch, old girl,' he said to the other.

'How do you know which is which?' whispered Sukie, who could hardly see anything. 'And why are there three of them, do you suppose?'

'The eternal triangle,' observed Sean cynically. 'And I don't know, I'm just making conversation, but I think this one's a female, she's giving me the eye.' And he suddenly caught hold of Sukie's wrist and pulled her towards him and kissed her hard on the mouth. She gasped with the pleasure and the suddenness of it all. He tasted delicious. She put her hand up to his long, dark curls and held his head in a fierce embrace.

'God, I want you,' he whispered urgently, as their lips parted.

'Come on then, what are we waiting for?' she whispered back.

They made their way slowly to the house, he stopping to kiss her neck and face at intervals. She felt a surging in her loins and reached out her hand for his cock. His erection was hard. She stroked it, he groaned involuntarily and pushed his tongue eagerly into her mouth. Their kissing became even more impassioned as their hands explored each other's bodies in the dark.

They reached the side entrance of the hotel and went quietly up to the room. It was luxurious and voluptuous, with a huge four-poster bed hung with drapes. The en-suite bathroom boasted a sunken whirlpool bath with gold taps.

Once inside, in the sanctuary of the bedroom, he started kissing her again in the dark. Sukie noticed he had suddenly become tentative, so she took the initiative. She pulled him towards the bed and sat him down on the edge. Then very slowly, she started to undress him. She removed his tie and his jacket and undid his shirt. His smooth body gleamed in the floodlights from the garden outside. She knelt down in front of him and kissed the muscular smoothness of his chest. Then she removed his shoes and socks and undid his belt and flies. She bent her head to nuzzle his cock straining in his pants. She pulled it out and kissed it lovingly. He groaned.

She slipped off her jacket. He pushed the top of her dress down, she undid her bra and watched his face as she exposed her breasts to him. He gasped at their fullness, and pulled her up to him. His mouth found her nipples and he sucked on them alternately. Then he pushed her dress to the floor and his hands found her crutch. Her flimsy panties were soaking with the juices released by her lust. She climbed onto the bed, still in her suspender belt, stockings and high heels, and lay back. He removed his trousers and pants and knelt on the bed naked before her. He made as though to enter her, but she pulled him up to her and took his erection into her mouth. He gasped with pleasure. She sucked at his cock for several minutes knowing from his stifled groans and abrupt movement of his head that she was bringing him continuously to the point of orgasm and he was somehow just holding on. Then she pushed him onto his back and they both started to explore each other's bodies lovingly, stroking and kissing and sucking. Finally, unable to wait any longer, he pushed his cock into her cunt and fucked her with long hard strokes. Then he lay on top of her and she took his buttocks in her hands and made him go faster. He plunged his tongue into her mouth as they both felt their pleasure increasing.

Suddenly he said, 'I can't hold on. I have to come, I have to.'

'Go on then,' she urged. 'I'm coming with you.'

He became masterful. 'Come on then, come on now, you bitch, come now.'

She felt him release the juices that drove her wild and his cock seemed to double in size as he reached his climax. She felt her vulva swell and her own orgasm approaching, then spasm after spasm of ecstasy. He came violently and cried out time and time again. Then they both collapsed warm and satisfied on top of each other. Finally he said, 'That was glorious.'

'Yes,' Sukie agreed, 'it was.'

She added mentally to herself in the dark, that was the best fuck I have ever had. I hope to God I don't fall in love with this young man.

40

'Larry, can I have a quick word?' Hugh looked anxiously into Larry Matthews's office where his PA was busy working at his desk with a huge graph in front of him.

Larry looked up over the top of his glasses. 'You look perturbed, oh ancient one,' he observed. Hugh ignored the insult and slid through the door, shutting it furtively behind him. 'To what do I owe the pleasure? It's not often the mountain comes to Muhammad. This calls for coffee. Sandra!' He rose and yelled into the corridor. 'Coffee in intensive care, pronto, there's a dear.' Hugh seated himself and waited for Larry to do the same. 'Cue,' said Larry.

'I've just had a call from Geoff's agent and that was followed by a note from Geoff himself.'

'Oh yes?' said Larry, 'and what's prompted this sudden rash of concern from the senior citizen brigade?' Geoff's agent was Jeremy Clifton, an almost hallowed figure in theatrical circles, mainly because of his venerable years and lengthy service.

'Geoff wants us to abandon the scenes with Claire and to replace them with an alternative story line – in other words, a different love interest for them both.' Hugh delivered his bombshell quietly and waited for the explosion that he knew was sure to follow. But Larry was choosing his moment.

'Does Martin know this?' he asked, without emotion.

'Yes, I rang him just now.'

'What did he say?' asked Larry, with interest.

'He's at the studios looking at a rough cut of the Amsterdam filming, so he'll be a while yet – lunch probably – but he said he'd abide by your decision.'

'It's nice to know I'm appreciated,' said Larry, leaning back in his chair with satisfaction.

'Aren't you going to explode?' asked Hugh faintly disappointed.

'Oh ye of little faith,' said Larry ominously quiet. 'Of course I am, and I've already reached a decision.'

'That's quick, even by your standards,' said Hugh impressed. 'What is it?'

'We'll go along with Geoffrey's demands.'

'What?' asked Hugh, shocked.

'Oh yes, who are we to thwart the demands and desires of our leading actor, or should I say ex-leading actor?' Larry's voice started to rise. 'Who the fuck does he think he is?' he demanded, thumping the desk. 'God All-fucking-mighty? Bruce fucking Willis? Kevin fucking Costner?' Hugh grinned and sat back to enjoy the firework display. 'I'll tell you what to do with his bloody note. Screw it – and Episodes Twelve and Thirteen into a large sharp ball and ram it up his middle-aged arse. I'll tell you what's going to happen in Episodes Twelve and bloody Thirteen. Claire and Jim are going to go a bundle on each other, Bella is going to do a big number on Jim, the two women are going to have a confrontation over him – as you, I believe, suggested at one time – I'm sorry I didn't take you seriously enough, I bow to your superior train of thought. Geoffrey fucking Armitage is going to be devastated because A, the bird he fancied is knocking off his American rival, and B, said American rival has taken all his business – and C,' he added with sudden inspiration, 'because aforementioned bird and rival have set up in opposition and put in a takeover bid for McMasters, and here you have your cliffhanger for your next series. And furthermore,' he continued, as he saw Hugh was about to interrupt, 'that ageing roué can find solace in the ample bosom of Bella Shand, his long-suffering estranged wife, thereby bringing contentment to millions of viewers. It was, if you recall, one of Geoff's fucking ultimata that resulted in their becoming estranged in the first place – because sir wanted to play opposite younger leading ladies – of course to feed his vanity. God, why the fuck have we put up with it? Because Geoffrey bloody Armitage was popular with the bloody great unwashed, that's why,' he said, answering his own question. 'Well, not any more, he ain't. He's blown it. This little amorous escapade of his that's hit the press has seen to that. The middle-aged matrons are not keen on their hero messing around and abusing the wife of his bosom – he's not got the clout he thinks he has with us. We have the perfect excuse, we reunite him with his fictional wife: doubly contented punters – happy, happy Bella, with bigger and better scenes to play – triumphant Geoffrey, his wish is our command, or do I mean the other way round?' He turned to Hugh. 'What do you think of the show so far?'

There was a pause. Then Hugh said solemnly, 'Larry, have I told you how much I love you?'

'No, and don't start now. I'm a happily unmarried man and I can't cope with any more menopausal middle-aged men. And anyway, what would Mona say? Sandra!' he bellowed. 'Where the fuck is that coffee? – Oh there it is,' he amended hurriedly as a startled Sandra appeared at the door bearing a tray of assorted goodies.

'There's no need to shout,' she said equably. Sandra was used to Larry and was more than a match for him. 'I've

305

brought you some Danish pastries. I thought you'd need some carbohydrate after all that noise – that's why I've taken so long,' she added apologetically, by way of explanation.

'Sandra, you are the woman of my dreams,' announced Larry elegiacally.

'I sincerely hope not,' said Sandra with feeling. 'It's all I can do to cope with you when you are awake.'

'Your Deirdre could learn a thing or two from my Sandra. We could get them together for a special training course. They could exchange methods –'

'We already spend Thursday evenings together, thank you very much,' said Sandra with some satisfaction.

'Doing what, pray?' asked Larry suspiciously.

'Judo classes,' announced Sandra complacently. 'I'm training for my black belt.'

Larry paused, his Danish pastry in midair, halfway to his mouth. 'Er, could we have a rain check on the dream section, Sandra, or should I say Alexandra. You're plainly way out of my league.'

'You can call me what you like,' said Sandra blithely as she went to the door, 'but I was christened plain Sandra, my mum calls me Sandy and my boyfriend, Kevin, is a black belt already,' she added as she left them.

The phone rang. Larry snatched it up.

'Yes, he's here, I'm here and you're not, otherwise all present and correct. Martin,' he mouthed to Hugh. 'Yes, it's all sorted out. We've, well, I've made the decision, but Hugh's one hundred per cent behind me. We're getting married – a June wedding, we thought – Deirdre and Sandra to be bridesmaids and Sandra's boyfriend, Kevin, to be best man. Thought you might give us away . . . Who to? . . . He can't wait,' he said aside to Hugh. 'Oh I don't know, do you think Anglia would take us? . . . Oh all right,

I'll be serious if I must,' he said peevishly. 'Listen, seriously, I've got the solution — get on your bike and get over here. I'm just about to do the re-writes — they'll make your hair curl, no, sorry, you haven't got any, have you? Get a transplant — you're going to need one.'

41

Claire may have sussed Jim out – she knew what made him tick, knew he was not the man for her – but Patsy was not so astute. She was totally smitten; she fell hook, line and sinker for him. The first day that Jim Dutton walked into the rehearsal room, she went weak at the knees, the room spun around her and her heart started knocking at her ribs. All the symptoms displayed by the heroines of the sensational romantic novels and historical romances she read were there. She watched breathlessly as his tall bronzed muscular frame loped into the room, looking around for a familiar face. Hugh approached him and shook his hand cordially, Larry went over and clapped him on the shoulder, Claire kissed him on the cheek, Scott took him by the arm to one side and muttered something in his ear. Jim was looking pleased, so it must have been complimentary. Then various cast members went up to him and welcomed him warmly.

Finally it was Patsy's turn. Jim turned to look at her and his eyes widened in appreciation. She was all pouting blonde prettiness – just Jim's type, and her figure was deliciously curvaceous. Jim mentally undressed her and assigned her to his bed that night, or if not the night after.

'Okay, everyone, let's gather round shall we?' called Larry loudly, and cast and production staff alike sat themselves at random around the long table, Claire ostentatiously seating

erself as far away from Geoff as possible. Patsy was almost
n ecstasy when Jim took her hand and led her to a place next
o him. She sat there in a beautiful dream, hardly daring to
ook at the glorious male, who was the embodiment of her
girlhood ideal. All her hurt and anger against Geoff, the
rumours about Jim and Claire – the visit to the porn house,
the fact that nearly all his scenes were with Claire – none
of it meant anything. It all faded away, to be replaced by a
fabulous fantasy in which she and Jim were in love, she
keeping house for him – perhaps even married. It was all
too blissful. Larry's voice broke into her reverie.

'Before we start – I'd like to hand out some rewrites.
Scenes two, six, nine, fourteen and thirty are to be replaced
in Episode Twelve and there are new scenes three, seven, ten,
fifteen, twenty-two, twenty-five and thirty-six for Episode
Thirteen. I should like to mention that these are at Geoff's
suggestion.' Geoff looked up startled. 'And we all think, and
I'm sure you will, too, that they are excellent, provide us with
two stunning new story lines and an exciting cliffhanger for
the new series. Could you please set about inserting them now,
as we'd like to hear how they read. Sorry they're so late –
we've been working against the clock.' And so saying he sat
down and braced himself for developments.

Geoff, of course, had absolutely no idea as to what the
rewrites comprised. Neither had Claire, nor indeed anyone.
Hugh had deliberately kept them in the dark, contenting
himself with ringing Geoff's agent and informing him that
Geoff's demands were being met, that they had resolved the
dilemma with a solution that would meet everyone's needs,
enhance the plot and diffuse the public interest in Geoff's
unfortunate domestic situation, which Hugh had been quick
to point out had seriously undermined Geoff's position in the
series and done the series irreparable damage. Jeremy Clifton,

being of the old school and with old-fashioned morals to match, had taken all of this on board without a murmur, had even actively encouraged it by suggesting that Patsy should be dropped and her place filled by a woman nearer to Geoff in age. Hugh promised to give the suggestion some thought and the scripts were biked round to the agent that very morning.

It had already occurred to Hugh that Patsy was a liability and he had no intention of renewing her contract for the next season. There was a concentrated silence for a few minutes as everyone removed and replaced pages of script. Larry observed Geoffrey trying to read a scene and said loudly, 'Are we ready?' This announcement was greeted with howls of protest and Geoff was forced to abandon his attempts and concentrate on getting the scenes in the right order.

To Patsy's overwhelming delight, Jim offered to help her, as the propinquity of his male loveliness had reduced her to a fumbling inadequacy and, try as she could, she was unable to insert the new pages. It was all finally sorted out and the reading began.

It soon became evident that Geoffrey was appalled at the amendments, but his sense of professionalism plus his pride as an actor precluded him from doing anything other than giving of his best. Bella, naturally, was thrilled at the resurgence of her character into the mainstream of the plot and read it for all it was worth. Their scenes crackled along as they had done in the first series. Likewise Jim and Claire turned in sparkling performances and the others all backed them up. Even Patsy managed not to fluff her two small scenes, although she was dismayed to find that her part had been savagely cut and she had no encounters with Jim. But she was determined not to be found wanting in front of him and for once put all her effort into her small contribution.

Simon seemed more rakish, Meg and Reg more down-to-earth and Jason more cheeky. At the end the whole room broke into applause. Bella was beaming.

'My God, you clever buggers,' she said to Larry and Hugh. 'We'll be back at the top of the ratings in no time. That's it, you've cracked it. Geoff, my darling, you were superb and may I say what a joy it is to be playing scenes opposite you again.'

'Thank you,' Geoffrey, looking shattered, accepted the compliment as best he could.

'Okay, lunch everyone. Back at two to start blocking,' yelled Larry.

Hugh always let Larry organize these sessions, mainly because of his underling's superior lung power, but also because he knew that Larry had a great air of authority and that no one would think of questioning his orders.

As they all crowded into the corridor and made for the stairs, Geoff collared Martin, the most timid of the triumvirate. 'What the hell is going on?' he muttered savagely in Martin's ear.

Martin looked shifty and said, 'Er, er – look, er, Geoffrey, we did the best we could with the time available. Aren't you pleased? I thought they worked splendidly.'

'Yes, well, you would wouldn't you?' Geoff said dismissively, realizing that it was Larry he should be speaking to, but Larry was nowhere to be seen, having discreetly fled back to the office block at the end of the road. There was no sign of Hugh in the canteen either, and Geoff knew he had to have the matter out there and then. Accordingly, he went to the nearest phone booth and rang Jeremy Clifton.

'I'm sorry, there is no one in the office to take your call, but if you'd like to leave your name and number, someone will contact you on our return from lunch. Please speak after

311

the tone,' said the voice tonelessly on the answering machine.

'Damn!' he said explosively. 'Yes, I would like to leave a message please, I would like to know what the hell this agency's playing at, who the fuck do you think you are and what the bloody fucking hell you propose to do about the script rewrites which have once again paired me with Miss Westcliff-on-Sea 1953, the escapee from Alcoholics Anonymous, and have handed the leading male role – on a plate – to our colonial friend, Mr Beefcake himself, Jim bloody Dutton. Perhaps you'd be kind enough to ring me – at your convenience, of course.'

He hung up, strode into the canteen and helped himself to food, he hardly knew what. Then he joined the table where the rest of the cast were sitting, to be greeted by universal acclaim.

'That was superb, old boy,' said Simon unreservedly. 'Good to see you back on form again.' Geoff did a double take at the back-handed compliment.

'Yes, you were wonderful,' breathed Meg. 'You know, it's a funny thing, but you're never so good as when you do scenes with Bella. There's a sort of, um, what do I mean – you know – feeling –'

'Chemistry,' said Amy firmly. 'Yes, there is, you just spark off together somehow. I suppose it's because you're from the same era, the same school of acting. It's lovely to watch.'

Geoff was forced to accept the universal admiration in spite of himself and despite the oblique references to his age. He suppressed his true feelings and, after smiling briefly in acknowledgement of their praise, sat down and tucked into his cauliflower cheese.

Patsy, meanwhile, was in seventh heaven. Jim continued his attentions towards her unabated during lunch, treating her to a dissertation on studio commissary lunches, LA style,

312

and life in tinsel town generally. She hardly spoke a word, but gazed at him adoringly. Jim, used as he was to female adulation, was flattered and knew that he was in for a treat in the sack. This kid was a pushover, he'd be able to do anything with her.

After lunch they returned to the rehearsal rooms, with those in the McMaster offices and residence scenes in one room and those in Claire and Jim's rival outfit, Livingstone's, and local hotel bar and showrooms in the other. This way Geoff and Claire saw nothing of each other for the rest of the afternoon. It also meant that Patsy and Jim were split up. So far as Patsy was concerned, this was an advantage, she would have been totally unable to perform if Jim had been present and she felt that she needed some time to herself to try to recover her senses. She comforted herself with the fact that there were still several days of rehearsals before the studio, when she would have ample opportunity to see him and did her best that afternoon to impress her peers. Geoff's remarks about her lack of acting ability had hurt her badly and she was determined to prove him wrong.

After she had finished her scene for Episode Twelve, she reluctantly picked up her things and, waving goodbye, left the rehearsal rooms. She bumped into Jim coming out of his rehearsal room to go to the lavatory.

'Hi!' he said cheerily. 'Hey, you never gave me your phone number. Now how do you expect me to call you later?'

Patsy's heart stopped. Oh my God, she thought to herself, did dreams really come true that quickly?

'Oh,' she giggled happily. 'Sorry, silly me,' and she delved into her bag and pulled out a printed card.

'My,' said Jim, looking at it wonderingly. It was mauve with silver lettering, and the object of much scornful mirth from the rest of the cast. 'Is this usual over here?'

'Oh no,' said Patsy proudly. 'I'm the only one who's got them in the company.'

'Fine,' said Jim. 'Well, okay, I'll call you – tonight okay?'

In her confusion Patsy dropped her bag and bent down to pick it up, thereby exhibiting her very ample bosom. Jim immediately got a hard-on and took advantage of the diversion to disappear to the loo where he had a struggle not to jerk himself off, and gave himself a stern talking to, persuading himself it would be all the better if he saved it up for later.

Patsy drove home in her little Peugeot on cloud nine. As soon as she got in, she ran a bath and spent the next two hours doing her hair and nails and deciding what to wear.

Geoff was called out in the middle of rehearsals by his agent, who needed to speak to him urgently on the phone.

'My dear boy, what seems to be the trouble? Hugh biked round copies of the scripts to me this morning. They're excellent for you. I'm so glad you're back playing opposite Bella. She really is a splendid actress, you know, and much better suited to you. I have to say I wasn't keen on your being paired with a succession of young girls – undignified, wouldn't you say? Also, you have to bear in mind this unfortunate business of the break-up of your marriage. The public doesn't like it, you know. And, of course, as you are doubtless aware, they are apt to confuse fact with fiction and seeing you reunited with your estranged screen wife, they will naturally assume that all is well in private. I feel it is a judicious move at this time and one that I applaud wholeheartedly.'

'Really!' said Geoff, scarcely believing his ears. 'That's how you feel, is it? Well, it's none of your fucking business what happens in my private life, if you must know, and I'd like to take this opportunity of thanking you for all you have done for me in the past and informing you that I no longer wish

314

to be represented by you. I am finding myself a new agent. You'll receive formal notice of the termination of our association in the post tomorrow morning!' and he slammed down the phone.

He did not return immediately to the rehearsal room, but went instead straight into the nearest production office and typed out the farewell letter to his agent of nearly twenty-five years, found an envelope, addressed it, took a stamp from his Filofax, then went out to post it in the nearby postbox. He was minus a wife, a family, a home, a mistress, a girlfriend and now an agent. Might as well make a clean sweep of it. He went back to the rehearsals and played the remaining scenes with Bella as though he were back at Stratford giving his Iago – which had not been well received at the time.

Jim could hardly wait for rehearsals to end. After they were over, he caught a cab back to the house in Shepherd's Bush and dashed inside. He phoned Patsy and told her to get her cute little tush over to his place as soon as possible, if not sooner. Patsy needed no second bidding. She hurriedly packed a suitcase and, slinging it into the back of the car, drove with all speed to Jim's abode.

It was the house of her dreams. Tasteful to a degree; she had only seen such glamour in the more expensive monthly magazines. Jim was amused by her naivety. She had arrived in a little black cocktail dress that left nothing to the imagination, and he had a tough job keeping his hands to himself. But a cocktail dress demanded a cocktail – so he mixed her a stiff one. About as stiff as his cock. She gulped it down, giggling happily and asked for a refill – and then another. Jim was more than delighted to oblige – this was going to be one helluva night! He produced some asparagus soup and garlic bread.

'I like garlic – it makes me feel sexy,' Patsy said, nicely

oiled by now. They sat down at the highly polished dining table. Jim had put a Suzanne Vega tape on and the atmosphere was warm and seductive. Patsy proclaimed the soup to be delicious, then spilt some down her dress.

'Ooops,' she said. 'Silly me.'

Jim was on his feet and at the back of the chair unzipping the dress in no time. 'Better clean it off now so it doesn't stain. It's such a pretty dress,' he said smoothly.

The dress was off and around her ankles, and Jim found himself gazing in awe at the biggest pair of tits he'd seen in a long time. And, jeez, they were for real. He scooped her up in his arms and carried her to the bedroom. He spent the next hour minutely examining Patsy's glorious body with his tongue, then fucking her every which way but loose. To Patsy, big was beautiful and Jim's was certainly the biggest cock she'd ever encountered. She experienced some difficulty in encompassing its width in her rosebud mouth, but she was determined not to be found wanting and finally managed to do so. They fucked several times that night. Patsy remembered hardly any of it except an exquisite pleasure followed by an hour or so of snatched sleep, before the enormous cock was pumping away inside her again. Her body would jerk convulsively as she felt the waves of pleasure ride over her before sinking down breathless but still tingling with pleasure into another satisfied sweaty sex-stained sleep.

The next morning, exhausted but happy, she got up early and padded into the kitchen to make him breakfast. Fifteen minutes later, she came into the bedroom bearing a tray of bacon, fried eggs and fried bread and a cup of lukewarm tea. Admittedly the fried stuff was swimming in grease and Jim's preferred breakfast consisted of orange juice, muesli and coffee, but he appreciated the gesture.

'Hey, you shouldn't have done all this,' he protested as she laid it on the bed in front of him.

'It's all part of the service.' She fluttered her eyelashes at him. 'I'll have supper ready for you when you get back, too – and if you tell me what you want washing and ironing – '

'What!' Jim sat bolt upright, spilling the tea in the saucer. Patsy smiled at him indulgently.

'I don't have to work today,' she said. 'I'm not called,' she added, as though to a small child. 'You're going to be a hardworking boy, so Patsy will look after you.'

Alarm bells were going off all over Jim's brain, which due to lack of sleep was not functioning on all cylinders.

'Hey, now wait a minute – ' he began.

'No, it's no trouble – I love to do it, I promise. I shall go out shopping and get you something really special for supper. What's your favourite?'

Jim's brain suddenly engaged in gear. He'd had this kind of trouble before, he remembered, with a crazed fan who was convinced she'd been engaged to him or some such whacky bullshit. He was not about to put himself through that again. He removed the tray and got out of bed. The erection that her initial appearance had provoked was subsiding rapidly at the unexpected turn of events. He grabbed his towelling robe and put it on. Then he very firmly took her by the arm and steered her in the direction of the bathroom.

'Holy cow,' he stopped dead at the sight of Patsy's open suitcase on the floor. 'Where the hell did that come from?'

'I sneaked out this morning in your raincoat and brought it in,' she confessed.

Jim stared at her. 'You snuck out?' he said horrified, preferring his own grammatical turn of phrase. 'Where do you think you are, Pacific Pallisades? Don't you know, dumbo, that the goddamn fucking British press has been

317

hanging around here ready to get pics of any bit of tail I bring home? Now get a tub, get some fucking clothes on and get outta here before I send for the cops!'

Patsy was transfixed with horror. 'I don't understand. What have I done . . . ?' she faltered.

'Gimme a break, will you? I can't handle fucking crazy dames at this hour of the a.m. Jeez, I need a fix,' he muttered to himself as he went into the kitchen to make himself some coffee. 'Go on – scram – and I don't want no further trouble from you, okay?' he said, looking back at her. 'I want you out of here in ten minutes, get it?' Patsy started to cry. 'Oh shit – that's all I need,' said Jim, as he disappeared into the kitchen.

Patsy, totally bewildered, got dressed. She packed her things hurriedly, ignoring his advice about the bath and sobbing quietly let herself out of the house. She staggered down the steps with the suitcase and pushed it onto the rear seat, and then with a tear-stained glance up at the windows of her temporary paradise, drove home, hardly able to see, the tears blurring her vision.

42

When Patsy got home, she went straight to her bed and, gathering all her toy animals around her, she cried her heart out. Around mid-morning she pulled herself together and went to repair the damage to her face. She was looking terrible, she decided. No man would ever look at her again. She started crying once more. She had been so in love with Jim, how could he turn on her like that after the wonderful night of love they had spent together? She had been so sure he had loved her in return. She was in the middle of trying to affix her eyelashes for the third time, an impossible task due to her constantly streaming eyes, when the phone rang. Jim! She thought exultantly, he'd rung to apologize for his extraordinary behaviour. It was just the strain of being in a foreign country and the lack of sleep that had done it. He was probably a moody man in any case. She'd have to get used to that. She rushed to the phone.

'Yes?' she said tremulously.

'Hello, Pat – it's me again, Anthony Snellor.'

'Oh,' said Patsy, bitterly disappointed.

'Er, listen, Pat, we're keen to get something in this weekend, we've heard the rumour about a certain person and a hunky American.'

Patsy was genuinely puzzled. 'Who?' she asked, her heart beating a little faster.

'Oh come on, Pat, don't be coy. The gentleman has good taste. Didn't take him long to suss out the prettiest girl in the cast, did it?'

Patsy still hadn't caught on. 'I don't know what you mean,' she said haughtily. 'Who are you talking about?' He'd better not mean that Claire Jenner.

'Well you, of course, who else would I be talking about? You're the prettiest girl by a mile. Is it the real thing, Pat? Have you finally met Mr Right?'

A thought slowly formed itself in Patsy's mind. Her native cunning was working overtime again.

'Yes,' she said simply. 'We're in love – he wants to marry me.'

Tony Snellor knew a load of hogwash when he heard it, and this was the biggest load he'd heard for some time, but as usual his nose hadn't let him down. This bint would be easy pickings, she was – what was the word – vulnerable, yes that was it, vulnerable. She would be putty in his hands.

'Listen, Pat, I've got a nice big fat cheque for you. I thought I might drop it round this morning, if that's all right with you – if you're alone, of course.' Patsy bit her lip.

'Oh yes, I'm alone. Jim's gone to rehearsals, that's why.'

Jim's dumped you, thought Snellor to himself gleefully, and you're going to talk to your Uncle Tony. You're going to tell him all about it and about everything else too!

'What time would be convenient, Pat?' he asked politely. 'Half an hour say?'

Patsy agreed that half an hour would be fine. She reckoned she could get her face in shape by then.

'See you then, Pat. Oh remind me of your address, will you?' said Tony, who was looking at it in front of him on a crumpled piece of paper. He'd long since checked it out. Patsy recited the details, and instructions on how to get there and, satisfied that there was no chance of his getting lost, she put down the phone and returned to the bathroom to make herself look glamorous as befitted the fiancée of the world's most handsome man.

Jim, meanwhile, had recovered his equilibrium somewhat. Having thrown out the rapidly congealing greasy plate of food Patsy had concocted, he had partaken of a shower and breakfasted on freshly squeezed orange juice, yoghurt and honey and assorted vitamins. He was just getting dressed when the phone rang.

'Shit,' he said to himself. 'If that's the screwball dame, I'll have to have my calls monitored.'

'Hello, Jimbo,' said a cut-glass voice.

'Claire baby, hi. Howya doing?'

'Jim, you remember I asked you to do me a favour?'

'Name it,' he said, relieved to be on terra firma again.

'Can you pick up some photographs for me on your way into rehearsals today?'

'Surely – where?'

'Funnily enough not far from you, the other side of the Bush – Limegrove – Ashton House – number sixty-one. I'll meet you there.'

'No problem. Why can't you get them, though?'

'It's the man you met the other day, Roger by name. He has some negatives of me in the altogether – er – the nude. Some of them are compromising. I think he may listen to reason if *you* ask for them back, you get my drift?'

'It'll be a pleasure,' said Jim, grinning to himself.

'Sal will be standing by as well to phone the police if necessary.'

Jim took a genuine delight in proving his superiority over

his fellow man whenever occasion demanded. He'd lost count of the fights he'd been in since his schooldays and at college, where he'd triumphed and come out smiling with hardly a scratch and just bruised knuckles to show for it.

'You're an angel,' Claire said relieved.

'When are you due at rehearsals?' he asked.

'We call it the fun factory – same time as you.'

'I like it,' said Jim and put down the phone.

Geoff had stayed the night at the Holiday Inn. He had been recognized at the bar and had been forced to retire early. He had spent the evening looking at his lines and trying to learn them. Then he tried watching television, but it was mainly football, in which he had no interest, and a truly dreadful 1970s Hollywood thriller, with the usual assortment of glamorous non-actresses and handsome smooth leading men, a plot that was impossible to follow and banal dialogue. He ordered food from room service and virtually emptied the mini bar. He then ordered more Scotch and drank himself into a torpor, finally falling asleep, sitting propped up in the bed with the light and TV on.

He woke in the early hours, with a stiff neck and a headache. He staggered out of bed and went to his briefcase, where he knew there would be painkillers. He took four washed down with the remains of the Scotch, and fell into a troubled sleep. The next morning he awoke early with an even worse headache. He ordered breakfast and dosed himself with more painkillers. After a long bath, he breakfasted on cereal and kippers, toast and marmalade and took two more pills with his coffee, just to be on the safe side. Thus fortified he sat back and surveyed the situation.

There was no way out of the script crisis. He'd asked for

it and he'd got it. He'd have to grin and bear it. He now
had no agent. Well, that didn't matter too much. He was
booked for another series, so he was all right for another year.
Sukie was divorcing him, she'd made that quite clear. He'd
wait until things had calmed down a little before he tried to
see the boys again. It was obvious from Claire's behaviour
at rehearsals that she'd washed her hands of him. There was
no hope there. As for Patsy, well, he was well rid of her. The
only course of action now open to him was to try to rent a
flat somewhere, not too far from the rehearsal rooms and
studios. He'd better start looking straightaway. There was
one consoling thought: things were as bad as they could be
– they couldn't get any worse.

Roger put the phone down after his conversation with Claire,
smiling to himself. He knew she'd come round. There was
nothing like the hero being injured in a fight to bring out the
maternal instinct in a woman. He rubbed his chin ruefully.
He looked in the mirror. He had a suspicion of a black eye,
too. Never mind, it could only help his cause. He went into
his studio. No, on second thoughts, he wanted to look his best.
There was a little dressing room that abutted on the studio.
He went in and searched the top of the dressing-table.
Panstick, great, just what was needed. He dabbed some on
gingerly. It covered the bruise perfectly, he blended it in
carefully and stood back to survey the results. He looked
terrific. What woman could resist him? Soon he would have
Claire eating out of his hand.

He'd been a fool to dump her, he could see that now. He'd
missed her dreadfully. It was only the pregnancy that had
unnerved him. He couldn't cope with that, he'd have to make
sure that didn't happen again. Claire was something special,

there was no doubt about that. What on earth had she been doing with an ageing roué like Geoff Armitage? He'd known that wouldn't last. He'd been disconcerted, he'd had to admit, to read that she'd found someone so quickly to replace him. He'd almost been jealous – well, not exactly jealous – come off it, more hurt pride really. And the trouble was, the other birds hadn't been up to scratch – and there'd been a few! Was he losing his touch or what? He preened himself in the mirror. Nah, he was a good-looking devil, a touch on the mature side, of course, but that's how they liked them. Experienced. Not bloody middle-aged like Geoff Armitage, that was going too far.

Satisfied by his reflection, he went back to his kitchenette and made fresh coffee. Claire loved fresh coffee. That's what he liked about her – the girl had class. He always liked having her on his arm and now that she was a bit of a celebrity – yeah, give the bimbos the Spanish archer, and get in amongst where it was at.

His business had taken a dive recently. Too much competition, that was the snag. Every bloody body thought they could become a photographer overnight. At one time, he'd had the profession sewn up, but now there were kids coming along who wouldn't know a reflector from a hole in the ground.

The door bell rang – that hadn't taken her long, she couldn't wait to see him – she was obviously distraught at what had happened at her house. He regretted now coming on so strong. He'd be gentle with her today. He went to the front door of his studio flat and opened it.

'Claire baby – what can I say, sweetheart? – can you forgive me? I just got carried away – you know.'

Claire stood looking radiant and smiling at him lovingly. 'Roger, my poor baby, were you very badly hurt, darling?'

324

and she flung her bag on the floor and herself into his arms.

'Aagh, ah, ow,' he said.

'Are you all right, angel?' she asked solicitously.

'Oh yeah, don't worry about me, I can look after myself – I'm fine, just fine. Come on in, I've got the coffee on.'

'Yes, lovely, I can smell it,' and she followed him in.

'Baby, let me look at you,' he said, when they were in the kitchen. He held her at arm's length. 'Wow, you look so good, so good – hey listen, I'm so sorry about last time – I just lost my head, you know – No, let me explain.'

'You don't have to, just pour the coffee. You remember how I like it, don't you?' she smiled winningly.

'What, whiskey at this time of the day?' he asked, surprised.

'Just a nip – for old times' sake,' she whispered, like a naughty little girl. Roger took the hint. 'Oh right, leave it with me,' and giving her a quick kiss, he started to hunt in a lower cupboard.

'Now, where did I put my bag?' she said, pretending to look around. 'Oh I know, in the hall. Stay there, I've got something for you,' and she darted out of the kitchen.

'Where the hell did I put the Irish?' he muttered, ransacking the lower shelf. 'Don't tell me I've drunk it all.' He felt a sharp pain as his left arm was twisted up behind his back.

'Looking for something, buddy?' asked Jim quietly, who had crept in unseen when Claire opened the front door for him under pretence of going to look for her bag. Sally had followed hot on Jim's heels and was waiting in the studio by the telephone.

'What the f – what's going on?' gasped Roger in considerable discomfort.

'Just take it easy, buddy, we're going for a little walk.' Jim pulled him up off his haunches and pushed him into the studio towards a filing cabinet. 'Just hand over the negatives, asshole, and you won't get hurt, okay?'

'What negatives? Ow – Jesus – hey, just watch what you're – Aahh, okay, okay, give me a chance, will you?' Claire joined them. 'Bitch!' Roger spat at her.

'You've changed your tune,' she remarked dryly. 'Where are they?'

'You better talk, buddy, or I'll break both your arms.'

'And Sal will ring the police if you don't tell us.'

'You can't force me – it'll take you several days to look through that lot,' Roger said, gesturing with his head towards the filing cabinet.

'That's why Sal's going to call the police. Jim is a witness to attempted rape.'

Ten minutes later they had the negatives and were on their way.

'Whatever did I see in that ghastly man?' asked Claire of Sally, as they were driving along preparatory to Sally being dropped off at a tube station.

'I did often mention it,' said Sally dryly.

'Not often enough,' replied Claire.

Snellor got to Patsy's place in exactly half an hour. By the time of his arrival, she was looking her most glamorous.

'Do come in, Tony,' she said graciously, holding open the door for him. 'Go straight through into the lounge.'

'Nice place you've got here, Pat,' said Snellor approvingly. He noted leatherette and chrome seats – plastic and chrome coffee tables and prints on the walls. This was right up his street, he'd been trying to persuade Mrs Snellor to modernize their place for years – to no avail. She clung tenaciously to the three-piece suite they'd had since they were married. He'd given up. It was like sex. She always had a headache. She had headaches so often, he was convinced she'd got a brain tumour.

'Glad you like it, Tone,' Patsy said with gratification. She'd spent a lot of time getting it just right.

'Does Jim like it?' he asked trying to catch her off guard.

'Why yes,' she replied without turning a hair, 'but I spend most of my time around at his place. He's used to something a bit classier in Hollywood – Beverly Hills, you know.'

'Oh I see, this not grand enough for him then? So, when's the happy day, Pat?'

'We're just good friends,' said Patsy simply.

Snellor stared at her. 'Come off it, Pat, you just said you were round at his place.'

'We're just good friends,' she repeated without emotion.

'Okay, have it your way.'

'Would you care for some coffee,' she asked with elaborate politeness.

'Oh ta, yeah, great. Actually I'd prefer a drink, if you've got one.'

She floated out in a cloud of heavy scent. Snellor wrinkled his famous nose. She returned shortly bearing a tray with Tia Maria on it. Snellor winced, he'd been hoping for vodka. Patsy seated herself carefully.

'Do you have my cheque, Tony?' she asked solemnly, as she poured the liqueur.

'Ah yes,' he said, trying to extract it from his inside pocket.

'Good, here's your drink.'

There was something unnerving about her calm exterior. The nose told him it was a cover-up. He handed her an envelope containing the cheque.

'Thank you, Tony. Now, what do you want to know?' Her stillness was alarming.

'Er, everything, Pat.'

'I do wish you'd call me by my proper name. I've mentioned it before.'

'Sorry, Patricia.'

'Patsy,' she corrected him.

'Patsy, of course. Right, Patsy, come on, let's have it.'

43

Sukie woke early, as was her custom. For a moment she couldn't think where she was. Overhead she could see the charming red and white lining of the heavy *toile de Jouy* drapes that hung over the bed and enveloped the sides, depicting a rustic scene also in red on a white ground. The posts of the bed were in limed oak, as was the antique furniture with which the room was superbly furnished. The bed was high off the ground and with a very hard sprung mattress. Sukie could not remember when she'd had a better night's sleep. She turned her head to see the tousled dark locks of her lover of the previous night, which was all that was visible of him. She smiled as she remembered the night, and stretched luxuriatingly. The early morning sunlight filtered through the lattice windows and she smelt the fresh sweetness of the spring garden. Suddenly there was the unmistakable cry of a peacock. It was all too impossibly romantic. Sean stirred and put out a hand to her. It found her shoulder, which he stroked lovingly.

'Good morning, princess,' he murmured from the depth of the pillow – 'Are you up to ordering tea?'

'I did it last night,' she whispered back.

'You're wonderful, you think of everything – what a woman,' and he snuggled down again.

She wanted to say, that for the last fifteen years her life had been such that she had been obliged to think of everything, but she decided against it. Why spoil this delicious idyll, why let the mundane things of life intrude? She wanted to savour this moment, she'd waited long enough for it. She thought of the boys at home in the patchy kitchen, which was due to be painted this weekend, she suddenly remembered. For a fleeting moment she wished they were with her here. How they would love this place. She promised herself she would bring them here one day in the summer. She'd love to treat them and they had been so good about recent events and Nicky would be mad about the peacocks. Yes, she would bring them here in the summer holidays.

'What are you thinking about?' he asked quietly.

'Sorry,' she replied, smiling apologetically, 'I was miles away.'

'What! When you have your very own Prince Charming by your side?'

'Oh is that who you are? I had been wondering.'

'Yes, didn't you see me last night? I was that rather energetic and debonair young frog that tried to attract your attention just before supper.'

'Yes, of course, I would have known you anywhere.'

He grinned and leaned over to embrace her. There was a discreet tap at the door. 'Curses,' he muttered. 'Just let me attend to this small matter, then I shall continue where I left off,' and he leapt out of bed. Sukie had a fleeting glimpse of a wiry muscular tanned body before he slipped on a thick beige towelling robe. It had been dark and she had felt rather than seen his body and she knew now that she had missed a treat. But now mundane matters had intruded after all. Sean opened the door and let in a rosy-cheeked chambermaid bearing a silver tray laden with breakfast.

'Good grief, what's all this?' asked Sean eyeing it with mock horror.

'Your last proper English breakfast for some time,' Sukie reminded him.

'My God, you're right. I'm a condemned man. Tomorrow I depart these shores for foreign climes and will doubtless be living off a diet of ship's biscuits and pemican – or do I mean ptarmigan? – or whatever other delights they had to offer in the fifteenth century. Never mind, it will be washed down with quantities of rum, so it won't matter.'

The girl set down the tray and blushingly accepted a tip from Sean from some loose coins that he'd found lying around on top of the bureau.

After breakfast they made love again and took a bath together. Everything seemed perfect to Sukie. They dressed, chatting happily, Sukie aware that she was breaking all sorts of rules, but she didn't care. She could hardly take her eyes off her handsome young lover, much less keep her hands off him. Then they wandered out into the grounds. The morning was sparkling and clear and everything seemed new-minted. The dew on the grass glistened in the early spring sunshine as they strolled through the gardens holding hands. At one point, Sukie drew his attention to some activity that was taking place by an old ruined arch.

'What are they doing?' she asked.

'Looks like a modelling shoot to me.' They walked towards them to get a better view.

'We mustn't disturb them,' she warned. There were two young men and a very stylish girl posing in casual wear against the lovely old stonework, which dated back to the twelfth century.

'I don't like the look of the photographer,' whispered Sukie. 'He looks like a poseur, something left over from the seventies.'

'Don't knock it,' said Sean. 'It was thanks to my way-out

hippy friend, Mike, that you and I got together in the first place.'

'Remind me to cover him with rapturous kisses of gratitude when I meet him,' she replied, giggling. 'Come on, let's go and find the peacocks.'

The movement of their departure attracted the photographer's attention and he turned around to see who was invading his space. The young man, he observed, was handsome by any standards and the woman looked familiar. Good-looking bird, bit mature for his taste, but he'd seen her somewhere before – where? Was she a model from way back? Nope. An actress? – Yes, that was it, an actress, an ex-actress. Now what the hell was her name? Roger gazed after her thoughtfully as she walked away. No, he couldn't think. It would come to him later. He resumed the shoot.

'That's right, Mildred darling – this way, chin up a little, up a bit more, that's it, lovely. Now give me some really hot looks . . . Come on, now . . . smoulder at me, come on . . . Now pout those lips and hot, hot, hot . . . That's my girl.'

Later on, Roger and his little unit had broken for coffee when he ran into Sukie and Sean again. They made an interesting and exotic couple, he thought.

'Sukie,' Sean called out over his shoulder as he was making his way to the main entrance with their bags, 'do you want coffee before we go?' Sukie shook her head.

Of course, that was it. Sukie Marlow! He had photographed her once. Not on her own, but with a whole bunch of other young hopefuls on the set at Shepperton Studios. They'd all been in a film together. What the hell was it – oh never mind. Sukie Marlow – he'd remembered her out of all of them. She seemed the most vivacious – whatever had become of her? Oh yes, he remembered, she'd married some actor. Roger stood still in his tracks. My God! She'd married Geoff

Armitage! The ageing Casanova that Claire had shacked up with. Well, the wife was doing all right for herself. He casually pointed the loaded camera that was hanging round his neck in their direction and snatched a few shots of them as they were walking towards the car. After they had driven off, he went in search of a phone.

'Are we ready to go again, guv?' asked his assistant.

'Yep, just hang on a tick, got to make a phone call. With you in a sec.'

Within a few minutes he was talking to his old friend Alan on the picture desk at the *Globe*.

'Got a few shots that might interest you, Alan old buddy, and a little bit of info your Ed might like to have about his person. Put him on, will you? – oh, and I'll be up in town by early afternoon, I'll drop by the office. See ya.'

44

'Trev, Trev, I've got it! The lot! The little tart has spilled the beans, we've got 'em by the short and curlies and no mistake. Wait till you hear this lot!'

'All right, all right, cool it, calm down. Take a seat and tell me in words of one syllable – not that you know any polysyllabic ones,' Trev added ungraciously.

Snellor bridled. He knew plenty, he was just never allowed to use them, that was the trouble. Polysyllabic! That was a good one in itself, maybe he could work that in somewhere. He didn't reply to the taunt, however, confining himself to a look of hurt and disapproval, and flinging himself into the nearest chair.

'Okay, then, let's have it,' commanded Trevor Grantly.

Snellor sat up immediately. 'Listen, Trev, you're not going to believe this. Geoff Armitage left the Jenner bird after he'd done a runner from his wife and moved in with her, tried to go back to his wife, wife wouldn't wear it, he tried to return to the Jenner gaff, she didn't want to know, so he turns up at our little tart's place, cos he's been knocking her off all along. She's now thrown him out, cos she's after the Hollywood import, who it transpires has been giving the Jenner bird one, that was after they had a night out in the red light district and ended up at a porno house. Bella's back on the booze again in a big way and Geoff's wife gets her leg over with a toy boy who's just landed a lead in that big movie.'

Snellor leaned back in the chair in some satisfaction to see the effect of his cornucopia of goodies on his boss. Cornucopia! He'd like to give that one an airing sometime.

There was a brief silence as Trevor attempted to digest the barrage of information that had just been hurled at him. Then he, too, sat back in his chair and stretched himself luxuriously. '*It is my birthday*,' he quoted dramatically.

Tony Snellor sat bolt upright. His face wore the appalled expression of a man who has neglected to send his boss a card for this auspicious occasion. 'Shit! – Sorry, I mean sorry, Trev – I forgot.'

Trevor ignored him. '*It is my birthday*,' he went on. '*I had thought t' have held it poor. But, since my Lord Is Antony again, I will be Cleopatra.*' Snellor was dumbfounded. 'I was Cleopatra at my public school,' Trevor explained, seeing his underling's horrified expression, 'and bloody good I was too.'

Tony Snellor had long since discovered that Trevor's superior grasp of the English language and his very considerable vocabulary, which sadly he never had occasion to use in his capacity as Editor of the *Globe*, but which had been put to good use in his early years as a news reporter on several of the 'heavies', had been acquired through a public school education. His parents, Liverpudlians by birth, had been in the wine trade and his father had come South and opened a chain of wine markets at the very moment when wine became the in drink. The resultant wealth had given Trevor's father the opportunity to give his son the superior education he himself had never had. It also explained Trevor's abstemious habits. Having had to endure the nickname of 'wino' and the aphorism '*in vino veritas*' every time he opened his mouth to speak, he resolved on a life of teetotalism at the

335

age of 16. Snellor, however, although having a vague idea that all forms of deviation were practised at public schools, had never suspected his boss of actually indulging in transvestism.

'In *Antony and Cleopatra*, the school play, you twat,' Trevor explained, seeing Tony's stunned expression. 'Run that by me again, will you – slowly?' Snellor did as he was told. Trevor listened thoughtfully and then said, 'If this is all true – it's dynamite! We could make or break that series – the producers will either decide to take it off air, for the sake of the morals of their hitherto unsuspecting viewers, or it will rocket even further up the ratings and become a smash hit. Either way, we're laughing. My God, they've got their own soap opera off-screen as well as on.'

'Hot stuff, isn't it?' said Snellor gleefully. 'Where do we start?'

'We don't "start" anywhere. We do a mass exposé – we go for broke – one foul swoop. Net them all at once. Let me see now: "Sex Crazed Soap Stars in Swap Shop Shock". Yeah – not bad, or, uhm, "TV bosses to pull plug on porno players". Or "Randy Romeo on Rampage in Rotterdam".'

'Amsterdam,' corrected Snellor.

'Shut up,' snapped Trevor. 'I'm trying it out for alliteration. "Clean up your act or get out, warn TV bosses".'

'That's not alliterative,' Snellor pointed out.

Trevor glared at him. 'I've told you before, leave the headlines to me. Once we've got the headline, we've got the story – it follows quite naturally. Right, let's get on with this. We'll devote the front page and a double page spread inside to it, more if necessary. Get on to the picture desk, see what they've got. Bella's back on the juice, you say? She's not having a fling then?'

'Don't think so, Trev.'

'That's probably why she drinks,' Trevor chuckled to himself. 'What about Meg and Reg – they up to anything?'

'Trev,' said Snellor admonishingly, 'he lost his wife two years ago and Meg's got a husband with Alzheimer's disease – he keeps wandering off.'

'I'm not surprised,' rejoined Trevor mercilessly. 'So would I with what's going on on that set – I'd want to get right out of it, too.' Even Snellor was slightly shocked.

'What pics are you after, then?'

'The porno house they visited – Bella with drink in hand – Jim Dutton in bathing trunks on beach in embrace with blonde bimbo – Geoff with Patsy, Geoff with his wife, Geoff with the Jenner girl, the Jenner girl with Jim Dutton, et cetera, et cetera. You sure you've got the full story? You haven't missed anything?'

'Isn't that enough, Trev?' protested Snellor.

'I was just wondering, you say our little tart is after Mr Beefcake – maybe we could catch them at it.'

'They make a good-looking pair,' observed Snellor sagely.

'Can we get off the subject of her tits, please, although, come to think of it,' he added thoughtfully, 'I've heard that Jim Dutton is a bit of a tit man himself. She's bound to make out. When she does, see if you can get her to spill the beans. Should make good reading!'

'She'll want more money,' said Snellor doubtfully.

'Nah,' replied Trevor scornfully. 'Just tell her they're planning to build the series around her and Jim Dutton, but they're not sure about their compatibility.'

Snellor looked doubtful. 'She won't know what that means – she hasn't got a lot up top.'

'You're kidding, aren't you?' replied Trevor derisively. 'She's in the Dolly Parton league. Get on to it. You're good on monosyllables.'

45

'She's got to go!' It was Bella speaking. She looked around
at the shocked faces of her fellow cast members. 'No, I'm
sorry, what other course of action do we have open to us?
We daren't make a move, she's monitoring our every action.
It's terrifying. One won't be able to utter – how can we?
– knowing everything we are saying is being fed straight to
the gutter press. It's outrageous! I've never in all my years
in the profession been responsible for the firing of a fellow
artiste – one can't dignify her with the appellation of actor,
but then I've never experienced anything like this before. No,
there's no other solution, she has to go! Otherwise the
situation will become intolerable. What does anyone else
think?'

'It explains everything,' said Claire slowly, as light began
to dawn. Patsy must have seen Geoff going into her hotel room
– how else could she have been sure? 'She must have been
spying on us. It's horrible,' she said emotionally. 'I mean
people's lives have been ruined.'

No one said anything for a while. Geoff, only too aware that
she was referring to her own, his wife's and the boys' lives
hung his head. He knew that in some ways it was his casual
treatment of Patsy that had partly provoked the whole ghastly
business. *Heav'n has no rage, like love to hatred turn'd, Nor Hell
a fury, like a woman scorn'd*, he thought. Dear God, he hoped

Claire wouldn't turn on him. But, of course, she already had. He was receiving his punishment at her hands in the shape of icy silences, snubs, and avoidance of any eye contact whatsoever. Would she ever speak to him again, he wondered, other than on-screen, of course? Did it really matter if she didn't? Did anything matter any more? He felt empty and cold inside. He supposed Bella was right – Patsy would have to go. He dearly wished the whole lot of them would go. He'd been doing this series for seven years now – surely he deserved something better than this? He was, or had been, a renowned classical actor, for God's sake. What was he doing slumming it with this bunch of fourth division actors? He should be giving his Lear at the Barbican or his Falstaff at Stratford, or perhaps a little-known Jacobean domestic tragedy at the Swan. This was all so tawdry, so tacky.

It was late Sunday afternoon and the leading members of the cast – Bella, Geoff, Claire, Jim, Meg and Reg, even Amy and Simon, were all sitting in Hugh and Mona's thankfully spacious living room, having been hurriedly summoned there after the publication of the exposé in that morning's *Sunday Globe*. Mona had supplied cocktails and snacks, although no one was hungry. Several copies of the offending newspaper were lying around the room. It was obvious from the tenor of the article and the amount of picture space that she occupied, that Patsy was the perpetrator of the débâcle. The extraordinary section where she claimed to be Jim's fiancée in one breath, followed by the ludicrous comment, 'We're just good friends,' in the next, confirmed that she was simply out for publicity for herself at the expense, it would seem, of her fellow cast members. They had forgathered, a solemn little group, appalled at the seedy headlines and apparently blatant attempt by the newspaper chiefs to sabotage the series in their self-appointed role as guardians of the country's morals. Hardly anyone had escaped. Even Meg and Reg had been roped in as horrified onlookers at the scene of dissipation and loose living by their cohorts. As both of them were almost entirely ignorant of all the events described, apart from the break-up of Geoff's marriage, and inclined to either absolute scepticism or total dismissal, the claims of the paper of their shocked reactions was both ludicrous and grossly misleading. Amy came in for innuendo in her relationship with Simon, which, as everyone knew, was restricted to the screen, but that didn't stop Tony Snellor, who managed by clever use of negatives to insinuate that Amy was as besotted with Simon off-screen as she was on. As Amy had a very steady relationship with an architect, whom she hoped to marry, this fabrication had upset her considerably and she arrived at the meeting red-eyed and visibly distressed. The article had covered the front page of the *Sunday Globe*, plus the next two inside sheets and the centre spread. *SOAP STARS IN STEAMY SEX SCANDAL* was the comparatively mild headline, but the revelations to follow were anything but. Described in *doubles entendres* were the nights of passion enjoyed by Claire and Jim, Claire and Geoff, Patsy and Jim, Patsy and Geoff. Bella was made out to be virtually an alcoholic past hope, and it was even hinted that Simon was gay. Not in so many words, of course. But just enough innuendo to keep the prurient reader guessing. As Simon prided himself on his smooth macho image and his hosts of teenage female fans, he was not best pleased and was all for offering the newspaper personal interviews with his numerous female conquests who would vouch for his heterosexuality.

Meg, as usual over-anxious to be fair, said, 'But how can we be sure it's Patsy. I mean, she's been exposed as well.'

Jim picked up one of the papers. 'There are certain relevant details in there that only she could give them,' he said softly.

Meg tilted her head, anticipating further clarification, but Jim would say nothing more.

Geoff was also able to confirm that the stories that concerned Patsy were the only ones with accurate detail, whereas the others, although correct, were vague. To Geoff's horror, the article had concluded with a picture of an actor called Sean Mallin who had landed a lead part in *Vasco da Gama*, the blockbuster movie currently filming on the Mediterranean. Alongside this was an old picture of Geoff with Sukie at an awards ceremony, and a caption noting significantly she was the casting director responsible for Sean's obtaining the part, and the fact that he had been spotted with her at the Castle Hotel. Geoff had been the victim of a nagging pain on observing the handsome features of the younger actor, and was a prey to doubts and fears. Was this the young man with whom she had been flirting? Was he her lover? What was she thinking of, consorting with boys half her age? He thought all this, blithely ignoring the fact that he had had numerous affairs during his marriage with girls many years his junior and that Sean was a mere ten years younger than his wife. He had not expected to feel jealous. But he did. He was consumed with a sort of impotent deep-seated rage that burned him every time he thought about even the vague possibility of Sukie and Sean in bed together. Now he suddenly rose from his seat in an agitated manner.

'Where do you think you're going?' asked Bella, who was awaiting a reply to her call for Patsy's dismissal.

'You don't need me here,' he said in low tones. 'I have some business to attend to,' and he started to leave the room.

'Just a minute.' Bella stopped him with a stentorian voice that had stood her in good stead when she had played Volumnia at the Birmingham Rep. 'This is an official meeting. You can't just walk out before we've come to a decision. For Christ's sake, pull yourself together, man. You've been behaving like a two-year-old. SIT DOWN!' she thundered. To everyone's surprise, Geoff did as he was told.

'All right,' said Hugh quietly, after a moment, 'this is an extremely unpleasant business, but I shall have to ask you all for a vote. Before I do, does anyone want to say anything else?'

Geoff said with venom, 'Get rid of the little bitch!' and the assembly wondered privately to whom he was referring.

Amy was next: 'I think Bella's right. She's tried to mess up people's lives, that can't be allowed to continue.' As Amy was normally as quiet as a mouse, everyone regarded this statement with due seriousness.

Simon cleared his throat. 'She's presumably in the pay of this ghastly newspaper – who knows what lies she's going to come out with next?'

Hugh looked at Meg. 'Megan, what have you to say? You have no axe to grind as you've escaped this horror.'

Meg shook her head sadly. 'Not entirely,' she said. 'They've lied about me as well. They never asked my opinion. How could I be shocked about something about which I knew nothing. And if I had've known, as far as I'm concerned it's none of my business what other people get up to, their private lives are their own affair and I resent being described as shocked when it's not true.'

'Here, here,' said Reg, who always backed her up. 'I won't know what to say to her when I see her again – well, I dare say I won't say anything, she don't deserve it.'

There was a silence, broken by Larry. 'I've had a wonderful idea,' he said quietly. Hugh looked at him gratefully. He'd been feeling like one of the conspirators in *Julius Caesar* up to this point. The rest turned towards Larry expectantly.

arry's ideas when they came were usually humdingers. You've heard about life mirroring art and so forth – well, ow about if we make our little Miss Hall the mole on screen s well as off! It'll mean rewriting a couple of scenes, of course, ut think about it: we discover that it is she that has been esponsible for the fake De La Tour being purchased. She ad access to the files, remember. We only need shoot one ny insert, she can be seen having a private conversation with ae forger – in Amsterdam – use some of the spare footage, aen any old corner of the studio for a mock-up of a bar, say n the Herenstraat.'

'Why would she have done it?' asked Hugh curiously, lready beginning to like the idea.

'Money,' said Larry simply, 'as in life. That way the public ets to know the truth in a roundabout way and we get rid f her.'

'But that amount?' said Hugh incredulously. 'We're talking bout millions here. There has to be a reason.'

'Political cause,' said Larry busking. 'She's part of an nternational terrorist group.'

'The IRA?' suggested Bella, starting to become involved.

Larry shook his head. 'Too near home. Better make it a undamentalist Islamic group, or leave it vague.'

'It's preposterous!' said Geoff scornfully.

'You think this whole series isn't?' Larry turned on him. And I should like to remind you, Geoff, that you have been lmost single-handedly responsible for the possible early lemise of this series. Just look at this garbage again, will you,' and he flung the paper on the floor in front of them, separating he cover from the centre pages so that they could review the whole horror.

IS IT CURTAINS FOR THIS SORRY SORDID ORTHRIGHT SAGA OF FAMILY STRIFE? Producers were meeting today to discuss whether or not to pull the plug on the steamy seamy soap . . . and so it went on.

'All right,' said Hugh, 'so she's involved with some unspecified terrorist group, or at least in their pay. I accept that and I dare say the punters might, but how do we get rid of her? There's only one more episode to go in this series and we would have to explain her absence somehow. Incredible as it may seem, she has quite a following.'

Larry was on the spot and he knew it. He thought on his feet. 'A desperate situation requires a desperate solution. I think we give her a nice little farewell scene. Gazing into the bathroom cabinet mirror, taking a cyanide pill, an overdose, what you will – big dramatic ending for her. What do you think?'

There was a horrified silence.

'You mean, kill her off?' Claire finally asked incredulously.

Larry regarded her with a half-humorous smile. 'Don't tell me you're confusing fact with fiction as well?'

'No, of course not,' said Claire hurriedly. 'It just seems, well, a bit drastic, that's all. Don't get me wrong. I've got no love for her, she's practically ruined my career, let's face it.'

'Well stop being sentimental then,' said Larry, giving her a wink. He turned to the others. 'Come on, you lot, she's going to love it. She'll have a death scene to play – every actor's dream.'

46

When Patsy received the script amendments for Episode
Thirteen she was thrilled. It took some time for the penny
to drop. All she saw at first was that she had three new scenes.
Admittedly she didn't have a word to say in any of them, but
she was on camera and in one of them, she was on her own
in close-up. Wow, it was working at last, they were finally
going to give her a big chance. An acting chance. She even
had a death scene. She had to lie on a bed absolutely still,
while the camera panned up to her face. Oh God, she'd never
had a death scene before. She hoped she'd be able to manage
it. What would her Auntie Thelma say? She couldn't wait
to tell her. She rushed to the phone.

'Auntie, guess what, you'll never guess what . . .'

Ten minutes later, she put down the phone, stunned. Of
course, if she were dead, that meant she wouldn't be in the
series any more. That's what Auntie Thelma had said. When
she'd done those scenes, she would be no more. No more in
the series. She couldn't take it in. They didn't want her. She
wondered dimly if it was anything to do with Sunday's
revelations in the *Globe*. Of course not, they couldn't possibly
suspect her, that was what was so clever, she'd been exposed
as well. It was thrilling. The whole world now knew her as
Jim Dutton's fiancée. It was wonderful. There'd already been
follow-ups in all the other tabloids. Her picture and Jim's had

featured on every front page. It was unbelievably exciting for a day or two. And then two extraordinary things had happened. Jim had come out with a denial. He'd come clean. He'd admitted that he had a brief flirtation with Patsy, but in no way was he involved with her. He absolutely stood by her statement saying they were just good friends. Then the next day a call had come from the production office to say that she would not be required at rehearsals. They were sending some rewrites around, but she needn't turn up until the final day at the studio. At first she thought it meant that her one scene had been cut, and when she received the script, she saw that it had, but that it had been replaced by three others and so she had been over the moon.

But now the full significance of what they had done to her dawned. It was Jim, of course. He didn't want her in the same show. No, it must be Geoff, he'd been so awful to her. Perhaps it was Claire, jealous of the massive publicity she'd been receiving recently. But what was she going to do? At Auntie Thelma's instigation, she phoned Deirdre, Hugh's secretary, to get an explanation, but Deirdre had been primed and was more than ready for her.

'Oh hello, Patsy, I thought you might call. Is it about the new Episode Thirteen? Yes, we're sorry we have to lose you, of course, but there's been a big planning meeting and there's going to be a whole new look to the series. A new format. More Americanized, to be built around Jim Dutton's character. To facilitate sales to America.'

America! That's just what she wanted. Oh no, this was too unfair. She was perfect to play opposite Jim. Surely they could see that.

'But, Deirdre,' she protested, 'I'm the most glamorous person in the series, they said so in the paper.'

Deirdre almost choked on her coffee, which she was

unwisely sipping as she took this call. She had known it would not be an easy one and she got herself a restorative to help her cope with it.

'Yes, we appreciate that, Patsy. You are, of course, very glamorous, we all know that.'

'So why can't I play opposite Jim then?' Patsy was almost in tears. 'I'm a Hollywood type, you know.'

Deirdre's glance raked the ceiling and walls in search of inspiration. She found it. Her eye alighted on a Hollywood calendar that Larry had given her.

'Jim feels that he wants a Katharine Hepburn type to play opposite him – and you're more, more –' she searched desperately through the calendar, 'more – Lana Turner, you know?'

'Oh.'

'Yes.'

'So, I'm not going to be in the new series then?'

'No, I'm afraid not.'

'They could always rush me off to hospital in time and I could recover.'

'Yes, I suppose they could, but that's not what's planned. I'm sorry.'

'My Auntie Thelma says that they have an option on me.'

'Yes, that's true, but it's not going to be taken up. I'm so sorry.' Deirdre was now beginning to feel like a murderess. 'But you must realize, Patsy, that this has been a wonderful chance for you. You've been in two series now. Most young actresses would have given their eye teeth to have had your opportunity.'

'Yes, I suppose so,' said Patsy dully. 'So I'm definitely not coming back then?'

'No, I'm afraid not,' Deirdre repeated. 'I really am very sorry.'

Finally Patsy had said goodbye and Deirdre had thankfully put down the phone. 'Oh God,' she said later to Hugh, 'it was dreadful – I felt like Medea.'

'I don't see the connection,' said Larry, who was also present. 'Didn't she kill her children or something equally gruesome?'

'Exactly,' said Deirdre. 'Well, that's how I felt! Do your own dirty work next time.' She cast a beady eye at Hugh who had the grace to look embarrassed. 'Do you know, I actually felt sorry for her.'

'Sorry? After what she's done to us? She's nearly made us all redundant, I'll remind you. Don't take after your namesake – didn't something frightful happen to her children as well?' exploded Larry.

'Who?' asked Deirdre. This was the first she'd heard of it.

'Deirdre of the Sorrows. I think she –'

'Oh do stop this wandering around in mythology – and, in any case, I think it was Niobe – I can't take any more, my head hurts,' said Hugh.

'Come on now, let's pull ourselves together,' Larry interposed. 'Patsy was a liability, it'll be a miracle if this series survives. I think we followed the only course of action open to us. Now all we have to do is maintain a dignified silence and hope that the press is good to us. So far we've obeyed all the rules. Husband and wife reunited, villain disposed of. Young love about to triumph and take over business and make pots of money. We only have to get Meg pregnant by Reg now to win the last sympathy vote –' Hugh groaned. 'Sorry, have I said something untoward?' asked Larry, concerned.

After Deirdre had left the room, he added, 'One thing that did impress me, old boy, was your wife's impeccable behaviour towards our leading lady.' Hugh looked guilty. 'Forgive me for mentioning it,' said Larry hurriedly.

348

'Oh that's all right. All that business with Bella finished ages ago.'

'Oh did it?' said Larry, with genuine interest. 'Well, there you go, I've obviously been watching too much television.'

'I suppose you wouldn't like my job, would you?' asked Hugh wearily.

'Certainly, when do you leave? Now let me see, what colour shall I re-do this office?' Hugh laughed weakly. 'No, seriously, you are a terrific producer and I'm very pleased about you and Mona, she's a dear person.'

'Yes, she is,' agreed Hugh, 'in every way.'

That afternoon, Patsy booked an appointment with her local GP. He was more than delighted to see her. For one thing, she was an extremely pretty girl and he didn't get too many of those in his surgery, and secondly, she was a minor celebrity, another rarity. Perhaps he could persuade her to open the summer fête for them. His wife was on the committee and it would gain him several brownie points if he secured the services of a star of *The McMasters*, however minor. Patsy was thrilled to be asked and agreed to do it. He was thrilled that she was thrilled and agreed to her request for sleeping pills. Yes, he'd seen the publicity she'd been receiving and yes, it must be a frightful strain for her. He didn't wonder she couldn't sleep.

Patsy left the surgery, happily clutching her prescription. This was her last chance to prove herself. She knew exactly what to do. She'd read somewhere in one of her old Hollywood magazines about a movie star, Rock Hudson, she thought, who'd had to play a drunk scene and he'd really got drunk so that he could do it convincingly. The scene, however, took several days to shoot so he'd had to stay drunk for days on end. She giggled at the thought of it. She couldn't begin to think how to act someone who was about to kill herself, so she hit upon the idea of taking some sleeping pills, not enough to kill her, of course, just enough to make her woozy. Then she wouldn't have to worry about the acting, it would be real and everyone would see how brilliant she was and then they'd write her back into the series. The first episode of the new series would be a shot of the ambulance tearing away, siren blaring. She shivered with delight. How dramatic! She called in at the chemist and picked up the prescription. She could hardly wait to get home and try them. She would have a practice tonight.

'I hope you didn't say anything about the end of picture party to her?' Larry later asked Deirdre in alarm.

'No, I didn't think of it, but I suppose she knows about it like everyone else. We can't stop her coming. After all, she's going to be at the studio on the day and she is a member of the cast still.'

'Yes, but we're recording her scenes in the afternoon, so she'll be released around tea time,' he replied with some satisfaction. 'But, as you say, she is a member of the cast, and if she turns up, she turns up, but I can't think she'll have the nerve. She'll be cut dead by most people, not Meg, of course. She wouldn't be able to resist being nice to her, but on the whole it really would be better for everyone's sake if she kept away.'

'Yes, I suppose you're right,' agreed Deirdre reluctantly. 'I can't help feeling sorry for her, though. I think she's just a victim of her own naivety and a grave shortage of brain cells.'

*　　*　　*

Patsy got back to her flat. She went straight to the bathroom to practise the scene. She opened the package and took out the bottle. She looked at herself in the mirror above the basin as instructed in the script, then opened the bottle and carefully tipped out some pills into her hand. Then, still watching herself, she popped them in her mouth. They tasted revolting. She grabbed the glass and filled it with water and gulped it down. Not bad. She'd have to practise again, though, tomorrow. She had a feeling it would look better if she crammed the pills into her mouth. She'd seen that on TV, she was sure. She wandered around the flat, tidying up for a while, and thought about making supper. But the acrid taste in her mouth had taken away her hunger. Then she started to feel a bit dizzy and decided to go to bed early. She fell asleep quickly and slept soundly.

47

It was the final studio day and there was an air of barely
suppressed hysteria. There were some dramatic scenes to
record that day, interspersed with Patsy's farewell. Her first
one was scheduled for straight after lunch. This meant that
the rest of the cast, who were not involved, could take a longer
lunch break. They would have preferred it if both her scenes
could have been recorded consecutively, obviating any further
encounters between her and them. This was not possible due
to availability and positioning of cameras and shortage of time,
which meant that, so far as possible, the episodes had to be
shot in sequence. There was a festive feel to the club room,
which was already bracing itself for the party that night.
Everything felt end-of-termish, teetering on the brink of the
holidays. The horrors of the exposé were forgotten in the
general atmosphere of gaiety that abounded in the make-up
room, the wardrobe department and the green room. On set,
however, all was quiet and concentrated. They had
successfully completed all the scenes in the McMasters' offices
and home the day before, and were now on to Livingstone Fine
Arts, Inc., the rival firm run by Jim and Claire, that looked
set to oust Paul McMaster from his hitherto unassailable
position as head of the old firm of McMasters, auctioneers
extraordinary, in the style of Sotheby's or Christie's. Claire
and Jim, buoyed up by the knowledge that their characters

and partnership were to form the basis of the main plot line for the new series, rattled through their numerous scenes in the morning, playing them for all they were worth, and accurately, which meant very little need for retakes.

'You look pleased with yourselves,' observed Bella, as they entered the make-up room after completing their morning's quota. 'And so you should – you were bloody good – both of you,' she added magnanimously. Since the rebirth of her character, Bella had become a new woman. Bright and charming, her expletives down to a minimum, she was even being, for her, abstemious, restricting her intake of alcohol to a couple of glasses of white wine a day. As a result she was looking and feeling better and the whole cast benefited. 'Worthy protagonists,' she proclaimed on viewing Claire and Jim in the Amsterdam filming.

Patsy had arrived at the studio groggy and dazed with sleep, having once again done a dummy run the night before. This time she had taken several pills – to get a more accurate feeling of what it would be like on the morrow. Completely drugged, she staggered off early to bed and had not woken until 10.30. Sonia, her mind on the forthcoming party, had made her up with barely an exchange of greetings.

'What are you wearing tonight?' Glynis called out from the far end of the make-up room.

'I've bought a new outfit especially. It's sort of dark green shot taffeta.'

'Oh yes?' jeered Glynis. 'And who are you trying to impress – not our Jimbo surely?' Everyone laughed including Sonia, who secretly had her eye on a cameraman named Clive. Patsy tried to rouse herself to defend her position as Jim's prospective wife, but was unequal to the occasion as the pills had left her feeling zonked. She slumped back in the chair again.

'You're looking a bit pale today, love,' Sonia said cheerfully. 'Good for your scene, though – I won't do too much to you.' Patsy tried to protest – she loved to wear lots of make-up – but this time she was unable to, sitting instead zombie-like as Sonia fussed over her.

Glynis, however, came to her rescue. 'She's got the shot to do with the forger first, Sonia,' she called out critically, all traces of bonhomie vanishing. Glynis relished her position as head of the department and made full use of every opportunity to exert her authority.

Sonia panicked. 'Oh yes, of course, sorry. I must concentrate on what I'm doing. Right, we'll give you the works, shall we?' she asked ingratiatingly. The exposé in the newspapers had provided the make-up department with a fund of gossip that would keep them going right through the summer break until the next series.

Glynis was not through yet, however. 'You can pale her up a bit for the death scene – we want a nice dramatic effect – and then you can take a look at those extras out there,' she said, jerking her head in the direction of the door.

Sonia mentally put aside for later her gorgeous green dress and the effect it was going to have on Clive, bowed her head and got on with her work. She was very much in awe of Glynis, who was possessed of a whiplash tongue.

Patsy subsided happily in the make-up chair. The voices in the room sounded as if they were coming from some far off planet. It was quite a pleasant feeling really and, leaning back against the headrest, she surrendered herself to Sonia's ministrations and dozed. Sonia woke her when she had finished.

'Go and get some lunch, love,' she said with concern. 'You look all done in.' Patsy thanked her and crawled out of the chair.

After she left the make-up room, Glynis, whose keen eyes had noted her departure said, 'Has she been drinking?'

Sonia was flustered at the idea of having an artiste who wasn't in control. 'Oh no, I think she's had a bad night, that's all. Probably getting into her part.'

Glynis nodded curtly. 'Keep an eye on her. Make sure she doesn't go to the club. That's all we need, to have to run over on the last day.'

Sonia quickly tidied away her equipment and left to search for her artiste. But although she scoured the building, she could not find Patsy anywhere. She wasn't in the club and Sonia even tried the nearest pub – to no avail. She obviously hadn't gone to lunch either, as there was no sign of her in the canteen or either of the crush bars. She eventually drew the conclusion that Patsy was sleeping in her dressing room. The best place for her, in Sonia's opinion, so she decided to leave well alone and went off to join her companions in the canteen.

After lunch, Patsy was called for her first scene. She appeared on set looking vague and disoriented after several minutes of Terri, the floor assistant, hammering on her door.

'Come along, dear,' said Scott, slightly irritated. He was personally glad to see the back of Patsy. Her scenes always took far too long as there had to be retake after retake until she got them right, and although he had escaped unscathed in the débâcle, since the tabloids were only interested in the lives of those in front of the cameras, all the furore made him uneasy. After all, there were plenty of skeletons rattling in his cupboard, and it just needed one of the top-floor boys to become interested and a moral purge of the entire unit would undoubtedly follow. He was also aware how close the series had come to being pulled and he liked his job here, thank you very much. More than that, he needed it. It was a very pleasant little setup he had here with Pam and he did not want

355

it disturbed. Thank God it was this wretched bimbo's last episode.

'Just stand over there with Pete,' he ordered, referring to the young man who was playing the forger. 'Face half away from us,' he instructed in exasperation then, with an impatient sigh, positioned her himself. 'Now just pretend to be in animated conversation with him – it doesn't matter what you talk about – it's mute – and mercifully brief,' he added under his breath. 'Okay, Bri, I'm going up to the gallery for a butchers,' and so saying he bounded up the stairs to the gallery.

'Actually, she looks quite good,' he said in surprise, when he got there and saw her on the monitors. 'She looks sort of frail and vulnerable. Quick, let's record it before she reverts to bland bimbo acting.'

The scene successfully over, Patsy was dismissed to her dressing room for an hour. She was starting to feel apprehensive. What if she couldn't do it? She closed the door of the dressing room behind her, her heart thumping. This was it, her big chance! She went to her bag and pulled out the little brown plastic phial containing the sleeping pills. Totally unaware of what she was doing, she walked into the bathroom that abutted on the dressing room. She looked steadily into the mirror. She saw a pale face with large round eyes staring back at her.

'Don't bother to do anything to her make-up,' Glynis instructed Sonia. 'Scott thinks she looks perfect the way she is.' Sonia had thankfully proceeded with the line of extras that Glynis had spitefully given her to make up for the next scene but one, and it was a race against time.

* * *

356

Patsy practised taking the pills several times until she was satisfied that she looked sufficiently distraught. By the time her call came, she had swallowed nearly twenty sleeping tablets.

Sonia had got her extras done on time and they shot a long dialogue scene between Jim and Claire in the restaurant. At the appointed hour, Terri came to get Patsy. She knocked on her dressing room door.

'I'm ready,' Patsy's slurred voice came faintly from within.

Terri opened the door. 'You feeling all right?' she asked, with genuine concern.

'Oh yes,' said Patsy happily – it was working. 'Just getting in the mood for my big scene.'

'Oh, right,' said Terri, impressed. 'You look great. Come on, we're ready for you.'

Terri led the way, then, seeing Patsy stagger a little, took hold of her arm and steered her towards the studio and onto the set. It was dark. Patsy leaned against the basin in the mock-up of the small hotel room. It was perfect, there was the bed all ready, just as she had imagined it. She positioned herself against the little hand basin. She was still clutching the phial of pills.

'We're coming to you in a minute,' whispered Terri. Patsy nodded. She could hear the sounds of a scene going on in another part of the studio floor.

'Quiet, everyone,' yelled Brian, the floor assistant. 'We're recording.' The red light shone up above all the studio exits, there was silence, then the scene was played. Another silence. Then Brian's voice, 'Going again, studio. Quiet, please, everyone.'

Oh when would they get to her? She was absolutely ready now. This time the other scene went well.

'Yes, okay, we've bought that. Just waiting for a clear – yeah, we have a clear – thank you, everyone. Onto the next set – er – hotel bedroom – thank you. Patsy, please.'

'She's already here,' called out Terri.

'Okay, thank you.'

The studio lights came on in the hotel room. This was it at last. Cameras started to glide into position.

'I better go down and organize this,' said Scott, sighing wearily. 'This day is turning out to be interminable.' And he hurried down to the studio floor. 'Okay, Patsy, now you know what you have to do, don't you? Just look in the mirror, take the pills, gulp down some water, look in the mirror again, then leave the shot. That's all. Then we'll have a recording break and pick you up again already on the bed. Okay? Have you given her the pills?' he asked Terri.

'Coming in,' she said, and produced a phial identical to the one Patsy was holding. 'Oh, it's okay, she's already been given some.'

'You have to take them all, Patsy, all right? Empty the phial.' He looked through the viewfinder of the camera and was satisfied. 'Okay, I'm on my way up.' He disappeared.

Brian on headcans was receiving his instructions. 'Yep, okay, Scott, I'll tell her. Patsy –' he said quietly, partly out of deference for the solemn nature of the scene that was about to be enacted, 'Scott says, shall we go for one straightaway?'

Patsy nodded. It was the first time a director had asked her opinion on anything and she liked it, the power she felt to be wanted at last. She was wanted and she was safe. She was ready. She was going to do this in one take.

'Camera ready?' asked Brian. 'Sound okay?' They all

358

odded and muttered affirmations. 'Okay, absolute silence, everyone – this is a difficult scene. We must have *quiet*!'

There was not a sound to be heard.

'Okay, Patsy,' said Brian, very quietly, still relaying instructions from the gallery, 'in your own time – and – ACTION!'

Patsy lifted her head and looked in the mirror. She suddenly realized she loved this studio and everyone in it. This was the last time she'd see it or them. Tears welled up in her eyes and started to course unbidden down her cheeks. She stared at her reflection.

Up in the gallery, they were mesmerized.

'Jesus H. Christ!' breathed Scott, as he gazed at the monitor.

Patsy undid the phial and emptied the rest of the pills into her hand. She crammed them into her mouth the way she had been practising for days. She reached out for the glass tumbler, filled it with water and knocked back the contents. Leaning both hands on the basin, tears pouring down her cheeks, she looked at the pale little face in the mirror. Suddenly she felt dreadfully tired, she could no longer stand. She had to lie down. She turned and looked at the bed longingly. Slowly, she walked towards it and climbed onto it.

'And . . . recording pause . . . and . . . thank you – Patsy that was terrific – Scott says – bloody marvellous.'

There were murmurs of approval from the studio technicians.

'Okay, studio, we're going on. Reposition cameras three and four. You okay there, Patsy?'

Patsy, now lying in her position for her close-up, nodded happily. She had done it, she'd proved that she could act. They'd all seen it. All she had to do now was lie as still as possible.

'Patsy,' whispered Brian, 'we'll be panning up the bed from your feet to your face, so don't move a muscle, will you – and try not to breathe.'

Patsy smiled her acquiescence. She could do anything now. She had received praise from the director and the crew. Anything was possible.

'Okay, we're going for it. Stand by, studio – absolute silence, please – and . . . ACTION.'

Patsy breathed a deep breath and then lay motionless.

'My God, I believe she's learnt to act,' gasped Scott in the gallery. 'Okay, cut. Provided it's clear, we've bought it.'

On the studio floor, Brian took charge.

'Thank you, Patsy. Thank you, studio – just waiting for a clear. Patsy?' He looked down at her sleeping figure.

Sonia, who'd been standing by, came over. 'I should leave her, she's had a bad night.'

'Yeah, she seemed exhausted to me,' agreed Terri.

''Sokay by me – thank you, everyone. That's a clear,' shouted Brian, suddenly receiving confirmation in his ear. 'Break for tea. Fifteen minutes only, please. Back at four twenty.'

Patsy was completely forgotten. The lights were dimmed on the hotel room set and everyone left the studio floor.

'Well, I've never seen anything like it,' said Scott in astonishment as he bit into a doughnut. 'The girl actually played the scene bloody well – pity she left it too late.'

After tea everyone returned to another set in the studio. The Penthouse suite, occupied by Jim's character, John Livingstone III. Nobody thought to check on Patsy. People were always falling asleep on sofas and beds in the studio. Exhausted actors who were appearing in the theatre at night would snatch a few precious moments between scenes; technicians who'd had too much to drink at lunchtime and weren't required for an hour or so. Nobody took any notice of, and indeed always respected, a tired fellow worker.

Thus Patsy slept on.

The studio broke for supper, returned to record the last scenes, completed the last shot and was finally wrapped for the day. A cheer went up and everyone dispersed to reassemble upstairs for the end of shoot party. It was in full swing when a worried-looking young security guard came into the club.

'Hi, Mark. You off duty? Come and join the fun. There's a mound of food.' Bella always prided herself on knowing everyone's names.

'Er . . . no thank you, Miss Shand, I . . . I need to see someone. Is Mr Travis around?' said Mark, looking very serious.

'Hugh? He's over there.'

'Thanks,' and Mark touched his cap and made his way through the noisy throng. 'Mr Travis, sir, please . . . I think there's something wrong,' Mark began.

'What is it, Mark? Wrong? What do you mean?'

'It's Patsy – Miss Hall . . . I think . . . I think . . .' His voice rose uncontrollably. 'I think she's dead!' His pronouncement produced an immediate silence in the little group surrounding Hugh and gradually spread across the whole room as people began to realize that something was wrong.

'What do you mean?' asked Hugh, horror-struck.

'Have you called for the nurse?' asked Larry immediately.

'I can't,' said Mark frantic. 'She's gone off duty.'

'Come on then, take us there,' said Larry briskly.

Mark hurried out followed by Larry, Hugh, Geoff and Jim, with Bella and Claire bringing up the rear in case the feminine touch was required, as Bella later put it.

The studio was in darkness but Mark had his torch.

'We need some more light,' said Hugh abruptly.

'It's all right,' said Mark. 'I know where the switches are.' He disappeared into the dark and in a little while the working lights came on. Long overhead strips of fluorescent light illuminated the pathetic scene in front of them. Everyone looked in silence.

Then with a broken sob, Claire said, 'Oh my God, what have we done?'

Epilogue

A tall fine figure of a man, with a remarkably even
golden tan and deep-set vivid blue eyes, was
threading his way through the hustle and bustle of
Mayfair. His light brown hair, flecked with gold,
was a touch too long for a banker or a barrister, and
proclaimed him at once a man connected with the
arts. Women's heads turned as he strode confidently
along, his gaze fixed firmly ahead, a slightly worried
look on his handsome chiselled features. He arrived
at his destination and glanced up briefly with an air
of ill-concealed pride at the name displayed above
the premises. 'John Livingstone & Paul McMaster'
it announced in discreet gold roman lettering on a
very dark green ground. He buzzed the intercom
and immediately gained admittance. A glorious
creature with auburn hair turned to greet him.

'You've taken your time,' she observed dryly. 'All
hell has broken loose here.'

'Hi, Sara,' he said equably.

'Geneva has been on the line. The Bellini is a
copy, your new secretary has just arrived,' she
continued as if he had not spoken, indicating a
delicious blonde who was eyeing him with a
predatory look, 'your wife rang to say she's filing

for divorce and Paul McMaster is downstairs waiting to see you. And he's hopping mad,' she added spitefully.

He glanced at the Francis Bacon that was the star exhibit in the window.

'So what's the good news?' he asked, grinning.

'There isn't any.'

'Oh yes there is. You're having supper with me tonight!'

'Over my dead body,' she retorted.

'That can be arranged.'

'We've had one corpse in this outfit. I hardly think we can handle another.'

'I can handle anything,' he said, leaning against the wall and narrowing his eyes at her.

'Well, start with Paul McMaster. He looks fit to burst out of his suit. Try to catch him before he turns into the Incredible Hulk, will you.'

'What the hell is going on here?' Paul appeared at the bottom of the basement stairs. 'How much longer do I have to wait in this black hole of Calcutta?'

'Hi, you down there,' said John Livingstone III, with another charming boyish grin. 'Thanks for bringing it home.'

'What?'

Livingstone jerked his head in the direction of the window. 'The Bacon. It looks really neat.'

'I should like to point out to you that it isn't paid for yet – nor is it likely to be.'

'Why ever not?'

'Because the firm of stockbrokers who ordered it has gone to the wall.'

'Holy Cow!' said Livingstone, the third of that name.

'You could put it like that,' said McMaster, 'although personally I prefer standard English.'

'Gimme a break, will ya? My wife's filing for divorce yet!'

'Are you surprised?' Paul arched an elegant eyebrow.

'Come again?' said J.L.

'My dear man, to my certain knowledge, you have been through all the thirty-five female employees of this company like a hot knife through butter. What do you expect her to do? Throw a hen party, a night on the town with the Chippendales?'

'Talking of which,' Sara interrupted glacially, 'there's a whole consignment arriving today.' Both men turned to her.

'Of what?' they asked in unison.

'Chippendales,' she said. 'Chairs – assorted – from an old lady in Harrogate.'

'I just know there ain't going to be a pair amongst the lot of them,' breathed J.L.

'We could start a new vogue, mix'n'match chairs. Give your dinner parties a cabriole leg-up – '

The rest of her witticism was lost as a car, driven at break-neck speed, crashed through the plate-glass window. Two masked men leaped out, snatched the painting and hurled themselves into a passing getaway car that drove off at high speed. Alarm bells were clanging – Sara screamed. So did the new secretary.

'Get the police,' yelled Paul McMaster.

'Yeah, and fast,' agreed J.L. 'Well, that takes

care of one problem – insurance,' he said casually. 'Now if you'll excuse me, I have a little matter of a fraudulent Bellini to attend to.'

'What about the woman you love?' asked Paul sarcastically as he dialled 999.

J.L. turned to look at him.

'Well, as she happens to be your wife, I guess you can answer that question better than I can.'

The theme tune crescendoed over Paul's startled expression. *The McMasters* was up and running again.